PRAISE FOR EMILY JANE'S

ON EARTH AS IT IS
ON TELEVISION

"Heartfelt, witty, and secretly romantic, *On Earth as It Is on Television* is a delightful and poignant story about what it is to be human and what we owe each other."

—Christina Lauren,
New York Times bestselling author of *Something Wilder*

"Weird and sweet, *On Earth as It Is on Television* is like a 2020s *White Noise*: loud and colorful Americana with a sprinkle of apocalyptic doom—plus cats. It takes aliens (or an Emily Jane) to help us see our society for the bizarre, sugary, microplastic-poisoned dream it is."

—Edgar Cantero,
New York Times bestselling author of *Meddling Kids*

"A very absurd, heartwarming, hilarious look at what makes us human. A tale laced with fatty foods, talking cats, mysterious aliens, and far too much television."

—*Geek Vibes Nation*

"Glittering, strange spaceships appear and hover over every major city on Earth; yes, that's familiar. What is unfamiliar about this debut from Emily Jane is the way first contact with an alien species brings people together and how it tears them apart—as well as the major role of cats. . . ."

—*Scientific American*

"A uniquely modern spin on the concept of aliens arriving on Earth. Both contemporary and fantastical, Emily Jane's story utterly charmed me. I hope when the aliens come, they're just like the Malorts."

—Maureen Kilmer, author of *Suburban Hell*

"Jane's novel subverts the classic first-contact story to explore humanity's responses to uncertainty in the modern age."

—*Library Journal*

"A painful and hopeful examination of first contact and second chances on the third rock from the sun. Jane skillfully weaves individual character threads into a poignant narrative tapestry of an unraveling world."

—Valerie Valdes, author of *Chilling Effect*

ON EARTH AS IT IS ON TELEVISION

A NOVEL

EMILY JANE

HYPERION AVENUE

LOS ANGELES   NEW YORK

First Hardcover Edition, June 2023
First Paperback Edition, May 2024
10 9 8 7 6 5 4 3 2 1
FAC-025438-24073
Printed in the United States of America

This book is set in Adobe Caslon Pro and Industry Inc.
Designed by Amy C. King

Library of Congress Control Number for Hardcover Edition: 2023930394
ISBN 978-1-368-10120-2

www.HyperionAvenueBooks.com

SUSTAINABLE FORESTRY INITIATIVE

Certified Sourcing

www.forests.org
SFI-01681

Logo Applies to Text Stock Only

For Steve

PREQUEL

The Crash

A WHITE TEMPEST swept the mountain. The dark road iced. The lines disappeared beneath fresh snow. The road was empty, but for a single car.

The car turned a sharp bend. Snow pummeled the windshield. The girl in the passenger seat pressed her hand to the glass.

"We're free, Ollie," she said. She felt ecstatic. Maudlin. Reverent. So many things. She was just a girl and not even that bright, folks said. Got by on her looks, folks said, except when she caught a fist, and her eye swelled shut tight.

Not any more though. Not ever again.

"Ain't no one'll come looking for us all the way out here," Oliver said. "That's for sure."

"California."

"California," he echoed.

She laughed, and her laugh made Oliver Smith think of the glint of sun on the waves that rolled in toward the white sand shores of Malibu, the Eden he envisioned when she said *California*. California. California. They listened to the songs on the radio as they fled, California songs, the siren of West Coast promise.

"What's that shit called?" he had asked, somewhere back in Missouri.

"What?"

"The thing they say. About like, going west and shit. About America. Like, 'Go west, young lad.' Like, you know, the mouse. Fievel and shit." He was high on skunk weed, which littered his parlance with extraneous *likes* and *shits*. He stayed high on skunk weed the whole drive west, until he'd run out, so that didn't explain what happened to them next on that snow-covered road.

"Manifest destiny," she said.

"Yes. Fucking yes. Manifest destiny."

Except like a lot of westward travelers, they'd reached a decent spot and settled. They settled just across the Nevada border because they ran out of cash, and he saw a sign on the window of a diner— LINE COOK WANTED—and the manager offered to lease them a little A-frame cabin, no deposit, no rent due until he got his first paycheck. *Hey, buddy, I been there, I know.* And it made him think that maybe the similarities amongst us all outshined the dissonance. We were all here or there, under the great big sky, hankering for California, or whatever vision we held in its stead.

"Damn, this snow is crazy."

The snow blew sideways, each flake illuminated by headlights, each flake different, a hundred thousand million billion galaxies of swirling snow. Oliver hugged the curve. He drove into the barrage. Snow covered the windshield as fast as his wipers could brush it off. He had never driven through snow like this. He had barely driven before the long drive west. He was eighteen.

She was seventeen. She wanted to go to cosmetology school. The name tripped him up. It made him think of the cosmos. His stoner brain got confused by linguistic commonalities. Cosmos/cosmetology. Astrology/astronomy. He envisioned tiny planets encapsulated inside shampoo suds; the ruthless clippering of solar systems; split, brittle universes trimmed away. She wanted to cut, color, make beautiful. *There's so much beauty in the world, Oliver.* She believed in beauty even when she couldn't see it. Behind the black eyes, the split lip, the swollen rainbow of purples and blues fading into sallow yellow, there was beauty.

He was eighteen and maybe, technically, theoretically might get charged with abducting a minor. He had gone to the library and opened up some dusty volume of criminal code that no one had read for a thousand years. He skimmed words that eluded his comprehension, until he saw the word *kidnapping*. Better not to know, he decided. Better to wipe the volume clean of fingerprints and get the F out of libraryville.

She still had a faint bruise on her cheek, from the last time Bill hit her.

What else? Ollie had asked her. *What else did he do to you? Tell me.*

Oh, Bill was just a little bit fisty. Occasionally punchy. Intermittently inspired to yank a lamp from the socket, swing it like a T-ball bat at a girl's head, and tie an electric cord necklace-tight around her pretty neck until she gasped and flailed and the oxygen fled her brain and she wondered whether her eyes would pop out. *Poppity-poppity*, the way it happened in cartoons, when a character got shot out the airlock into space.

Is that it? What else? What are you not telling me, Jo?

She was less than a year younger than Oliver but she was also way, way younger. Eons younger. Oliver had traveled all the way to Seattle. He had gone to Florida twice. He had slept with three girls. He had held six fast-food jobs and gotten fired from two. He had spent a month in juvie. Jo had lived her whole life in the same trailer. She had never traveled farther than Pittsburgh. She had never had a job or smoked hash or gotten fucked by anyone but Bill.

Did he? That fucker. Tell me he didn't. I'm gonna fucking kill that motherfucker.

Oliver's profanity did not reflect the literal facts. Mother was all dried up, a shriveled husk of a cunt, Bill said, when he cornered Jo after school. Bill had it wrong too. His old lady wasn't old. She was a MILF. But her heart had shriveled, and she kept her mind soaked with white zin and vodka tonics. Everyone found a way to cope. Or they ran. Or transformed. Or died.

Mother belonged to Jo, but not to Oliver. Oliver had his own mother, and she was *all right, I guess. I mean, she's whatever,* was how Oliver described it. She watched a lot of soap operas. Her feet always hurt. She subsisted on salty snack foods, sandwich cookies, diet sodas. Infrequently, she fell prey to maternal guilt. She felt ashamed by the deviation between the mother she actually was and the mother that TV suggested she ought to be. She stalked Oliver through the house. She pounced. *My boy, oh, my little boy, so precious.* Her adulations sounded forced. She hugged him, too tightly, for too long. She offered him sugary treats. She wept a bit. Then she reverted to her natural state of ignoring Oliver, a state that they both generally preferred.

Oliver's mother and Jo's mother had both gotten fucked, literally and figuratively, by the same boozy deadbeat no-longer-in-the-picture dad. Dad hung around long enough for Oliver and Jo to know who Oliver and Jo were in relation to each other, and then he ducked out, *So long, suckers.* Mothers couldn't demand child support when mothers couldn't even find him. Oliver's mother got food stamps and then she got depressed and then she got Prozac. Jo's mother got Bill. For a few years. Until Bill decided he liked Jo better.

Oliver did not *fucking kill that motherfucker.* He didn't have a kill mode. Blood made him squeamish. He considered the cops, but he didn't trust them. They had him sent to juvie just because he was handy with a can of spray paint and had sprayed up the side of an old warehouse building. He sprayed his name; OLIVER in a grove of spray-paint trees; OLIVER against a neon sunrise. The building was old, gray, dirty, boring. He made it better. He made art. The cops didn't give a crap about art. They called him a vandal, cuffed him, tossed him in the squad car back seat. Twelve-year-old Oliver hadn't hit puberty. Arrest felt like a video game—*Oliver Gets Arrested RPG*. Oliver would beat the level and move on to fight the big boss, Mom. He grinned while they took his photos and prints, a big goofy tween-boy grin. But then they called him a delinquent and locked him up, and when he got out they had painted over his art. They had washed the wall in bland gray. So, no, he didn't trust the cops.

He said to Jo: We're going. We're going and we're never coming back.

Jo: No. What? No.

Jo: How can we?

Jo: What about your mom? She's all right. Don't you want to tell her?

Jo: But I'm seventeen.

He said: Fuck, Jo. You can't even open your eye. We're going. We're fucking going.

Jo: Where? Where do we go?

He said: Wherever you want.

Jo (she thought about it first, for a long while): There's this song. It's like, *Oh, Shenandoah, I long to see you. Aaaawayyyy, you rolling river.* You know it?

He said: Yeah, I know it.

Jo: So there. Shenandoah. Or whatever. That's where I want to go.

Except Shenandoah was too close. Too easy to get pulled back. Also, Oliver forgot the map, and he smoked a J on the way out of town, and they just kind of wound up driving west. Or west pulled them in its direction. West was like, *Over this way, here I am, yo. Your destiny.*

Which is messed up, considering what happened next.

"It's pretty," she said. She gazed out the window into the swirling white. "It's not Shenandoah. But it's pretty." She had never seen the Shenandoah Valley, but it had always existed in her mind as a painting she had seen once, of lush green cliffs and waterfalls beneath a Creamsicle sky, a dreamland place of sprites and fairies, where the world softly glowed, where all of life was luminescent. She conjured that place when she drifted to sleep, and at the whisky-midnight hour when the rattle of her doorknob woke her, and in the morning after, when she examined her face in the bathroom mirror. *Who are you?* She dabbed ointment on her split lip. She smoothed concealer over the bruise, but she could still see its violet edges. She thought: What if I was a fairy? She thought: What if there was no Bill? If there had never been any Bill. If her dad had stuck around. If her mom went to night school and became a nurse practitioner and bought a little brick bungalow with a tulip garden and took her on vacation every summer, to Jamaica, Madrid, Disney World. If her brain worked better. If it didn't go fuzzy-blank, stranding her in suddenly unfamiliar spots, mid-sentence, holding in her hand an object that she believed was a spoon. Was it really a spoon? Usually, no. Her brain had confused the pen for a spoon, the spoon for a sock, the sock for her purse, which she continually misplaced. If her brain worked better, she might go to night school and become a nurse practitioner herself, but everyone said she was too dumb. She hadn't always been too dumb. If she still had smarts, she might have hatched her own escape plan, and Oliver might have kept on spray-painting and smoking joints and playing *Fortnite* in his mother's basement. If she still had smarts, she might have understood how none of what had happened was her fault.

"Yeah. It's pretty," Oliver said. "But damn. I can't see shit."

"Maybe you should pull over."

"Pull over *where?*" The road had no shoulder. It had a snow-covered cliff that descended into darkness.

"We could just stop."

"Like in the middle of the road."

"Until it lets up."

"But what if it doesn't? If it keeps snowing all night. If the battery dies. Then we'd have to, like, find a bear and kill it and cut it open and climb inside it to keep warm. And that sounds fucking gross."

Oliver had unrealistic expectations, inherent to eighteen-year-old guy-dom, of continued life. A battery might die. A bear might die. But not him. He would prevail. At the very least, death would happen the way it did in the video games: with a new life. A fresh start.

"I am not getting inside a dead bear," she said.

"Oh, you would. If that was your only option. You'd do it."

"We should have stayed in Tahoe."

"And what? Got a hotel? We don't have money for that."

"Well, we could have, um, um . . ." Her brain circuits shorted out. For a moment, she forgot herself. She stared past her shadow reflection on the dark window glass, at the snowstorm beyond. She saw, beyond the blanketed treetops, up in the clouds, a colored light. Then the light was gone. "It's pretty," she said. "Even if it's not Shenandoah. Uh . . . wait, what were we talking about?"

"You were saying how you wanted to cut open a bear and climb inside it to keep warm," Oliver joked.

"Screw you. What were we really talking about?"

"I'm serious. Bear-corpse sleeping bags."

"You're full of it."

"Yup."

"Hey, turn the radio up," Jo said. "This song—"

"What, you like this?" Oliver said. He feigned derision, but he turned the volume up, steeping the car in disco beat. Oliver liked rap music, he told himself. Not this pansy disco stuff. He imagined himself too hard-core, too modern, too worldly to bother with classic disco.

Secretly, he liked it.

"It's Blondie."

"Lame."

"I love this song!"

"Uh-huh."

"It makes me feel like . . ." She couldn't explain it. She envisioned herself busting out of herself, shedding the skins of her past, herself in a constant phase of blooming. She played what-if. What if she existed at a different point in space-time, in a Bill-less world stricken with disco-mania. What if she wore roller skates to work. If she wheeled around in a halter top and high-waist bells, if she feathered her hair, if she wasn't broken inside, if she found true love. But she couldn't sculpt speech from feelings. She sputtered out.

"Like what? Like you want to dance?" He knew she had never gone dancing. "Or like, you want to drive really fast? Lots of songs make me feel like that."

"Yeah, 'cuz that's a good idea."

"Should I? How fast you think we can go around these curves? Sixty? Seventy?"

"Faster, Ollie!" she joked. "Faster *faster faster!*"

"I bet we could take that next curve at seventy-five. You think?"

"Oh, at least." She laughed.

"All right, hang on," he said, but he didn't speed up. He slowed down. He wasn't an idiot. "Hey, grab that pop, will ya? I'm thirsty."

"Is it—"

"From the back seat. Can you reach it without unbuckling?"

"No. But—"

"I can wait."

"It's fine. I'll grab it." She unclicked her seat belt. She lunged over the seat. Oliver held his breath. She retrieved his bottle of Fizz Wizard Cherry Cola. "Here you go."

"Can you open it?" He didn't want to take his hands off the wheel.

"Give me a sec." She buckled her seat belt. She opened the bottle. Foam fountained out of the bottle, over her hand. She slurped it up. She held the bottle to Oliver's lips. He drank. It was the last good sensation he remembered. Warm cherry pop, bubbling over his tongue, down his throat.

"Thanks," he said.

She screwed the cap on tight. "You ever seen flakes this big?" she asked.

The flakes came quarter-sized. The earth had disappeared entirely. There was nothing out there but them, in their old beat-up car, no chains on its tires, its bumper affixed in place with duct tape. Nothing but them, the trees, the hazy light-orb of a snowbound house, the buried road, the disco beat.

"Nope."

"Me neither. I—"

The car hit a patch of ice. The tires slipped. Oliver hit the brakes, and for a moment it seemed as if the car would skid to a stop. The oppressive sky acquired a strange glow. Snowflakes formed as flowers, crystals, pearls. The car seemed to slow, and Oliver's thoughts seemed to accelerate. His mind reeled fast visions of tomorrow: the hash-brown sausage breakfast; the new truck with four-wheel drive; the art studio, canvas and clay, spray-paint murals, metallic swirl acrylics; his sister, the cosmetologist, the cosmologist. The cosmos tasted like warm cherry pop. Then he understood. It wasn't the car that had slowed down. Time had slowed down. The car kept on sliding at a fast clip.

The road curved, but the car didn't. The car plunged straight ahead. It sailed off the road, over the cliff edge, nothing beneath its wheels but an abyss of snow and space, pure and empty.

The radio played, and Oliver's mind said, *Yes. No reason not to admit that you like disco now.*

He had never gone dancing.

He felt his heart sync to the beat of music.

Snowflakes formed pearls, disco ball mirrors, shattered shards of glass.

Jo grasped her brother's arm. She gazed out, past the windshield, into the blizzard, her destiny made manifest by each trifling snowflake moment of her life. Her mind traced them back. *You ever seen flakes this big?* She screwed the pop bottle cap tight. She turned on the radio. She didn't stay in a Tahoe hotel. She climbed into the passenger seat. She let Oliver convince her. *You've got to get out of here, Jo. I'll come with you. We'll go together.* Shenandoah, she said. Someplace mountainous, a land of tall trees. She didn't get a second lock for her bedroom door. She didn't block it with a chair. She feared Bill's wrath, his hot breath, his rage. She didn't stab fingernails into his sockets and rip out his eyes. She didn't run fast enough that he couldn't seize her and smash her head against the concrete stoop. She didn't run away the first time Oliver had said, *Hey, what if we ran away? I know a kid who's got a fake ID. I know how to drive.* She said *Oliver, you're only twelve* and *What would we do? Join the circus?* She didn't join the circus, and now she was in this clown car, no ropes, no nets, sailing off a cliff.

* * *

Time slowed, and then it sped back up. The car flipped. It rolled down the steep, snowy hill. It crashed against a tree. Its headlights blinked out. Smoke spiraled up from its crushed hood. There was a muffled scream, and then silence. There was nothing there, nothing anywhere but blizzard, and faint flashing light, imperceptible to human eyes, out there beyond the clouds, in that great cold empty that stretched on for nearly ever.

EPISODE 1

The Brother

THE WEATHERMAN ON the local news said the cherry blossoms would come early this year. They would erupt in a blaze of pastel pink. It was February, almost spring, almost balmy. The Brookwood windows had never gotten opened this early. Nurse Betsy Martin planned to open them after breakfast. Fresh air was good for the constitution. Fresh air smelled like freedom, even when freedom was an illusion.

In Brookwood the windows all had bars.

Betsy Martin sorted pills into paper cups. A trainee watched over her shoulder.

"So the list says who gets what pills?"

Her trainee was overly enthusiastic. He had a passion for nursing. He had not worked nearly enough twelve-hour shifts.

"You have to print the list out every day," Betsy said. "Don't get lazy and use the same old copy. The doctors change the dosages sometimes, so if you use an old copy it might be wrong."

"Got it."

"And you want to double-check again when you give them the pills. Just to be sure you didn't make a mistake."

Betsy made the rounds. She double-checked pills. She handed them out. She made little check marks next to the names on her printed list. With some patients she lingered, waiting to make sure they didn't spit out or chipmunk pills. With others she had to coax. She threatened withdrawal of TV privileges if they chose to take their pills *the hard way*. Betsy Martin abhorred *the hard way*, which explained why she still worked at Brookwood after twenty-some years, even though she didn't like the job. She had almost enrolled in premed, but medical school seemed like too hard of a climb. Finding a new job required too much work. Brookwood was bland, flat, unchanging. Some patients came and went, but others lingered, their minds static. Like the catatonic fellow, the last stop on Betsy's pill rounds.

Oliver Smith.

He sat in a wheelchair near the window, staring out. Except he wasn't really staring out, because there wasn't anything in there, behind his glazed eyes. He was like a vegetable that could still chew; a paraplegic who could, if led, shuffle into the shower room and stand there, slack-jawed and pitiful, while you sponged him off. His limbs technically functioned, but his brain did nothing to guide them. His brain seemed to do nothing at all.

"Last one," Betsy said. "You want to check the list?"

"Okay, looks like we've got the right pills," the trainee said. "We've got your pills, Mr. Smith."

The patient stared, unblinking.

"Oliver can't hear you," Betsy said.

"Oh."

"He's deaf. Well, kind of. His eardrums work, but whatever they hear doesn't make it to his brain. Same with his eyes. They're there, and maybe they see something, but you wouldn't know it. They never move."

Oliver's eyes stared straight ahead at whatever emptiness lay straight ahead. His mouth could chew and swallow, and every once in a while something resembling speech came out of it, not that his jumbled sounds ever made any sense.

"What happened to him?" the trainee asked.

"Car crash. His car went off a cliff. Somehow, this guy managed to climb out of the wreck and all the way back to the road. With broken ribs. During the middle of a blizzard, mind you. He was out there in the cold for a couple of days. They said it was a miracle he survived." Betsy shook her head. "Sure doesn't look like a miracle to me. If it was me, I tell you . . ." Too hard a climb, up the side of that snowy cliff, with nothing but Brookwood waiting for you at the top. "He's been here about twenty years now. Almost as long as me."

Betsy peeled Oliver's lip back. She had a green pill, a blue one, a gelatin capsule. She stuck each on his tongue, *one-two-three now swallow*. Oliver tended to drool, but if Betsy tilted his head back and poured water in his mouth, she could make his throat obey.

"You're all set, Oliver." She turned to the trainee. "We're all done with pills until lunchtime. Next up, we're going to check the schedule to see who's got physical therapy this morning, and then—"

"Um, Betsy," the trainee said.

"What?"

"Look. His eyes—"

"Mm-hmm. That's just how they look. All clouded up." The new nurses always remarked about Oliver's eyes. They had a creepy film, like the eyes of a corpse.

"No," the trainee said. "It's not that. His eyes are moving."

"What? Oliver? His eyes don't move," Betsy said. But she looked down at Oliver, just to be sure. "What the heck?"

His eyes moved.

"I thought you said they never moved," the trainee said.

Oliver's gaze slowly shifted. His eyes scanned the room.

"They don't. They just stare straight ahead. This is just . . . it's just . . ."

She shivered. She crouched down in front of Oliver. She waved her hand in front of his eyes. His brain did not seem to register her presence, but his eyes kept on scanning. And they looked different than she had ever seen them, brighter, less milky. As if the clouds behind them had begun to part.

"I'll be darned. I've never seen Oliver's eyes move at all. Not like this, for sure. Not once in twenty years."

The Husband

WOULD YOU BELIEVE in alien life, if it didn't come right out and smack you in the ass? Blaine wouldn't, his wife said. He remembered that later; how she gave a little smack as he walked past, en route to the kitchen to grab that tray of sliders.

He remembered how she had speared each slider with a plastic toothpick molded to the shape of a tiny sword. His wife, who hailed from a land of infinite plastic, Blaine joked. To their guests, he alluded to a vague thrift-store origin: recycled vintage toothpicks, to be washed and reused at the next happy hour. The toothpicks were, in fact, new, but Blaine felt embarrassed by this wanton consumption of disposable plastics. After their guests departed, he collected all the tiny swords and hand-washed them. He suggested to the wife that maybe—*maybe*—they should gravitate away from plastic and toward more compostable toothpick options. The wife looked slightly hurt. *But, Blaine*, she said, *don't you love them? They're so cute!*

* * *

So where was he when it happened? What did he remember?

He had just eaten lunch: leftover sliders.

The weather had turned unnaturally hot for February. Blaine remembered hot breeze, littered with last year's dead leaves. The climate change models said southwest Ohio would become southwest Missouri, or Oklahoma, and it hadn't happened yet, but here was a sneak peek. Blaine ate lunch in the van with the windows down. Blaine's work partner,

Dave, in the passenger seat, chattered about spy drones. Microscopic spy drones that collected data for the deep state, carnal stuff, shower stuff. You ever pick your nose when you think no one's watching? You slip that salty bit into your mouth? Those drones got that video footage.

Dave was a flat-earther and an RVK adherent. He believed that the tap water was contaminated with slow-release poisons and that Mount Rushmore was a projection designed to conceal a secret military base and that the conspiracy cult figurehead Harvey Kayman had come back from the dead by way of an interdimensional portal. He believed in all of it long before it all happened. He was born believing. He was born with the cord wrapped round his neck, head stuck in the birth canal. The doctors had to cut him out. *My kids too*, Blaine told him. This was about the only thing they had in common. The C-section. The same employer. The same moment in the van on that hot February day when the radio blared:

TOOOOOOOOOOOOOOOOOOOOOOOOOOOOONE

THIS IS THE EMERGENCY BROADCAST SYSTEM

TOOOOOOOOOOOOOOOOOOOOOOOOOOOOONE

Where were you when it happened?

The daughter, Avril: I don't know, it was weird. Gym class? I kind of blacked out.

The son, Jas: They let us go home early! And we all got to pick extra candy from the points jar and Mom couldn't come and get me, so I went home with Foster—and we got to play video games all afternoon! Dad!

The dad, Blaine, had parked the van in an industrial lot along the river. Smokestack scenery imprinted his memory. The brick-walled warehouse, the smoke pillars, bare branches stark against the blue sky.

The branches would blossom early that year from unnatural February warmth, but the blossoms would freeze up, fall off. He remembered dead brown petals on the cold spring earth. He remembered the river that day, blue as the sky. But it wasn't. His memory tricked. The river always ran brown.

TOOOOOOOOOOOOOOOOOOOOOOOOOOOOOONE

It had to be, what, a test, right?

Blaine believed in Occam's razor. The simplest explanation was the incontrovertible truth. He ripped open a packet. He squirted ketchup on his slider. The wife had a point about the ease of the ketchup packet.

But landfills, he said.

But unnecessary packaging.

The simplest explanation for his reliance on single-serving condiments was that the reusable condiment containers had been requisitioned for the kids' sparkle-slime mixing endeavors and the wife always requested extra ketchup packets with takeout, and there they were in the cupboard, ready to grab when he packed his lunch.

The wife's name was Anne; classic yet succinct; a short, definitive name. She was, when he thought about her in the abstract, The Wife. But when she appeared in the flesh, she was Anne; *Anne,* said in a swooning voice; *Anne,* who made his heart pound, two kids and a decade-plus later.

Dave believed that surely the end had come. He turned the radio up, so he could hear it outside the van. He lit a cigarette, a menthol, half genetically engineered tobacco shreds soaked in chemicals, half fiberglass. His eyes gleamed with apocalyptic possibilities. He had a nuclear fallout shelter in his backyard, a stockpile of automatic weapons. Yes, and a crossbow.

Shouldn't we all have crossbows, he had said, *you know, just in case?*

THIS IS THE EMERGENCY BROADCAST SYSTEM

TOOOOOOOOOOOOOOOOOOOOOOOOOOOOOONE

The *TONE* didn't just get to the point. It blared through sliders two, three, four, and Blaine ate too fast. He didn't chew well. He knew in his heart that maybe the explanation wasn't so simple and it would be awkward to hear it mid-bite, mouth full.

TOOOOOOOOOOOOOOOOOOOOOOOOOOOOOONE

He finished up, got out of the van, stretched his arms up toward that pristine February sky. Score one, global warming. He could get used to this Missouri winter.

"You check your phone?" Dave asked. Dave had already tried to dive headfirst into the truthy waters of the internet and smashed, instead, into a solid wall of no-service. "Check your phone. Check your phone, dude. You got service?"

Any good apocalypse naturally began with an abrupt severance of internet service.

Dave paced, checked, paced, checked, et cetera. He had a theory: flesh-devouring nanotech swarms. Nanites could gobble a whole House of Representatives in, oh, point-two nanoseconds. Dave seemed a little too gleeful, like he already knew, somehow, that the murderous swarms would, for inexplicable reasons, spare him.

Blaine checked his phone. He had the dread zero bars of no service. News apps, social media, email, even the weather had gotten stuck, twenty minutes in the past, at 11:52 EST on the first day of February, sixty-one degrees Fahrenheit, which, Blaine calculated, was sixteen degrees Celsius.

Blaine believed in science, and thus the metric system. It was obviously superior. It was *how they get you,* Dave had said, as if it was superiorly obvious. *I pledge allegiance,* he said, with his hand on his heart, *to inches and miles.*

THIS IS THE EMERGENCY BROADCAST SYSTEM

TOOOOOOOOOOOOOOOOOOOOOOOOOOOOONE

Neither of them had service, but then Blaine got a text from his wife: *Are you watching the news?*

The wife texted in complete sentences, in case a litigation discovery request required the production of text messages that could not be withheld on grounds of privilege, the wife said. But the simplest explanation was that the wife was compulsively anal about written grammar and punctuation.

Blaine had dumb text fingers. Or, a single texting finger incapable of tapping a simple reply in the time it took his ambidextrous wife to send a four-batch of texts:

I am freaking out.
If you are not watching the news, you should turn it on right now.
I love you.
Whatever happens, Blaine, I love you.

No, he had not watched the news, and he loved her too, and *Do not freak out,* he told her, and then he told himself, as he started to freak. Dave climbed into the van, driver's seat. He tapped the wheel impatiently. Come on, come on, come on. They hadn't taken water samples yet, Blaine said, and it seemed like a waste to drive all the way out again.

TOOOOOOOOOOOOOOOOOOOOOOOOOOOOONE

He glanced up at the sky. Somewhere, beyond all that blue, there was life. Myriad life proliferated through the galaxies. It was all very far away. Space was unfathomably vast. A V-flock of black bird shapes flapped past, east to west.

"The wrong direction," Dave said. "If they were real birds." But they weren't. No such thing. The "bird," according to Dave, was just an aircraft carrier for nano-drones.

Blaine climbed into the van because, seriously, Dave would drive off without him. Dave peeled out of the parking lot. The radio blared its uninformative emergency alert. Blaine's phone stayed frozen at 11:52 a.m. They turned onto the main road.

"Does the street seem empty? The street seems empty," Dave declared.

The traffic lights flashed yellow.

TOOOOOOOOOOOOOOOOOOOOOOOOOOOOOOONE

Where were you when it happened?

Halfway to the highway, river on one side, sloped hill on the other colored brown with winter grass, the roadside dappled by Midwest commerce. The Whippety-Dip soft-serve joint. The pony keg. The used car lot guarded by a massive painted puma, festooned by colored plastic flags. The billboards: ARE YOU PREGNANT AND SCARED? (That one was tricksy.) INJURED? CALL HOMERUN HOWIE MASON! HE'LL KNOCK YOUR LEGAL PROBLEMS OUT OF THE PARK! The billboard lawyer wore a baseball jersey beneath his blazer. He had a baseball bat, a profitable twinkle in his eye.

Funny, the things that mattered before it happened, and the things that mattered after.

TOOOOOOOOOOOOOOOOOOOOOOOOOOOOOOONE

THIS IS THE EMERGENCY BROADCAST SYSTEM

THIS IS NOT A TEST

A VESSEL HAS APPEARED IN THE AIRSPACE OVER OUR NATION'S CAPITAL

SEEK SHELTER

REPEAT

SEEK SHELTER, IMMEDIATELY

THIS IS NOT A TEST

TOOOOOOOOOOOOOOOOOOOOOOOOOOOONE

The van slowed. They coasted to a stop in the shadow of the puma. Dave shook his head, unbelievable. Unbelievable. The message repeated.

THIS IS NOT A TEST

A VESSEL HAS APPEARED . . .

The Stepchild

WHERE WERE YOU when it happened?

She had a fight with her boyfriend. But that happened later, after they'd drank a fifth of Jack P.'s gin and her boyfriend just wanted to play *Super Smash Bros.* and she was like, WTF, Justin. Hello? Aliens? Hello? How are you not freaking out?

Heather freaked out. If Justin was a good boyfriend and not just a douchey gamer, he would have held her in his arms, murmured strong helpful encouragements, and followed up with an afternoon leisure-fuck.

He was not/did not.

His excuses sucked:

"But I just want to finish my game."

"But we *just* had sex." Yesterday. For like two minutes and forty-five seconds. Not that she had timed it, exactly.

"But what's the big deal, Heather? I mean, *of course* there are aliens. Didn't you watch, like, *The X-Files?*"

When the alien ship appeared over LA and the power went out in Malibu, Heather's first thought was *Holy crap, it's happening, finally!* She felt shivery, hopeful almost. Nothing real ever happened, but now it was. The old shitty cycle had abruptly ended. This new one still had potential. It could be the beginning of a brilliant new epoch. And she was a part of it.

She and Justin went out into the yard and stripped off their clothes and dove naked into the pool. Jack P. had taken Heather's mom to Carmel for a week, and Heather's stepbrother, Alex, was away at some fancy-schmancy college prep school, so they had the pool to themselves. Heather floated on her back and stared up at the shadow of the great ship in the sky. The lights on the ship flashed blue red green. Beyond them, the stars glittered. It felt like she and Justin had the whole world to themselves. Then she felt something bump against her arm and she looked over and saw her stepdad's newest pool float, green inflatable plastic in the shape of a gecko, which (she was pretty sure) was not amphibious, and her exuberance fizzled into annoyance. The pool belonged to Jack P., not to her. The world didn't belong to her at all, and she hated it.

She swam to the edge. "Let's get out."

"But we just got *in*. Come on, stay in the pool. You know what we've never done in the pool?"

They had, but it hadn't worked right and, of course, he had forgotten.

Heather climbed out. She drip-dried. She stared out, at the vessel. She wanted to rekindle her excitement, but instead she just felt cranky. She felt like she had last Malibu Christmas, when Jack P. and her mom couldn't quit petting each other and Jack P.'s brainiac kid Alex got a brand-new Tesla with a big red bow on top while she got a pair of Rollerblades. *Won't that be so fun? Rolling around in those?* It wouldn't be fun, and she sold them on eBay. Sure, she already had a car, but it was used, boring, and not a Tesla. She felt cranky and hungry, and she wanted a blueberry scone, but Justin had eaten the last one.

Justin climbed out of the pool. He walked dripping into the house. He came back out with the bottle of gin.

"Power's still out. But hey, doesn't your stepdad have a generator?"

Jack P. had everything. Jack P. had won big on *Jeopardy!* when he was young, and after that he kept on winning. He won studio contracts for the reality TV programs he produced. He won the affection of Heather's mother. He won awards. Best Reality TV series. Best Television Director. Best Ever Dad. Heather had given him that last award when she was just a little kid, right after he married her mother and she was still young and dumb enough to think that Jack P. was cool. She'd colored a lopsided trophy in yellow crayon and wrote his name in bubble letters, *Jack P.*, surrounded by pink and purple stars. But then Jack P. had the award framed and hung it on the wall where Heather couldn't not see it, and every time she saw it she felt cranky.

"If you can find it," she said. "I don't know where it is."

Justin climbed up onto the diving board. He tested its spring.

"I think I'll call in to work," he said, as if the focal feature of alien arrival was its impact on his schedule valet-parking cars at the Twin Palms Resort.

He dove, swam, procrastinated. When he tried to call, his phone didn't work.

"That's lame," Heather said.

"Try your phone."

"You can get it if you want."

He did. Her phone didn't work either.

"This is bunk." Justin dove back into the pool. Heather scrolled through news feeds that would not update. She took a series of spaceship selfies. Sun-kissed, bare-shouldered Malibu Heather against the backdrop of alien invasion.

"You think they're gonna, like, destroy LA?" she asked. She didn't feel afraid. Jack P.'s backyard did not feel like insurrection ground zero. She had seen this movie before. It ended with maybe a crater in place of a city or two, but the people like her, out in the burbs, they were all fine. Maybe a little dusty, with a cinematic smear of dirt across the cheek, a torn shirt sleeve. In the end, they kissed and wept happy triumph tears.

"Like, what, in that movie *Independence Day*? I dunno." Justin shrugged.

"I know you don't *know*. But what do you think?"

"I think they're, like, violating the Prime Directive."

"The what?"

"The Prime Directive. You know?"

"No." She reclined beside the pool. She dipped her toes in the cool water. This was the boring part of the movie, where you waited for the laser blast, the boom, the buildings crumbling, the mushroom clouds; first you had to sit and listen to boring conversations about the prime whatever.

"Don't you watch TV?"

"I watch *good* TV."

"It's from *Star Trek*."

"Of course it is."

"But, like, it's part of the cultural lexigon." Justin tried to sound smart by using words like *lexicon* but he pronounced them wrong. Heather found this Justin feature cute at first, but the more words she heard him confidently butcher, the more it annoyed her. "It's, like, a more advanced culture isn't supposed to interfere with, like, less advanced people. Or creatures. Life-forms. 'Cause it inpeeds their ability to develop naturally."

"Uh-huh."

"I'm serious. It's, like, *unnatural*. We're supposed to evolve on our own."

Justin had inconsistent viewpoints regarding sticking to the natural course of evolution. He had, for example, paid a kid to write his essays and earn him As in English class.

"Yeah, but that wasn't what I asked. I asked if you thought they were gonna destroy LA."

"Oh. I dunno. But if they were gonna, you'd think they wouldn't still just be hovering there. It would have happened already."

The Husband

"BUDDY, HEY," BLAINE said. "Hey. Buddy. Dave, man. The message said—"

THIS IS NOT A TEST

A VESSEL HAS APPEARED . . .

SEEK SHELTER

REPEAT

For a moment, Dave stared, aghast, motionless. Then his action switch flipped back on. He turned the radio off. He hit the gas, flipped a U-turn, steered the van into the pony keg. *Fill 'er up.* A glaze-eyed attendant with a shoulder-length mullet loaded six-packs into the back of the van. The attendant hadn't heard. No radio in the pony keg. The wireless cut out. His phone kept glitching. He would remember, later, when he picked up his last paycheck from the pony keg and bought a one-way ticket on a bus headed south, how those two fellows bought every six-pack, every wine bottle, every candy bar, all loaded into the back of the city van. They cleaned the place out. Then told him, on their way out: He better get out too. It wasn't a test.

Dave drove crazy fast. The empty road filled up with Daves. Cars did sixty in a thirty-five. Trucks straddled the yellow line. Dave maneuvered around them all. A cop appeared in the rearview mirror. The cop pulled up beside the speeding city van, zipped past them, raced away.

Blaine switched the radio back on.

THIS IS NOT A TEST

A VESSEL HAS APPEARED...

SEEK SHELTER

REPEAT

He switched it off.

"When do you think they'll tell us, like, what's actually happening?" he asked Dave.

Dave ignored the *when* part. "No," he declared. "No, they'll never tell." Not the truth, the whole truth, and nothing but. Dave had secret sources: internet decoders, shortwave radio gurus. Folks who could gather all the clues and gestalt them into truth. Whatever they heard from official sources would just be watered-down lies. Fake news, dude.

Blaine tried to call the wife. *Hello, you've reached...* her voicemail said. He heard fear in her voice. But it was just a recording. The same recording she'd had since forever ago. He hung up. He called again. *Hello, you've reached...* She sounded almost panicked. *Damn it Dave,* Blaine thought. *Damn it.* The simplest explanation said he'd projected his own panic and fear onto the voicemail message. But Dave rubbed off. He made everything smell like conspiracy.

They passed a Value Valley, where lines had already formed at the pumps. The parking lot had begun to fill up. *Suckers,* Dave said. If you didn't stock up on toilet paper now, you wouldn't find any for weeks. Dave had forty-eight rolls in his basement. If he stretched them, everyone else would be dead before he had to resort to leaves.

"But maybe it's not the end," Blaine said. The simplest explanation said a vessel had appeared and that didn't mean squat. There was no next thing until a next thing happened and it hadn't yet. And when it did, well, maybe it would be excellent and Star Treky. A welcome, good humans of Earth, to the peaceful galactic federation of hooray-you-don't-have-to-work-a-pointless-shit-job-as-slave-to-the-capitalist-regime event. But the galactic federation didn't mesh with the flat-earth theory. (*Truth*, Dave said. *Flat-Earth Truth. Have you been all the way around it? I didn't think so.*)

Blaine tried again to call the wife. He left a voicemail message. He fretted about her. He fretted about their kids. He tried to call the school. The line was busy. The kids didn't have phones because *Honey they're obviously too young, I mean Avril loses at least six gloves every winter, and Jas?* Jas was the impressionable sort. He could get recruited by anarchist skinheads. He could get convinced that Earth was flat.

Dave drove the side roads. The freeway would be hazardous, he said. Full of crazies, he said, as he grabbed a six-pack, cracked open a midday beer, lit a menthol in the city van. They turned the radio on and off. It offered nothing but the same alarming tone, the amorphous message of invasion. Blaine's phone offered nothing but a temporal snapshot: 11:52, back before the world as they knew it had begun to end.

"Whaddaya think?" Dave inhaled deep, minty fiberglass. "Whaddaya think is gonna happen?"

It didn't matter what Blaine thought. Dave had asked as a segue to what Dave thought: the eradication of the human race, or at least all but the craftiest, Daviest among them. Or, depending on our luck, the aliens would just enslave us, probe us, rape us, guinea-pig us. Or things would get blasty. A few laser bursts, a few nuclear warheads, it all ended the same: with us kaput.

* * *

What did you think, when it happened? Do you remember?

Blaine remembered menthol. He remembered a car pulled off to the side of the road, hazards blinking, smoke rising from the hood. How Dave said, *That poor guy*, as if a smoking engine meant the difference between life and death and Dave drove right past him anyway. Sped up, actually. Blaine remembered thinking how the simplest explanation was Orson-Wellesian, a modern day *War of the Worlds* radio event. The simplest explanation said *hoax* and tomorrow he and Dave would share a good laugh, a laugh that would endure (*Hey, remember that time when you maxed out your credit card to buy apocalypse beer?!*) alongside Dave's disappointment.

The van pulled up in front of Blaine's house. He couldn't remember exactly how they got there. The past had already begun to erase itself. His house looked suburbanly cartoonish, with its trim winter lawn, its two-car garage. It looked like the house in the scene in the movie when the alien ship fired its red death ray down, straight down at that placid house, to signify the end of lawn mowers and barbecues and barking dogs and everything else that house meant. He saw, in his mind's eye, the darkening sky, the kids pointing up at the ominous shadow above, their bikes abandoned in the cul-de-sac. Duck and cover, babies. Then, in a flash, they were gone. The sun blazed bright in the vacant sky.

"Take some beer," Dave said. "Take half. Hell, take more." Dave was just one man, in a house by himself. How much beer could he guzzle while the world ended?

The Brother

OLIVER.

Oliver.

"Oliver."

You ever seen flakes this big?

"Oliver? Are you done with breakfast?"

A blizzard came, and the snow kept falling and falling, faster, faster.

"Guess you didn't like the oatmeal, huh, Oliver? Well, next time we'll tell 'em to hold the brown sugar."

The snow kept falling and falling. It covered the cafeteria tables. It blanketed his oatmeal. He didn't understand. Why had they served him this bowl of snow, with a patch of grainy brown in the middle, a dirty center?

"Oliver, if you're done with breakfast, can you give me a little nod? Can you do that for me? Can you nod?"

The napkin dabbed at the corner of his lip, where he couldn't feel right. Because of the cold, he tried to tell them. But he couldn't make his voice work. Because the cold made him numb because the snow kept falling.

"Well, shoot." Nurse Betsy Martin examined Oliver. "After your neat little trick this morning I was hopeful you might still be in there. But I guess not, huh? Oh well."

She looked disappointed in him. Oliver clenched his jaw. He tried to see through the snow, to the other side, where the nurse lived. He tried tried tried and he felt so cold, so exhausted, but then his head moved. Up-down-up-down. A nod.

"Well, I'll be," the nurse said. "Did you just nod, Oliver? There's a good boy. Maybe you're in there after all."

Oliver felt out there. He was not in anywhere. His heart felt cold and cracked. He was not a good boy, not good not good not good *holy moly. SLAM. SMASH.* His arm flung out. *SMASH.* The water cup toppled onto the linoleum, but it didn't break. Plastic cups only at Brookwood.

The pooled water became a mop. The cafeteria table became a wood-framed chair, bolted to the floor, padded seats encased in protective plastic. The nurse became a television, the channel: cartoons. The bombastic rooster paraded the barnyard, whistling humming swinging that wooden plank. The rooster slapped that sleeping dog *yee-ooww* on his bee-hind. The inmates howled. The inmates became patients became inmates. The windows wore iron bars. No jumping, the signs said. Oliver read them but he could not read them. The day became the night became the day while Oliver contemplated jumping. The rooster plotted and raged. Games of Uno, games of checkers, games of chess. Inmates versus patients. Oliver rocked in his chair. That green pill, they said, would calm his seas, would settle the rocking. *That's a joke, I say that's a joke, son.* Linoleum became planks. Brookwood became a boat. Oliver felt seasick. Along came the white pill, for nausea. Oliver's insides became a slip-and-slide.

The nurse thanked the plastic seat cover. She sprayed him clean. She dressed him in institutional whites that had become grays after years of trips through the wash. This, the doctors agreed, engendered healing. But fresh white conjured snow, inside Oliver's head. The snow fell and kept falling. It glazed the chessboard. It buried the Uno cards. Brookwood slippers left barnyard tracks, from the barn to the doghouse to the Ping-Pong table, all covered in snowy drifts. Oliver shivered. The bathrobe on his shoulders became an ineffectual blanket.

The blanket was a quarter-strip of worn fleece, cut small because *no hanging*. No blanket-noose. The bathrobes had no belts. The pants had embedded elastic bands, but they still slipped down because Oliver didn't eat enough because maybe if he starved to death the snow would stop, finally.

The nurse said no, they would just stick a needle into his vein and stuff him full of nutritional fluids. They were civilized, and civilized meant maintaining life at all costs, even when life would rather snuff itself out with a bathrobe-blanket-noose.

Inside it snowed, but outside the sun peeked through the window bars. Green bulb buds poked through the Brookwood mud. Purple-white snowdrops lifted their heads to gaze up at the February sky. Patients or inmates filed out into the yard. Fresh air, the nurses said. The high walls said *sorry you can't leave*. Once Upon a Time of Lobotomies, the walls wore barbed-wire crowns. But Brookwood was too civilized for barbed wire now. Oliver cowered in his scrap blanket. He sought a corner of shade, in which to rock. Patients or inmates played H-O-R-S-E with a squishy plastic ball, the kind that couldn't break noses. Once Oliver had *SMASH*-smashed his nose against the cement. The snow wouldn't stop, so he closed his eyes and let himself fall flat. His flayed arms made an Oliver angel. His nose bled all over. The *when* bled into a later when all the days bled together. He couldn't discern them, through all this snow. The blood left a stain. Some things stain, Oliver, the doctor had said. Some things left marks on your permanent record. The doctor scribbled marks on Oliver's chart, and the marks changed the shape and color of the pills placed on Oliver's tongue and none of it made sense. A veritable blizzard of confusion, it all was.

Until it wasn't quite. Until the day when all the inmates or patients began to screech, weep, point up at the darkening sky. *Holy moly.*

"Yelling like a pack of crazed chimps." The nurse stared up. "What's the—"

Holy moly.

Oliver rocked, shivered. Damn, that snow that snow that snow seemed to let up a bit. There was a subtle shift in the wind, almost imperceptible. The sky got darker, but the light got brighter. The headlights around the bend illumined a brutal swirl of snow. Oliver screamed. The nurses screamed. Get them in! Get them all in. Get them *holy moly.*

Next: mayhem.

An inmate or patient squirreled up the wall, flung a leg over the top; see, we should have kept that barbed wire. A stampede of Brookwood slippers crushed those snowdrops. The snowflakes *you ever seen flakes this big* got smaller.

They're all unique, she had told him once.

They're all unique.

A memory broke free from his snowbound mind.

Someone grabbed his arm, pulled him along. Inside, inside. As if the inside could protect them now.

The yard became the big room where everyone gathered at the windows, stared out through the bars. *Get back, get back,* the nurse refrain, but none of them listened, not even the nurses. The rooster cawed *pay attention to me, boy! I'm not talkin' just to hear my head roar* and then snow. The rooster became snow. The TV screen became snow. The snow became a blackout. The inmates howled. The blackout became the sky, as something passed over.

Something immense, sky-sized. The window-bar shadows on the snow-swept floor had a colored hue, pinkish then blue then green. Oliver had a strange thought. *Break out,* the thought said. Pry those shadows apart. Leap out. Bask in the kaleidoscopic light. Oliver felt a strange fuzziness inside his head, like peach fuzz sprouting along the skin of his thoughts. He felt light, feathery. He drifted up, out of his chair. He gazed up. The sky became the ceiling. The snow tapered. He caught the last few flakes in his outstretched hands. He took a cautious step, leery of black ice. His legs teetered. *Pay attention to me, boy!* He saw the phantom outline of a rooster on the TV screen. His paper shoulders pulled back. His rail chest puffed out. I say I say, his slippered feet became rooster talons. He strutted the length of the big room *faster, Ollie, faster, faster* to the far side, to the window. He touched his fingers to the glass. He pressed his face against it. He stared up.

Farewell, sky.

The snow clouds had parted, exposing the silvery chassis of the outer world. What had been sky was now boundless metal, molten yet solid, rippling with colored light. Oliver felt like a bug inside a bottle inside a dream, and in the dream the snow stopped and the plows and salt trucks rumbled past and his car pulled safe into the driveway and nothing shattered. Not his heart, not nothing. He seized the window bars. For a moment there was no window beyond them, just space; him and space and the brand-new sky. Then a hundred million billion shards of glass re-formed into a solid pane, and Oliver did not know if this un-breaking had happened to the window, or to him.

His hands steadied. His noodle arms stiffened. He squeezed the bars and pulled, and he knew he could never pull them apart, tear them from the wall, shimmy between them. He knew because the blizzard had blown out of his head. He squeezed and pulled to squeeze and pull. He yelled to yell. He started to cry. What did it mean? *Faster, Ollie, faster faster.* What did it mean? To be alive in the universe. To find one's self alive, and not alone. *Holy moly.*

The Husband

DAVE DROVE OFF in the city van. Blaine stacked six-packs in the garage, then went inside. His hands shook as he turned on the TV. The TV bleeped, then turned itself off. He pressed the power button. Nothing happened. He flicked the light switch. Nothing happened. He went into the kitchen. The stove clock displayed numberless black. The power had gone out. Preview: apocalypse.

No, Blaine told himself. No, it didn't happen like this. The apocalypse didn't happen. Occam's razor said the power cut out on the regular, for regular reasons like windstorms and electrocuted squirrels and poor infrastructure investments. This, Blaine had tried to convince the wife, was why they needed a landline.

No, the wife insisted. What, a landline? How quaint. What year was it anyway, 1938? The other houses on their street suggested yes. The other houses spawned from the Sears catalog. They had bungalow porches, detached garages, casement windows, crystal doorknobs. Their house was built new, atop the bones of a hoarder's lair. They bought the old house and tore it down. The old house reeked of the forty-some cats that lived and died between the towers of magazines, Beanie Boos, plastic cutlery packages, takeout menus, et cetera that sprawled mega-city style across its rotting floors. It doesn't smell *that* bad, the wife said wistfully. But the floors were irreparable, so they had to tear it down. Blaine thought maybe they should look at what else the Sears catalog had to offer. No, the wife insisted. They would buy the hoarder's house. They would tear it down and build anew.

The wife had very particular, very strong ideas. Blaine couldn't argue when she set her mind on something. She was a straight red laser beam.

He tried to call the wife again, but her phone didn't even ring. It went straight to voicemail. *Hello, you've reached the voicemail of . . .* The wife's recording sounded unduly, almost insultingly professional. Blaine started to leave a message but the system cut him off. *Thank you, goodbye.* He set the phone down. He heard a startling knock on the front door.

What would Dave do?

Dave had a spy hole, an arsenal, a Rottweiler bitch who'd tear an intruder's nutsack off with her teeth.

Blaine crept toward the door. *Rat-a-tat-tat.* He opened without looking first. Occam's razor said Avril had lost her key.

"Oh, Blaine!" Elena, the neighbor, flung her arms around him. "This is just terrifying. Do you have any idea what's happening? I guess I don't need to leave this note. I thought you were at work. John got stuck on his way home. There was a terrible wreck on the freeway. He said people just abandoned their cars. It's a literal parking lot. I told him, leave ours. Just get home. Walk if you have to. He wouldn't let me pick him up. And now I can't reach him! My phone is useless. The satellites must be . . . well, who knows. Anyway, I just ran down to leave this note. I've got your kids."

She might have led with that. "Oh, good," Blaine said. "Thanks."

"The school said to pick them up. So. Well. They're fine. Jas is fine. Thrilled, actually, since school got out early. Him and Foster are playing some video game—"

"You have power?"

"No, it's a handheld. And Avril is— Well, she's, I mean, anyone would be disturbed. I am. Do you want to come get them? I'm sure

Foster would rather Jas stay, but, you know, family . . ."

Blaine would come get them, he decided, but on the short walk to Elena and John's house they passed two other neighbors, one heading out to stock up on supplies and the other returning with a back seat full of paper products and canned goods. So instead of heading home with his children, Blaine found himself backing out of a driveway in Elena's minivan with a two-page supply list and a Ziploc bag full of cash, assorted credit cards, and a bad, bad, bad feeling that everything he knew was on the precipice of ending; and surely the Value Valley had sold out of at least half the things on the list. The toilet paper, the hard liquor, the canned stews, medicines, toothpaste. At best he could hope for long-shelf-life perishables, the flavored yogurt tubes, the processed cheese slices, the soy milk creamers.

At best or at worst he could hope that someone had driven a truck through the entrance to initiate the new era of looting so he could grab some supplies before they all sold out.

He turned the car radio on—*TOOOOOOOOOOOOOOOOO OOOOOOOOOOONE*—then off. Then on again. He raced through stations. They all played the same emergency message. He let it run, volume low, in case it changed to something informative. He waited and cursed at the dead traffic lights. All the lights had lost power, and the houses and businesses. The Value Valley had lost power. The gas pumps had shut off, but people still waited in line for them to come back on. The cars, at least, still worked, which meant no electromagnetic spaceship blast. At least not yet.

Blaine parked at the far end of a packed parking lot. He jogged up to the back of the line that snaked around the Value Valley's concrete-box exterior. He took his phone out of his pocket and tried to call the wife. The wife's voicemail rejected him. *This voicemail box is full. Better luck next time, sweetie.* It didn't make sense that her mailbox could be full, or that Blaine's phone could stay set at 11:52 a.m., or that a vessel could appear in the airspace over the capital. If they could traverse the vast reaches of space, couldn't they at least cloak the ship?

Well, yeah, Blaine's brain responded, in the voice of Dave. *If they didn't want us to know. And they want us to know because, well, the simplest explanation is . . .*

Dave would plant a grove of land mines in his front yard. Dave would splatter the barbed-wire fence around his yard with the bug-guts of a thousand aliens before he'd let them beam him anywhere or take his land.

The line didn't move. Blaine checked his phone. *11:52.* Still no service bars, no internet connections. He had a vague, empty feeling inside, the feeling that came from the absence of memes, video clips, updates to the newsfeed. Also, the absence of the wife. The wife would have ideas, instructions. *Well, don't just stand there, Blaine. The line isn't moving. You need to* think the way the wife would think. *Think*, he told himself, as he stood there idly, as he checked his non-functioning phone. The gregarious humans flocked to the megastore, but the wife would know about some mom-and-pop grocery with full shelves and no lines, some specialty market, medical supply site, toilet paper warehouse, distillery, or other destination perceptible only by special wife magic, which Elena didn't have. *Go to the Value Valley*, Elena had said, and so Blaine went. But even if he could think like his wife, he knew it wouldn't work out the same. He would arrive at the mom-and-pop grocery just as mom and pop hammered the last nail into the boards meant to keep the looters away.

The line inched. A few people trickled out of the store with carts half-full. Then someone yelled, and the people near the entrance surged. The front of the line erupted into a horde. People fled, converged, yelled. Commotion trickled through the line, to the futile back. *What's happening?*

The wife would have known this would happen. She would have warned him in advance, and he never would have been near the scene. He would have heard about it later from the neighbor who saw the last shopping cart emerge from the building, nearly empty, who saw the lone security guard and the gaggle of Value Valley greeters and stockers in their cheery green vests aligned at the entrance, shaking their heads in fear, locking the door. They didn't get paid enough for whatever this was, and what it was they still didn't know. A chunk of concrete flew toward the window. The glass shattered. A woman got trampled, Blaine heard later from a neighbor who had a friend at the front of the line who saw it. People smashed through the windows. They streamed between the shards of broken glass, into the building. Blaine turned away. He hurried back to Elena's minivan. He climbed inside. He drove over the strip of grass that framed the parking lot, out into the street. His heart pounded and he had no canned goods, no toilet paper, nothing but a massive pile of beer. *Thank you, Dave.* Maybe he could trade it.

The radio played *TOOOOOOOOOOOOOOOOOOOOOOOOOOOOOOONE.* It didn't say much more. It said that maybe, the world was ending. Time to go a-looting.

But Blaine felt done. He steered the minivan toward home.

* * *

Blaine began to really seriously worry when the sun went down but his phone still said 11:52 and the wife still hadn't come home and the power still hadn't come back. Before it got dark, *THIS IS NOT A TEST* had felt like a test. *NOT A TEST* hailed from Daveville, Fringe County, somewhere out along the obscure edges of the flat earth, a land antithetical to the rational, scientific principles in which Blaine placed his faith. *Don't you think it's weird that you're, you know, technically a scientist,* he had asked Dave once. Dave answered with a shrug, followed by a *You know what's really weird* followed by a story about microscopic explosive devices embedded in certain potato chip flavors. It didn't matter which brand. All the brands did it. The micro-explosions destroyed cells and caused cancers. An obvious correlation existed between the increased consumption of cheddar bacon chips and rising cancer rates.

NOT A TEST made Blaine think of explosive cheese powder, which made his heart doubt, even though his heart also felt that something not-test-like must be happening to provoke this sustained emergency radio broadcast. The kids thought it was definitely-definitely-definitely not a test. Avril hated tests. She had to take them in a special windowless room at school, on special fill-in-the-bubble paper while all the other kids used computer screens because screens made her eyes hurt when they weren't TV, and now she had an anti-testing bias. Jas thought that any minute now, alien invaders resembling man-sized cockroach-eel-scorpion hybrids would invade their city-neighborhood-house, and he meant to repel them.

"But when will the electricity come back, Dad? And how do I make giant bug zappers if I don't have electricity?"

Jas collected all the household batteries. He drew crayon schematics. He strung soda cans on a shoelace line in front of the door, to alert them if anyone tried to enter.

"Okay, that's enough sugar." Dad put his foot down after several hundred grams. "Geez, how much soda did you drink?"

How much did it matter if the world was ending?

They lit candles. They went out onto the back patio. The air had gotten cooler, but it still felt warm for February, warm enough to make Blaine think that maybe he could survive in the powerless post-apocalyptic Midwest. It felt like summer, Jas said, so they should have hot dogs and roast marshmallows. Blaine built a fire in the fire-bowl. He skewered hot dogs. He roasted them, while Avril sat and drew by the firelight, and Jas patrolled the dark corners of the yard. The invaders might not come from the street. They might pour over the fence, or rappel down from the trees.

"But when will Mom come home?" Avril asked. She sculpted an eye in her sketchbook. The eye belonged to a winged, lionesque creature. It had a name that Blaine couldn't remember. *Oh, that's a nice lion*, he would say, and Avril would scowl and tell him it wasn't a lion, it was a *fill-in-the-blank*, similar to all the kids' other amalgamated exotic animal creations.

"I don't know. Mom's probably just . . . Well, I'm sure she'll be home soon."

"You don't sound sure, Dad."

Surely, the wife was out there accomplishing productive things. Surely she would return home with a sedan full of camping equipment or a generator or a family set of crossbows. Blaine gazed up at the sky, the same sky beneath which the wife was presently bartering for their future survival, the same sky in which a vessel had allegedly appeared. There was no evidence of the ship now, there, in the backyard. There was only firelight shadow, dark and stars, more stars than ever. The power must have gone out everywhere.

"I don't think the aliens are bad," Avril said. "They probably just want to check us out and see what we're like. Like when we go to see the animals at the zoo." Except the zoo animals didn't exist in the wild. They got snatched and caged. "Here, Dad, look at my drawing."

"That's pretty," Blaine said, glancing at the drawing.

"It's not pretty. It's a *lineagle*. It's fierce and majestic."

"Well, you did a nice job of making it fierce and—"

The house whirred. The porch light flickered on. All the lights came on.

"Dad! Dad! The lights!" Jas bounded up to the porch.

"I liked it better in the dark," Avril said.

"That's because you're a freak."

"Jas—"

"But, Dad, it's true. And you said that if something was true, then we should say it—"

"That's not what I meant. I meant that—"

"I *am* a freak," Avril said.

"See, Dad?"

"But Jas is a *jerk*."

"Hey!"

"Kids!"

Jas tore the lineagle from his sister's sketchbook. He leapt back. Avril swiped. She grabbed the picture, but Jas held tight. The lineagle ripped in two. Avril punched her brother in the gut.

"Kids! Stop!"

The kids circled each other, snarling.

"She punched me!"

"He's a killer! He killed the lineagle!"

"Stop it!" Blaine yelled. He wished the wife was there. The wife always seemed to know the exact right combination of magic words to defuse any child spat. The wife would never let the kids devolve into vicious hyenas. Avril swung with her claws out. Jas kicked.

"Both of you! Stop it!" Blaine had a limited repertoire of magic words. He could only think of one: TV. "Stop it! We're going inside. You can watch TV until your mom gets home."

The children retracted their claws. Their hackles smoothed. They ran inside. They loved TV. All children loved TV, but these children *adored* TV. Blaine had caught them, when the television was turned off, stroking its plastic casing, singing it a soft lullaby. They made valentines for the TV, red and pink construction paper hearts, which the wife laminated and strung up around it. BE MINE, TV. JAS + AVRIL + TV FOREVER. TV was the central unifying force in a homeland of sibling discord.

Blaine gathered the half-eaten hot dogs, the skewers, the empty soda cans. He tried to recall when/how the children had snuck more soda. He followed them inside.

"Dad!"

"Dad! Dad!"

They yelled from the living room.

"Dad! Come see!"

"Come see, Dad!"

"Dad! It's aliens!"

Blaine ran into the living room. Avril stood transfixed, inches from the beloved TV. Jas jumped up and down on the couch, shouting, pointing.

"Aliens! Aliens! Aliens!"

The television played live video feed: Washington, DC, filmed from a distance. It was nighttime there, and the city was dark, the building windows black, the streetlights out, the usual white-red streams of traffic light absent. The only light came from the vessel that hovered over the city. The vessel was massive, miles wide, wheel shaped, fatter in the center but still several stories high around its perimeter. Its surface was smooth and silvery, but also colored. The color seemed to shift, silver-red to silver-green to silver-blue, forming a halo of light. The ship itself pulsed softly.

"Dad! Dad! Aliens! Dad! Aliens!"

Jas did a twirling trampoline leap across the couch. His stray hand smacked into the lampshade. The lamp crashed onto the floor.

"Oh no! Dad! I'm sorry! I—"

"It's fine, just . . ." Blaine slumped onto the couch.

Jas flopped down beside him.

They stared at the vessel on the TV screen.

"Avril, I can't see!" Jas whined. The vessel throbbed—silvery green, silvery blue.

"Avril—"

Avril's hand glided across the screen, as if she wanted to pet the vessel through the glass. She pulled her hand back, dissatisfied. She tiptoed backward to the couch, to her father. She curled up beside him. They all stared.

"Dad?"

"Yeah?"

"Is that a real spaceship? Because—"

"I don't know," Blaine said. It looked real. Occam's razor said . . . what, exactly? He grabbed the remote. He changed the channel. There it glowed, one channel up: the vessel. He flipped through the channels. They all played the same alien spaceship programming. The vessel whirred. Then on the lower-right corner of the screen, a second video frame appeared.

"Are we on? The connection— Oh, we're live. Okay, then."

A reporter turned to face the camera. She stood in front of a farmland backdrop, a red barn, cows grazing in the dark distance. She looked frazzled, and afraid. It was nighttime, but the light beyond her shifted, silvery green to red to blue.

"Reporting live from CBN News, outside Fredericksburg, Virginia. I'm about an hour south of Washington, DC. At 11:52 a.m. Eastern Standard Time, a massive spaceship-like object appeared in the airspace above the capital. You can see it, if you pan up—"

The camera panned up. In the space behind and above the reporter, miles away over the city, the vessel glimmered.

"The object has not moved. It has not taken further aggressive action. It . . . We've gotten reports that it is surrounded by some sort of disruptive force field. At this time we don't know any more. Our communications systems have been nonfunctional all day, though they are starting to come back on in certain places. Power is still down in the district. Evacuation orders have been issued for DC and the surrounding suburbs, but—"

The reporter stopped. Someone offscreen handed her a phone. She listened, nodded. She closed her eyes for a moment. She took a deep breath before she spoke.

"Just in. The spaceship above DC is not the only one. We have reports of . . . six? Six. At least six additional ships confirmed. Los Angeles. Mexico City. London. Delhi. Tokyo. Is that . . . right. São Paulo, Brazil. The same as the one over DC. Several miles wide. All just hovering there. So far, there have been no attacks—"

"Did you hear that?"

"—other than the widespread loss of electricity. We lost all power in the areas surrounding DC. We've gotten in similar reports of power outages elsewhere. This may be a worldwide—"

Blaine muted the TV.

"Hey!"

"Dad—"

"Dad, we want to—"

"Shhhhhh. Listen."

The children's ears perked for the jingle-ling of alien invaders. They heard a clang.

"Did you hear that?"

"It's the cans! The soda cans!"

Clank-clang-tink-tink.

"We've trapped one!" Jas squealed. "Dad! We've trapped one!"

"Jas, it's probably just the wind."

"Avril, you go get a knife. I'll take the fireplace poker, and Dad—"

"No, Avril, do not go get a knife," Blaine said.

"Well, how is she supposed to kill it if—"

"She's not killing anything. There's nothing out there but—" *Tink-clank-tink-clank.* "But cans. Just cans, blowing around in the wind."

"But, Dad, what if it's aliens? You don't know it's not aliens—and if we don't kill them they might eat us!"

"Jas, I hardly think that—"

Tink-clank-tink.

Knock-knock-knock.

"Oh my god, they're knocking!"

Avril dropped to the ground and rolled under the coffee table. Jas grabbed the fireplace poker. Blaine headed toward the door.

"Dad, get back!" Jas yelled. "Don't open it!"

"Do you really think"—*knock-knock-knock*—"that aliens would knock? It's probably just one of the neighbors or—"

Blaine opened the door. Jas screamed.

Anne screamed as the fireplace poker sailed over her shoulder.

"Jas! What the—"

"Mom?"

"Anne!"

"Mom!"

The wife was tangled up in a string of cans. Jas flung himself at her.

Avril squirmed out from under the coffee table. She scurried to the door, to her mother. "Mom." She nestled her head into the wife's armpit.

"I nearly wasn't. *Jas.*"

"Sorry, Mom."

"You could have killed me."

"I thought there were aliens outside and I, I didn't want them to eat us and, and, and—

The wife stroked the boy's soft head. She pulled him close. Blaine waited for her to say something wifey, something like *You've got to think before you act, Jas. Brain first, then the legs and arms, just like we practiced,* but she didn't. She stared, silently, at Blaine but also kind of through Blaine, at some nothing spot on the wall behind him. She looked upset, more upset than he had seen her since Jas knocked over the hutch and all the good dinnerware and wineglasses and champagne flutes shattered into a million jagged shards.

"Anne, I was so worried," Blaine said. He hugged her.

"Yeah . . ." she said.

He kissed her furrowed brow. "I tried to call. My phone was—"

"Yeah." The wife nodded vacantly. "They're all . . . I mean, mine stopped working . . ."

Blaine stepped back. He glanced past the wife. He half expected an RV, a tank, a truck and trailer loaded full with solar panels, weaponry, assorted livestock, a family-size eight-wheeled ark built for post–alien apocalypse survival. There was nothing behind her but dark yard.

"What happened? Did you drive . . . Or, well, come on in."

Blaine led her inside. Avril clung to her arm. Jas unwound the string-and-can trap, which had gotten caught on the buttons on his mother's coat. It had worked well. He strung it back up along the front stoop.

"I was . . ." The wife stared absently. Then she shook her head, as if she meant to shake all the alarming thoughts out of it. Her eyes snapped back. "I was at work. And then when, you know—"

"Yeah."

"I tried to drive straight home. But there was a horrible wreck on the freeway."

"Yeah, I heard about that."

"A semitruck. It flipped over, and all these cars piled up, and . . . it was terrifying." She shook her head again. She bit her lip.

"Oh, Mom." Avril started to cry.

"It's okay, honey. It's fine. I'm fine, okay?"

"Okay."

"Don't cry."

"Okay."

"I'm fine. I just . . . Well, I got stuck behind the pileup. And then everyone started to get out of their cars, I guess, freaking out about the emergency broadcast. And no one had cell service. They were all just leaving their cars on the freeway. So, well, I got out and walked."

"You walked all the way here."

The wife nodded. "All the way. And . . . this was so dumb . . ."The wife laughed, but she seemed more distraught than amused.

"What?"

"I locked my purse in the car."

"Oh no. How did you—"

"When I got out. I must have hit the lock button on the door. So dumb. I don't know how it happened, really. But my purse was on the seat, and I didn't grab it, and then it was too late. The door was locked. And so—"

"Mom!" Avril yelped. "Mom, you're bleeding!"

The wife frowned. "I am?"

"Your arm!"

The wife had a deep gash in her forearm, halfway up on the soft inner side. Dark blood oozed out of it.

"Oh . . ." The wife made a puzzled expression. "Yeah . . . that's right . . . I, I tripped."

"You tripped?"

"And I hit some sort of . . . There was a piece of glass in the road. That was what happened."

"Oh no, Anne," Blaine said. He inspected the wound. "Is the glass—"

"I pulled it out."

"This is really deep. We need to get you to the hospital, get it sewn up."

"Is your car—"

"No. Shoot. It's at work. We could get a ride from Elena and John, or—"

"No," the wife said. "No. Tonight? We can't. Not with what's going on. The emergency broadcast said to take shelter, and—"

"But, Anne, you probably need stitches. I really think you need to go to the hospital."

"No."

"Anne—"

"No." The wife pinched her lips together. She had made up her mind. "No. You'll just have to stitch it up."

"I can't—"

"*I'll* stitch you up, Mom!" Jas hollered, from the doorway.

"You can," the wife said, to Blaine. "You can. You will."

* * *

He did. He cleaned the wound. He threaded a sewing needle. The kids crowded around.

"You don't want to watch," Blaine told them. They wanted to watch. They wriggled closer. "Come on, get back. Give us some space."

"Blaine, if they want to watch—"

The wife saw an educational opportunity. Sewing 101. Home economics for the alien invasion era. Blood dribbled down her arm, onto the table. Blaine felt queasy. He stared at his wife's bleeding arm, the blood-cherry to top off the whole surreal day. They had no neutral thread colors, only bright primaries. The wife chose yellow.

"Just jab it in," she said.

Blaine pinched the flaps of her skin together. He held his breath. He stuck the needle through. The children gasped.

"Dad!"

"Wow!"

"Dad! You should sew a picture, Dad!" Like a duckling. A daffodil. A crescent moon, sewn into the torn flesh of their mother's arm.

"Or a flying saucer, Dad! Sew that!"

"It would be," the wife remarked, "commemorative."

* * *

When, after they pried the children away from beloved TV and sent them upstairs to bed, after they drank a six-pack of lousy beer and abandoned the toothbrush ritual in favor of a prebedtime bag of Chizz-Wizard Cheese Product Puffs and caught the children downstairs, fondling the television, and sent them back up to bed again, they checked the news one last time, there were twelve vessels. Twelve cities. The first seven, plus Cairo, New York, Mumbai, Manila, Lagos. Twelve vessels hovered, silent, over darkened cities.

"How can you expect us to just go to bed?" the children protested, from behind their bedroom door. "What if the aliens sneak through the window while we're sleeping? What if they come down the chimney, like Santa? How could we possibly sleep?"

Blaine felt the same way when he climbed into bed. He felt like he might never sleep again, but he also felt exhausted. The wife was already in bed.

"Like Santa," she said. She laughed. "I hope that . . . that things go on. You know . . . things like . . . I love Santa. I love Christmas. All the holidays. It's all just so . . ."

"They will," Blaine said. He didn't feel convinced at all, but he tried to sound certain. The wife needed reassurance. She rarely needed reassurance.

He kissed her. He pulled the covers up around them. The wife stared absently at the ceiling. Beyond the ceiling, up there in the airspace, the extraterrestrials stared down and said nothing. The absence of any message terrified him. The waiting terrified him. It made him remember his boyhood, when his father went dark. He could never anticipate when it might happen. One week his father would arrive home from work at a regular hour, fry up some chicken, overcook the broccoli, crack jokes at the kitchen table while he fiddled with the crosswords and Blaine finished his homework, and life was good. The next week his father would buy a boat, or go skydiving, or call home from Albuquerque. *Have you been? Hot damn it's nice, I just started driving and driving and then I got to thinking: What if we moved? We could buy one of those adobe houses and I could really devote myself to art and Blaine could* try not to get too excited. He'd had a tough time when the boat never happened. He had told his friends at school and envisioned boating slumber parties, but of course Mom made Dad take it back. Those weeks, hot damn, Blaine could handle them. But then his father turned, swept up by a sudden dark storm. Blaine might say something simple, something harmless, like *Can you pass the maple syrup* and his father would get up and stomp out of the room, slam the door, refuse to come out. Blaine might say something less benign like *So, on the math test, I got a C. But next time, Dad, I swear* his father didn't want to hear it. His father stared at him with those dark eyes and said nothing, made him wait, for days or weeks. Then, out of nowhere, his father would say *That's okay, son, I'm sure you'll do better next time.* Or he would say *A lousy C? You'll never go to college with those shit grades. It's all over for you now.* But at least once he said it Blaine felt relief. The waiting, the not knowing, that part was way harder.

"How's your arm?" he asked. The wife wore a half-dozen strips of Captain Barksford cartoon Band-Aids.

"It's fine. It's great!"

"It doesn't hurt too much? Because I think I've still got some Vicodin left over from—"

"Oh no, I don't need that. It's really fine."

"Are you sure, because—"

"Really. If I need it, I know where to find it. Now kiss me."

He kissed her, and an overwhelming sense of gratitude swirled around his brain. He felt so grateful for Anne; forthright, stoic Anne; Anne who journeyed miles in her work shoes with a bleeding arm to make it home; Anne the child-whisperer; Anne who wanted to kiss him, and for a moment it didn't matter that there was life, possibly hostile, definitely intelligent, invading the airspace of Earth's prominent cities.

Then the kiss ended, and it mattered again.

"I'll never fall asleep," he said.

Anne wore a silk mask to sleep. She pulled it down over her eyes. She nestled up beside him.

"Sure you will," she said. "Just close your eyes."

He turned off the light. He wrapped his arm around her shoulder. He closed his eyes.

He slept.

* * *

He dreamed of a monstrous alien spacecraft, hundreds of miles wide, huge enough to blanket the sky. Then the spacecraft shrunk down, drone-sized. It flew through the window into his house. The kids steered it with a remote control. It shot up the furniture with laser beam blasts. It circled around and around his head like a pesky UFO fly. *BZZZZ! ZZZZZ! DAD! BZZZZZ!* He tried to bat it away.

"Dad!"

BZZZZZ!!!

"Dad!"

"Huh!"

BZZZZ

"Wake up!"

The bed shook. He opened his eyes.

The children stared down at him. Jas pointed fingers at his eyeballs. "Dad!"

"He was going to pry your eyes open," Avril tattled.

"Only because you wouldn't wake up. Dad! Mr. Meow-mitts is gone!"

"He's gone! Our chonky boi is gone!"

"We can't find him anywhere!"

"What if they ate him, Dad?"

"He is a hamb sandwich."

"What if the aliens stole Mr. Meow-mitts so they could eat him because—"

"Okay, stop—"

"—because—"

"Just stop. The cat is . . ."

"But, Dad—"

"Shhhhh. No one ate the cat. What time is it?" Blaine reached for his phone. It was pitch-black outside. It felt like an hour at which no child should ever be awake. The phone suggested, misleadingly, that it was still 11:52.

"It's technically morning," Avril said.

"Anne…" Blaine rolled over. The wife's side of the bed was wifeless, and overrun by children. The clock on her bedside table flashed 8:18, but they had not reset it when the power came back.

Blaine got out of bed. The children slithered beneath the bed to check for the cat. They came out dusty.

"You should really clean under there, Dad. What if Mr. Meow-mitts is allergic to dust, and that's why he's gone? Then how could you ever forgive yourself for letting it get so filthy?"

He had tried to persuade the wife to hire a housecleaner, but she'd objected. Something about strangers in the house, and the exploitation of cheap labor markets, and the children needing to learn the value of hard manual labor. Every six months she would shove cleaning solution and paper towels at the children, and they would pretend to clean for a few minutes and then sneak off to watch TV. No one had ever dusted the under-bed realm.

The children decided to check each room methodically, and the dad had to help them. They had to stick together. When people split up, they got picked off. The aliens would be waiting for them to split up; hidden in closets, drifting past windows, lurking behind the shower curtain, definitely, smacking the skin-like folds that framed their flesh-sucking mouths. No, the children could not conduct a cat-hunt on their own.

"But what about Mom?"

"What about Mom?"

"She's already awake, right? Why couldn't you ask her?"

"Geez, Dad." Avril rolled her eyes. She pointed at the dark window. "Because. Come on."

They toured the closet, the upstairs bathroom, the office–slash–guest bedroom, the kids' room. The kids shared the room because they didn't like to be apart because apart they couldn't torture each other as easily. The kids slept in a bunk bed, and which one got top bunk on any particular day depended upon an elaborate system of points, known only to them. The kid on the bottom bunk got stepped on, when the top bunk kid climbed up the wrong way from the center of the bottom mattress.

"Mr. Meow-mitts wasn't in here when we went to sleep," Avril said.

"I thought Avril had him in her bed."

"And I thought Jas had him."

"We were both wrong. But Avril was more wrong."

"Hey!" She pinched her brother.

"Ow!" He flicked her in the nose.

It baffled Blaine, how his children could love and loathe each other so much.

They searched every corner and toy chest and dresser drawer in the kids' room, and Blaine kept thinking how ridiculous it was for them to roam the house in the middle of the night in search of a (very likely peacefully slumbering) cat when twelve (or more?) giant alien vessels occupied the airspace of Earth's larger/largest cities, and how ridiculous it was that they had all tried to sleep through Alien-Invasion Night #1, and how aliens had traveled from distant galaxies, across the vast where-no-man-has-gone-before reaches of space, to visit their B-list Earth, where the wild animals became frequently extinct but the domesticated ones got their own special matching rain boots and slickers, and their own wall plaque awards for "Floofiest" and "Best Peets," and ate boneless chicken (*chimkin,* the children called it) breasts cut into tiny bites and arranged geometrically on the one good piece of dishware that remained after Jas had broken the rest of it. And if the aliens somehow knew—if the aliens could peer into the eccentricities of human-run Earth-life and see the absurdly misguided turn it had taken—how could they just keep hovering there, lasers holstered?

"But did Mr. Meow-mitts eat his chimkin dinner?" Avril asked.

"Dad?"

"I just gave him dry food."

"Dry food!"

"Dad!"

"Were you trying to scare Mr. Meow-mitts away?"

This was how far things had devolved already.

The dry food in Mr. Meow-mitts's bowl was predictably untouched. Jas picked up a cat-food kibblet. He stared at it. He sniffed it, detective-like.

"He's starving!" Avril declared.

"Did he eat any of it?"

"Did you see him eat it?"

"When was the last time you saw him?"

"I didn't see him when we came home."

"Poor Mr. Meow-mitts! He must be terrified and starving."

The crisis intensified. They searched every cupboard, every closet, every under-furniture squeeze space. They scoured the basement and the garage. They put on their coats and shoes and went out onto the back patio. The light was off, but a placid flame flickered in the fire bowl. The wife held her hands over it.

"Anne?"

Her face was shadowed. Ember light danced in her dark eyes.

"I couldn't sleep," she said.

He sat down beside her.

"Dad!"

"Dad!"

"The cat!"

The children were relentless.

"I'm going to keep Mom company while you search."

"But, Dad—"

"I'll be right here."

The children grumbled, but they scurried off. They stalked the dark yard, calling the cat's name.

"You okay?" Blaine asked his wife.

"Yes. No. I'm just . . ." Her hands trembled slightly. "I . . . I thought I had it all figured out, you know? But this . . ." She gazed out, beyond the soft sphere of firelight, at the prowling children, the bare-limbed trees, the slate-shingled rooftops, the chimneys and streetlights and windowpanes pooled with silvery moonlight. "I guess . . . I expected things would turn out differently."

"We don't know how things will turn out."

"But . . . I know. You're right. We don't . . ."

He scooted close. He took the wife's hands in his own.

"But whatever happens, Anne," he said, "whatever happens with all of this, we'll be together."

Mr. Meow-mitts

MR. MEOW-MITTS FELT terrified and starving. He wanted his fur-coated cat spot on the armchair by the vent. He wanted his chicken dinner. His feet hurt. He kept running, despite the ache. A racket tormented his cat brain. It sounded like cymbals, with his head sandwiched between them. It sounded like a voice. The voice said *run cat run run run*. It didn't tell him why. It told his legs to go, and his legs went.

Where was he when it happened?

In the sun, on the back deck. Then, *ka-blam!* His cat-zistence altered irrevocably. His sundeck cat-sized, tossing him overboard into the damp lawn. The riptide of his own meowmentum swept him away.

Instinct, some would speculate, later, when they began to puzzle together what had happened. The house cat decampment paralleled the upstream swim of salmon, the seasonal migration of butterflies and birds.

Mind control, others conjectured. Aliens trained their brain-control-beams on a lesser life-form, as a test-run for the real deal.

This supposition suffered a fatal fallacy. Cats were not a lesser life-form.

Cats were *on a different wavelength, yo*. They were *far out*, as evinced by the pictorial representation of cats in deep space, often with rainbow laser eyes and/or galactic pizza. The frequent appearance of cats in psychedelic space scenes was not coincidental. It was, rather, the predictable consequence of similar vibrations. Cats vibrated on a trippy deep-space frequency. You could hear it in the purr.

Mr. Meow-mitts did not feel cosmically mellow as he ran down an unfamiliar dark street, late at night, his belly empty, his toe beans tender and cold. He wanted chicken, but even dry food sounded like bliss. He wanted *the children* who knew just the right spot on his head to scratch, or *the wife* with her spectacular nails, but he would take *the husband*, whose hands were too big and clammy to scratch well. He wanted to understand the mechanism that propelled him, but he did not. He understood only the need. He needed to go.

He went on, late into the night. He traveled long lonely streets. He squeezed beneath fences. He crossed train tracks, and even a small creek. His poor feet got muddy and damp. He ran up a slope, across a field, toward a sheltering grove of trees.

He sensed the others, long before he got there. He could feel the patter of their hearts inside his own. He could feel the hum of their collective purr. He sprinted through the field, his own little heart clattering. His hunger receded. His ache numbed. He ran into the trees. Their eyes turned to greet him, hundreds of eyes, from the ground, from the trees, the glowing eyes of at least a hundred gathered cats.

The humans would never theorize about the meaning of this gathering, because they would never realize that it happened. They would know only that their cats had disappeared, and that when their cats returned, *if* they returned, some of them came back different.

The Stepchild

THE FIGHT HAD happened like this:

Justin said: *I'm going down there.*

Heather said, reasonably: *There?!?! You're going* toward *the ship? Are you crazy? Or just stupid?*

Then he got all prickly and acted like a big jerk. Then he ignored her entirely while he played *Super Smash Bros.* for *like four hours, gawd, Justin, turn it off already*!!! It wasn't *his* generator. The generator belonged to Jack P., and, besides, they ought to save it for *important* things.

"What are you saying? That video games aren't important? Who made you the arbitert of what's important?"

"Arbiter."

"What?"

"It's *arbiter*, not *arbitert. Arbitert* is not a word, Justin."

"Yeah, I said arbriter. Sheesh. Why you gotta be such a snob?"

Justin did not think that the aliens intended annihilation, but if they did, he wanted to go out in a blazing battlefield of Kirbys and Links and Marios and Jigglypuffs. He wasn't going to waste the last hours of his life with *Serious Boring Shit.* His tone insinuated. He passed judgment. Heather would dump him, she decided, when everything got back to normal. Except maybe normal would never come back, and the last normalest hours of Heather's existence would pass in an irritated haze of jerky boyfriend pot smoke and video game ditties. She deliberated on disconnecting the generator, but the forced shift of Justin's attention from his preferred apocalypse partner to her would impede her righteous outrage. She did not want to relinquish her right to feel justifiably maligned. Also, she wanted refrigeration and climate control. She wanted electric lights. She felt exclusive, in her house on the Malibu hillside, a spark of light in the alien darkness. Even though the house belonged to Jack P. But now the brave new world of intergalactic travel had appeared in the skies above them. With the power and satellites out, Carmel, where Jack P. had taken her mother, might well be a distant universe. Maybe Jack P. would never come back.

Heather hoped that he didn't.

Justin passed out on the couch with the TV still on. Heather turned it off. She felt annoyed that the historic arrival of extraterrestrial life had gotten irreparably tainted by video-gaming. She felt annoyed by herself for expecting relevance, meaning, anything beyond the same thumb-twiddling bullshit that defined her existence. She felt annoyed by Justin's wanton expenditure of generator power. She felt annoyed by everything about him. He was like Jack P. Junior, she thought. Except dumber, less sophisticated, plagued by acne.

Jack P. was *just the most exciting man* her mother claimed to have ever met. Jack P. had a swimming pool with a pool house containing every conceivable inflatable pool float ever invented. Jack P. had a private jet. Okay, he shared it. Like a time-share for jets. But still. He also had a time-share in Baja and a time-share in West Palm Beach and a sphynx—a hairless slonk named Bastet who ate only fresh fish and had his own cush seat on the private jet and wore a collar chain made of pure gold. Bastet, of course, had gone to Carmel, too.

He likes the cat better than he likes me, Heather had complained to her mother. Her mother just smiled and shook her head, *Oh, no, of course he doesn't dear,* as she stroked the regal, furless feline head.

Heather went outside. She opened the pool house door. She found a float in the form of a human-sized pizza. Better than the lizard float. She kind of liked it, but also she hated it because Jack P. had picked it out. He had seen it on some website and had chuckled to himself and a week later it showed up in a box on his front porch. At least he had never used it. Because if he did, ugh, gross: tanning-bed man chest with unsightly groves of graying fur, splayed like a Jack P. sardine across the floating pizza. The float was still unopened in its box. She took it out, inflated it, tossed it into the empty pool. Maybe aliens would obliterate Carmel, and Jack P. would never come home, and her mom and Bastet would join a roving post-apocalyptic motorcycle gang. Maybe her brainiac stepbrother would get abducted from his prep school dorm room and she would get to keep the Malibu house.

Homeowner step 1: Turn on pool lights.

Homeowner step 2: Take out trash. Aka Justin. He slept with his mouth open. She hadn't wanted to admit it, but he was a mouth-breather.

He snored.

She didn't want him to leave.

She just wanted him to want her more than he wanted video games.

Heather slipped into the pool. She climbed, ungracefully, onto the pizza float. The Malibu night air felt cool against her wet skin. The Malibu sky sparkled with more stars than she had ever seen.

She thought about aliens, about their alien world that circled one of those distant stars. It probably sucked, that world. It probably reeked of armpits and banana peels and that was why they had come here. Well, they should probably go back.

Or somewhere else. The universe was a big place.

Malibu was a tiny dream on the cliff edge of California, and someday the Pacific Ocean would rise up and swallow it whole. But for now, it was a fairy dream of generator lights, a luminous backyard pool, an open bottle of Jack P.'s pricy Napa cab on the pool deck. She paddled toward it.

The sliding back door opened. Justin stepped out.

"Hey," he said. He had shoes on. He had his hoodie tucked beneath his armpit, and a scone in his hand, even though he had claimed to have eaten the last one hours before, when she had gone looking.

"Yeah. Hey."

"I'm going."

"Going?"

"Yeah. Like, down to LA. Man. Fuck. I gotta go down there, where the ship is. To see it. You know?"

"No."

"You should come. It's like, I mean, alien life! How fucking crazy is that? I gotta go see it, you know, closer up. We could go together. Maybe we could take Jack P.'s Lamborghini and—"

"No. Besides, I thought you were like, 'Oh, of course there's alien life, Heather, so why not just play video games all night?'"

"I was digesting."

"Whatever. But I'm not going."

"What? No . . . why?"

"It's stupid. You want to go down there? You're just going to get yourself killed."

"If they were going to kill us, don't you think they would have? They would have just killed us all already. No, this has got to be something different! And I don't want to waste any more time up here—"

"Waste any more time? Are you serious?"

"I just mean, like, I want to be a part of it. Whatever it is. And . . . and I want you to come."

"What, so you can get laid again before you get yourself killed?"

"No, I just, we can like, it'll be like—"

"No. LA? No way. That's fucking stupid, Justin."

"Damn." Justin shook his head. "Why you gotta be such a bitch?"

"Fuck you. I'm not being a bitch," Heather said. "You're acting like a moron. You're gonna go down there and get yourself killed. But you know what? I don't give a shit. Go."

"Heather—"

"Go! Go on! Go!"

He went.

And Heather was all alone, floating in the lonely pool in her stepdad's backyard. All alone in the great big universe, teeming with life.

The Husband

BLAINE SLEPT LATE the next day and woke to an empty bed. He reached, instinctively, for his phone, which suggested he had slept in till 11:52. He had decided to assume that work and school had gotten canceled, though he had no way to confirm. His useless phone still had no service.

Blaine put on his slippers and went downstairs, where the children had requisitioned the dining room table for arts and crafts. They pasted photographs of Mr. Meow-mitts onto rainbow paw-print Lost Pet signs with hand-drawn photo frames, speared hearts, crayon Meow-mitts duplicates, extraneous biographies; *Mr. Meow-mitts, aka Colonel Meowerson, aka Mitters, Master of Peets and Beans, born on the third of March; Mr. Meow-mitts is a sworn enemy of the cell phone charger, because really it's a snake; Mr. Meow-mitts barfed in Dad's shoe, but Dad didn't know until . . . Call our dad if you find Mr. Meow-mitts,* the signs instructed, providing his telephone number, *because he won't let us have cell phones because he says we're too young, which is really unfair.* Also, untrue; their single-digit ages served as a handy excuse for the real reason—the children's idolization of the television. A gift of cell phones would dissolve any semblance of control or separation between children and screens. Children and screens would fuse irreparably.

The house smelled like bacon. The wife could eat bacon like a former high-school linebacker on Super Bowl Sunday. She ordered it in multiples of five-pound value packs. She wrapped chicken breasts in bacon shawls. She layered bacon strips between Hasselback potatoes.

She assembled salads with equal parts lettuce and bacon. Every sand-wich became a BLT, except for peanut butter, which didn't get the lettuce or tomato because that would taste weird and gross. *But The Environment*, Blaine would say sometimes. *But a pound of meat takes a dozenish pounds of grain to make, and grazing leads to deforestation, and all those methane farts . . .* The wife would pat his head, *Oh, hello, small-child husband*, and shove a crunchy strip of bacon in her mouth. *Oh yes, baby, of course* she believed in pig-farm-induced environmental degradation, wasn't he a sweetie, but in the end she couldn't *not* eat the bacon because bacon was just so delicious.

"I made you some bacon," the wife said when he walked into the kitchen. She stood at the window. Rain drizzled from a dull winter sky. "But I ate it. Sorry. I can make more if you want."

"No, that's fine."

"But there's still pancakes."

Blaine wrapped his arms around her. He rested his chin on her head. He could feel the soft thump of her heart in his hand.

"Have some pancakes," she said.

He heard a slight tremor in her voice. "I will. But how's your arm? Are you—"

"I'm fine," she said. She stepped away from him. She opened the refrigerator door, pretended to look.

"Are you sure? Because—"

"Are any of us really fine? The . . . *aliens* or whatever are fucking *here*. There are fourteen ships, probably more because, like, no one's heard from China or Russia, and, and, and we're just . . ."

She pulled another pound of bacon out of the fridge, a bottle of Fizz Wizard Cherry Cola, a package of American cheese in individually wrapped slices. She stood in front of the open fridge with these things in her hands and panic on her face and tears in her eyes.

"Hey, hey now," Blaine said. He gathered the wife and her precious processed foods in his arms. "We are fine. We're going to be fine."

"But what if . . ."

"What if what? If they're hostile? I mean, we don't know that they are, or, I mean, we're all still here. And if they are, well, we'll do what we need to do, okay, Anne? Whatever we need to do."

"I just . . . I love our life here, Blaine. Just like it is. And I don't want to lose you guys."

"You won't," he said. "I promise, you won't."

She buried her weepy face in his robe. For a minute, maybe two, she cried, and Blaine held her thin shaking frame in his arms, and it struck him that he had never seen her cry before. Not like this. Then, abruptly, she stopped. She flipped, back to regular wife mode.

"You should get those pancakes before they get cold," she said. "I'm going to fry up another pound of bacon. If we don't eat it now, we'll have it with dinner. Then we'll go hang up the missing pet signs—*Kids! Grab the laminator! We're going to need the laminator!*—and then let's make popcorn and watch movies! Here, do you want syrup? I'll warm it up for you. And coffee!"

The wife produced a hot plate of heart-shaped pancakes dusted with powdered sugar, a mug of coffee, a ramekin of piping maple syrup. Blaine carried breakfast past the crafting children, into the living room. He turned on the TV, promptly muting the volume so the children wouldn't flock.

Foot pitter-patter sprang forth. Even muted, the television lured them.

"Dad!"

"Dad!"

"Spaceships!"

"Hey, I want the remote!"

"No, you had it last time!"

"Did not!"

"It's mine, you jerk!"

Whack! Slap!

"Hey! Cut it out!" the dad growled. It was his remote. He sometimes let the children borrow it, but not today, after this display of remote-inspired savagery.

On the television, the mammoth spacecraft hovered over London. The footage shifted, to Cairo, Tokyo, Manila, New York.

"Will *we* get one, Dad?"

"Yeah, when are they coming here?"

"I don't know."

"Well, if they come, we need to be ready!"

"Yeah, Dad!"

"We can't just sit here and watch TV!"

The children, galvanized by the dad's inequitable confiscation of the remote, boomeranged around the living room, obstructing the dad's TV view. Also, they had a plan: How to Prepare for Alien Invasion, scripted in crayon and now laminated and displayed on the refrigerator.

"Okay, but can I at least eat breakfast? Geez."

Yes, but not in peace. The children mothed around the TV light, claws out. They were barbarous moths, and opportunists; when one's gaze fixed intently on the TV, the other would pinch, poke, or prod a spit-wet finger into the other one's ear.

The spacecraft footage on the TV shifted back to DC. The confirmed ships now totaled fourteen, but there might have been more. Certain large countries (China, Russia) had fallen silent. The satellites malfunctioned. The reporter, via landline telephone from a Maryland town outside DC because the video feed cut out and the Wi-Fi went glitchy, speculated electromagnetic interference. The mere presence of the spacecraft confused our primitive communications systems. Certain cellular devices had stopped working altogether, as of yesterday, at the hour of the extraterrestrial arrival.

The news channels played landline interviews of various Important People, many of whom had evacuated or retreated to secure locations in the countryside, underground bunkers, or private compounds where the aliens would at least have to climb over/beam through barbed-wire fencing to reach them. Everyone Important had theories as to why the aliens had come and what they wanted. To invite us into a great galactic federation, an idealistic billionaire surmised, from his secret mountaintop fortress. Or some of us, at least. Would the gratuitous violence endemic to certain nation-states disqualify them? Or would their inhumanity serve to exclude us all? Or would our brutality be the defining trait that would compel these visitors to embrace us? Maybe they were Klingons, warriors, bellicose, here to stamp out all those pansy socialists so that the bloodthirsty among us could reach their full Ayn-Randian potential. But why bother with us at all, a scientist conjectured. To a species that could travel across the galaxies, humans had little to offer. Our Goldilocks planet, on the other hand, had minerals, water, edible plants and animals, the miracle of habitability. Most likely the aliens had come to strip us for parts, or to move in. *Hello, Earth! Meet your new squatters.* If they occupied the planet long enough, it would be theirs. Which was how, one senator remarked, many Earth nations had been formed. By squatters. Which was why, another senator insisted, we ought to destroy them now. Fire the nukes, the lasers, the napalm. Send those alien bastards an Ebola welcome gift. Sure, we would sacrifice a few cities, a few hundred-thousand-million lives. Better to show our strength than lose everybody, the senator argued, from his fortified bomb shelter fifty meters beneath the doomed surface of Earth.

"Yeah!"

"Yeah!"

"We should get 'em!" The children cheered.

"No. No!" Blaine said. Were all children, he wondered, so blood-thirsty? The ruthless little zealots raised their fists and chanted: *Nuke E.T.! Nuke E.T.!* Blaine blamed TV for their proclivity toward violence. He had not installed appropriate parental controls. He had caught them watching wrestling shows, had seen the lust in their eyes when one wrestler raised a metal folding chair against another.

"Nuke E.T.!"

"Bomb them now!"

"No! That's . . . do you even know what that is? Nuking?"

"It's like, you know, microwaving," Avril said.

Jas went, "KAPOW!"

"No. It's . . . it's bad," Science Dad tried to explain. "It's a very bad type of weapon that we shouldn't use generally, and we definitely shouldn't shoot it at an alien vessel that we know absolutely nothing about. I mean, we have no idea why they're here, or what would happen if we fired weapons at that ship. It could backfire. It would destroy DC, at least. Tons of people would die from the radiation. And the aliens might retaliate. They could wipe us all out. Do you understand?"

Jas blinked.

"KAPOW!"

* * *

The wife fried up all the bacon. She laminated Lost Pet posters. She dressed the children in slickers and galoshes and they ventured out into the great wet world while Blaine lay in a finally-some-peace-for-Dad lump on the couch and stared at spacecraft on the television.

He felt, concurrently, terrified, astounded, and indifferent. He knew that the spacecraft had to be real, because they looked real, because the television and everyone on it treated them as real, because of Occam's razor. The alternatives to real—elaborate stunt, mass delusion—were at this point convoluted and improbable. This wasn't a radio broadcast in 1938. His damned phone still didn't work. The maxim of simplicity pointed to real live space aliens. Yet he had seen aliens on TV so often that it all felt as if it could not be real. It felt like *Star Trek* and *Independence Day* and *Starship Troopers* and maybe he ought to make the popcorn and bust out the Swedish Fish and the Campette Choco-Bites and mix them all up together, the way the wife did. *This is the way*, she said: one part popcorn, two parts candy, shake them all up while the popcorn is still hot so that maybe, maybe if you're lucky, you'll get a melty sticky candy patch at the bottom of the bowl.

The wife came home and did just that: popcorn, candy, movie. They watched *Aliens*, which made Blaine feel guilty because should he really let his vicious single-digit children watch something so horrific? But the children had seen *Aliens* a dozen times. They owned the DVD. They bought a collection of DVDs with their own money at a garage sale (for our dad, they told the neighbor), and they watched the gory scary violent ones in snippets, when their parents showered or mowed the lawn or labored in the kitchen under the false impression that the children were watching nature documentaries. By the time Blaine caught them, they'd already watched *Aliens* in its entirety twice.

The wife knitted while she watched. The kids wanted a rainbow sweater for Mr. Meow-mitts, for when he returned, or to lure him back. *Mr. Meow-mitts, we made a pretty sweater for you*, they would call from the backyard, and the cat would see the rainbow knit and come trotting home. After the sweater and the movie, the wife baked cupcakes. She blended frostings with purple and green food colorings, because aliens had purple-and-green skin. She helped the children frost the cupcakes with alien faces. The children's cupcakes had monstrous globs of frosting and dozens of eyes. The wife's cupcakes looked magazine-perfect. Blaine had grown accustomed to feeling comparatively unproductive amid the flurry of wife-accomplishments. The wife's lawyer job paid more than his water treatment job with the city, and required more hours, and between those extra work hours the wife managed to run five-plus miles every day, juggle domestic baking/gardening/knitting/sewing tasks, attend PTO meetings, host parties, eat prodigious volumes of prepackaged snack products, and binge-watch years of television—the good shows *and* the crap ones. The wife was one of those physiologically rare creatures who required less sleep than most, especially Blaine, who aimed for a regular nine hours. The wife subsisted on four, and her eyes never had dark circles, and she never nodded off on the couch in the middle of the afternoon, like her husband, and sometimes he felt sorry for her. She would never know the splendor of the unintended midday couch nap.

"Dad."

"Dad!"

"Wake up!"

"Wake up, Dad!"

"Mom says you have to get ready!"

Blaine's eyes popped open.

"What? What's happening?"

His heart pounded. His mind flashed back to *Nuke E. T.! Bomb them now!* "Mom says you have to bathe us," Jas said, "because she did it last time." And because the children had poured half the tub water onto the floor—because there was a hurricane, they said, and hurricanes caused flooding. The wife had gotten stuck with flood cleanup.

"Mom says you have to clean up the bathroom after, because we're having a party."

"We're having a party?"

"Just a little one!" the wife called from the kitchen. "I thought we should all be together!"

Blaine ran the bath. He threw in bath bombs, a couple too many, because what if the aliens blasted them, and the bath bombs went to waste? He shook that unsettling thought from his mind. The children climbed into the tub. The children insisted on bathing together, and with every bath Blaine wondered whether/when they would get too old for shared bath time. When the first advanced to double digits, most definitely, he told the wife, and she shrugged, as if she didn't quite understand what the word *inappropriate* meant. *But whatever you think is best*, she told Blaine, *we'll do that.*

The children wanted to bathe together so that they could torment each other in an aquatic setting. They squirted, splashed, jostled, got water in the eyes. Tears flowed, but the tears were a crocodile show for Dad. The show always ended with soap in the mouth, water on the floor, slippery children tempting concussions as they leapt from the tub, and the parent chasing them down the hall with the towel. He had to pin them down to brush their hair. They were gremlins made exceptionally rabid by bathwater.

"But now we need the tinfoil," Avril said after Blaine had crammed the damp children into their clothes.

"And the tape measure."

"What for?"

"Step three."

"Step three?"

"Of the plan. Duh. Dad, you really should read the plan."

"That's why it's on the fridge."

"Otherwise how will you prepare for the invasion?"

The wife prepared with pigs-in-blankets wrapped in bacon. She dredged pub cheese through crispy onion, forming cheese ball centerpieces for plates of circle crackers. She made deep-fried mac-and-cheese balls. She scooped the innards from halved oranges and filled the empty peels with vodka Jell-O. She set out bowls of cherry tomatoes, olives, grapes.

"Everything's spherical . . ." Blaine observed.

"I'm trying to maintain a consistent aesthetic," the wife said as she poured spherical cheese puffs into a party bowl. She sprinkled the cheese puffs with Sixlets candies. "So that . . . I mean, what if this is our last party?"

The wife didn't usually indulge in what-ifs, because she was too busy frosting triple-layer cakes and carving multi-melon ball salads set in scalloped melon rinds.

"I don't think we need to worry about that," Blaine said, trying to sound more relaxed and jovial than he felt. "I mean, the kids will make sure we're prepared. They're already on step three."

Step three involved protective outerwear. Like a Faraday cage for your body, Jas explained, except it's not a cage, and they didn't have the right metals. They had to improvise. Blaine wondered how the children had learned of the Faraday cage, or deduced its potential usefulness against alien incursions, or concluded that it would protect their single-digit selves from electromagnetic attacks. They had no electrical parts, though they did look like robots in their finished step-three suits. They both wore tinfoil frocks with decorative shoulder pads, tinfoil legwarmers and armbands, helmets crafted out of foil pie pans. They had made foil smocks and hats for Mom and Dad, and for their friends who would attend the party—Foster, Gabriella, Ivan, and Lane—but not the accompanying parents, whose names the children did not know. The children claimed not to recognize the parents, though the children had known these parents for almost their entire lives.

"You better put it on, Dad," Avril said, handing Blaine the foil armor.

"Or else, KAPOW!"

Step four involved Faraday-caging the house. Fortunately, the wife bought tinfoil and everything else in bulk, so they had half a dozen two-hundred-foot rolls of the stuff in the basement.

"But can you carry the ladder, Dad?" Jas asked. "So we can get to the roof?"

Rain battered the roof.

"Why don't you kids go watch TV until the party starts?"

Good enough. Aliens couldn't get them during a TV break. But the TV channels all played the same thing: INVASION EARTH! MYSTERIOUS SPACESHIPS THREATEN EARTH'S MAJOR CITIES: LONDON, NEW YORK, LA, TOKYO, CAIRO, DELHI, and, by the time the first guest knocked on the door, Shanghai and Beijing.

Blaine greeted guests in his tinfoil suit and hat because the kids got cranky when he tried to take it off.

"Not until we complete step four, Dad. Until then, you won't be safe!"

The wife had invited their closest neighborhood friends: John, Elena, and their son, Foster, from up the street; Jeff, Marshall, and their kids, Gabby and Ivan, who went to school with Avril and Jas; Greg and Rebecca; and Matty and her daughter, Lane. The kids all put on their Faraday suits. They gathered cupcakes and ran upstairs, where they could lick the frosting off and toss the sticky cake in the trash without their parents accusing them of waste. The adults gathered glasses of wine and beer, plates of spherical finger foods, and tiny cocktail forks with which to spear them. They assembled in the living room, where the TV played a background soundtrack of *What do the Aliens Want?*

"What do you think they want?" Jeff asked. "Damn, is this little fried thing here a mac-and-cheese ball? It's divine."

"You think?" Anne said. "I feel like I should have added some bacon."

"No, it's really perfect."

"I think they're testing us," said Rebecca. "Otherwise they would have done something by now. They're waiting to see what we do."

"What, like if we fire off our nukes?"

"Or even just how we react on TV. What are people saying? Does everyone freak out?"

"But how would they not know that by now? I mean, if they can travel all the way here from some other solar system, they can definitely pick up our transmissions. So they'd have to know something about us."

"What makes you think they traveled here from a different solar system? Maybe they've been here all along."

"What, like, hiding?"

"Cloaked."

"Dark side of the moon."

"Or under the ocean. They could've been at the bottom of an ocean trench and we'd have no idea."

"These Jell-O shots are delicious."

"And adorable. How did you—"

"Oh, I didn't," Blaine said. "The wife."

"Anne—"

"I think she's in the kitchen."

The wife had slipped away.

"She always makes the best—" Jell-O shots, hors d'oeuvres,

child pea-pod costumes for the elementary school play, matching family sweater sets. Whatever it was, the wife excelled.

"I know."

"Yes."

"Mm-hmm." Elena sidelined the Jell-O orange slice. She peeled the bacon from a pig-in-blanket, eyeing it with subdued malice. It was hard to despise the wife's excellence when she left home-baked casseroles and brownies on your doorstep, when she shoveled the snow from your walkway, when she exclaimed, with genuine glee, how thrilled she was that you came to her party and she noticed that you had gotten your hair cut and that you had been working out and darling, you looked *gorgeous*. But the wife looked more gorgeous, and it was hard not to despise her, when she sprinted up the frozen street at six a.m. in her spandex pants, looking chipper. *Do you think Elena likes me?* the wife would ask, and then the wife would self-answer with: *I think I'll bake her a pie. Cherry or lemon curd? You know what? I think I'll bake both.* But then two pies became six or eight pies, and the wife devoured at least one, all by herself, in a single midnight sitting.

The wife had not slipped back when Blaine finished his drink. He got up and walked to the kitchen. The wife wasn't there. Blaine cracked a beer and refilled his glass. As he turned back toward the living room, he noticed that the back door had gotten left slightly ajar. He reached for the door, to close it. He heard a voice outside.

"John, I'm so . . ."

The wife's voice. He couldn't make out the rest of her words. He opened the door. The wife stood on the back patio with John, Elena's husband. They stood a little too close together, though Blaine did not notice it at the time. It only occurred to him later, weeks later, when he saw his wife standing on the sidewalk in front of the pizza parlor and he thought back to the interrupted moment on the patio, to how close the two of them had stood, and to the glance that the two of them exchanged when Blaine intruded.

The wife looked over at John. John's eyes flickered and then retreated. He crossed his arms.

"What are you—" Blaine started to ask.

The wife headed him off.

"The cat. I just came out to call the cat."

"Oh. Is he—"

"No." She shook her head.

"I just came out for some fresh air," John said. The fresh air drizzled and blustered. "This whole thing . . . I don't know what to make of it. . . ."

"I know," the wife agreed. "It's crazy! And *of course* our cat is missing! Mr. Meow-mitts! Here kitty, kitty, kitty! Darn it! I hope he comes home soon. But let's all go inside. It's cold out!"

They went inside. The wife refilled her wineglass. Children paraded into the kitchen. They all wore tinfoil suits, except for Jas, who had stripped down shirtless and colored his chest and face green to play the role of the alien.

"Puny hoomans!" Jas yelled. "Pitiful hoomans! We will kill you all! We will eat your brains!"

"Quick, everyone!" Avril said to the tinfoil-suited children. "Gather your weapons!" She opened the silverware drawers and began handing out utensils.

"Not the knives!" Blaine instructed. "Whatever you're doing about the aliens, you don't need the knives."

"But, Dad—"

"Dad—"

"How are we supposed to—"

"The adults need the knives," the wife said. "I mean, if the aliens want to cut anyone up, who do you think they'll go after?"

"It's true," Blaine agreed. "Children are smaller. Harder to experiment on."

Harder to placate. They slipped clandestine butter knives beneath their Faraday vests and scurried back upstairs. Blaine went back into the living room, where all the adults stared at the DC spaceship on TV.

"Something's happening," Matty said.

"What's happening?"

"It's—"

"Oh shit, oh shit—"

The alien vessel over Washington, which had done nothing but hover and flash since its arrival, began to spin. It circled slowly at first, then faster and faster. The red-blue-green lights became a multicolored blur. The white stone memorials picked up the colors and seemed to spin as well. The news reporters sounded panicked. *It's spinning. We don't know what's happening. We don't—* The audio feed cut out. The video feed played a silent shot of spinning spaceship.

"Oh my god, what if they—"

"Those people—"

"Those poor people in DC—"

"What if it—"

"Don't say it—"

The spacecraft became a blur.

Blaine's heart pounded. He glanced around, for Anne. He needed Anne. He wanted Anne in his arms and what if the ship laser-blasted DC? What if the laser blast spread death across the land, red molten laser death that crackled across the highways and incinerated the towns and suburbs and forests and turned all the humans to charred bone and ash? The cat was out there somewhere, a wet cat stranded in the February damp. And then, in an instant, the cat would be a charred lump of smoldering fur. The tinfoil Faraday suits couldn't save his kids. The forks and knives and soda-can traps would melt. Upstairs, the clueless children cackled. Blaine's mind spun and blurred, oh Anne where are you Anne and then the wife was right beside him, digging her claws in his arm flesh, her eyes wide with terror.

The spacecraft blur spun up, lights flashing, a hurricane force. Twisters formed in the water beneath it. Trees uprooted and windows exploded out of buildings. Then, just when Blaine thought the ship's bottom would open to unleash its fiery laser blast, the ship was gone.

The airspace over the capital was empty. Nothing there but gray clouds, dark sky, scattered stars.

Then the stars disappeared too, as the city lights flashed on.

. . . it's gone the spaceship is gone . . .

. . . where . . .

. . . what happened . . . can you hear me? What happened?

The audio recording cut in and out.

. . . is it . . .

. . . the others . . .

The video feed cut to London, where above the city a spacecraft spun at insane speeds and then, in a blink, spun away.

. . . they're gone. They're all leaving. They're . . .

Blaine had stopped breathing.

The wife gasped. Her claws dug deeper into Blaine's arm, but he couldn't feel them. He felt a gut-punch of terror and relief.

He felt a strange emptiness in his heart, a gaping sense that once again, they were all alone.

EPISODE 2

The Cat

THE CALICO STOOD on the corner of a busy intersection. Elusive adventure rumbled past on a motorcycle. The calico admired the motorcycle. It had a swift, mouse-like quality. But he didn't like the intersection. He didn't like the outside world.

But you are an adventure cat.

You are awake.

The calico didn't like the insistent voice in his head. His heart pattered. He bounded down the sidewalk to where the sidewalk ended. He watched the thunderous cars and trucks that roared across the road. His brain, though incapable of comprehending its uniqueness, was singular among the many species of Earth. His thoughts floated along an inimitable pattern of waves. His wakeful perceptions interfaced with an alpha-wave dreamland. His neural circuits forged and re-formed with psychedelic malleability. The cat was, invariably, tripped out.

* * *

The cat detested the noise, the traffic, the wind, the pavement, the intensity into which he found himself unwittingly thrust. He wanted to retreat to his peaceful window seat overlooking the front lawn of his Roland Park home, where nothing happened but snoozes and scratches.

But no. You are an adventure cat.

Go.

Go. Find. Your. Friend.

The cat's window seat faced east. In the mornings he basked in resplendent sunlight and he dreamed. He dreamed of bird calls, flutters, swift darts, flicks of tail, dreams devoid of plotlines—technicolor dreams, saturated in greens and blues and magentas, where everything appeared more vibrant than it did in his waking life.

His window seat had a striped cushion, which the humans kept snatching and washing and vacuuming around. The vacuum came once each week. He loathed it. He had endeavored to chew through its tail while it slumbered, but the humans caught him. *Bouchard! No, Bouchard! You'll get shocked!*

Bouchard: a fine, stately name that warranted wet food and a designated garden catnip plot marked by its own little wrought-iron sign. BOUCHARD'S GARDEN. Bouchard had never ventured into his garden because he despised the outside, albeit not in the same manner that he loathed the vacuum. He detested damp paws and wide-open spaces, but, unlike the vacuum, he appreciated the *existence* of outside, so long as it stayed out where it belonged. *He* belonged in, on his cushion or his couch, his many beds, armchairs, carpets, coiled by the fire or in front of the heating vent, sprawled across the counter or the stairway, where he might make a human trip and fall. *Bouchard, what did I tell you about sleeping on the stairs!*

It did not matter, for Bouchard was a cat. He could not, at that time, comprehend human speech even if he cared to, which, he did not.

* * *

What happened to him, two days earlier, was this:

Having just dozed off in his sunlit window seat, something jolted Bouchard awake. He startled and jumped up, right into the window. He smacked against the glass and fell back. His furious heart rattled. His brain felt strange *sooooooo straaaaaaaange* as if it might leap out of his head and flap away. His thoughts swarmed and tangled. He turned circles, confused.

Bouchard.

Go.

Go now.

He saw the human housekeeper dragging the vacuum cleaner toward him. The vacuum cleaner snarled. Bouchard yowled.

"What are you freaking out about?" the housekeeper said, as Bouchard bolted across the room. "The vacuum's not even on."

Bouchard, who did not like the outdoors, felt, for the first time in his life, an overwhelming desire to get out. He felt more wakeful than he had ever felt before. He sprinted erratically through the house. His head throbbed. His thoughts whirled. They formed a thought tornado, sweeping up words and images, seeding his mind with ideas. He had to get out. He had never tried to get out, and he didn't know how but then—suddenly—he did. He recalled the plastic flap in the back door, the cat-sized tunnel installed by his human to accommodate a whim Bouchard had never had. He ran to the back door and dove through it. He emerged outside. He stared up at the sky. It had changed. He understood this now. He had changed. Everything had changed. He sprinted through the yard, reveling in the feeling of the wind in his whiskers, the herald scent of early spring, the yellow-chested orioles that scattered in his path. He ran out of the yard, onto the sidewalk.

Bouchard.

Go.

He went, and he kept on going.

He wanted to go home, but his legs carried him somewhere else. His paws brought him here, to this desolate corner of motor-ville, where every passing beast growled louder than the vacuum.

I want to go home, Bouchard thought, *to my window seat, to my sleepy life.*

But his mind, or something in it, told him *go.*

Go.

You. Bouchard.

You. Will. Find. A friend.

He wanted home, but not home, not exactly. Home was nostalgia; a fond dream of a long sleep from which he now had woken. Bouchard felt fully alert, agile, aware. All his whiskers tingled.

* * *

Bouchard had the plush body of an indoor housecat who had only dreamed of birding. But instinct awakened, along with something else, some latent twinkle in the darkest reaches of his brain. He turned around. He ran another way, and as he ran he saw connections; between the road and the cars and the changing lights; between the shrubs and the dirt; the dying grass, the late patch of grimy snow, the shards of a broken bottle; between the clouds and the wind and the birds. He saw how one thing caused another thing caused another thing caused a cascade of events, each hinging on the incident before it, all of them inescapable. His eyes saw lines of light. His ears heard harmonizing chords in the chaos of rush hour traffic. He felt, at once, the rightness and wrongness of all of it, existing concurrently. He understood the feeling, cold and beautiful, empty and brimming, the dichotomous yin and yang of life and its absence.

Bouchard turned from the sidewalk into a gas station. He observed a strip of median, planted with boxwoods, littered with cigarette butts.

He asked himself: How did I awaken?

But the *how* was a black blank slate.

He saw a semitruck with its door left open.

You. Will. Find. A friend.

He galloped toward it. He hopped up into the cab. He curled himself beneath the ledge of seat. He held his breath. A man climbed in, slammed the door shut, turned the key. The truck purred. The man smelled of rubber and ammonia, of tobacco and coffee, pancakes, gasoline. The man couldn't smell Bouchard because humans had terrible noses. The man didn't notice Bouchard until Bouchard made him sneeze.

Ahhh-chooo!

"What the—"

The man opened the door and shooed Bouchard out. Bouchard stood and watched the truck drive away.

It's okay, he told himself. *You'll find a friend.*

The Brother

THE ALIEN SHIP appeared in the sky over the capital, and some humans fled in terror. Some humans gazed up, unable to turn their eyes away, suddenly as catatonic as Oliver had been for two decades when confronted with the specter of extraterrestrial life. Other humans traveled toward the ship, with disregard for their own continued survival, in defiance of evacuation orders, enrapt, engulfed in gleeful frenzy. *The aliens had come*, and these humans waved flags and welcome banners. They carried signs. They chanted, cheered, danced in the streets. The National Mall was impassible, a dark carnival, flecked with the starry glimmer of solar lanterns, glazed by the slow-motion laser shifting of red-blue-green spaceship lights. Humans beat drums. They played guitars. They sang. A DJ played techno beats through generator-powered speakers. Alien invasion became both rave and rapture, a dance festival, a spiritual assembly of believers. The aliens had come to save us, to usher in a new era of galactic peace. They had come to judge us, as modern harbingers of apocalyptic doom, on ships instead of horses, to escort God's chosen up to the heavens, to abandon the sinful dregs on a dying Earth.

Then the alien ship left. And slowly, anticlimactically, the crowds dispersed.

Now, days later, the bacchanal that had overwhelmed DC had re-formed merely to decline into an unruly after-party; a small crowd of protestors encamped at the Washington Monument; a stray sign-waving herald of alien doom wandering the sidewalks; an excess of litter in the street; an abundance of runaway cats. The world felt, in many respects, unchanged.

But not Oliver.

Oliver was transformed.

"Would you like to tell me how you're feeling today, Oliver?"

The doctors didn't understand how it had happened. The doctors had concluded that Oliver would never speak or eat or read like a normal human, and yet here he was, responsive, having just bathed, shaved, and fed himself, eluding them.

This doctor had a clipboard, but the clipboard was really a *tablet* upon which the doctor wrote, with something called a *stylus*. These words—*tablet, stylus*—emerged from the snow-swept valleys of Oliver's mind. The blizzard had shorted his electrical brain circuits, was how one doctor had described it to another. Except he hadn't said *blizzard*. He had said *accident*, and Oliver hadn't understood any of it at the time. He only began to understand it now.

"I'm fine," Oliver said. "I'm good, actually."

His voice felt like cold rust. His fingers hadn't entirely thawed out. They still curled into bloodless claws. *Opposable*, he thought. He ran the word across his limp fish tongue, muttering, "Opposable opposable opposable."

The word tasted like a strange dream. The doctor dropped the stylus, reached down, pincered it between his forefinger and thumb. The doctor looked nervous. He kept glancing at the door, the window, the ceiling, the glowing clipboard tablet.

"Opposable," Oliver whispered.

"What's that now?"

"Nothing."

"Mm-hmm. Okay."

"How are you feeling?" Oliver asked.

The doctor's brow furrowed.

In the courtyard, a tree had gotten sucked out of the ground. There it lay, roots exposed, dying.

The top-floor windows on the south side of Brookwood had blown out, littering the sidewalk with shattered safety glass. The patients housed on that floor had to share rooms until the windows got replaced. More patients arrived every day. Seven more just yesterday, the nurses said. Too many to handle. Oliver overheard them in the hallway, and they didn't stop talking when they saw him because he was just an empty husk filled with snow.

Inside Brookwood, things unraveled. A patient on floor two tried to gnaw off his own finger. Janitors walked out because why would they clean up this piss for shit wages when life was so damned short. *We're not alone,* they yelled on their way out. *We're not fucking alone!* And on the way in. *We're not fucking alone! Doctor, I'm crazy,* a new patient would declare as he handed admission papers to the receptionist. *I'm crazy, doctor. I saw a spaceship in the sky.*

The really, really crazy-crazy people had raved about spaceships in the sky for years. *I know you think there are spaceships, Crazy Bob,* the doctors and nurses corrected, *but there aren't. They're just in your head. You understand that, right? How they're not real?* But now things had gotten all confused. The doctors got up mid-therapy to check the window for alien vessels. The Crazy Bobs hurled globs of tapioca at the wall. They pounded the cafeteria tables, chanting *A-lee-ens! A-lee-ens!* Until the less crazy people joined in, or began to weep.

The chicken nuggets all resembled crispy UFOs.

"Can you explain to me, Oliver, what happened? How you came to—well, it's very unusual, for a patient in the condition you were in to ever recover any functionality. So . . ."

"I don't know what happened," Oliver said. What did the doctor expect? The storm had just blown away. "I'm not a meteorologist."

"Meteorologist." The doctor scribbled the word on his pad. He frowned. "You think, maybe ... meteorology is a part of this all?"

"Um ..."

"Why did you say that, Oliver? Does that word have some meaning to you?"

"Mm-mmm." Oliver shrugged.

"I'm just trying to understand."

They were all just trying to understand. No newspapers at Brookwood. No news channels no internet access no radio. Patients required peace and solace to improve, a respite from the twenty-four-hour cycles of modern life. But Oliver had wandered into the employee breakroom, had found a newspaper left behind on the counter, had poured himself a cup of coffee from the employee carafe, two packets of creamer, six sugar packets, a plastic stir straw. It tasted like a memory. He had stared at the front page, absorbing without reading because he had forgotten how reading felt. Still, the words came crawling out from his snowpack brain. Aliens. Spacecraft. Intention. Departure. Until a nurse caught him. *What are you doing in here, Oliver? Is that coffee? Are you reading?*

"It just ... things just ..."

"Yes?"

"Changed. Can I have a cup of coffee?"

"Is that ... well ..." The doctor read something from his tablet, something about Oliver and chemical combinations in Oliver's brain. "I suppose. I suppose that would be okay."

The doctor had his own special doctor coffee station on a little table in his doctor office. His hands shook, as he fixed two cups.

"I don't think they wanted to kill us," Oliver said.

"Who? What?" Coffee splashed over the cup rim, onto the table.

"The aliens."

"Oliver . . ."

"Can I have more sugar? I like it sweet."

"You do . . . that's . . ." The doctor scrambled for his tablet. He wrote this down. *Oliver likes it sweet.* He set a bowl of sugar on the table. Oliver glopped sweet white snow into his coffee cup.

"Oliver, what do you know? About the aliens?"

"Mm-mmm." Oliver shrugged. "Just what I saw. The ship. The newspaper said . . ."

"How is the coffee?"

"Good."

"It's not the real thing. The coffee. It's instant coffee."

"Oh."

"You said the newspaper. You read it?"

"I don't know. I saw it."

"And is that why you said . . . You don't think they want to kill us?"

"No . . . it's . . ."

"I mean, maybe that's the point. To get our guards down. Because . . . But anyway, the newspaper. How did it make you feel?"

When he came to the hospital, the doctors showed him pictures, and he saw snow and said nothing. They showed him ink splatters and he saw snow. His eyes had frozen. He couldn't even blink. Words = snow. Doctors were snow, but they didn't wear hats or mittens or snow bibs and Oliver got agitated and he screamed and wept inside his head, though no sound escaped the muffling snow.

"I felt . . . normal?" *Normal.* He turned the word over on his tongue silently. *Normal. Normal. Normal.* He didn't quite know what it meant, but it felt like the right word.

"So what made you say that, that you don't think they want to kill us?"

He saw something indescribable, an indescribable fear, bleeding out the doctor's eyes, blood-ink splattering the doctor's face. He gazed at the Rorschach fear splatter, and he knew that the doctor had thought otherwise.

They want to kill us, the doctor had thought.

"They didn't," Oliver said.

"They didn't."

"They didn't kill us."

"But don't you think . . ."

Some of the patients felt not so sure.

Two patients refused to leave their bunk room because their bunk room was a bomb shelter, the only surviving bunk room in the catastrophic Brookwood wreckage. *But what makes you think this will happen?* the doctors asked, but their questioning lacked its customary patronizing tone. Really, they wanted to know: What would happen? The insane could claim an inside knowledge of alien conquest matters. The insane raved about aliens back when all pompous doctors waved their science flags and pointed at the empty sky. *See, kids? Nothing up there!*

Other patients planned their graduation from the human evolutionary level. One staged a reenactment of Heaven's Gate. He pilfered meds and shook them up in a gallon of milk, but the milk tasted bitter and wrong, and no one drank it. One patient made WELCOME ALIENS signs. WELCOME TO EARTH! GREETINGS, FELLOW LIFE-FORMS! PLEASE KILL US QUICKLY, WE ARE WIMPS AND CAN'T HANDLE PAIN!

One patient tore the duct tape/pee pad from a top-floor window and leapt out, headfirst, *SMACK-CRUNCH-GLUSH* against the sidewalk.

"Will they clean him up?" Oliver asked the doctor.

"Will who clean who up?"

"Anyone. Who cleans? The . . . the . . . the janitor."

The janitor had gotten iced in, but Oliver scraped him out. Out came the mop the rags and rubber gloves the garbage cart the scent of lemon-pine. The more his brain thawed, the more it thawed. The faster it thawed. A spring flood of words washed through his brain.

"Yes, the janitor cleans. Do you feel like . . . would you like to talk about . . ."

Here the doctor would have asked, in a pre-alien era, what it was that made him feel unclean. Was cleanliness or uncleanliness a problem area? Did the problem stem from his mother, his father, his deeply ingrained feelings of inadequacy? Instead, the doctor got up, carried his coffee mug over to his desk, took something out, poured a splash into the mug.

"Will the janitor clean up Rick?"

"Rick."

"Who jumped out the window. On the sidewalk, his blood . . ."

"It's stained. It's a stain."

"I can see it from my window."

"They'd have to . . . to pull up the sidewalk square. Pour fresh cement. Does it bother you?"

"I don't know."

"It'd bother me." The doctor shook his head. "You know, this place . . ."

Oliver knew. *Pew pew pew pew,* fired his neurons. The doctor had a framed photograph on his desk, of the doctor and a woman and a gap-toothed child, standing against a snow-and-evergreen backdrop. He had a picture of mountains on his wall.

"You should get out of here," Oliver said. "If that's what you want."

The doctor glanced up at the mountains.

"We'd been saving up for a cabin. Somewhere in the Shenandoah. You ever been there?"

"No."

"Those Blue Ridge Mountains. They're gorgeous. I could set up a small practice. Life is short, you know?"

"Yeah." He knew. "Can I go?" Oliver asked.

The doctor glanced at the wall clock. Life was short.

"We still have another twenty minutes."

"No. I mean . . . can I go? To the . . . the . . . the Shenandoah . . . Valley?"

A song broke loose in Oliver's brain and he *needed* to go he *had* to go he *had* to see it. *Shenandoah. Shenandoah. Shenandoah* sang the palpitations of his battered heart.

"You want to . . . Uh, well, look. Oliver. You're here, you know."

"In Brookwood."

"Brookwood. And I'm just trying to understand what happened to you. You were—"

"A prisoner. Am I? Am I a prisoner?"

"A prisoner? No. No! This is a hospital. We're here to, you know, this is about treatment. We want our patients to get better."

"I am better."

"I can see that. But . . . well, I'm just trying to understand why, Oliver. One day you were, well, catatonic. Nonresponsive. It was like, like your mind wasn't there. But now, all of a sudden . . . the alien ships show up, and then, well, it just raises questions. It's very unusual. For a patient as . . . as nonresponsive as you were to come back so suddenly."

"But I'm not a prisoner."

"Well. No. No. But there are policies, you know? For your own protection. You can't just go out there and start, well, we have to make sure first that you won't immediately relapse. And then you'd need to move into a transitional housing situation—"

"So can I do that?"

"Well, eventually, yes. When there's capacity. But we'll have to check and see if . . ."

Oliver got up. He walked over toward the window. He looked out, at the mountain-less cityscape, at the courtyard with its uprooted dying tree. The cement looked mottled, gray with splotches of brown, as if the blood had splattered everywhere, had stained every surface, and Oliver felt as if he should have felt scared or sad, or cold. But instead he felt free.

The Husband

SCHOOL GOT CANCELED Friday, but the next week Blaine dropped the children off like nothing had happened. The children had leftover alien-head cupcakes in their lunch boxes and a stack of laminated Lost Pet flyers to disseminate among their classmates. They had an altogether unreasonable expectation that they would find the missing Mr. Meow-mitts hiding out inside the Pleasant View Elementary School building.

Jas explained the logic:

(1) Aliens wouldn't visit boring places.

(2) School was boring.

(3) School was a safe place to hide from alien invaders.

Conclusion: Mr. Meow-mitts had sought refuge at the children's school.

Moreover, boring school had taught the children logic, which they concurrently employed to illustrate why Mom and Dad should not send them back to dangerous school:

(1) Aliens were obviously smart.

(2) It was smart to be efficient.

(3) It would be more efficient to abduct all the children all together, from school, than to pluck them from their individual abodes.

Conclusion: Children should stay home from school until the alien crisis had fully and formally resolved.

"Because they could come back at any time, Dad," Jas had said, at five a.m. on a dark Sunday morning. He poked Blaine with his cold little finger. "Dad. At. Any. Time."

"What time is it? What are you . . . Where's your mom?" He flapped his arm at the wife's empty side of the bed.

"She's out running."

"It's too early."

"You don't want me to get abducted, do you, Dad? You don't want them to experiment on me and implant, you know, weird things in my body. Do you? Dad? That's why Avril and I wrote this No-School Commitment Form. All you've got to do is sign right here."

Blaine refused. Jas pretended to agree to stay quiet so Dad could fall back asleep, but every few minutes he stampeded up and down the stairs, *clomp-clomp-clomp*ed across the floor, dunked a basketball in the bathtub, steered the remote-control fire engine through the hallway, et cetera. The wife intervened, when she returned from the six or twelve miles she had run through the dark damp neighborhood: TV. *Remember TV?* And don't you forget whose TV it is. Children had no legal right to own or contract, and even if Jas could convince his dad to sign, he had no means of enforcement. And, most importantly, TV belonged to Dad.

On Monday, the school parking lot was pandemonium. People ignored the painted lines. They double-parked in the driveway. They drove across the schoolyard grass to escape. The parking lot parent volunteer had not shown up. The usual stratum of greeting teachers had diminished. Blaine had to coax the children out of the car.

"TV. Think about it. TV."

He turned onto the highway twenty minutes late. There were wrecks, of course. One-two-three-four of them. Fender benders. The offending drivers let their stopped cars block lanes. Every rubbernecker driving both directions had to slow down and survey. The wife had smartly avoided rush hour. The wife had sped downtown in the wee dark hours to win the first-to-work prize. The wife had won that prize nearly every morning for eight years running. The prize had won her an early partnership, a corner office with a river view, and first pick from the pastry spread delivered to the firm's twenty-third-floor office every morning at seven a.m. By seven, the wife had already billed two hours.

Children: Why doesn't Mom ever drive us to school?

Dad: Because your mother is crazy.

Mom: Yep, crazy for eclairs!

Children: How come Mom gets donuts for breakfast every day but we only get donuts on some days?

A compelling question. Fresh-fried donuts got delivered to the house at dawn with increasing regularity, though sometimes the wife fried them up herself at a time that would be, for a regular person, the middle of the night. For her, it was first breakfast.

Sometimes, Blaine wondered what the wife saw in a person as regular as himself. He rated, objectively, moderately above average; seven or eight on the looks scale, B+ for intelligence, room for improvement. *But you're perfect*, the wife would say. *You're adorable. Just look at those cute little hairs on your chest!* There was a guy at the summer swim club—handsome, six-pack, smooth-chested—who could do a double flip off the diving board. A partner at the wife's firm wrote novels and owned a ski chalet. Even their neighbor John up the street ran triathlons for fun. Blaine jogged a few miles here and there. He tinkered in carpentry. His birdhouse had a hole in the roof. His custom bookshelf stuck out an inch too far from the wall. He loved the wife and read sex articles on how to please the wife with cunnilingus, and she seemed to enjoy herself, but she approached even the blandest endeavors with such orgiastic intensity that he could not help but wonder.

Blaine took the downtown exit, through the tunnel, onto

Third Street, now forty minutes late. He got stuck at a light, and then another. The lights usually operated on a timer, but this morning they had a strong and irrational preference for red. He glanced out the window. He saw a couple standing on the street corner, face-to-face. The woman stared up at the man. She reached out and placed her hand on his shoulder. She had the same coat as the wife, Blaine noticed. She had the wife's hat. *Anne,* he thought, for a second.

Then the cars behind him started honking. He turned and saw empty road in front of him. The green light turned yellow. He slammed on the gas. He glanced back at the street corner receding in his rearview mirror, but he couldn't see the wife. He *hadn't* seen the wife, he told himself. Lots of women had that same coat-hat combination. The wife was warm inside at her desk with her jelly-filled donut and her cream-filled donut and her sugary, sugary coffee. The wife liked it sweet—sweet enough to overpower donut sweetness. And everyone knew that liars and adulterers took their coffee black.

See, the wife had said, once, sipping her diabetes-tempting breakfast beverage, *this is how you know you can trust me.*

Blaine arrived at work nearly an hour late, but the time-punch had an out-of-order sign taped to it. The manager who usually reveled in reprimanding late arrivals had not shown up at all. A third of the office had not shown up. One employee had decided to take a morning nap in his cubicle. Another had affixed a three-foot cross to the front of her desk next to a stack of pamphlets. *The Second Coming of Christ,* the pamphlets said. Blaine wanted to take one, just to see if they said that Christ had come and gone, or had passed by but would come right back after he picked up some galactic lunch, or if the ships sailed to Earth as false prophets on a mission to confuse. But he left the pamphlets untouched. He didn't want to invite discussion. He wanted to get on with work so he could get it done and go home so he could come back to work again tomorrow, and he felt a sudden dark dread pit in his stomach, a sense that he should not have come to this office place, a sense that everything had already gone wrong and he just couldn't see it yet.

He pulled his phone from his pocket to check for wife-texts, for something, some solace from the overwhelming uncertainty and desolation that had just subsumed him. But there were no texts, no news, nothing but the slow tick of empty time.

He sat down at his desk and tried to decide how long he could sit at his desk and look semi-productive, or even pre-productive, contemplative of his next important work move.

Then Dave appeared. "Welp. Got a full schedule today." Dave slapped the testing schedule down onto Blaine's desk. He grinned, a perfectly ordinary sort of grin that could only exist as a front to conceal some underlying scheme. "Let's get going."

They went outside and climbed into the city van that Blaine had expected he would never see again. The van should have gotten absorbed in the mushrooming of Dave's apocalyptic prepper compound, yet here it was, with a confounding Dave in the driver's seat.

"Mind if I smoke?" Dave asked, heedless to the no-smoking signage in the city van. "You know what? I'm gonna smoke."

He lit a menthol as they pulled out of the water treatment building parking lot. He drove too fast, in the wrong direction.

"Hey, I thought we were going to—"

"Nope," Dave said. He flicked ash out the window. The ash blew right back in. "I mean, we will. But I gotta meet a guy first. Say, you got your phone on?"

"Yeah."

"Better turn it off. So you don't get implicated."

"Dave, do you really think—"

Dave had already thought through to the point of illicit smoking in the city van, which he had commandeered for some elusive mission, and there was no going back, no leaping out the passenger door like some pansy. Blaine had committed, fully, tacitly, by virtue of his non-refusal to not commit at the moment of the mission's inception, which dated back to Arrival Day, when they bought out the pony keg. Blaine had a tower of beer in his garage now. He knew he should have felt alarmed, as they sped in the wrong direction, Dave humming along to Radio Station Cock-Rock, befouling the city van with his menthol. But it all felt strangely normal. The sudden momentous appearance and then disappearance of alien vessels felt entirely normal. The world had changed, and yet here he was, at work, kind of. The song on the radio ended. *Beam 'em up*, the DJ said, playing a soundtrack of UFO bleeps, laser beams, the squelch of deep probing. *Beam 'em up, we're doin' butt stuff!*

Dave drove too fast, west along the river, past the rust factories, the road-salt silos, the great mounds of gravel, over some railroad tracks and more railroad tracks, into the weedy parking lot of an out-of-service HVAC business that operated out of a concrete warehouse, its one front window boarded up, its peeling paint re-coated in graffiti. HAVE U SEEN DIS WHERE-HOUSE B4? the graffiti asked, and Blaine felt another cold chill up his spine.

"You turn your phone off?" Dave asked.

"Yeah."

"It's better to leave it behind altogether, you know? Because they can still track you even when it's off. I left mine in the office."

"So what are we doing here?"

"Planetary defenses." Dave opened the van door and gestured for Blaine to get out.

"You know, I think I'll just wait in the van."

"Your loss, man."

Dave disappeared into the warehouse. Blaine steered the radio dial from Beam-Me-Up-for-Butt-Stuff to Monday-morning Disco. He warmed his hands over the vents. He thought about the wife who was not the wife on the corner of Third Street. He tried to calculate how many doppelgangers the wife might have, spread across the whole Earth, encompassed within the more expansive overlapping sphere of women who owned the same coat. The numbers turned astronomical. The calculation morphed to a calculation of life in the universe; the number of planets exceeding billions, the habitable Goldilocks spheres, the jackpot winners that spawned life, intelligent life—intelligent life that did *not* wipe itself out—and, among those, the masters of space travel. Life elsewhere in the universe had already been speculated an inevitability—calculated by women and men with more advanced degrees in science than Blaine had even heard of—to exist or have existed on Mars, and beneath the icy surface of Jupiter's moon Europa. But how that inevitability correlated to alien spacecraft depended on planetary estimates and probabilities published out there, somewhere on the internet, which Blaine couldn't access because he had turned his phone off in furtherance of or willful blindness to his work partner's shady dealings.

"I know you're thinking this is shady," Dave said, hoisting unmarked wooden crates into the back of the city van. "But it's not. It's essential. It's fundamental to the continuity of human civilization."

Dave, in a pre-alien-invasion iteration, had endorsed the eradication of human civilization, wholesale destruction being the only salve to humanity's obvious maladies, among which: its disco music, its sweater-wearing pets with inappropriately anthropomorphic names, its tree-kissing, hybrid-car-driving recycle-Nazis. Dave said this to his hybrid-car-driving work partner, after said partner had fished

Dave's discarded aluminum can out of the trash like a *libtarded raccoon*. Yet now that humanity's greatest threat had shifted from ABBA to aliens, our civilization was worthy of survival. And dependent, Dave explained, as he climbed into the van and seized control of the radio dial, on crafty survivalists like Dave.

"You know what's going to happen, right?"

"No," Blaine said. Not knowing terrified him, but terror itself felt commonplace, indigenous to the highway-spangled land of texting drivers and mass shootings. "No, what's going to happen?"

"Well, clearly those aliens made a deal with the government."

The deep state had, yet again, betrayed its people.

"But they're gone," Blaine said as the van peeled out of the parking lot.

And that terrified him too, because what did it say about humanity? Intelligent life had snubbed us.

"Oh, they're coming back," Dave said. "I mean, some of them are still here for sure. You know, in hiding."

"But you think the ships are coming back?"

"I *know* they're coming back. And then it's *pew-pew-pew-pew! PTCHOW!*" Dave gestured the coming detonations. The van swerved. Blaine grabbed the wheel and swerved it back, and he thought how on every road in every city-state-country across the whole Earth there was a Dave—a pewing, ptchowing, swerving Dave—but among them how many had a Blaine in the passenger seat to grab the wheel? Terrifying.

"But how do you know?" Blaine asked.

A mistake. Dave rolled his eyes. It was obvious, to anyone with eyes to roll. The aliens had negotiated a plea deal with the global elites; the elites got to keep their mansions, their sports cars, their private jets, and in exchange they would give the rest of us up, no contest. The point-one-percent subsisted mostly on nuts and berries and fermented greens and supplements anyhow, and those things were gross and un-American. The aliens wouldn't want them.

"But I bet you're wondering," Dave went on, "why did they leave? I mean, they made the deal. Why fly off, instead of staying to enslave us now?"

At a stoplight, Dave lit another menthol. He stretched, arching his unrestricted back. He was a slave to the seat belt once, in his pre-alien resistance-fighter days. The city told him to buckle, so he buckled. Now, he was unfettered. He wouldn't stand slave to the traffic light, either, damn it, when, judging by the distance of approaching traffic, it was clearly objectively probably safe enough to pull out into the intersection.

So he did.

"What are you doing? Dave!"

"Looks fine to me. See? We're fine."

"But the light's red!"

"Fuck the light."

"No. No, you can't just ignore the light!" Regardless of the safety risk that, in that particular instant, had seemed minimal, Blaine didn't want his partner to get fired. He liked Dave, kind of, at least enough to not wish him ill. Dave remembered his kids' birthdays and sent home cheapo plastic toys for them, like those plastic eggs filled with play-slime that fused with the carpet fibers and embedded itself in the couch cushions and leeched toxic chemicals into the children's fingers, but the children sure liked that stuff. Last fall Dave spotted an injured deer that lay dying in the road, and he pulled the city van over and barricaded the road so no one could hit it, and he stayed with it, stroking its soft head as it bled out from its torn center, until animal control showed up. Also, Dave seemed like the sort who, if fired, might fire back.

"Look, I'm not going to be a pawn to the Alien-Government-Industrial Complex. You know the traffic light is all about control, right? That's its central purpose. To watch and manipulate you. Well, not me. I've joined a band of resistance fighters. Now, I'm not going to ask you to join us," Dave said, before he launched into an hours-long soliloquy as to why Blaine should really, seriously consider, for the sake of his country and his children, joining them.

The speech continued through the morning, as they drove to the first testing site and then the next, ignoring red-light recording devices and stop-sign spies as Dave sucked down a pack of menthols and infused the city van with the aroma of minty cancer. Blaine half listened, but his mind wandered. He thought about his missing cat, and what he would do if the cat turned out like that deer on the road, broken, dying, just another pitiable mass of flesh and fur in a broken, dying world. *But Mr. Meow-mitts*, the children would ask, *can't they fix him? Can't the vet equip him with a new cat-heart, a fresh set of lungs, a gut transplant?* We could do these things, we humans. We could bring forth miracle life, life renewed, if confronted by necessity. And yet our creatures broke, and died, and so often we stood by and watched, as Blaine had from inside the van, while the bleeding deer gasped its last breaths. We stood by, and these aliens couldn't even bother to do that. They took one glance at our broken, dying planet and sailed past, like the drivers who slowed down to check out the wreck on the opposite side of the road, peered idly out the window, *Oh look honey there's blood, there's death*, but soon enough they forgot. We were too far gone.

Were we too far gone?

All those billions of planets, those Goldilocks planets, all that proliferating life. If some of it survived, a miracle. If it launched itself out across vast uninhabitable space, shouldn't we expect it to be better than ourselves? Not just intellectually, technologically, but also morally? Yet here we were, on our still-dying Earth, and the aliens had gone on.

Unless one believed Dave.

"It's dog-eat-dog," Dave said. "Except the dogs are aliens." Which made Blaine wonder if the aliens kept doglike pets, for companionship and not merely sustenance, and if those pets had made the long-space-distance trip, vacation destination Earth, but, oh, darn, Earth's got roaches, and it's so filthy and teeming with diseases, no way are we staying there.

The Ohio River looked particularly orangish brown. The tributaries had algae problems, increasingly frequent, blooming up again now even though winter should have dispelled them. The second inspection site would fail its water test again for sure. The company had failed their last two tests: unacceptable phosphate levels, copper, arsenic, fun stuff. It paid the fine, gladly. Cheaper than the treatment, the site rep said, followed by an *Oops, wasn't supposed to say that out loud.*

In the afternoon, Dave and Blaine returned to the water treatment building. They filled out paperwork and tested samples. Dave transferred the unmarked crates from the city van to his own truck and left early.

"See you tomorrow," Blaine said.

"I guess," Dave replied. "We've got to keep up appearances, right?"

Blaine left at the regular time. He got in his car. He drove to the car wash. He filled up the gas tank. Everything was regular, he told himself. It's all regular and normal if you can just believe it's regular and normal and lots of women own that same coat as his wife. He picked up groceries, pursuant to the list texted by same wife. She wanted soft tacos fried up in crispy exterior taco shells with crispy melty cheese. Dang she ate a lot of bacon. She organized the grocery text by aisle, so he never had to circle back or check off. He could move ahead in a forward trajectory, through to the checkout line, down the street in his nice clean car, past the billboard lawyer, HOMERUN HOWIE MASON, HE'LL KNOCK YOUR LEGAL PROBLEMS OUT OF THE PARK! Onto another street, lined with big bare oaks, greening February grass, Sears catalog houses. Out the window, he saw the house that belonged to their friends Greg and Rebecca. Greg stood in the lawn with a shovel and an ax. Blaine waved. He pulled over, rolled down his window.

"Hey there," Blaine called, in a very regular voice. "Getting an early start with the yard this year?"

"I'm going to dig up the tree," Greg said. "Chop it down and dig it up."

The tree, one of those offensive tree-beasts that shed inedible berries and spawned profligate shoots and suckers to entangle your lawn mower blades, occupied the thin stretch of grass between the sidewalk and the street.

"Can you? I thought the tree technically belongs to the city, from where it's planted."

"I don't give a shit," Greg said.

"You might get fined."

"Whatever." Greg shrugged. "Say, can I ask you something?"

"Sure."

"How much you think this house would go for?"

"Your house?"

"Yeah."

"I have no idea. Anne might. Why? You're not thinking of moving are you?"

"No, no. I mean, it wouldn't make sense. With all our family here.

And Rebecca's new job. I was just curious, you know, about the price."

"Right. Yeah. It does seem like prices have gone up in the neighborhood."

"I'm sure it'll be worth more without this damned tree here." Greg scowled at the tree. "Anyhow, tell Anne thanks for dropping off that lasagna."

"Sure," Blaine said. When had the wife baked lasagna?

"We'll see you at the party Friday."

"Right." *The party?*

"Have a good night!"

Blaine drove home. Spiderweb strings of cola cans barricaded his front door. He found a similar situation at the back door. He got trapped on his way through.

"Hey!" he called into the house. The string had caught him on two different buttons. "A little help!"

The children ran up, dressed in their aluminum armor and pie-pan helmets, brandishing their butter knives and salad forks.

"Halt!"

"You can't come in!"

"Unless you say the password."

"Um, what's the password?"

"You know the password, Dad."

"If you're really *Dad*."

Blaine unhooked a strip of string from one button but his foot got stuck on another string.

"Okay, this is ridiculous. You can't just block the door like this. If people need to get in and out—"

"I can get through. See?" Jas wriggled through a gap in the string.

"If you were really Dad, you could make it through," Avril said.

"*Hoomans* can get through."

"Humans?"

"Hoomans."

"And chonky bois."

"Wait, did Mr. Meow-mitts—"

"He's back!"

"He came back!"

"Come and see!"

"Yeah, come on, Dad!"

He became *Dad* again when the children got excited enough. Jas squeezed back through the string-and-can trap. Blaine unwound himself. He untied the top strings and climbed over. By the time he got in, the children had forgotten the cat and remembered TV. He walked past them, up the stairs, into his bedroom.

"Anne?"

"Shhhh."

His wife sat on the bed with their cat in her lap. The cat was wearing the rainbow sweater she had knitted for it. One of her hands stroked the length of its back. The other scratched beneath its chin. The cat purred, and its purr sounded otherworldly.

"Meow-mitts," Blaine whispered. The name, in the presence of this creature, felt reverent. Mr. Meow-mitts had fled because the universe was frightening—surely his alpha-wave brain had sensed the threat—and then he returned because the universe was frightening, and this small house, with its alien-repelling can-traps and makeshift Faraday-suited children and bacon smells, was the best place in the whole great universe to be.

Blaine sat down on the bed. He slid his arm around Anne. Anne gazed into the cat's eyes. She leaned over the cat and whispered something into its ear.

"Where did you find him?" Blaine asked quietly.

"On the porch. When we got home. He was waiting."

"Good. Good, I'm glad."

"Listen to him purr," Anne said. She nestled her head against Blaine's shoulder. He listened. "He's amazing. It's all so amazing. Isn't it?"

The Brother

OLIVER DUG HIS fingernails into his palms. A stray flake drifted from the popcorn ceiling sky. He heard a figment of a distant disco beat. He rolled the cuffs of his jeans. They hung too long. Floor-moppers, the social worker had said, scrunching her nose. But Oliver liked the color of them, deep blue like the sea, like a line in a book he had read as a child, about colors. He remembered that line—*deep blue like the sea*—somehow, when he had forgotten so much else.

Because the brain, Oliver, the doctor had said, *the brain is a weird thing.* The doctors couldn't tell him what made his brain start motoring along again, after it had stalled out for so long. The doctors had colored pictures of his brain and the colors had changed—a rainbow miracle—but the doctors couldn't say why.

Of course, they had a theory.

Oliver ran the treadmill, suctioned up to various cords, meters, monitors, while he watched the green blip of his heartbeat on a tiny TV screen, while the doctors played twenty questions. The answer couldn't be aliens, but the answer was almost always aliens.

Other doctors idled in the breakroom, circling the donut box, or took the day off to go play golf, even though the Brookwood doctor-patient ratio had recently gotten skewed with the influx of patients and the increase of doctor sick days at the golf course.

A room had opened up at one of the transition houses. The doctors were glad to send Oliver on his way. The treadmill and the brain scans said that Oliver could trade his pajama-slipper-robe ensemble for jeans,

T-shirt, sweater, sneakers. He tucked the T-shirt into his jeans, to see how it felt. Was Oliver a shirt-tucker? Oliver did not know what or who Oliver was.

He un-tucked the shirt. No, Oliver was not a tucker. Oliver didn't like the shirt, its scratchy cotton weave, its boxy largeness, the list of corporate sponsors on its back.

"Well, you can buy yourself a new shirt, Oliver, once you're out," the social worker told him. "You've got enough money for that."

He had something called *a trust*, but the social worker couldn't tell him anything more. The social worker showed him a piece of paper with numbers on it, dollar symbols. Monthly, you see, Oliver? Also something called *disability*. The word made Oliver feel weak in the arms, and his shoes felt too big. They were too big, but he could buy new shoes too, if that was how he felt about things.

The social worker put that paper in a folder with a bunch of other papers. She put the folder in another folder with a bunch of other folders. She called a taxi. They waited outside, six squares down from the bloodstain. The taxi came. They climbed inside, Oliver with his life's possessions: sneakers, jeans, T-shirt, sweater, folders, papers. Also, a vinyl square inside the back pocket of his jeans, with an ID card, and a debit card, and business cards for Brookwood and for the social worker and for his doctor. *Call me any time*, his doctor had said, but Oliver sensed that his doctor didn't really mean it. The ways of the world grew clearer.

The taxi dropped them off at a store that sold everything. The social worker got a cart, maneuvered through aisles of clothes, shoes, here, you need a suitcase, Oliver. He had to pick—black, red, navy, stripes. He had to redefine the man he wanted to be, when he didn't remember the man he had been, or anything, really, beyond the endless Brookwood snowdrifts. He had fragments—a car, the shadow of a woman in the passenger seat, a kitchen table patterned with blue-green atomic bursts, a name carved along the table edge that he couldn't read. He could read, just not that name part. *Sale*, he read. *Twenty percent off men's slacks.* Would he be a slacks man, or a jeans man?

"When you get a job, Oliver," the social worker said. *When you get a job.* He saw a flash of polyester shirt and paper hat, a deep fryer, a silver basket of fries. He wanted jeans, but the social worker helped him pick a suit, stiff and black, off the rack. She steered him to the fitting room.

"Don't you look so nice," she said. A changed man.

Then back into a cab, across the city, to a house. Transitional House, the social worker said. She keyed numbers into a keypad on the front door. The door opened. The house smelled like lots of different men. Like Brookwood, but with dirty laundry, oregano and garlic, cologne. Just in time for dinner.

Oliver sat at a table, one of two tables crammed together in the dining room of the house, crammed between the men who lived there. *Transitional. Transitional.* He turned the word over in his mind, until it became something else. *Transformational.* One man said grace. Another man rolled his eyes. He spooned spaghetti onto plates. Two scoops, two meatballs, a hunk of garlic bread, a glass of milk. The plates got passed around. Oliver twirled a noodle around his fork. He remembered a napkin on the lap. He remembered a spoon in a nurse's hand, special delivery to destination mouth, cold oatmeal and a blue pill and darn it, Oliver, don't just let it dribble down your chin like that. This time he didn't. This spaghetti, this buttery garlic bread, this meal was transformational.

"My name is Oliver. I was in Brookwood. For ... they said it was for about twenty years. But I don't remember. I was catatonic. And then ..."

"Oliver."

"Welcome."

"Welcome."

"And then . . ."

"What happened?"

"Don't prod. Let the man speak."

"I don't know," Oliver said. "I was catatonic. And then all of a sudden, I wasn't."

Aliens, the transitional men agreed.

"But how?"

How didn't matter. Aliens had burned away the heavy fog of catatonia, and now Oliver was free.

"Well, kind of," one of the men said. "In transition, from not free to free."

Except maybe, Oliver thought, in thoughts that clumped into mushy half-formed words, *none of them had been, or ever would be, free*. Something always tethered them. Some tragedy some pain some false looping narrative. There, in his mind again: the atomic kitchen table, and on it a foil pouch of fruit punch, an ashtray, a hand, fingernails painted pink, tap-tap-tapping. *I go through enough shit, Oliver. Enough shit, without you* yes him too. He was tethered to some pain in his past, though he could scarcely remember it. But it felt like he would never break free of it, not fully.

Now the narrative that tethered them was a true story, the story of the aliens that had come to our planet. The story replayed daily on the televisions, the news, the talk shows, the halls of Congress, the subways, the factories, the dining rooms where transitional men, with their plates of spaghetti and meatballs, gathered to discuss what it had meant, and what would happen next.

They had all seen the ship. They had gone outside and stared up at the flashing lights. They had considered that it meant that they had lost their minds, again. Everyone everywhere was running, screaming, losing their minds. It took a lot of crazy to produce a delusion like that.

Oliver had seen the ship, but he had also felt it, in his head. He felt a *wub-wub-wub*. He felt a crack, and then a trickle, and then for a moment he thought he had pissed himself, but he hadn't. It was just his skin, alternating hot-cold, getting prickly, until the prickly bristled up into his brain and he thought, *Oh shit, I'm in the loony bin.* Thus he had, in a sense, an out-of-body experience.

"Like an abduction," suggested a short man with a trim beard.

"I don't know," Oliver said. "Maybe. Maybe it was like that." He had felt himself phase in and out, but maybe the snowstorm had done the phasing. He didn't understand it.

"But you don't remember anything," asked a guy with a red bandanna, "from your life before, before Brookwood?"

"Not really. Snippets. It's jumbled."

"She said you were in a bad wreck," a balding man with round eyeglasses told Oliver.

"Who?"

"Audra. The social worker."

"I think . . . maybe. I don't remember."

"Yeah, she said you were in a bad wreck, and that you were like, like, more vegetable than man."

"Hey, that—that's not how she put it."

"I was just—"

"Don't be a jerk."

"Guys, kind words," said the man with the red bandanna. "Kind words."

"But that's right," Oliver said. He saw a flash of the soft-tipped spoon, chug-chug-chug, into mouth-station. He remembered the wet spittle down his chin, the nurse's face as she sponged him clean. "I was. More vegetable than man."

"But now you're like . . . You're like—"

"That's wild, man."

"It has to be them." The transitional man looked up, as if they were up there still, beyond the ceiling, whirring and flashing.

Something in the ships', whatever, like, radio waves. Electromagnetimagic. Infrarariums. Satellspectragrams. Alpha beta brain beams. Transverse temporal thought alteration. The transitional men amalgamated science-sounding words and syllables to make new words and phrases to explain it, to explain the miracle of Oliver's recovery. Oliver appreciated their ingenuity, their kind, forthcoming words. The doctors had given him, mostly, troubled stares, puzzled questions, probes into what he thought it all meant, how he felt about it, could he examine this ink splotch and tell them, did he look at it and see aliens? Mostly the doctors told him nothing useful, but it came from a place of confrontation, of confusion in the shifting sands of what they thought was medical science. But maybe it wasn't. Maybe Western medicine had gotten it all wrong, so they had to believe that Oliver had gotten it wrong, and now, like a good American boy, he had pulled himself up by and from his institutional-slipper-straps and decided to finally get things right.

The transitional men also told him nothing useful, except their nothing useful came from a place of fascination, with a second helping of meatballs. The meatballs came frozen in a bag, someone said, apologetically, but the meatballs at Brookwood had come frozen and then got boiled up in a giant vat and then got mushed down into a meat-paste and fed to Oliver by a soft spoon. So, yes, he would have another.

The transitional men had stories. They told him how they had a job busing dishes at a tapas place on K Street and that when the sky went dark people dropped their glasses, threw their napkins on the floor, and ran out screaming.

They told him how they cowered in the Metro station, them and a million other frightened sobbing people. But the train never came. Someone had leapt into the track a few stations down, *leap-smack-splat*, shards of bone in the rails, blood on the wall. The trains stopped running and people walked, through the darkened tunnels, their path illuminated by the flashlight beams of otherwise useless phones.

They told him how they went back to work after, but the hotel or sandwich shop or grocery store where they worked was short-staffed. People called in sick. Or they never called. Or they internet-shopped and played games on their phones in the hotel lobby instead of stocking bathrooms with travel-sized shampoos. Or they hoarded toilet paper in the grocery stock room, for that beltway suit who looked like they would pay. Twenty-five dollars? Higher. Forty, for a ten-pack.

Insanity, the transitional men agreed, though they didn't use the *I*-word. Had those suits not heard of leaves?

Two of the transitional men had transitioned backward. One went back to Brookwood.

"Richard. Tall guy. Ears that stick out—like. Didja see him?"

The other man, Carl Lesniak, well . . .

"Let's not talk about Carl, okay?"

"We were just saying—"

One transitional man got up from the table, stomped away. Tears slid down a chin, plop-plop into a glass of milk.

"Why there was space for you. Oliver. That's why."

* * *

Oliver tucked himself into bed. The bed had belonged to Carl. Carl's sheets had gotten washed, but a smell still lingered. It reminded Oliver of snow. He lay shivering between the smelly threadbare sheets, beneath the weak blanket, the water-stained ceiling, the sky up there devoid of visible spaceships. *Let's not think about Carl,* he thought. *Let's not think about snow.* His mind circled back to what his mind had strived to avoid; the covered streets, the buried houses, the wind blowing it sideways, Carl wandering around out there without a coat. He got up, crept past the transitional snores of his roommate, pulled back the blind. He looked down at the black asphalt, the barren rooftops of parked cars, the steady streetlamps, the dark sky spotted with innocuous clouds. He returned to bed.

But he couldn't sleep. He coiled into an Oliver ball, legs pressed to his belly for warmth, blanket pulled up over his ears. He lay and thought and thought, and his mind was a vacuum, but, also, a puzzle box.

The atomic table. The fruit punch pouch. The ashtray. The wicked cherry of a cigarette, pressed into his back-hand flesh. Had he done that to himself? Oliver slipped his hand out from beneath the blanket. He held it up to the moonlight. He examined the scar, a small sphere at the base of his ring finger.

He didn't know much about himself, but he had a sense that he was good and nice. Oliver was nice. It felt right and true and relieving, to know something about himself, to begin to unravel his mysteries. He lay and thought and thought about the scar on his hand, the last weeks at Brookwood where his snowdrop mind blossomed, the first flower of the spring. He thought about how the spaceships came and then his broken brain started working again. He thought about the explanations posited by transitional men: infrarariums. Satellspectragrams. Magnetlectricmagic-words. He folded them over, turned them around in his mind. Transverse temporal thought alteration. Causation versus correlation versus random chance. The transitional man who identified the distinction explained. The spaceships made him better. Or the happenstance of spaceships related to the dispersion of his catatonia but did not cause it; the spaceships snapped him out of it, but the spaceships might have been a tidal wave, a pair of perfect breasts, a Godzilla smashing the Brookwood rooftop. Or the departure of his mental whiteout and the arrival of spaceships had occurred coincidentally, neither bearing any relation to the other, beyond timing, and the connection imposed by his not-very-smart brain.

Except was his brain really not very smart? Because the things the transitional men explained made enough sense for him to ascribe a low probability to coincidence. He would not bet his trust fund on coincidence. He shivered, and the man in the bed beside his gave a snort, and Oliver understood then how Brookwood was that icy embankment where your car spun out and got stuck; how this transitional place was the mechanic's shop where they fixed up your car, but sometimes you had to wait months or years for the right part, and it still reeked of crazy men, of their garlic dinners, their sweat-pit shirt-stains, their somnambulant snorts and farts, their tears, their moments, teetering on the brink of Crazy. He understood how he needed to transition quickly, to slink out in the middle of the night so no one could see just how rapidly he had bloomed, and in seeing doubt in their own slowly thawing paths, their own fragile selves. *You should get out of here. If that's what you want.* He recalled the picture on his doctor's wall in Brookwood, the blue-ridged mountains unfolding against a dusky sky. He stared at the picture in his mind until the picture became real, rock and trees, winding roads, green valleys. If he climbed those mountain peaks, he could see all the way to the Atlantic, all the way across the land and sea, and up, into space.

"Oliver?"

His thoughts scattered at the sound of his roommate's voice.

"Yeah?"

"Are you awake?"

"Yeah."

"I had a bad dream."

"I'm sorry."

"There was a tiger, and, and . . . I couldn't see it. But I knew, you know? It was out there in the trees, somewhere, watching. Stalking me."

Oliver understood how this dream was symbolic, how the tiger was a great ship that had flown away. But it was out there somewhere, waiting, biding, plotting. Maybe. But who understood the minds that steered the ships and tigers?

"You know . . . there are no tigers in DC."

"At the zoo."

"But they're locked up."

"But they might get out. That happens."

"I know. But I wouldn't worry. There would be an alert. *Tiger on the loose* or something."

"Yeah, yeah, you're right," the roommate said as Oliver wondered what he had meant when he said the word *alert*.

Oliver's mouth had said the word before the word could register in his brain. The inventory of his brain surprised him.

"But . . . life is short," the roommate said. "And it's like, a tiger could, like, make it way frickin' shorter. I wanna get out of here, you know?"

"Yeah. Where would you go?"

"Anywhere but DC. I want, like . . . land. Trees, fields. Like, horses maybe? Goats. I'd like goats."

"That sounds nice."

"Yeah. It does. Well . . . good night."

"Good night."

Oliver still couldn't sleep. He crept out of bed. He went to the window. He looked out. He saw a shadow moving through the otherwise empty street; the shadow of a tiger, he thought. But it was just a cat.

The Husband

WEEKS PASSED, AND February blossomed into March, and the spaceships did not return. Dave stockpiled weapons and prattled about deep state conspiracies. The children forgot about their tinfoil Faraday suits. Most of the string-and-can traps got hauled away with the recycling. Mr. Meow-mitts prowled through the house on high alert in his rainbow sweater. *He's acting weird*, the kids said. Jas, with a screwdriver in hand: *Yeah, Dad, can you fix him?* As if Dad could disassemble the cat, rearrange his wiring, and screw him back together, good as new.

The wife was also acting weird, but Blaine told himself that weird was normal for the wife. Like three years back, when she went on that baking bender, whipping up triple-layer chocolate cakes and peanut-butter bars and cherry cheesecakes and savory scones. It started with a school bake sale and ended with the purchase of a fifty-pound box of chocolate, found and opened by two sneaky children, who ate at least a pound each before they got sick all over the carpet. Or a few years before that, when the wife, in an uncharacteristically un-wife-like move, left her cell phone on the roof of the car, where it stayed until she turned onto the highway, and the wife punished her inattention by withholding new phone privileges from herself for a whole month, but she treated herself to a brand-new moped, chrome and aqua blue, which still sat in the garage, mostly unused, looking pretty.

The wife had never slept much, but lately it seemed like she slept even less. She seemed distracted. She texted to say she'd be home late from work.

Anne: *I'll be late again tonight. I'm sorry. I ordered a pizza for you and the children.*

Blaine: *Thanks. Another late meeting?*

Anne: *...*

Anne: *Yes, it's my client on the west coast, so we are meeting late because of the time difference.*

Blaine: *Gotcha. Drive safe!*

Except the wife came home smelling like pesto, and when he kissed her she tasted like wine. It was a dinner meeting, she explained, as she helped herself to a slice of pizza. And that night, as they lay in bed, Anne nestled between his arms, her breath soft on his chest, her legs intertwined with his, he started to wonder. He wondered back to the corner of Third Street, to the woman in his wife's coat and hat, staring up, enrapt, by another man.

"I love you, Blaine," Anne whispered.

"I love you, Anne," he whispered back, and that coat, that hat, that Third Street corner ceased to matter. It didn't matter that he tasted late-night-meeting wine on his wife's lips. It was a weird time, and maybe Anne had responded weirdly to it, but so had everyone.

The thing was, a human had to have compassion. Blaine's mother had said this, after his dad emptied out the bank accounts, went on a scratcher-ticket spree, stayed out several nights doing who knows what, and then crashed his car into the garage. Blaine heard the crash from bed at six a.m. on a summer Saturday. He ran outside and found his father slumped over the wheel, the garage corner collapsed over the smoldering hood, the back seat packed with paper grocery bags overflowing with lottery ticket scratchers. *A human had to show compassion* was why Blaine's mother insisted that his father come inside, that he stay and rest and recover at home, instead of checking him into one of those awful facilities. Blaine's father didn't belong in an institution, she said, and she wouldn't do that to him. She wouldn't make him take those pills that made him slow and dull. He wasn't a crazy man, she told Blaine, just differently minded, and deserving of our understanding.

She cultivated, in her son, a disposition of understanding. It was entirely understandable that Anne would sleep less and eat more bacon and forget things, like the children's appointments at the hairdresser, or the windows being left open when a thunderstorm blew through, or her cell phone, which she left sitting on her office desk. *Oh shoot, honestly, I don't know what's going on with me*, she would say, but Blaine understood. He'd replied with *Let's all go out for ice cream*, or *Let's have some quality family TV time*. The children fondled the remote control and haggled for selection rights, agreeing, eventually, on three episodes of *Adventure Time*, and Blaine cuddled beside Anne and watched the cartoon exploits of Jake the rubber-bodied dog and Finn the human and sometimes Blaine caught his wife staring off at some blank spot above or beyond the TV. Sometimes she had a look in her eyes—one part sad, one part fear—and she bit her lower lip. He had never seen her bite her lip before. But it was a weird time.

"Do you want to talk about it?" he asked her, late at night, after the children had faked their bedtime and snuck back downstairs to worship TV.

"What, the kids being up? I told them—"

"No. The spaceships."

"What about them?"

"It's just . . . you've seemed a little distracted."

"I'm fine, Blaine. Really. It's just been . . . work. It's work."

"It's just, I was thinking it might be because of the spaceships.

Because it's like, it's crazy! I mean, the way they showed up and then just disappeared. The whole thing is crazy and now no one has any idea what's going to happen, and—"

"Well, no one ever knew what was going to happen."

"Yeah. I mean, I guess that's true."

"I'm just trying to be pragmatic," Anne said. "You're correct, it all must have seemed . . . or was very weird. But now the spaceships are gone, and we're still here, and there's work to be done. We need to get that lawn mower repaired. We need pansies for the pots out front. We need to have the kitchen cabinets painted. The kids need haircuts. We just have to . . . we just have to go on with things."

The wife shoveled cookies into her mouth as she said this, one-two-three-five-eight cookies. She chugged a glass of milk. He gazed at her, across the table, her big eyes, her pink lips, her slim shoulders, her breasts. He needed her.

"I need the kids to go to bed," Blaine said, "so we can go upstairs and I can take all your clothes off and—"

"I need that, too," she said. She belched. She yelled, "Kids! Kids, you have two minutes to get upstairs or no TV tomorrow! You hear me! Two minutes!" She turned to Blaine. "You know, if you think it might help to talk about the spaceships, there's that town hall tomorrow night at school. You could take the kids. I think Elena is taking Foster. You should go."

"I might do that. Can you come with us?"

"Well . . . I might be able to meet you there at the end," the wife said. "But I have a meeting. It might go late."

The wife's meeting went late. Blaine fed the children cheeseburgers—buns, burgers, and cheese all arranged in separate no-touch corners of the plate, the way the children liked them. He pried the children away from TV, loaded them into the car, and drove them to the school town hall event, *Aliens and Us.* The school had recycled the title from a prior town hall, *Immigrants and Us,* a divisive title, considering the population of immigrant students at Pleasant View Elementary.

They arrived in the auditorium at the start of a PowerPoint presentation illustrated with the same spaceship photos that everyone had seen a bazillion times over the past weeks. They sat in the back, on folding chairs, two rows behind Elena and Foster. Aliens had come to Earth, the principal explained, over the course of sixteen PowerPoint slides, but what did that *mean* for us? Specifically, for the students of Pleasant View Elementary? For one, school would continue as usual, except that the school had a counselor, available for an hour every Tuesday afternoon, for any student experiencing adjustment difficulties. Second, students were discouraged from coming to school dressed in space alien costumes. The school would no longer permit springy antennae headbands, or fake weaponry that made laser-blasting noises. Third—

"But where are the aliens?" Jas whispered.

"Jas, honey, I don't think anyone knows. That's why—"

"Well, that's not very professional," Avril said.

"Yeah, Dad."

"Maybe," Blaine whispered. "But until we know why they came, then we'll never know why they left. And even then—"

"Yeah, but where *are* the aliens?"

"The principal said they'd be here."

"Yeah, she said the town hall was for 'aliens and us,' so—"

"Oh! I see." Literal extraterrestrials, alongside the *and Us.* "No that's not what the principal meant. She meant it was about, like, the effect the aliens had. On us. When they came."

"I feel exactly the same," Avril said loudly.

People in the rows ahead turned to look. Someone shushed. Elena saw them and waved.

"So there aren't any aliens at the town hall?" Jas said, equally loudly. "That's lame."

"Shhhhh."

"I only wanted to come 'cuz I thought we'd get to meet them."

"Yeah. Dad."

Blaine wondered how the children had gotten so misled as to believe that their elementary school had landed extraterrestrial guest speakers for its event. What did they teach these children? Well, it is a public school, people said, as if that did or should explain it. *I went to a public school*, the wife had said when Blaine had brought up the topic. *What's wrong with public? I went to public school and look at me.* The wife could throw pretzels high in the air and catch them in her mouth, which she did one night as they debated their children's educational fate. She had learned that nifty pretzel trick at public school.

Jas hid under the metal folding chair. He didn't want to listen to the *and Us* part if it wasn't buttressed by real live aliens. Avril had an open notebook on her lap. She watched the stage, appearing enrapt. She nodded. She scribbled something in her notebook.

"Pssst. Dad."

"What?"

How cute, she's taking notes to study for the post–town hall exam, Blaine thought, at first.

"How do you spell *annihilate*?"

"Uh . . ."

"I'm writing a screenplay."

"A television screenplay," Jas said from beneath the chair.

"Shut up, butt brain. It might be a movie. It might be an online video, too."

"You shut up."

"And in it, there's aliens, and they, um, annihilate us all."

The principal wanted to talk about fear. The children felt fear, and that was normal. Spaceships could be scary. But they weren't scary, and the children had no reason to feel afraid. There was nothing scary about circular logic.

Also, Pleasant View Elementary would, starting next quarter, implement quarterly invasion drills, mixed in with their fire drills and their active-shooter drills, and their subconscious-bias education. Students should not assume that just because the spaceships likely possessed weaponry capable of destroying a planet (the principal did not verbalize this idea, but the slides implied it through the use of menacing spaceship graphics) that they would. For all we knew, the aliens had traveled here on a Star Trekian mission to seek out new life and new civilizations, in which case we ought to welcome such visitors, so to present Earth's myriad cultures as convivial and inclusive. Even if they weren't, we owed it to the galaxy to put on a good face.

"So what?" a parent asked, during the Q and A. "If they come back? We invite them down for wine and fondue?"

The audience snickered.

"We all gather around the campfire and sing 'Kumbaya'?"

"Speaking of 'Kumbaya'—"

The audience had questions about a certain incident, regarding a certain teacher who no one named, but who everyone knew was the second-grade teacher who had "taken" an administrative leave of absence after teaching his students how the spaceships' arrival and subsequent departure symbolized God's judgment and wrath—an incident after which all those students came home with questions about rivers of blood and locusts, and whether the forthcoming emergence of the seventeen-year cicada brood was akin to a locust infestation for the

Midwestern/mid-Atlantic region, because they didn't get locusts everywhere. Some regions had to find a viable bug substitute. The school administration had prepared for this question with slide deck pictures comparing the biblical locust to the local cicada, which no public school child should fear. The pictures prompted twenty minutes of debate, during which the administration kept trying, unsuccessfully, to move on to its final topic of Educational Initiatives to Prepare for a Pan-Planetary Future (which translated to accelerated math and science courses), after which Blaine wondered where the last hour of his life had gone to, and how and why he had consented to its squandering.

"Well, that was an hour I'll never get back," Elena said to Blaine as children in springy antennae headbands and their parents streamed out of the auditorium. Blaine's own children were now both hidden under their folding chairs.

"We're practicing," they explained.

"For the invasion drill."

Elena's son, Foster, lay sprawled across a span of chairs with a bag of sandwich cookies. He twisted a cookie apart, licked up the frosting center, and tossed the damp cookie ends back into the bag.

Elena rolled her eyes. "He's feral," she said covertly, though Foster probably heard her. "He's like a feral animal."

"Yeah, I think that's how it works. You flying solo tonight?"

"John said he had to work late."

Maybe, a less understanding, less distracted version of Blaine might have noticed the note of doubt in Elena's voice. But Blaine, from his utopian forty-hour work week, empathized with those poor striving professionals tethered to their all-hours jobs. Also, Jas had gotten his Captain Barksford Junior Explorer wristwatch entangled in his father's shoelace.

"What are you— How did you even—"

"Dad, stop pulling!"

"I'm not pulling. You're pulling. Can you just stay still so—"

Jas tugged and writhed.

"I knew it," Avril said, smirking. "I knew you'd break the watch."

"Hey! Shut up!"

"You shut up!"

"When I get loose, I'm gonna—"

"You're not," Blaine said. He crouched down and untied his shoe-lace. "You need to quit it. Both of you. Or . . . or no TV."

The children glared at each other, but at least they didn't scratch or pinch on the walk out to the car. They climbed in.

Blaine texted the wife: *On our way home now.*

The wife texted right back: *I am leaving work now. I'll see you soon!*

"But, Dad," Jas said while they waited in the car line of cranky parents to exit the parking lot. "What about ice cream?"

"Yeah, Dad."

"What about it?"

"Can we get it?"

"No."

"Can we get it?"

"No."

"Please?"

"No."

"Pretty please? With hot fudge and a cherry on top?"

"What if the spaceships come back tomorrow, Dad?"

"What if they come back and kill us? And you didn't let us get ice cream."

"You made us miss our last ever chance to get ice cream."

"How would you feel then, Dad?"

He felt bleary. He felt stretched thin. He felt a hole in himself; a gaping, abyssal trench that spanned his depths, and maybe the hole had been there always, but only just now, in this honking line, as his beseeching children chipped away at his dad reserves, had he telescoped down and seen it.

By the time they finally escaped the line, he felt ready for ice cream. Instead of heading home, they drove to the Frosty Freeze. Avril ordered a chocolate-vanilla twist with chocolate chips, and Jas ordered blue raspberry with sprinkles, and they all knew that each child would want the other child's ice cream but neither child would agree to swap. Blaine ordered Frosty-Freezes for him and the wife, and they came in Styrofoam cups with plastic straws, and Blaine felt guilty about plastics and the environment, but he could see his wife's face light up, her glee at the gift of ice cream, her lips pressed against the plastic straw, her eyes gazing up at his.

He could see her just like that. And then he did. See her. Just like that.

He pulled to a stop at a yellow light. He glanced out the window. There was a pizza parlor on the corner. Not the best pizza, the wife had said. Their crust was too thick. Their door opened, and a woman stepped out. She wore the wife's coat, and the wife's hat. She had a plastic to-go cup, with a plastic straw pressed between her lips.

"Mom!" Avril banged the glass. "It's Mom!"

But lots of women had that hat, that coat, those lips. Thousands of women, probably, in the great universe of women.

"It's not—" he started to say.

"Mom!" Avril yelled. Jas leaned over her lap. He pounded on the window.

"Dad! The window—" The back seat windows had child locks. "Open it!" *Bang bang bang.* "Mom!"

"But it's not—"

But it was. She stepped forward. A streetlamp illuminated her face. Only one woman had that exact face. Her face. His wife.

Then, behind her, the pizza parlor door opened again, and a man emerged. Blaine couldn't see his face clearly in the shadow of the building, its interior glow behind him. But he had seen that man. In his house. In his backyard, on invasion-party night, standing too close to his wife. He knew that man. He knew enough that he didn't want to wait and see what happened next. What happened: the light turned green. The car behind Blaine sounded its horn. Blaine slammed on the gas. His car flew into the intersection. The children screamed. Avril's ice cream tumbled onto the floor mat. Blaine glanced back, in his side view mirror. He didn't want to, but his eyes made him do it, and there she was, his wife, standing on the corner, sipping her soda, with that man's arm around her shoulder.

* * *

A human had to have compassion, and there had to be a perfectly reasonable, perfectly innocent reason why the wife had—

He had only glimpsed through the side view mirror, in the dark, as his car sped away, as Avril cried over spilt ice cream, after a long day of deep-state speeches, illicit weapon stockpiling, child wrangling, town hall PowerPoint contradictions. His brain felt dizzy. His brain had a huge dark hole. Call it stress, call it fear, uncertainty, disillusion. Per Occam's razor—

He had not seen kissing. He could not say, indisputably, what he had seen. Like one of those pilots, in the pre-undeniable-spaceship era, who had spotted a disk-shaped blur from the cockpit, flying at irregular speeds, defying the laws of physics, but visible only for a second. An explainable blip on the radar. Not saying it's not a spaceship, but . . . *It's not a spaceship*, his wife had said when he showed her the article from a semi-reputable source that reported the pilot's claims uncorroborated by verifiable proof. He had no verifiable proof that his wife had done anything improper, much less adulterous, and how could he confront her with suspicion and conjecture?

He had seen this confrontation play out between his own parents, when his father (post scratcher-ticket binge) became convinced that his mother (yes, she had cheated once or twice, but who could blame her) was tits-deep in a torrid affair with the mailman. Never mind that the mailman was not always the same mailman and was, in fact, sometimes a mailwoman. Whoever it was, Blaine's father waited for them at the mailbox and stalked them up the street, until his wife found out, *What the heck is wrong with you?* So maybe whatever the heck was wrong with him was wrong with Blaine. These things ran in families. He could not say, indisputably, that he wasn't crazy. Only a crazy person could make that sort of claim.

So when the wife arrived home, he said: "Here, I brought you a Frosty-Freeze."

And the kids said: "Mom! We saw you!"

"We saw you at the pizza parlor!"

"Mom!"

"Did you bring us pizza?"

And the wife said: "Well, darn, I ate it all," without signs of fluster, and of course she had an explanation to dovetail nicely with her text message. She had worked late, and her colleague worked late, and they thought, let's grab some pizza because their families had already eaten without them and they could talk about work stuff while they ate and bill the hour. She didn't like that pizza parlor, but her colleague liked thick crust.

"Which colleague?"

Oh, it was *mumble mumble.*

"Sorry, who?"

"Oh, uh, Roger."

But the man Blaine had seen with the wife wasn't Roger, and the wife would never let a fellow like Roger slap his meaty arm around her shoulder. Blaine knew the wife well enough to know that, at least.

Blaine didn't press. The better strategy was to wait, and to dig. To wait until he'd dug deep enough to find the proof, and confront the wife then, when she had no avenue of escape. She climbed into bed beside him, cuddled up to him, pressed her lips against his neck.

"What a day," she said.

"Yeah."

"But at least I'm home now. Home with you."

"Yeah."

"There's no place I'd rather be," she said. Her hand plunged down beneath the covers. Her lips swooped.

"Yeah." Blaine's own hands felt clammy and his own lips felt chapped and his poor brain made him limp all over.

"You're tired," the wife observed, giving a squeeze.

"Yeah. Sorry." He understood the cyclical demise of a relationship; suspicion to limpness to sexual dissatisfaction to extramarital satisfiers to suspicion to et cetera, the vicious circle of the lovers' drain. Once it started . . .

The wife gave a pat. She swung her leg over his leg. Already it felt platonic.

"Well. That's okay," the wife said, but she didn't sound okay. She sounded like a wife with something to hide, and it made him suspicious. He thought about routes to the proof. If only Dave was right, about birds. He could contract some nano-drone bird carriers and send them on a detective mission. The wife would never suspect the hawk outside her office window, the cardinal watching from the trees, the small swift hummingbird that snapped spy photos of the wife and her—

"Tomorrow?" he offered. "I'm sure tomorrow—"

"Right. Yes! Tomorrow!"

She flopped over to her side. He slung an arm across her, pulling her close, the way his body wanted. He inhaled her hair-smell. He loved that smell, the sea kelp scent of her shampoo, the salt hint of sweat on her scalp, and something else, something like sunshine and spring breeze, as if the sweet floral world had imprinted itself upon her.

"I love you, Blaine," she said.

"I love you, too," he said. He thought about her adulterous secrets and where she might hide the scraps of them. Her emails and texts, if she didn't diligently, almost obsessively, delete them, to the point of inconvenience, because he might text her something notable, say, what date and time they could expect the plumber, and she would promptly delete the text. Or at least, she had last week, and the plumber knocked on the door (getting his coat sleeve caught in the string-and-can trap), and no one answered so they had to reschedule. But if the wife had multiple lovers and the plumber was one—

Her office was an impenetrable fortress. Her car was unbuggable, if he could even procure a bug . . . unless he could enlist the children, but the children couldn't keep their traps shut. *Mom! Mom, guess what! We bugged your car, Mom!*

He found himself, in the morning, rummaging through her dirty laundry. He inspected sweaters for stray beard hairs. He examined the texture of her underwear. He smelled it.

"Dad!"

"Dad! What are you doing up there!"

He jumped. The kids were downstairs, but they sounded closer. "I'll be right down!"

He buried the guilty underwear at the bottom of the basket. The underwear smelled like regular wife. The guilt belonged to him, his reward for sniffing when he should have spoken. *So, honey, the other night. Your coat. Your hat. That man you were with* . . . But the crafty wife would dismiss him with reasonable explanations. She would placate him with bacon and hand jobs. He would circle right back to another sleepless night of wondering. He wondered why he had to wonder about this. Of all things, infidelity. When he should be suffering spaceship-induced insomnia, like everyone else.

He saw Elena and Foster, out walking their dog during the post-work dog-walking hour, before the wife returned home. "So . . . How are you holding up?"

"Well. You know." Elena shrugged. She glanced up at the empty sky, gave a casual head nod to the absence of aliens.

"Yeah. Yeah, I know."

"At least our cat came home. He'd run away, but . . ."

"Hey, yeah, ours, too."

She looked at the horizon. "I just keep thinking . . ."

"Me too."

"About . . . what if they come back." Her dog ran stupid circles around her, tail flapping, tongue slopping out to lick the breeze. She passed the leash from hand to hand.

"Yeah. Do you think they will?"

"Well . . . I mean, why else would they have come all this way? Just to spy on us and then leave?"

The word *spy* was a quiver of guilt through Blaine's brain. "Yeah. I mean. That wouldn't make any sense, right? There has to be something else going on. How's, uh, John holding up?"

"He says he's just crazy busy with work."

Blaine parsed the meaning of her response. The way she said *He says* implied that the thing he said might not be the entire truth.

"Hmm. Anne too. It seems like she's had to work even later than usual."

"Oh? I swear she's Superwoman. Thank her for those cookies when you see her, by the way." Blaine wondered: *What cookies?* "Not that I needed them. But they were delicious."

But of course the wife would Superwoman an affair with mollifying cookies.

"I'll be sure to tell her. Well. At least our spouses got to skip last night's town hall, right?"

"It was the worst. I told John. Better for him that he missed it. Lucky bastard. Not only did he miss it, but he also got pizza."

"Oh?"

"From that pizza parlor on Montgomery. What is it called? The place with the thick crust. His favorite."

"Lucky for him."

"Yeah. I'm hoping these long hours will end soon. He keeps talking about taking a long vacation."

"Oh? Where to?"

"The Florida Keys. He wants someplace with no Wi-Fi. Very rustic."

"That sounds awesome."

"Yeah. He said he wanted it to be a surprise, but I overheard him talking to a travel agent."

"That's very—"

"Nineteen nineties, right? What happened to travel agents? I was like, John, you know there's this little thing called the internet, right? But whatever. Time to shop for swimsuits!"

Elena left, leaving Blaine to ponder the meaning of what John said, of thick crust pizza, travel agents, Florida Keys vacations, John who had to "work late" when the wife also "worked late" and somehow in between it all she managed to bake and deliver cookies. But she didn't leave any cookies behind, at home, for Blaine.

The wife got home not too-too late that night, and she brought sushi.

"Vegetables tempura, and those crispy rolls that— Hey," she said, "is everything all right?"

"Yeah," Blaine lied. "Everything's fine."

"You like tempura, right? Because—"

"Tempura's great."

"It's just that you look . . . I don't know, a little pouty?"

Blaine frowned. "I look pouty."

"Yeah."

"Well, I'm not," he said.

"Do you want to tell me why?"

"Why what? There's nothing to tell."

"Good. Great! But you're totally pouting."

"I am not."

"You are."

"Okay. Well. You baked cookies."

"Cookies?"

"For Elena. You baked cookies for Elena," he said, as if this explained everything.

The wife blinked.

"And . . . you didn't leave me any."

"Oh. Oh! Right! Cookies! All the baking, sometimes it's just a blur! Gosh, I'm sorry. I . . . Well, so what happened—"

She popped a crispy crab-and-cream-cheese roll into her mouth.

"What happened?" He visualized the wife naked beneath her apron, scooping an erotic finger of cookie dough, slipping that finger between her lover's lips.

"Sorry . . . god, this is delicious . . . what happened was I dropped them."

"You dropped them."

"Well, not the ones I gave to Elena. Those ones I wrapped up in a pretty tin, and I'd already texted her a picture of them, and then when I took the second tray out of the oven I dropped it."

"Oh."

"I don't know what happened. I'm not usually such a klutz. It was . . . anyway, those ones would have been for you, but I dropped them and they were still hot and gooey, so I couldn't just brush them off. I'm sorry." She patted his arm and pecked his cheek, that crafty wife with her credible story.

"That's okay," he said. "That's sweet. That's . . . Well, it's the thought that counts."

The thought counted, people said. But *idiom* was only a few letters shy of *idiotic,* which described how Blaine felt about applauding the wife's purportedly generous thought when the wife's actions deprived him of cookies. Blaine felt sore, despite what he said, and he felt douchey and duplicitous for trying to pretend not to feel sore, but how he felt about it didn't matter. What mattered was that the betting markets wagered 3:1 the spaceships would return within the year and blow us all to kablooey. It mattered that underground bunker installations and bomb shelter sales and sales of hunting rifles, water filtration devices, camo vests, fishing rods, survivalist handbooks, vegetable seeds, extraterrestrial cosplay accessories, rosaries, plastic figurines of Jesus high-fiving a big-eyed gray-skinned classic model alien, spaceship earrings with flashing red-blue-green LED lights, hard liquors, edible marijuana gummies, E.T. costumes for dogs, et cetera, had all blasted sky-high toward outer-space-level profits. It mattered that the wife got a *work call*, she said. Halfway through dinner. *Honey, I've got to take this, it's work*, she said, and she scampered upstairs, and locked herself in the bathroom with the tub water running. It mattered that Blaine seized the wife's shady immersion in a bathroom work call as an opportunity to scavenge her drawers and pockets.

He found her drawers pristine, all her clothes pressed, folded, arranged within the drawers in color-pleasing palettes. Her suits hung in plastic dry-cleaning bags in her closet. Her jewelry box was mostly pearls with some scattered sapphires and diamonds. Her coat pockets lacked the tinfoil-wrapper crumbles and tissue drifts that plagued his own. Her purse, somehow, repelled all debris, crumbs, receipts, Post-it notes reduced to illegible faded scraps, business cards for businesses long defunct. The wife had owned the same purse for as long as he had known her, and yet it had no ink stains, no inkless pen shells, nothing not practical, useful, necessary.

Except.

In the pocket, he found a single scrap, with a telephone number scrawled across it, in the wife's handwriting.

He jotted the number down on an old business card he kept in his own wallet. He folded the scrap and shoved it back into his wife's purse. In the bathroom, the faucet turned off.

"Dad!" Avril yelled from downstairs.

"Mom! Dad!"

"Mom! Dad! Come downstairs!"

"Come and see!"

"The TV . . ."

TV, TV, blah-blah-blah-blah TV. The children talked over

each other, so he couldn't hear what either was saying beyond the repeated reference to *beloved TV.* He hurried down the stairs. He heard the bathroom door open behind him.

"Mom!"

"Dad!"

"TV! TV!"

"Blaine! Will you—"

The children stood predictably close, close enough that he could almost see the transference of static from screen to children. He could almost see the electric bristle in the screen-glow air. The TV played snow, for a second, and then the news burst through. The children swooned. Avril pressed the remote to her lips.

BREAKING NEWS . . .

"Hey! Blaine!" the wife called from the stairs.

BREAKING NEWS—

"Dad!"

"Hey, gimme the remote!"

"No! Dad there's—"

"Blaine, could you—"

"I want to watch *Adventure Time*—"

"Shut up! I'm trying to—"

"Hey! Blaine! Kids! Could you—"

"Shhh! I can't hear it!"

Avril jammed her thumb into the remote as she waved it high above her brother's reach. The volume turned up-up-up-up!

BREAKING NEWS

"Ow, my ears!"

"Blaine!"

"Dad!"

—PRESIDENT HAS JUST CONFIRMED—

"Make her turn it down!"

"You suck! You just want—"

"Ow! Hey!"

"Ow! Dad! She just kicked me!"

"Well, he hit me first!"

"But—"

—HAS KNOWN ABOUT THE PRESENCE OF ALIENS ON OUR PLANET FOR YEARS—

The Stepchild

JACK P. DID not get incinerated by alien lasers and the revolt-o-meter of kissy-face PDA between him and Heather's mom had escalated to an unparalleled level of saliva-smeared disgust and Alex the Brainiac had flown back to Malibu from his elite fancy-boy prep school for spring break to brag about his courtship by Harvard *and* Stanford and Justin had devoted himself to some pro-E.T. coalition of astronomers and astrologists and spent his every waking hour coddling or diddling or picking up carryout sushi for Dr. Fringe or whoever claimed they could reach E.T. with the right blend of supercomputing and crystals and housecats because the housecats had some involvement with all of this, which was, like, whatever, asinine.

He wasn't her boyfriend anymore anyway.

She secured his copy of *Super Smash Bros.* and, oh, oops! down the toilet it went, but Jack P. chastised her. *If it's yellow, let it mellow!* As if his weasel nose could smell, somehow, that *Super Smash Bros.* didn't get the turd-flush it deserved. *We've got to conserve!* Jack P. insisted, with respect to water, even though he drank it out of plastic bottles. Drought had stricken. The Los Angeles hills had already started to burn. Everything had gone up in a blaze all at once. Heather smoldered.

She had nothing to do.

She had taken a gap year on the premise that extra time would afford her the opportunity to do, *you know, Mom, real stuff. Like real-life stuff, instead of all that academia.* She had taken the gap year after Justin said, *Hey, you should take a gap year*, which, at the time, meant *We'll hang out at the beach and smoke blunts*, but now Justin was off crystalizing or whatever and she had nothing to do.

"That's your problem." Mom diagnosed it. "You have nothing to do."

The remedy, per Mom, required expunging unwanted clothes from Heather's walk-in closet, attending mother-daughter Pilates sessions, and logging volunteer hours at the animal shelter.

"It's overrun," Mom said. "All those poor cats. That spacecraft must have done something to their little brains. Just like what happened to Bastet." Jack P.'s beloved Bastet had disappeared into the wilds of Carmel and never returned, and no one had tried to return him despite the $5,000 reward, and Heather's mom seemed more distraught about the cat than she had ever been about anything that had ever happened to Heather.

It was just a cat.

Mom dropped her off in front of the shelter en route to couples' massage therapy with Jack P., followed by a dinner reservation at Bluegreenery, followed by whatever gross face-sucking they had planned for after.

"You're not picking me up?"

"It took us forever to get a reservation! I swear, every restaurant claims to be short-staffed and the reservation lists for the good ones are, like, weeks long. Anyway, you can call an Uber! But don't bother Alex. He's got important stuff to work on."

"I would have driven here myself if—"

Except, really, she would have driven maybe kind of near the animal shelter and then changed her mind. She would have gotten herself a boba tea and a pedicure and gone home, buoyed by the fleeting victory of self-pampering, until Alex made some remark about diverting a fraction of his Bitcoin investments toward building schools in Pakistan and she became shit. Absolute shit, with pretty red toenails.

Mom waited for Heather to enter the building. Knowing Mom, she waited around for a few minutes after that. Heather devised a fictional runaway cat. Pumpkin, she called him. That big scary spaceship had frightened poor Pumpkin away and she couldn't find him anywhere and she was just despondent. The fabricated story, repeated, began to materialize as real-ish emotion. She felt a pseudo-genuine despair for her fake missing cat. The shelter, of course, had not found the cat, but perhaps could offer a replacement cat, something floofy and chip-less.

She had to wait nearly an hour for her Uber ride, and then the cat meowled the whole ride home. It expelled great tufts of gray floof in the back seat, which made her sneezy. It ruined her passenger rating, undoubtedly.

She carried the cat up to her bedroom. She let it out of its carrier. Some small broken part of her had expected it to love her instantly, to leap up into her arms and serenade her with the adoration-purr. She didn't think to shut her bedroom door. Out it ran, down the hall, gone, the little bastard.

"Say, is there a cat roaming around?" Jack P. asked, the next morning. "I could swear I saw a cat this morning?"

Jack P.'s tone implied that he had seen it. His choice of question over declaration exemplified his feigned diffidence, his overarching need to appear likeable and accommodating.

"I don't think there's any cat," Heather replied. "Why would there be a cat? I mean, since Bastet is gone . . . You're probably just seeing things."

"Hmmm." Jack P. nodded and looked puzzled. "Well, I have been working an awful lot, and everyone says, if you aren't getting enough sleep . . ." Which was a weird thing to say, for Jack P., who routinely subsisted on inhuman sleep-morsels and somehow managed to still seem annoyingly chipper. He took the eggs out of the fridge. Crack, crack, crack, crack. Toast, juice, butter, bacon, coffee. *How about just some cereal?* Heather's mom would say. *Yogurt with fruit. Tofu scramble. Just think about your heart, darling. You only get one.*

Jack P. was a trigger for teenage girls who dabbled in eating disorders.

"You only live once," Jack P. said, slopping butter onto an extraneous side-waffle. He chuckled, oddly, as if the whole concept of mortality was a kind of cosmic knock-knock joke.

Knock-knock.

Who's there?

Death.

Death who?

It's Death How, not Death Who. And he's bringing waffles! Har har har.

Jack P. told idiotic knock-knock jokes that he had clearly invented himself. Heather could not discern whether he fancied himself clever, or whether he knew his jokes sucked but told them so as to seem relatable. Her opinion waffled.

Har har har.

To make things even worse, Jack P. cooked breakfast for Heather, and her mom, and Alex. He cooked four separate breakfasts serving four distinct palates and dietary regimens, miraculously hot and ready at the exact same time. They enjoyed a family breakfast on the pool deck, beneath the Goldilocks sun, overlooking the glistening Pacific. The iconic palm trees fluttered. The lapping breeze blew the wildfire smoke southeast, away from Malibu. Heather felt nauseated.

"So, I forgot to mention," her mother began, sipping the perfect foam off the top of her latte. "At the salon the other day I saw Marissa—you remember her? She was at our table at the leukemia benefit last fall."

"Oh yes," Jack P. said. "She was charming." He dipped his bacon in a ramekin of maple syrup.

"She's moving. To Antigua!"

"What, the island? Do you think they can get TV out there, in the middle of the ocean?"

"It's TV, Jack," Heather said. *What a doofus.* "It's everywhere."

"Why's she moving?" Alex asked. "Is she concerned about the spaceships coming back? I read this article in *Forbes* the other day"—*I read this article in* Forbes *blah blah blah*—"about the recent uptick in home sales in remote areas, which corresponds with the spaceships' departure."

"She said she just wanted a change of scenery," Heather's mother said. "But . . . it's so curious, isn't it, that the spaceships never came back."

"It sure is, darling." Jack P. nodded. His eyes had a contemplative gleam. He slurped his coffee, which he drank extra creamy, with about a thousand sugars.

"I mean, how long has it been now?" Mom asked this same question once every three or four days, as if she couldn't count and didn't own a calendar, which she obviously did. Jack P.'s pointless conversational hypothetical posturing had obviously rubbed off. "I would think by now they would have at least sent a message. Or that the government would tell us something definitive."

"Well, they did say they knew about an alien presence," Jack P. reminded them. "Maybe that's all they know."

"Oh, come on, Jack," Heather said. "Of course they know more."

"Hmmm." Jack P. nodded. "Maybe they do. But maybe the government has told us what they know."

Heather rolled her eyes. "We are, like, living in the same country, right?" she asked.

Jack P. blinked.

"I mean, this is *America*."

"Land of the free, home of the brave!" Jack P. said. "I just love that. It has such a great ring to it. Land of the free."

"Well, I'm sure if the government knows more," said Heather's mother, "it's got a good reason not to say so."

"Like maybe the aliens are still here," Alex said. "If they were, and people knew, it might lead to chaos."

"That's a good point, son."

"Heck," Alex continued, "the ships themselves might even still be here. It's not unfathomable that they would possess advanced cloaking technology. Or they could be hiding in the ocean. If those ships can handle space, it stands to reason that they can handle the ocean. They could be down in the Mariana Trench right now and we'd never know it. Or maybe that's where they came from in the first place."

"What, from the ocean? You're saying that the aliens came from the ocean?"

"Not originally. But one theory is that they came to Earth a long time ago. They were here before the general population of humans knew. They could have even been living among us, disguised as humans. They might have been here for decades. Centuries, even."

"Well, hopefully," Heather said, "if there is an alien presence or whatever, the government will round the aliens up and make them tell us. Because it just isn't fair that—"

"That seems excessive," Alex interrupted. "Besides, I speculate their motivation is benign."

"I concur," said Jack P.

"Ugh." Heather groaned.

They all looked at her.

"What?"

"What?"

"Nothing." She just. Hated. When. They. Spoke like that. They couldn't just *agree*. They had to *concur*. *Good* wasn't good enough. It had to be *benign*.

"Well, it's not especially polite," Heather's mom said. "To groan like that."

"She probably just had something caught in her throat," Jack P. said. "It's perfectly fine. Besides, it's a disconcerting time to be alive on Earth. Perceptions of humanity's place and purpose in the universe have been understandably upended." Jack P. slathered butter onto his scrambled eggs. He took a bite. He washed it down with a hundred-calorie gulp of coffee.

"Perhaps we can determine the extraterrestrials' motivation by the result," Alex said. "They're clearly quite intelligent. They likely possessed some knowledge of our culture and psychology before they revealed their presence. We've been left to question our place in the universe because they wanted us to question it."

"Or maybe," Jack P. said, chuckling to himself, "they just don't know what the heck they're doing."

Heather didn't know what the heck she was doing after breakfast when she wandered the house and yard for a wasted hour in search of the cat that wasn't there and didn't want to be there. She didn't blame it. *She* didn't want to be there. She wanted a family that was, well, she didn't know exactly what this ideal family would look like, but it would definitely not include a brilliant stepbrother who idolized quality family time and a gooberish human garbage disposal of a stepdad who harbored a creepy obsession with television game shows and a massive yet uncultivated collection of plastic action figures all still in their original packaging.

She didn't know what she was doing when she spent—okay,

wasted—an entire afternoon swiping through internet posts and photos of her high-school friends, and their friends, and Alex's friends, and Justin's friends, and other girls her age whom she had met once or twice at a party, and all of whom were enrolled in some rigorous physics academy or perfecting their Portuguese in an immersive six-month stint at a Brazilian organic farming co-op or interning at a movie studio or writing a novel inspired by the revelation of intelligent extraterrestrial life or volunteering their computer equipment and coding skills in a coordinated grassroots effort to contact said extraterrestrial life or at the very least doing the music festival circuit, getting drunk-stoned-high AF in light-up booty shorts on a nightly fucking basis, watching the sun rise over the changed Earth. They were all out there, alive, living. Whereas she was here, not living, not becoming, not doing. A. Damn. Thing.

Fuck.

Heather also didn't know what she was doing when she decided, after failing to find the cat that she claimed had never existed and torturing herself with photos of everyone whose lives were better than hers—which she knew academically was not everyone and in fact included a very small subset of the privileged world but which sure *felt* like everyone—to call Justin, the same Justin who had ditched her when the aliens came to go party in the streets of LA, and endeavor to persuade him to meet her at the beach, with his vape.

"Duuuude . . ." was what he said, in his suddenly adorable surfer-boy accent.

"Yeah, we could, like, hang out for a while at the beach, and then maybe get some fro-yo after or, like, whatever you want."

"Yeah. But like, seriously. You flushed my video game down the toilet. That's so fucked, Heather. I'm just . . . I'm done. I'm done with this shit."

"So, is that . . ."

"I don't want to see you. Don't call me again, 'kay?"

He didn't wait for her okay. He hung up.

She did know what she was doing when she opened up a bottle of the good wine Jack P. had brought back from his Carmel fuck-fest with her mom. They had done Carmel, Pebble Beach, Big Sur, lunch in the city by the bay, then a couple of glorious nights in Sonoma, sipping many-hundred-dollar bottles on the sun-soaked wine-country patio while everyone everywhere else in the world freaked the fuck out about alien life, and whether it would come back to crush theirs. Yes, Heather knew that she would finish that bottle before dinner, that she would say something rude and cruel during dinner, that the others would stare at her, aghast, that Jack P. would attempt to smooth everything over, that Alex would corner her after dinner and profess his loyal brother-liness and attempt to convince her, with his intimidating vocabulary, how empathetic he was about whatever isolated incident it was that had caused her to feel upset, that Alex would retire to his studies and Jack P. and her mom would retire to their television watching and petting rituals, and that she would find herself alone.

Alone.

So alone.

Despite all that life.

It was everywhere, wasn't it?

It was in the second bottle, which she opened, without asking. Seek forgiveness, not permission, they said. In vino, there is life, they said. Whoever they were. Getting the maxim wrong.

The truth was, she kind of swayed drunkenly as she opened it, and then she went outside, past the pool deck, over the fence, to the dark spot enshrouded by dry shrubs and brush, where she could sit and smoke cigarettes without having to worry about Jack P. traipsing out and asking whether she really ought to reconsider her tobacco habit. A smart, capable girl like her knew better, didn't she?

She didn't feel smart or capable. She felt dulled by the glut of time, by too much wine, too much sleep, general aimlessness. She sat and stared out at the black water that stretched all the way to the end of the earth. She thought about A-Day. Arrival Day. One day before D for Departure Day. She thought about Justin paddling naked in the pool, the sun on his shoulders, and the sense she had, at that spot in space-time, that things might happen in her life, remarkable things laden with meaning. They meant something. Her. Justin. Young. Capable. Fortunate, and yet, in her mind, deserving. Possessing an electrical generator, an ample supply of quality wine, a stockpile of assorted liquors. Poised to bear witness, from the cliff-edge of Malibu, to whatever transpired.

Nothing transpired.

The wine and the liquor and the generator, the house, the swimming pool, the Malibu view, they all belonged to Jack P. Her mom belonged to Jack P. That glimmer of A-Day possibility was borrowed. It didn't belong to her. It had, in actuality, barely fluttered past her, but her stagnant present seized it, and with it ascribed a retroactive import, basting the past with layers of fresh meaning. She felt nostalgic for an alternate-universe A-Day. She yearned for a Justin more smitten with her than with Nintendo. She wondered whether she could finish the whole bottle of wine, and how fast. She hadn't bothered with a glass. She swigged, lit a cigarette. She heard the distinctive rustle of nerdy stepbrother feet.

"Hey." Alex emerged from the bushes. "Are you smoking?"

"Duh."

"Can I bum one?"

Was this a trick? He sat down on the rocks beside her. She offered her package of smokes.

"Your funeral."

"Yeah, I know," Alex said, lighting a cigarette. "Don't tell my dad, okay?"

"Why, you don't want Jack P. to be like"—she did her best Jack P. chipper voice—"'Son, you're such a bright young lad, you sure know better, don't you?'"

"Ha, yeah that's exactly what he'd say. And I do, you know?"

"Obviously."

"But sometimes the stress is just . . ."

"Yeah." She glanced at her stepbrother. He gazed out across the dark Pacific. "What is it? I mean, like, what are you stressed about?"

"School, mostly. But . . . it's not really that. It's like . . . what is the point, exactly? You spend all this time studying and working and, like, building up your résumé, and for what? Ever since the spaceships came . . . I don't even know if I want to get my MBA."

He surprised her. He had always seemed so annoyingly sure about his business school trajectory.

"You don't?"

"I don't. I don't think that's what I want."

"What do you want? Don't say you want to take a gap year. That would be a terrible idea."

Alex laughed. "I think it was smart."

"You do?"

"Totally. Taking time to figure out where you're going and what you want to do with yourself? It's smart. And mature."

Maybe, Heather thought, *if* her objective had included figuring things out, and not just getting baked, tanned, and laid. But she let herself enjoy the compliment. Maybe she could figure things out. She still had time. Maybe she could make it true.

"Thanks."

"I was thinking . . . maybe I'll travel," Alex said. "And then . . . I don't know. Maybe medicine? Or I could go to veterinary school. I always liked cats, and, you know, horses, dogs. It'd be cool to do something where I got to work with animals."

"I think that's a good idea."

"You do?"

"I mean, as long as you don't mind crushing Jack P.'s lifelong ambition of having a stockbroker son with his own business-markets TV show."

"Ha! Yeah. No. Except . . . has my dad seemed upset at all lately?"

"No," Heather said. Jack P. had seemed exactly like Jack P. Except she hadn't really observed. She had prejudged his Jack P.-ness and skimmed past him, seeing nothing beyond her own preexisting conceptions of who Jack P. was and what that meant. "He seems pretty much the same to me."

"Huh. Well, that's good. It just . . . I got the sense that he was upset or something. He says he's fine but . . . you're right. He's probably fine."

"So . . ." Heather snubbed her cigarette out on the rock, cautious of stray wildfire-fueling embers. She took a gulp of wine from the bottle. "Where do you think you'll travel to?"

"Everywhere. I want to go everywhere. I was thinking Japan, for starters. Then maybe Thailand, Vietnam. Hey, you should come with me!"

"Me?"

"Yeah. We could travel all summer. I was thinking Asia, but we could start wherever."

"That sounds . . . yeah. Maybe?"

"Well, think about it."

"Wine?" She took a drink, then offered Alex the bottle.

"I'm good. I'm beat. I think I'm going to bed."

"Okay. Cool." She drank his offering.

He got up. He walked back toward the pool deck. "I'm serious," he said, "about traveling. We'd have a blast. And there's no one I'd rather go with than you."

Then he was gone. Heather took another drink. She sat alone in the dark with her bottle. She lit another cigarette. She let it burn slow. She felt almost happy, almost hopeful as she imagined herself on a bathwater beach in Phuket, on a neon Tokyo street corner, on a backpacking trek through the jungles of Vietnam, bantering with Alex, sampling street-vendor deep-fried crickets with Alex, exploring the far crazy reaches of the wondrous Earth, with her brother. Her stepbrother. Her brother.

She spat on the cherry of the last dying cigarette. She buried it beneath the dirt. She staggered back through the brush, onto the pool deck.

She stopped.

She saw Jack P. He stood in the doorway. He stared out at the sea. He was on the phone.

"They never tried to reach me," he said, into the receiver. He turned, paced. His brow furrowed. Heather crept along the edge of the pool deck, into the shadows of the house. She crouched down low beneath a potted palm, where she could listen unseen.

"No, I have no idea," Jack P said to the phone. "No ... No ... I've heard from the others, but I think we're all in the same boat. Don't you love that? 'In the same boat.' Fuck ... Yeah, that's how I feel, too ... Well, obviously someone has been working with the government ... Yeah, I know. *Jeopardy!* ... Give me a few days to see if I can figure it out, and then ... Okay ... Okay ... and then if that happens, well, I'm sure we can work something out. Maybe I'll take one for the team.... Okay ... I'll be in touch."

He hung up.

Heather sank down onto the cement. She cradled her bottle. Such good wine. He was so weird. Her stepdad. Her mother loved that about him. But his weirdness rubbed Heather wrong. She knew. She had always known. There was something not quite right about Jack P.

Now she finally understood it.

He wasn't human. He was one of them.

The Brother

THE TRANSITIONAL MEN had to keep each other safe. Support. Intervention. Steps to a better (saner) tomorrow. If one man refused to leave bed or started muttering about demonic Chihuahua insurrections or avian nanotech missiles—or threatened to hurl himself, ingloriously, out the third-story window—the Transition House manual offered boilerplate supportive language. *I believe in you, buddy*, the men said to each other. *Let's quiet our minds. A hug heals the soul.* The windows had locks, and decorative metal bars, so the men couldn't smash their way out. A fire code violation, Oliver thought, and felt perplexed by the strange complexity of his mind to have retrieved this assembly of words. *Fire. Code. Violation.* But he knew, his murky heart knew, this didn't matter. Transitional men could transition to charred corpses in their burning beds, and no one would care much. No one cared much about Carl Lesniak when the transitional men called 9-1-1. 9-1-1 said: *We are experiencing a high volume of calls. Please stay on the line.* Transitional men had been mindful of the windows, when Carl started ranting, but they hadn't considered bathrooms and kitchen knives. The paramedic who zipped up the body bag said: *That was the knife he used? Hot damn, that thing's about as sharp as a spoon.*

But the Transitional House felt almost like family. To try to keep safe, to be kept, to share dinner around the big table, to drift to sleep to the hacksaw sound of his roommate's snores. It felt warm and relaxing, and then like a warm bath that had lasted too long. Oliver had reached the pruning stage. He had to get out.

In the city all around him, in the everywhere all around that city, folks had to get out. Oliver could feel it, at the bus stop, at the nonprofit bakery that hired convicts and crazies to transition them back to a life of work, in the park where he sat and watched the brazen squirrels, the leaves bud and blossom, the spry heads of spring tulips, all emerging, restless. In the subway, in the trains and tunnels, kids sprayed their tags in broad day. A business-suited man carved his name into the plastic seat. A couple boarded with two big dogs, malamutes, not for service, and someone yelled: *Jesus, this isn't a fucking dog park!* But it didn't matter. The driver shrugged: *I like dogs.* The cops had bank robbers and anti-E.T. protest rallies and armed men running naked through the National Mall to contend with.

At the transitional bakery, Oliver twisted dough into pretzel loops and his coworkers made weed butter and talked about the government's complicity. Those fuckers had known all along. Or, maybe as far back as Roosevelt but at least as far back as Bush-Cheney-Rumsfeld, and those fuckers had conspired to keep it all hush-hush. They had funded alien flicks and TV shows. They were *X-Files* masters of misdirection. They saturated the sci-fi markets with fake spaceship stories, and the real stories drowned beneath the flood of entertainment media. No one who saw them ever believed them. But now the ex-cons and crazies could baste their pastechi and cheese tarts with weed butter right out in the open. Folks wanted to get good and high in case/for when the aliens came and snatched them away.

The transitional men gathered around the living room TV after dinner, to watch and discuss reruns of the Breaking News. The news said the aliens had come to visit years ago, and the government had known. The news said a hundred thousand–plus heavily redacted FOIA pages from the D-oh-D said some of the aliens were probably still here, among us. Like sleeper agents, the news speculated, waiting for something to activate them. The FOIA production didn't admit or deny this, so maybe it was true. *Like you*, Oliver, one of the transitional men joked. But only once. No one else said anything after that, but they all wondered. They all examined the suddenly responsive Oliver among them through a lens of suspicion. Even Oliver, as he watched his fingers pincer a fork, as he stared down at his hairy legs and feet grounded on the shower tiles where Carl had died, as he wiped steam from the bathroom mirror to reveal the curiosity of his own face. Oliver couldn't admit or deny. He had been snowed in, and now he wasn't. He could scarcely remember his past. So maybe it was true. Maybe he was E.T. Oliver, Oliver the Spaceman.

The Transition House manual directed acceptance and compassion. Everyone had tried to leap off a bridge, or stolen pills from the pharmacy, or intentionally driven their truck into a field of grazing sheep, or come to Earth as an alien sleeper agent, and none of them had the right to judge. They all had a mission: move on. Make a new life. They suspected Oliver, but he was also one of them, not bound by his alien past, free to move on, if he so chose.

He could think of nothing else.

He saw, in his mind, a cabin in the woods. He could see the steep slope of its roof, but the image was otherwise murky. He tried to focus, but his gaze shifted down. He saw ferns and weeds, lanky grasses, a pebbled path, a blackberry bramble. He heard the thrum of crickets, and in the background, music. His heart cracked and the vision ended, stranding him with his own broken pieces, his fractured self, and the overwhelming sense that he had to get out.

While the transitional men watched and discussed in the living room, Oliver slunk upstairs. He packed his suitcase with all his clothes, his toothbrush, his umbrella. The entirety of his possessions fit in a single bag. He smoothed the covers on his bed. He thought about

Carl, who had left no note. Carl who left with a threat, and made the threat come true. He thought about writing a note: *Dear Transitional Men, thank you for your kindness. But I had to go.* But they might take it wrong. If they didn't, someone might come looking. Someone might analyze his handwriting for the telltale slope of an alien E. Better to drop a postcard from the road.

He crept down the stairs with his suitcase. He opened the back door, hid his suitcase beneath an overgrown bush, went back inside, ate ice cream with the transitional men. They had Neapolitan and Cherry Garcia. Oliver ate both. He washed the dishes. He said good night. He waited in bed, until his roommate's snores escalated to a chainsaw volume. Then he left. Out the back door, over the fence, down the sidewalk, wheeling the suitcase behind him. Good night, Transitional House. Goodbye, good luck. Already, he felt like a new man. He walked six blocks to the bus stop. He saw a bus traveling the opposite direction, and he ran across the street to catch it. The bus delivered him to Georgetown. He got off. He caught another bus headed somewhere else. Somewhere, buses came and went from a station, and where they went to was far, far away. Where to? He stopped to ask. He caught a bus bound for a bus bound for Baltimore. He knew nothing of Baltimore. He knew no one there, had never been, had thought he'd have more time to sleep on the bus, but in the blink of a dream he was there, awake, bleary-eyed beneath the bright fluorescents, disembarking, dragging his suitcase along a gum-stained sidewalk, past tarp and shopping cart encampments, beneath the steel-glass towers where the office lights began to turn on and the street-level coffee shops and breakfast joints opened their doors and the sky turned purple-mauve, then gauzy pink, *good morning, Baltimore.* He bought himself a breakfast sandwich.

"You want sausage, ham, bacon?"

The world was overfull with questions, and Oliver had no answers. Every situation demanded self-reflection. Was Oliver a sausage man? Was he fried or sunny-side up? Was he for cheddar or American? Was he a man, or was he an alien sleeper agent, and, if agent, what would he order to maintain the illusion of his humanity?

"Um . . . I'll have . . . sausage?"

"Sausage. Right. One sausage sammie! You want hash browns?"

Oliver sat on a park bench with his egg and sausage sandwich, sans hash browns. A cat jumped up onto the bench beside him, a fat calico with one green eye and one blue eye. Oliver broke off a piece of sausage and set it on the bench. The cat gobbled it up.

"You like that? Here, have the rest." Oliver left the last bites of sausage for the cat.

He got up to leave. He didn't realize it at the time, but the cat followed after him.

Oliver rented a room in a dismal downtown motel, five hundred a week for dark maroon carpets, bulbs burnt out, unmentionable stains on the bedspreads, roaches scuttling in the vents. He slept through the day, and in the evening he woke up and wondered what Oliver would do, as he transitioned into this new life. He could hear TV clatter through the thin walls, creaky plumbing, voices screaming on the street beneath his window. He opened the window and climbed out, onto a fire escape. He looked down. He saw a cat sitting on the sidewalk in front of the hotel. It looked like the same calico he had shared his breakfast with, but he couldn't tell for sure.

From somewhere, someone yelled, "It's comin' for you, boy—those deep-state assassins, all their cronies . . . better watch your back."

The cat startled and ran off. Oliver shivered. He crouched down. He peered through the metal slats at a man on the opposite sidewalk.

"Yeah, boy," the man yelled. "You better watch your back!"

He looked authoritative, at first glance, in his long trench coat and his glasses. But then he took a fustian leap over a discarded takeout box, and his coat billowed open, exposing stained tatters beneath.

He's crazy, Oliver thought, and again, he wondered at the presumption, at his mystery self, who had conjured this judgment, who felt an inexplicable fear of these assassins and their cronies. He looked over his shoulder, up, down, out across the streets at the unlit windows of tenements and residential motels. A roach scurried across the fire escape railing. Oliver crawled back inside. He sat on the rayon bedspread on the hard, creaky bed.

He thought: *What am I doing with my life?*

He thought: *What is coming? Will it come for me?*

TV blared from beyond the brittle wall, loud enough to make the wall crumble like a cracker, but for the layers of wallpaper and roaches to hold it together. On another wall, a fist pounded. *Turn it down!* Humans passed through the hallway, a man, a lady. *Hundred for half an hour,* she said. *Extra if you want . . .*

Time passed. TVs turned on and off. Humans came and went. Oliver explored the contents of his sparse room. He found a Bible in the desk drawer. Someone had scrawled black marker messages in its pages, in jumbo letters: *Aliens. Aliens. God is Aliens. Jesus = Aliens. Angels are douchey aliens who can't get it up. WTF GOD? Where are our FUCKING spaceships?* Someone had ripped out several pages but left a note of apology: *Needed something to roll so we could snort some blow, sorry GOD! But what did u expect? U made blow so good!*

Was Oliver a religious man? A man who feared God, who loved God, who would endeavor to serve, in the limited capacity of his flesh-and-bone self, God's will? He thumbed through Bible pages. He read passages. The words felt familiar, but not right. They brought a vision of a wooden pew, of a small hand full of bit pencils, of loafered feet.

A hoarse whisper telling him to quit it. *Quit swinging your feet. This is church.* He closed the Bible and returned it to its drawer. He put on his shoes. He went out, down the dim stairwell, past the plexiglass lobby desk, into the night.

The crazy man had moved on, and Oliver felt safer now. He felt like what? Like pizza. His brain tossed a memory: a wooden booth, a hand plucking a straw from a table dispenser. The hand tore paper from the straw's tip, held it to a boy's lips. He blew. *Oliver, quit it. For Christ's sakes, be civilized.* And then, for an instant, he saw the face of a girl. She stared back at him with mischievous bright eyes. She held a straw to her lips. She blew him a paper message.

His addled flesh-bone self lacked the capacity to decode the message. But he felt it in his heart—allegiance, regret, despair.

He walked the Baltimore streets, littered with despair, confusion, resignation, desperate furor, and religious zeal, like the streets of DC, but grittier, more sirens. He saw the illuminated yellow awning of a pizza joint, pizza by the slice.

"It's all confusion, man," the guy at the counter told him. "It's all confused. Had a guy rob this place last week, but for fucking pizza. Like, gimme four slices and then he won't pay. What the fuck is that? I tell you. You want pepperoni? You want mushroom? That's what we got."

There was a tip jar on the counter. It felt right to drop in a bill and some change. It felt like he was beginning to understand himself. He ate in, two slices of pepperoni and a root beer. He walked back toward the hotel. On one side of the hotel, there was a dark alley that dead-ended in a copse of dumpsters. Oliver approached the alley. He saw something dart across it. He heard an agonized meow. It sounded mournful, a cry for help. But also a greeting, a message meant for him.

"Meow?" he said to the darkness.

The darkness meowed back.

Oliver turned into the alley. He crept. His eyes searched, until they spotted, beneath a dumpster, two yellow orbs. The eyes of a cat.

"Meow?"

Meow.

He lowered himself down, onto his knees and hands. He sank further, until his cheek touched cool asphalt.

"Meow?"

Meow.

He stared at the cat. The cat's eyes had looked yellow, but closer up their color shifted, one to blue and the other to green. It was the calico. It stared back, and then it extended its paw.

"Meow."

Meow. It's you. Oliver. It bowed its head, revealing a gash on the back of its neck.

"Oh. Oh, no. I see."

It trotted toward him. He held out his hands, palms up. *Meow.* He scooped the injured cat up in his arms.

"I've got you, buddy," he told it. "You're safe now. It's all okay."

The Husband

THE WIFE WAS not okay. Things were not okay with the wife. Blaine teetered on the fence of accusation. The wife said she needed to make a call. A work call, that she had to take outside, never mind the cold blustery damp, or the late hour, or the children, up past bedtime, combing the Pleasant View Elementary yearbook, singling out the freak kids whom they suspected of extraterrestrialism.

"But how will we expose them?" Jas asked his sister.

"Well, like, how do you think?" Avril rolled her eyes. Wasn't it obvious? "We'll have to find a way to cut them and then peel off their human skin."

"No," Blaine tried to explain. "No, no, no, no, and no. And NO. No peeling skin. Damn it!" What the heck was wrong with their children?! Because, NO, he told the budding psychopath Earth-nationalists as the wife waved her arms around and chirped *work-call work-call work-call work-call*, and he thought: *Holy shit, I married that obnoxious earliest of early birds, the predawn whistler that wakes the neighborhood at four a.m. on a Saturday. Work-call work-call.* The wife was that bird. She slammed the door shut. He shouted one last *NO* at the children. He ran upstairs, to the bedroom window, to spy. He saw the wife hurry down the driveway. She turned right. She shoved her hands in her jacket pockets, but they did not emerge with a telephone. They stayed shoved, as she hurried up the street, two-three-four houses up, until he couldn't see her anymore.

He wanted to run after her, to catch her not-on-a-work-call. He would say: *What is going on, Anne? Tell me the truth.* Or *I know you're cheating. Don't try to hide it.* He would leave the children alone in the house because he wouldn't go far. He wouldn't leave the block. The children would be perfectly fine, if they didn't strangle each other, break each other's fingers, poke out each other's eyes. At least the house contained no other children whose skin they could cut and attempt to peel off.

He never had to reach a decision point because the children had run upstairs after him.

"What are you doing?"

"Yeah, Dad?"

"Are you spying on Mom?"

"You're spying on Mom, aren't you?"

"I'm not spying," Blaine said. "I was just . . . I was looking out the window."

"What's out there?"

"Are there any spaceships?"

"No. It's boring out there."

"Then why are you looking?"

"Um . . . because I'm boring. I'm a boring adult, and I like to look out the window when there's nothing out there to see."

"That's really dumb."

"That's what happens when you grow up. You get boring and dumb."

"That's not going to happen to me," Jas declared. "When I grow up, I'm going to be a cat."

Avril rolled her eyes and declared her brother's cat plan the asinine product of having shit-for-brains, but Blaine caught her, minutes later, before the wife had returned from her fabricated work-call outing, coloring the grown-up incarnation of her own future cat self.

"What's that thing on your, um, the cat's stomach?" he asked. The Avril-cat wore a scribbly white garment beneath a gray blazer.

"The chumbis."

"That, um, white thing is a chumbis?"

"No, Dad, ugh. The chumbis is under that."

"So, the chumbis is, uh—"

"It's, like, the awesome soft belly that I'll have, when I'm a cat. You know, the soft, swinging part. See?" She rubbed the exposed chumbis of Mr. Meow-mitts, who lay sprawled on the couch, his cat eyes fixed on the television. "The white part is my blouse. It's lacy."

"That's great."

"I'm a lawyer cat."

"Great."

"But I'm not going to wear heels, like Mom. Because they don't make heels to fit peets."

"Peets?"

"Dad, hello? What planet do you live on?"

"What are you talking about, 'peets'?"

"I'll bet he's one of them," Jas said. "I'll bet he's an alien, and that's why he doesn't know about peets."

"You know . . ." Avril's mistrustful eyes examined her father for irregularities. She reached out and pinched a fold of his arm skin between her fingers. "You know, he might be."

Only one way to know for sure. They would cut him while he slept and try to peel his skin off.

"I'm not," Blaine said. "I swear."

"That's what an alien would say."

"Exactly."

"Seriously, what are peets?"

"The feet, Dad."

"Yeah, Dad. The feet."

Mr. Meow-mitts arched his back and stretched his legs long, exhibiting his padded cat feet.

"Aww, himb long," Avril said. "I accempt."

"I accept himb's peet offering."

"What a nice long boi."

Avril would grow into a lawyer cat, and Jas deliberated between circus cat, astronaut cat, detective cat, and the not-at-all-improbable option of dinosaur-cat. For a few brief minutes, they all existed in harmony, Jas, Avril, Blaine, the long boi, all except for the wife, who was outside somewhere, not on a business call, doing god-knows-what. Blaine's heart went haywire and his gut was full of roiling acid and he felt like any second he might explode, because *fuck* it was all so awful. His wife, and her fucking coat. Her work calls. Her perfunctory attempts to conceal her infidelity, which made him the furious cuckold, and he hated it. He hated it. Because he loved her so, so much.

He had loved her from practically the moment he first saw her. He saw her in the back of a dive bar, the Comet, fumbling with the pool cue. She had no idea, she said. This wooden stick, this blue cube, was she supposed to rub them together? And why? *You rest the cue between your fingertips*, he explained, *and you stab the balls to knock them into the holes.* He wanted to help position her shot, to wrap his arms around her arms, to smell her silky hair. He didn't try, though, because he wasn't a creep. She said: *Why don't you just toss the balls? Wouldn't that be easier than trying to knock them in with this silly stick?* She swiped the eight-ball and threw a three-point shot into the corner pocket. He laughed. She chugged a beer and started outside to smoke. *Well, aren't you coming?* She dragged him along. He tried to check his principled revulsion to nicotine products. She smoked two in a row, and they looked good on her. She looked good. She blew perfect smoke rings. Her pink lips left a lipstick ring on the filter, and maybe smoking wasn't so bad after all, he thought. Later, when she swapped cigarettes for bubble gum, she explained how she had just wanted to try smoking on, to see how it fit, as if smoking was a jaunty vest or a pair of sling-backs. She snubbed out her cigarette and tried on a vodka tonic, and then a Long Island iced tea, and then *how about a game of pool*, she asked him, slightly slurring. She wobbled over to the pool table, snatched the cue, jabbed her finger in the cube of billiard chalk. She wanted to make it interesting. She slapped a twenty down on the table. He wouldn't take her money, if (when) he won.

He didn't take it, because *That was how I hustled your father. Avril, Jas, are you paying attention? That was how* she told the children, when they were seemingly too young to understand, except that they both got in trouble at school, for hustling dodgeball games, betting cookies and chocolate milk.

He lost sixty dollars the night he met her, but he won her phone number, and then he won a date, and he felt like the luckiest man in the entire world. She was uninhibited, could drink him under the table, could crush him at Skee-Ball, pinball, miniature golf. *This is why I'm going into law*, she told him. He didn't understand how law had anything to do with her mastery of recreational pseudo-sportsball games. She was a second-year law student with a big law internship lined up. She had plans to work in international law, to move from Ohio to New York to London to Switzerland, to become a James Bondian secret agent, to drive fast in a fancy car with flamethrower headlights. He never quite knew when she was joking. Everything she told him sounded kind of like a joke, but also kind of serious, and he loved that about her. *You know what I love about you?* she asked him, during a game of boccie, and it threw him off. His toss wasn't even close. She loved something about him? She loved him? She loved him, because he was so earnest, so practical, so unpretentious, so quintessentially good. *So unlike her family,* she said.

So, what about your family? he asked when they got engaged, one year and two-hundred-plus games of pool after they first met, and she suggested a small wedding, just them and a judge, and his mom and a couple of friends. That was the practical thing to do, she'd said. She took a big firm job at a place with a local office because that was the practical thing, and she wanted to be practical, for their future.

Her family? No, she didn't want to invite them. She was done with them. They were not earnest, not unpretentious, not good, at their core. *Maybe,* she said, in a rare visible moment of self-doubt, *she wasn't either.*

He didn't buy it. Good was not an immutable quality, a core element of one's existence. Good was not genetic or mystical or intrinsic. Good was the choice made, the action taken, the love displayed when Anne read the vows she had written herself, when she chose the stay-put firm job over the international one that would require moving and travel and long weeks away from Blaine, when she let him win at putt-putt or baked his favorite cookies or nestled close to him late at night and said something like *this place, here, in bed, with you—this is my favorite place in the whole universe.*

"You want to rub the chumbis?"

"What?"

"The chumbis, Dad. It's exposed." Avril stroked the cat's fat-sack.

"Awww, Mr. Meow-mitts, my boi, my boi."

Mr. Meow-mitts purred.

"Go on, Dad," Jas urged. "He says it's okay."

Blaine reached slowly toward the cat. He placed his hand, gently, on the cat's belly. He rubbed. The claws came down. Blaine jerked his hand away.

"Ow! Hey!" Avril giggled. A beaded line of blood appeared on the back of Blaine's hand. "Why'd you have to—"

"He changed his mind," Jas said.

"He's a changeable boi. Isn't himb? My longling. My hamb." Avril stuck her hand smack in the middle of the sharp-pointed cat danger zone. She rubbed the chumbis. The cat's happy motor rumbled.

The front door opened. In came the wife. "Guess what!"

She flung her coat in the closet. She kicked off her shoes. Blaine wanted to rage. *Where were you? Who is he?* Even though he knew. *How could you want him, when you have me? Am I not enough?* He wanted to cry. He thought he knew the answer: *No, you're not enough.* His very ordinary self could never satisfy this gorgeous, extraordinary wife. He was a buffoon to think that he could, in the end, be anything more than the mundane fellow who packed the kids' lunches and vacuumed the rugs and lost every pool game, every round of Skee-Ball, dodgeball, tennis, bowling, badminton that he ever played against the wife, unless, out of pity, she let him win. He existed, as husband, to make the wife look good, but eventually she would realize or had already realized that she would look better with someone more muscly on her arm, someone without a creeping pattern baldness, someone with preternaturally white teeth and protein-shake shoulders, someone rich and refined, someone other than John, who seemed fairly unspectacular but was maybe just a stepping-stone on the wife's way to that someone.

"What?" he asked.

The wife slid across the floors, into the living room. She threw her arms around Blaine. She hugged him tight. "We're going on vacation!"

She let go. She plopped onto the couch beside the cat.

"Vacation?"

"Spring break vacation! Be excited!"

"I *am* excited."

"You don't sound excited." The wife's hand fondled the chumbis.

"I am. I am excited."

"We're leaving on Sunday!"

"But . . . I thought you had some big work thing. And I have work. And the kids have school. Spring break isn't until the week after next. And where are we going, anyway?"

"It's, um, well—"

"Disney World?" Avril asked.

"Disney World! Right, Mom?" Jas declared.

"Well, it's, sure. Yes!"

"I knew it!"

"I mean, it's, it'll be kind of like Disney World," the wife said, but the kids had stopped listening at *well*. The kids were going to Disney World. The kids were halfway up the stairs, on their way to pack their bags.

"Okay, but really," Blaine said after they had scampered off. "Because . . . you know the work call. I mean, I know that's what you said you were doing, but—" But really she had planned one last family hurrah, a Disney pre-divorce, chocolate pancake princess breakfasts and overpriced plastic mouse ears to pacify the children before Mom bid farewell to their boring dad.

"I know," Anne said. "I know, I said it was a work call. I'm sorry about all the subterfuge. I was . . . I was just trying to plan something, and I didn't want to say anything. In case it didn't work out."

"But . . ."

"But what?"

The wife's coat. Her hat. Her, standing on the corner, sipping her soda, while that other man slung his arm around her shoulder.

"But . . . I . . ."

"What? What is it?" Her gleeful Disney vacation smile faded. "What's going on?"

"I . . . You tell me. What's going on?"

She looked at him, askance. Her eyes studied his. "What . . . do . . . you mean?"

"I mean . . . I saw you, Anne. On the night of that godawful town hall. The kids and I were, well, we went for ice cream and we passed by that pizza parlor, the one with the thick crust, and I saw you."

"You did?"

"With John."

"Oh."

"He . . . he had his arm around you."

"Oh."

"And then, earlier, there was that party, and you guys were outside together. And you've been acting so . . . look, if you love him—"

"*Love* him?"

"Or if I, if I'm— I know these things happen. I just want to know—"

"Wait, you think I . . . that I *love John*?"

"Well, I don't know what I think exactly, but what I saw was—"

"Oh gosh, you think I'm cheating on you! Oh, Blaine!" Anne got up. She threw her arms around his neck. "I don't— There's nothing going on, I mean, John is just a friend. And, well, what you saw, his arm, he was just, it was just a friend thing. Really. He was comforting me because I've been so stressed-out and that's why I reached out to him to begin with. I mean, not for comforting, because I have you, and, and you're all I need, really, seriously, Blaine. But he has a, um, a cousin who has time-shares, vacation rentals, like that stuff, and we were just planning. We were vacation planning."

"So you're telling me we're going on vacation with John and Elena?"

"With them? No. *No!* I mean, they're going on vacation too, but we're not going together. We were just planning the logistics, helping each other out, you know?"

"Yeah . . ."

"Oh, Blaine!" Anne kissed him. She pressed herself against him. "You don't think, you didn't really think I was having an affair, did you?"

"I . . . I guess . . ."

"You know I love you more than anything. You and the kids. I love you more than anything in the universe," she said, and while Blaine still felt doubt, that vexatious mosquito, buzzing around the dark back corners of his mind, it was impossible not to believe her.

The Stepchild

HEATHER'S PHONE RANG during morning yoga. She had embarrassingly deliberately neglected to turn it silent. She leapt up, toppling her water bottle with a graceless flail while the professed devotees of hot-flow tranquility pretended not to be annoyed. She ran through the studio, out the door, onto the sidewalk, and saw a number she didn't recognize.

"Hello?"

"Hello, this is Agent Raquel Innes with the US Department of Homeland Security. I'm trying to reach . . ."

Heather almost dropped the phone.

She hadn't expected anyone to call when she filled out that form on the website. She had submitted it between glugs of wine, to dispel the boredom, to obtain that fleeting happy squirt of dopamine, enough to convince her brain that she had done something worthwhile, that she was worthwhile. She had expected the form to languish on the clunky government servers for half a decade until some clerk dredged it up, printed it out, stamped it RESOLVED.

Or, that was how she told the story to herself, now, in her present state of progressive clarity. She would never discriminate against aliens. She would never snitch on her stepdad, just because she envied his capacity for devouring salty snack foods.

Except they did call, and they sounded *very* official even though her brain could not quite register the content of what this Agent of Homeland Security was saying.

"... have investigated your claim and found it to be credible ..."

"What now?"

"... found it to be credible and ..."

Her feet were cold. She felt suddenly exposed, standing there barefoot on the dirty sidewalk, while the women of Malibu did sun salutations behind the window glass, while the sun itself glared down, as if to chastise her. She had believed in its singularity. The miracle of life on Earth. But that miracle was just the middle-school smart kid who grew up to discover that the smarts she thought had set her apart, above and beyond the others, were commonplace, and that in that place, her smarts ranked subpar.

"So, what, you're going to *what*, exactly?"

"Can you hear me?"

"I'm sorry, I'm outside. It's loud ..."

"It says here in the documentation of your report that the extra-terrestrial resides with you. Is that correct?"

"What? Um ..."

"It lives with you. The extraterrestrial."

"Oh, yeah, I mean, I guess."

"We will be assigning a special agent to follow up. In the meantime, we suggest that you do not make any direct contact. The extraterrestrial may be dangerous ..."

The extraterrestrial. Jack P.

Heather turned her ringer off. She walked back inside. She felt numb, outside, inside. She moved through the motions. Mountain pose. Plank. Upward dog. Downward dog. Warrior. She was not a warrior. She was not a snitch except she was a snitch, and she knew her phone was ringing. She could sense it, inside her purse, silenced, howling.

Yoga class ended. She waited to check until she got back to her car. Her plebeian little Honda Civic. She would never own a Tesla like

Alex or be brilliant like Alex. Harvard would never be her fallback choice. Her heart would never brim over with feelings of family love and togetherness. Her mother had called, texted, texted, was calling right now again.

"Hello?"

"Heather? Heather, something terrible has happened. They've . . . they've taken Jack. Oh my god, Heather, I—"

Her mother sobbed.

She feigned shock. "Mom, who? Why?"

"These agents. They . . . they came to the front door. They said they're Homeland Security and . . . and they told Jack to come with them, and he went and they wouldn't let me call a lawyer or go with him and it's just . . . It's preposterous!"

"Well, but like, why did they even take him? Did they tell you?"

"They said . . . Oh Jesus, Heather. They said it was because he's an alien."

"That's ridiculous!" She tried to sound astonished. "It can't be true. I mean, he has a kid. So, like, that doesn't even make sense, that he could be an alien and have a kid. And he was on *Jeopardy!* It's totally absurd that an alien would launch a television career by winning on *Jeopardy!*"

"Well, yes, that would be brazen. . . . But it's beside the point, what he is. He's an American. And they have no right! Carting him away like that without any due process! Depriving him of a lawyer! It's just uncivilized. They wouldn't even let me talk to him! He's a good person. He deserves better than this. Doesn't he? Heather?"

The Husband

THE NEXT DAY, Friday, the wife traded in her sedan for a minivan.

"What? Did you . . . You got a minivan?" Blaine said, over the phone, as he drove the city van through early rush-hour-traffic snarls.

Dave chuckled. "It's a waste, man."

"That's . . . I mean, we didn't talk about it first," Blaine said to the wife. "And I thought you hated minivans."

"She should have bought a tank," Dave said. "Or at least a Humvee."

"A Humvee? So she could use it to destroy the earth?" Blaine said. "I mean a minivan is bad enough but . . . Oh, that's just Dave. I was talking to Dave. Okay . . . My wife says hello."

"Hiya, Annie," Dave yelled. "Congrats on your new van! Baby steps. But you'll come around."

Dave himself had purchased a Humvee, after his efforts to procure a tank failed. Dave had sights set. Dave was about to make moves. He had ammo stockpiles, tactical equipment, survival gear, everything in camouflage. He had excavated the lawn behind his house and buried two conjoined shipping containers, one for supplies and one for himself, to live in, underground, for when the alien combatants occupied the streets of suburbia. But Dave had built the shelter as a contingency, for use if his militia group disbanded, or scattered, or fell in an alien massacre.

"You really ought to join us," Dave said right after highlighting said potential alien massacre, as if it was a militia group selling point. Blaine could not quite tell from Dave's descriptions whether the militia group was a militia group or a cult or a cosplay club. The group called itself the Whitesnake Raiders, a name that Dave had forbidden Blaine from uttering outside the confines of the city van, which Dave inspected assiduously, every morning, for bugs and tracking devices. The Whitesnake Raiders had a compound "in the hills somewhere," at which it trained its raiders in shooting, archery, guerilla warfare tactics, crop rotation, beer brewing, mushroom gathering, animal husbandry, saponification, et cetera, et cetera, like summer scout camp except for grown men with thick beards and rifle collections. The men got badges, and if they earned enough badges they got a sash with a jumbo-sized special badge, and a snake rank promotion, Garter to Mambas to Python, Cobra, Viper, King Rattler. There could only be one King Rattler. Dave was an Anaconda, thanks to his armament efforts. Dave had won third place in the Whitesnake Raiders' recent alien-incursion drill—a three-night raider campout, barbecue, and "E.T. slaughter" operation. Dave laid real traps in the woods to catch fake aliens, but his traps caught a real deer, which the raiders killed, cooked, and ate.

"I don't think I would fit in," Blaine said.

"Sure you would!" Dave clapped him hard on the back. "You're one of us. You're a man."

Women and children could come too, Dave explained, but they couldn't *be* snakes. They could be spiders, squirrels, or wildcats. They ran their own cosplay drills, wherein they got pretend-captured and had to escape. The snakes, in contrast, ran offensive drills; it was assumed they would never get caught.

"I'm headed up there tomorrow," Dave said as the city van pulled into the lot. He lit a menthol, inside the van, in clear view of their office windows. He had given up giving a shit about the human rules. Not that he ever really had, but he had at least pretended.

"Where, to—"

"Whitesnake Ridge."

"Whitesnake Ridge."

"Yup. You sure you don't want to come, bring the family? It'll be safer there, when the E.T.I. come back." E.T.I. was the Whitesnake Raider acronym for the enemy, the Extraterrestrial Invaders.

"I'm sure."

"Well . . ."

"Yeah."

"Look, man." Dave turned and looked at Blaine. "You've been a good partner. I've enjoyed our long hours together in this van."

"Yeah, me too."

"But there's a season. And it ain't city season no more. It ain't our season, unless we make it. You sure you don't want to come?" Dave said.

"Yeah." Blaine nodded.

"Well, if you change your mind . . ." Dave climbed out of the van. He walked toward his car, not bothering to go into the office, punch the time clock, collect the remains of his urban life. When he reached his car he stopped and looked back, one last time. The last time, Blaine knew, though Dave never said the word goodbye.

"To each his own, man. And to the aliens, death. Right?"

Blaine waved goodbye and went inside. He labeled the samples for testing. He filled out his time card for the next week, recording one week of vacation. He punched the clock. He drove home, feeling empty and unsettled, regretting his lack of resolve, his marginal motivation to do anything, much less prepare for alien insurgency. While Dave trained for battle and devised plans to drive E.T.I. off the edge of the flat Earth, Blaine watched TV with the children. They watched back-to-back-to-back-to-back *Adventure Time* episodes. They watched until their eyes hurt and their shirts turned to smocks of cat hair and their bodies atrophied into couch-potato sludge. The wife, at least, could watch TV and knit, or watch TV with calisthenics, or watch in the kitchen while she baked chocolate cupcakes with cream cheese centers and crispy bacon tops.

The wife had still not disclosed the vacation destination.

"Let's let it be Disney World," she said.

"But is it? Because if it's not—"

"Shhhhhh."

"The kids will be—"

"The kids will be fine. They'll be great! They'll love it!"

"Okay, but how should I pack? I mean, if it's Disney World it'll be warm, and I'd pack shorts and sandals and—"

"Just, um, pack a little bit of everything. Pack all your favorite stuff. That way you'll be prepared. That's why I bought the minivan. So we could fit everything!"

The wife was definitely not okay. She was definitely losing her mind, at least a little bit, but the same could be said of everybody. Dave had signed up for a year at Camp Militia Cult. Their friends Rebecca and Greg had just listed their house for sale and rented a flat in Costa Rica. Their friends Jeff and Marshall had gotten super OCD about decluttering, cleaning, and sanitizing, as if a sparse and spotless kitchen could keep the alien threat away. John and Elena had also sprung for a surprise vacation. Blaine stopped fretting about the wife's new minivan the moment he saw, parked in John and Elena's driveway, a brand-new forty-foot RV. A monster-house on wheels. A middle finger to the environment. The sight of it annoyed and repulsed him, but he also felt a bit jealous.

"Did you see it?" he asked the wife when she got home. "It's . . . it's just excessive! Who needs an RV that big? Who needs an RV at all? What ever happened to a good old tent?"

"I think it's fantastic," the wife said.

"Yeah, Dad," the children agreed. "How come we don't get an RV?"

"Because you're going to Disney World instead," the wife said, perpetuating the spring break vacation myth. "Now go upstairs! Finish packing!"

The wife wanted to listen to background adult television while she packed items of questionable importance to a spring-break vacation at a destination she was pretending was Disney World. She packed coats, hats, boots, tools, books, baby photos. Their wedding album. Her entire jewelry collection. She was definitely losing her mind, and yet she managed to stay breezy about it. She managed to concurrently pack and snack and listen to the TV talking heads debate the import and concealment of earlier alien visitations. The pertinent documents came highly redacted; big chunks of FOIA black interspersed with disjointed snippets of real talk. *Real talk*, one news commentator said, to the other: You think the government knows who these aliens are? Where they are? What they're doing? Government officials kept their mouths shut, except they let it slip that they had identified *persons of interest. Is that what we're calling them?* One news commentator said derisively. *Persons?* The wife's brow sprouted a furrow. She poured herself a second glass of wine. She ate an entire box of bacon-cheddar crackers. She filled a second suitcase and moved on to the third. Blaine intervened.

"Okay, you need to stop," he said.

"Stop what? I'm just trying to get ready. I just want us to be completely prepared."

"For vacation."

"For vacation!"

"We're leaving Sunday, right? It's Friday night."

"Yes! So?"

"You've packed a bunch already. Why don't you just, I don't know, relax for a while?"

"I'm drinking. See?" She gulped back half a glass of red.

"Yes, but you're also overpacking. You're obviously stressed-out."

"I'm not . . . Well, everyone's stressed-out! This, this alien thing! It's stressful! What if they come back, Blaine? What then?"

"I don't know. But I do know that stressing yourself out now won't make things any better. So maybe you should save the rest of the packing for tomorrow and just take a break and relax this evening."

"That is such a Blaine thing to say," the wife said, and to her credit, she tried. But she got fidgety. She couldn't sit still. Blaine turned the TV off. He poured more wine. He lit candles and put jazz on the record player. He volunteered for bedtime duty, but after he tucked the children in and came back downstairs, he found the wife pacing in front of the TV. She looked harried. Government authorities had identified persons of interest, the TV news said, and they could not be permitted to roam freely through our midst. Extraterrestrial imposters had no constitutional rights. Congress-humans had introduced bills. Constituents demanded it. Round them up, turn them in, keep them caged, interrogate. By all means necessary. Americans needed to know what threat these imposters posed. Americans needed answers.

"They'll get tortured!" The wife shoved a handful of Chizz-Wizard Cheese Product Puffs into her mouth.

"Well, I mean, I'm sure if they talk—"

"But what if they don't know anything? Don't they have rights? Isn't America supposed to be civilized? How is this legal?"

"I'm sure there's . . . Well, I mean, you're the lawyer. Is it legal?"

"I'm not that kind of lawyer! I'm a corporate lawyer! But—"

"Look, Anne, it's going to be fine. It'll all be fine. It'll be better. If we can find these aliens and they can explain, then maybe we'll know more. Maybe this looming uncertainty—"

Looming uncertainty, Blaine thought, had defined every hour-day-week of his life since the inexplicable spaceships flashed their blue-green-red lights over Earth's great cities. It had enveloped them all, like a plague, upending every assumption, every expectation, every conviction that humanity had about the absence or presence of life in the universe, and what that life would do if it found us. No one expected it would be so flighty. No one expected the remarkable incidence of first contact to be followed by a nebulous wait. Aliens were supposed to come and conquer, or come and welcome, not come and leave without explanation, without any stated return date. This uncertainty, Blaine assumed, tormented the wife far more than it bothered him, and he couldn't fall asleep at night anymore without a couple of drinks and a melatonin gummy. The wife was so spectacularly organized, such a masterful planner, an obstinate shining grand-prize supermom, that this prolonged uncertainty would, undoubtedly, drive her mad.

She couldn't sleep at all. She made frantic drunken love, after which Blaine gobbled his sleep gummies and passed out.

In the middle of the night he woke, briefly, to an empty spot on her side of the bed, and in the morning it was still empty. The wife was downstairs, frying up pounds of bacon. The foyer was stacked with suitcases.

"I've decided to get an early start," she said.

"How long have you been up?" he asked. "Did you sleep at all?"

"Well, I had to finish packing."

"But—"

"So we can leave early. Today! We'll leave today!"

"Today?"

"Come on, Blaine, where's your sense of adventure? It'll be great! It'll be like vacation!"

"What do you mean, it'll be '*like* vacation'?"

"Oh, just that, well, it'll be like vacation because it *is* vacation. Right? Here, have some bacon!"

"I'm not packed."

"Sure you are! I packed for you. While you slept. I tried to be very quiet, so I wouldn't wake you. So now you're all ready! You just need to eat your bacon and get dressed and then we'll go!"

"But, Mom!"

"Mom!"

"Mr. Meow-mitts!"

The kids ran into the kitchen, pulling the cat behind them on a plastic sled.

"Yes! Of course! We'll have to make a spot for him in the van."

"We're taking the cat," Blaine said, confused. "We're taking the cat on vacation?"

"Yeah, Dad."

"Duh."

"We can't go to Disney World without the cat, *Dad*."

"This is . . . No!" Blaine said. "This is absurd! We're going to drive, what, like, fifteen hours in the car, with the cat? Will they even let the cat into the hotel? Are we taking his litter box? We can't take a cat on vacation!"

"But, *Dad*!" Jas screamed. He ran from the room, sobbing.

The wife shoved a crispy slab of bacon into her mouth. Avril crouched beside the sled. She stroked the chumbis.

"Really, Dad," she said. "How could you? Mr. Meow-mitts is family. Mr. Meow-mitts would never suggest that we all go on vacation without *you*."

His wife looked sad on his behalf. "Avril, honey—"

"No. No, of course he wouldn't! Because he's a cat!"

"Avril, why don't you and Mr. Meow-mitts go watch TV so your dad and I can—"

"Whatever."

Avril hitched the sled to her waist and crawled away. The cat leapt from the departing sled. It weaved between the wife's legs.

"This is just . . . We can't . . . the cat . . ." Blaine stammered.

Anne squeezed his arm. She smoothed his bed-hair. She looked up at him with her bright beautiful eyes, eyes that said *I'm not crazy* but that also looked, maybe, more than a little bit crazy.

"This is just . . . a thing . . . a thing you're saying to the kids, to, you know . . ."

"Sure. Yes. Of course," the wife said, and Blaine looked down at her, nodded, smiled. His inner voice instructed: *Good, of course, just play along.* Just like the wife, pretending to take the cat to fake Disney World. He would pretend it all made sense. He would eat his bacon like a good little Blaine and pretend they'd booked Mr. Meow-mitts his own vacation week of secluded luxury at the cat-kennel.

You've gotten really good at pretending, haven't you, Blaine?

He heard a voice inside his head, but the voice felt as if it had traveled to his brain from some external place. The voice had a feline quality, but Blaine pretended it didn't.

You know we're not really going on vacation, don't you? You do know what this is about?

Mr. Meow-mitts stopped weaving and stared at Blaine.

"Well, I guess I'll go get ready . . ." Blaine said. "For vacation . . ."

And yet, he knew, as he showered, dressed, brushed his teeth, as he carried half a dozen large suitcases plus several small ones out to the driveway, as he Tetris'ed the luggage into the brand-new minivan, as he walked back into his house, one last time, he knew that this was the last time, that a week-long vacation would distend into a much longer, weirder stretch of life, that he had known in his heart all along. But pretense came easier than rigorous examination. Love eschewed an inquisition. And he loved her. He loved Anne. He knew that much at least.

"Say you love him, Dad."

"Say you love Mr. Meow-mitts."

Blaine sat in the passenger seat. The children crowded the open door. Avril cradled the cat.

"Okay. I love him."

"Like you mean it, Dad."

"I. Love. Mr. Meow-mitts."

"Now hold out your arms and say, 'I accempt this chonk offering.'"

"Um . . ."

"Say it."

"I accempt this chonk offering," he said.

"Good. Here." Avril set the cat down on Blaine's lap. She closed the passenger door. The kids and the wife climbed into the car.

"Off we go!" the wife declared. The minivan powered on. She checked the mirrors. She looked giddy and sad and terrified and overly confident, the look of someone at risk of crashing the brand-new minivan into the garage door. The van accelerated.

"Stop, stop!" Blaine yelled as they careened forward, toward the house.

The wife hit the brakes just in time.

"It's fine," she said. "It's fine. We'll all be just fine."

She backed the van up, and they pulled out of the driveway. They drove up the street. Blaine watched their house recede in the side-view mirror. Then it was gone. They drove past the Sears model houses and

Craftsman cottages on their street, and then the houses were behind them. They passed John and Elena's house, John and Elena's RV behemoth. Elena stood in the yard, her arms full of cardboard boxes, her expression burdened by an impending vacation that wasn't, really. She looked up as they passed. Her eyes met Blaine's. He raised his hand, a bewildered wave, the last.

* * *

They had already merged onto the highway when Blaine realized his phone was not in his pocket.

"My phone!" he said. "It's not—"

"Is it not in your pocket?" Anne asked.

"I could have sworn it was there. Well, at least we haven't gone far. There's an exit right up there. We can turn around and—"

"Oh, no, I don't think so," Anne said.

"What do you mean? Hey! Hey, you're passing the exit!"

"We're not going back."

"Anne—"

"We're not going back for your phone."

"But I need it, and we just left and—"

"Blaine, no. No. We're not going back. You can't have your phone. You'll just have to . . . well, you'll adapt."

A cat claw pierced through his jeans and dug into the skin of his thigh.

"I don't understand," he said.

"Well," the wife replied, "neither do I."

The Brother

OLIVER DID NOT know the cat's name. It had no collar, though the fur around its neck grew thinner, as if a collar had once encircled it. It was fat, floofy, with calico patterning. Its eyes looked yellow at first, but as the light shifted one eye turned green and the other blue. It had a fresh cut on the back of its neck, still oozing.

"Where did you come from?" Oliver asked it. He had left it alone, on his bed in the roach motel, while he ventured out for supplies: the canned food, the catnip mouse, the litter box, the antibacterial ointment. He dabbed ointment on the cat's wound.

"It's okay," he said. "I don't know where I came from either."

Except that night Oliver dreamed of an A-frame building surrounded by tall pines. He dreamed of fresh snow out the window, white and glistening beneath a stark blue sky. *Oliver, let's make waffles.* The television chattered. He had his feet up, two socked towers rising over coffee table kingdom, land of scattered playing cards, remote controls, empty beer can, ashtray, bong. She approached behind him, leaned over the couch, arms draped around his shoulders. *Oliver, we made it. We made it out.* Dream time shifted. He smelled butter, syrup, ganja. She wore a thrift-store terry-cloth robe, maroon, monogramed. He tried to read the initials but then he knew: They didn't belong to her. He stood at the window, stared out at the glittering snowscape, watched a clump of tree snow slide down its needle bed. He watched a bird alight. *It's not Shenandoah,* his dream self said. *So. Well. It's farther. It's better, maybe,* she said, but already the sun had retreated, the glitter-white turned dull beneath the future's shadow. Already he knew. *Maybe* was a hard *no*. *Snow,* his dream self said. A loner flake drifted past the window. The mug in his hand felt lukewarm. His mind felt clogged with worry. The snow. The cyclops car, bald-tired, no chains, duct tape on the bumper. The rent. The grease-stench on his skin. The phone service disconnected. *But we made it out,* she said, and his brain screamed, *No no no please!*

But ABBA, she said, and his dream filled with music.

And when he awoke, the stray cat slept on the bed, on the pillow, feet-length from his face, and Oliver felt a weird humming inside his head, a *whir-whir-whir-whir,* like a motor. *Running on cat fumes,* he thought.

The cat opened its eyes, yawned. *What did you dream, Oliver?*

"How's your neck?" he asked the cat. The cat bent his head down for Oliver to see the scab. "Better. Good. You want breakfast?"

They dined on cat food and dry cereal. They watched TV. The TV news said that Russia had rounded up a dozen E.T. suspects, had dragged them away from their beds in the middle of the night. But maybe this was how the Russian government dealt with its human dissidents. But maybe America would be safer if—

Oliver changed the channel. He watched cartoons. The cartoons had a strange wizard and an elastic dog and a dancing handheld video-game creature. The cartoons made Oliver feel at ease and connected to something larger than himself. Some other larger thing might come and drag him away from his cheap motel bed in the middle of the night. Something might interrogate him, but Oliver didn't know the answers. He still needed to pry the answers from his own muddled mind.

The cat sat on Oliver's lap. It stared at the TV. He stroked it.

What will you do with your life, Oliver?

"What will I do with my life, cat?" he asked aloud. He had a flash memory: a wood-framed window, trees glazed with snow, disco music, his own voice speaking from a distant past. *Something better. Something better than this, someday. I want to make something for myself.*

He had made, in his mind, a twenty-year blizzard. He had made it out of the Transition House. He had made it out of Brookwood, and yet he was, in a sense, still there.

Are you, Oliver? I mean, you're not crazy. Just because you're hearing me inside your head.

A roach scuttled across the floor and disappeared beneath the dresser. A roach on the floor meant a thousand more in the walls. Roaches would keep on scuttling, even if the humans all got wiped out by aliens, or by something else. Roaches could provide an adequate protein source, if pulverized to roach pulp and reconstituted into some chickenesque product, for feeding the E.T.s' human slave labor force. Oliver saw a brief vision of himself working the roach-nugget assembly line, followed by a vision of Oliver the factory overseer, blowing the break-time whistle.

Who are you, Oliver?

He did not want to work in food production. His arms did not stretch like rubber bands. He had made nothing worthwhile, that he knew of, in the elapsed first half of his life. If he got lucky enough for a second half. If the authorities did not capture and interrogate him on suspicion of alienism. But, he had to admit to himself, his remarkable recovery *was* suspicious.

He lifted the cat, gently, from lap to bed. He went into the bathroom. A roach lingered in the bathtub. A dead one, he saw, when he looked closer. He examined his face in the mirror. His eyes had a clever spark. His nose hooked slightly left, the bent of an ancient break. His features could be best described as unremarkable, exceedingly ordinary, neither handsome nor unattractive, chameleon in quality. His dark hair sprouted patches of gray. The cat jumped up onto the sink. It lapped water from the dripping faucet.

"Better than from the bowl, huh?" Oliver glanced over at the bowl of water he had left on the floor for the cat. A roach perched on the edge. "It's not a swimming pool, buddy," he said. But the roach was dumb and it dove right in. "We've got to get out of here."

The dream/memory flashed back. *We had to get out of there.* A waffle on a plastic plate, drenched in syrup. The maroon sleeve of her robe. *I know. I just wish that . . .* He had a sense that he had been trying to *get out of here* for a long time, for forever; that the struggle to *get out of here* defined his pre-Brookwood existence; that the struggle resumed when his mind snapped back, and here he was, fleeing, again.

"But why? What am I doing?"

He had an identification card in his wallet, with his picture. He studied the card. Oliver Smith. That last name sure wouldn't help him find any answers, said the repository of stock knowledge that had resurfaced in his mind. The world contained a hundred billion Smiths and at least a million of those were named Oliver. This Oliver Smith was age thirty-eight. This Oliver Smith had in his wallet a Social Security card, freshly printed, a debit card, a business card for a financial advisor named Chaz Landry, a stack of twenty-dollar bills.

You're keeping that all in the same place?

"I probably shouldn't keep this all in the same place, huh?"

He stared at the numbers on the Social Security card. He repeated them over and over in his mind, chiseling them into his memory. He stuck the card in a pocket in his suitcase. He scratched the cat's head.

"I'm going out. Will you stay? Will you be good?"

He left the cat in his room with the TV on. He walked the streets of Baltimore. He wandered into stores. He bought a wallet with a chain.

He bought a prepaid phone, a space-age cat-carrier backpack with a plexi-bubble viewing window, a pair of sunglasses, a lamb shawarma, and tabbouleh salad. He walked back to the roach hotel.

"You want some shawarma?" He fed tidbits of lamb to the cat and pondered the strangeness of this tiny predator eating creatures so much larger than itself. When he finished eating, he called the number on the back of his debit card.

Hello. Thank you for calling the First Bank of Lake Orange.

"Hi, um, my name is Oliver Smith. I'm—"

If you are calling to check your account balance, please press one now.

"Oh." Oliver had mistaken the automated voice for a real human. He had forgotten how things worked; banks, phone calls, robotic answering. He pressed one. He keyed in his birthdate, his account number, the last four digits of his social.

Thank you for calling. The balance of your account is—

"How many thousand?"

To hear the balance again, press two. To return to the main menu—

Oliver listened again. He had $47,294; a vast sum.

"I could buy a house. . . ."

Except that he had no idea how much a house might cost, or whether he wanted one. He had only the knowledge, innate, almost visceral, that he possessed, according to the automated voice, unreasonable cash, more than he had ever had or expected, in his limited temporal span of consciousness, and it felt strange. It felt like a twenty-dollar bottle of champagne and a pack of Swisher Sweets, like a new pair of sneakers, like the car stereo that made the windows shake. It felt like a spotlight illuminating the disconnect between the Oliver Smith whose life had begun to resurface in his memory and the Oliver Smith that existed here and now, in a Baltimore roach motel, two months after the spaceships came and went.

"Forty-seven thousand." He said the number out loud. "It doesn't make sense."

How do you think you paid for Brookwood all those years, buddy? You know that place wasn't free, right?

Right. Brookwood, Brokewood, Drain-Your-Account-Drywood. He recalled the patients talking. No cable. Shit food. All the hazardous choke-sized pieces removed from every board game. *But still, better than State,* the patients said. Better than the underfunded government-run psychiatric suck-hole where taxpayer dollars bought semi-edible cereals and grade-F meats.

Oliver took the financial advisor business card out of his wallet. He called the telephone number listed on the card.

"Hello, thanks for calling First Bank of Lake Orange Brokerage and Investments, you've reached Chaz Landry."

"Hi, um, yeah, s-so . . ." His thoughts kept getting tripped up by forty-seven thousand.

"Hello? This is Chaz Landry."

"Yeah, so, I . . . I found your business card. In my wallet. I . . . I don't know why. Maybe, I have an account, or—"

"Should we look you up? We can look you up, no prob."

"I . . . I might have forgotten, so—"

"It's fine. People forget about their accounts all the time. It's totally understandable. All that stuff can be hard to keep track of. So if you didn't report the account, you know, I wouldn't worry about it."

"Okay. I'm . . . I won't."

"Good. I need your name and *soash*."

"My soash?"

"Your social. Gimme a sec. Okay, shoot."

Oliver recited his Social Security number. Chaz Landry said something unfathomable about trusts and deposits and investments and how the accountant had handled all the reporting, it looked like, so Oliver didn't need to fret about the IRS.

"Wait, what?"

"Every month. That's how the trust is set up."

"I don't understand."

"You want to see? I can Skype you, so you can see the account statement."

"You can what?"

"Or if you have email."

"I . . . I don't think I . . ."

Did he? The present-slash-future made no sense. He had a vague recollection of email. Maybe Oliver Smith had email, but it had gotten misplaced in the blizzard.

"Or if you want to grab a copy of the account statement, we can go through it."

"I don't have it."

"The recent one. We mailed it out last month. The address on record . . ." The address belonged to some law firm in Ohio.

"Look, can you just . . . just explain again."

"Sure, Mr. Smith. Of course. The trust provides for monthly transfers into your bank account. The deposit amount is indexed to match inflation, so right now it's around six grand, but next year, whatever the inflation is, you understand?"

"Yes." Oliver didn't.

"I'll have another copy of the statement mailed out. You want me to send it to a different address, Mr. Smith?"

"Um, no. That's fine but . . . I just . . . I'm sorry, this is all very, well, so, how long will the, um, transfers last? When will they stop?"

"They won't."

"I don't understand."

"They last for the life of the trust, which is the same as your life, Mr. Smith."

Oliver hung up. He sat on the hard motel bed. He stared at the shawarma dregs in the takeout container. He stared at the blank TV screen. He didn't understand. Trust, accounts, indexed to inflation, gibberish. It felt like a delusion constructed by a psychotic mind of the state psychiatric ward. Oliver Smith was broke. He was strapped. He was a boy with a couple of stolen candy bars and a pack of beef jerky in the baggy front pocket of his shoplifting sweatshirt. He was poor and he didn't know how he knew it, but he knew it in his bones. He stared at his luxury shawarma. He stared at his futuristic cat-mobile backpack. His brain said: *Yes, this is amazing, we must have it.* But, concurrently: *You can't afford that shit, dude, how you gonna pay rent?* And the thoughts felt like his own but not his, and it all felt so confusing that he almost wished the blizzard would start back up.

"I don't understand," Oliver said.

Yep, it's a doozy.

"Wait, did you just . . ." Oliver looked at the cat.

The cat blinked. *Why, yes, it is my voice you're hearing in your head. I know, Oliver, it sounds crazy.*

"Am I . . . crazy?"

Well, twenty years locked up in an insane asylum . . . I can't say that you're not crazy, but . . .

"But I was . . ." Blizzard brained. A memory void, all the frames wiped blank, except a few ink splatter snippets, a fragment of nurse with mashed potatoes on an airplane spoon, an atrophied naked man in a stall-less shower, sponge-bathed, hosed off. A catatonic.

Catatonic. Cat-a-tonic. Cat. A. Tonic. I love that. Cat a cat a cat a tonic!

"I wouldn't know, would I?"

Ding ding ding ding ding! We have a winner!

"If I'm crazy. If it's just in my head or"—he stared at the cat—"if it's you."

Murrrrrowr.

The Husband

"PEETS AND BEANS and peets and beans and peets and beans and cat fat sacks!"

The children beatboxed. The children had embarked on an ecstatic voyage to child-heaven, aka Disney World. They had brand-new portable television tablets. They had a back seat cat and plenteous snack products: powdered donuts, meat sticks, Funyuns, sour-apple candy strings.

"Chimp-kin chimp-kin chimp-kin chimp-kin chimp-kin chimp-kin chew it up!"

Americana flashed by, a rolling panorama of cornfields, barns and silos, fast food exits, outlet shopping, sprawling big box parking lots.

"It's amazing," Anne said. "So much pavement. So much plastic! How'd they do it? It's masterful."

Blaine tried, as they sped west, away from Florida, to ignore the sense that every facet of his regular suburban family life was, in truth, a fiction. The wife would not tell him why she had packed the family photo albums and winter coats for Orlando spring break, or why she refused to turn the van around so he could retrieve his phone. She proclaimed, in an excessively chipper voice, *that they could talk about it later!!!* Then she turned the radio volume up, even though the radio played mostly advertisements for basement bomb shelter renovations and invest-in-gold schemes and pharmaceuticals, and Blaine could have streamed superior commercial-free music through his phone. The wife's phone had the same streaming capabilities.

What about your phone, Blaine started to say, but the wife just turned the advertisement volume up.

Some other husband might have turned the volume off—*Damn it!* Said husband might have seized the wheel, started yelling, *We're going back for my phone! What the hell is going on?! Why are you acting so crazy?!* But Blaine had learned, at an early age, to endure household eccentricities; to revel, for example, in the sudden manic surfacing of a bedridden father who emerged from his lightless room to purchase forty-some pounds of candy bars, every candy bar in the Value Valley checkout line, *We bought those suckers out, son, ha ha ha!* The wife's eccentricities—her prodigious bacon consumption, her capacity for wakefulness, her television obsession, her fondness of disposable plastics, her productivity and general excellence—all seemed rather benign, in comparison to the Where'd Your Father Go / What Did Your Father Destroy Now? Game that Blaine had played throughout his youth. The wife's eccentricities were not only mild, but rather adorable, and flattering. She was the most remarkable creature Blaine had ever met, and she had chosen to marry him. So when the wife turned the radio volume so high as to preclude any possibility of conversation, Blaine stifled the burgeoning realization that the wife was, perhaps, even more remarkable than he had realized, and he stared out the window and thought about what attractions he wanted to visit first, when they got to Disney World.

The wife drove tirelessly. Blaine fell asleep in Indiana and woke up in Illinois. The road signs said CHAMPAIGN, SPRINGFIELD, ST. LOUIS. The wife veered off 70, onto some back country road.

"I thought we would try the back roads," she said.

Blaine did not ask why.

"Uh-huh," he said, and "Hey, pass the snack bag up here," and the kids howled.

"Don't eat the donuts, Dad!"

"Not the donuts!"

Blaine perused, with dissatisfaction. The snack bag had devolved into a bag of mostly empty wrappers.

"Hey," the wife said, "hand me a meat stick."

The children had devoured every stick of meat.

"Sorry. We can stop and stock up if—"

"No, no, we should keep going."

"Anne—"

"We just have to get . . ." Blaine looked at his wife, her creased brow, her eyes uncharacteristically forlorn. "Disney World! We just have to get a little bit closer!"

In the back seat, the children got into a sparring match over which Disney cartoon characters qualified as spectacularly awesome and which sucky-suck-suck-sucked. Avril scratched. Jas yanked out a few strands of her hair. Mr. Meow-mitts leapt into the front seat. He curled himself into a cat-ball on the wife's lap.

"You want me to move him, since you're driving?"

"No," Anne said. "He's fine. He's . . . he's a good . . ." The cat purred. Its paws kneaded her leg. "Hey, that tickles! Meow-mitts!" The car swerved. "Okay, maybe you'd better grab him."

Blaine plucked the cat from his wife's lap. The cat latched its claws into her jeans. He had to pry it loose. It was surprisingly spry, for such a hefty, lazy cat.

"Come on, mister," Blaine said. "Sheesh, has he always been this big?"

"Chonky," the children clarified.

"Himbs a hefty chonk."

"A mega-chonkster."

"Sir Chonks-a-lot."

"Mr. Meow-beans the chonka-donka."

"Senator Chimpkin Chonk."

And so forth, until Blaine tried to change the topic and the children accused him of anti-chonk bias.

"You need to respect the chonk, Dad."

"Respect it."

"You've got a lot to learn, *Dad.*"

He had a lot to learn about a lot, because the world was a stranger place than he had imagined, encapsulated inside the bubble of his mild-mannered suburban dad persona. He had understood the eminent threats—climate change, viruses, fanaticism, gun violence, cancer, et cetera—common in the news, explored in documentaries and satirical journalism, and had shielded his ordinary suburban family from these threats with the protective buffer of spaghetti dinners, ice cream treats, baseball games, bike rides, movies, camping trips, all manner of generally acceptable and pleasant family-friendly endeavors, all of which served to defuse any latent spark of doubt, that perhaps things were strange after all. That there were, as his father had once proclaimed, in Davian fashion, after a three-week light bulb–smashing smoke-detector-dismantling spree that culminated in a drunk-tank night at the county jail, Space Aliens living among us. Watching us through our own light bulbs. Recording our conversations with their fake smoke detector bugs. Blaine had not so much forgotten the incident as he had disregarded it as the ravings of a mad dad, resolving that he himself, once he assumed the role of paterfamilias, would project a steadfast dependability, replete with all standard offerings of ordinary American family life.

But then, after they had stopped driving for the day and checked into a roadside motel in the forested outlands of St. Louis, the wife casually climbed onto the sink counter and casually dismantled the smoke alarm. Then, with similar nonchalance, she unscrewed and inspected each light bulb in their motel room.

The children bounded between the motel beds. "Whatcha doin'?"

"Yeah, Mom?"

The wife had insisted on a brief screen-time respite. But also, she needed to check the television.

"I'm just checking for bugs."

"What kind of bugs?"

"Oh, you know, fire bugs! But not the good type that we get at home in the summer. These are bad ones."

"Can we check?"

"I want to squish them!"

"Why don't you two check for bed bugs!"

The children went to work. Blaine stood and watched and hoped they wouldn't find bed bugs. He had set a suitcase down on the bed, and the bugs could squirm inside, stow away, multiply, and infest everything in the van.

"Well," the wife said, "everything looks clear."

"Can we watch TV now?"

"I've never watched this TV before."

"You think it's the same as our TV at home?"

"I love TV," the children both said, at the same time. "Jinx!"

Punching ensued, but TV quelled the conflict. TV pacified the children's violent impulses. It entertained and subdued them. It taught them to expect happy endings, on Earth as it is on television. The recognition that beloved TV had prepared them for a future of unrealistic expectations didn't come until later, years after the realization that the family was not, and never had been, bound for Disney World. And even then, lives still played in episodic format, in reels of summer sitcom days, seasons binged, plotline twists, the best series always canceled too soon.

"The thing was," the wife said, outside, while inside the motel room the children stood too close to the TV, "I didn't want it to end. I don't want it to end. Not ever!" she said, in media res, before revealing the past plot points to Blaine.

He nodded because he was her husband and he understood how it felt, to not want a thing to end. "I know. But . . ."

Here, the scene should have flashed back to the start of the thing that the wife feared ending. Instead, the wife started to weep, and as she wept, she tore the wrapper from a Chocolate S'more-Campette candy bar and devoured big marshmallowy bites between her sobs and gulps, and Blaine held her in his arms and stroked her back, like the good understanding husband that he was. He didn't ask her—had never asked her—how she could eat like that and stay so thin.

She cried and finished her candy bar and cried and started another. Then, halfway through, she turned to face the motel room door, as if realizing just then how dangerous the door might be. She took several big steps back, past the minivan, into the parking lot, pulling Blaine along with her.

"What? What is it?" he asked.

"The light."

"The light."

"The light bulb. Over the door. I didn't check it. So they might be listening. I mean, it's highly unlikely, but—"

"Anne—"

"I'm not crazy."

"I never said . . ." He stared at her, his big-eyed beautiful wife. She had chocolate on her lip.

"I just wanted . . . like in . . . in one of those shows where the humans fall in love, and, and . . ."

The humans.

"Anne?"

"What if they catch me? What if they try to peel off my skin?"

"Anne—"

"Because it doesn't work like that. And I wasn't, you know, I felt bad lying all these years, but—"

"Anne—"

"But you know I love you? Right?"

"I know. But, Anne?"

"What?"

"Tell me."

* * *

Blaine grabbed a six pack of warm pony-keg apocalypse beer from the back of the minivan. He sat down beside the wife, on a strip of curb along the edge of the motel parking lot, away from the light bulbs. She chugged half a can before she spoke a word, but what did that equate, for the super wife? A mere sip. Her eyes shone with exotic curiosity and moonlight. She looked up at the stars.

"I love beer," she said. "It comes in a can! How magical is that!"

"You don't . . . where you're from . . ." He faltered. "I don't even know what to ask."

"I don't. I'm sorry. I get sidetracked. Everything here is like TV, and then there's TV, and it's all just so . . . awesomely insane. Insanely delightful. Delightfully weird. This language makes me so happy! English! I love it! I'm sorry. I'll tell you."

She took his big hand in her smaller one. "I'm not human."

EPISODE 3

The Wife

THE HUSBAND STUDIED her. She could feel his heartbeat in her palm. She knew she looked human, except sometimes she had a gleam in her eyes. He saw it, she knew, from the way he looked at her now.

"Okay . . ." he said.

"Okay?"

"Well . . . what are you?"

"I'm, well, an alien. Like, from space."

"But what, I mean, if you're not human . . ."

"Oh, right! The name is, well, it's unpronounceable. It sounds kind of like . . ." Anne made a noise that sounded like *gmlowrghatortns*.

Blaine tried to repeat it.

"No, no," Anne said. She made the noise again. Blaine tried to repeat it, but he could not even begin to pronounce it.

"I can't, um, can you say it one more time?"

"So, if you were going to try and pronounce it in English, it would probably sound something like . . . Malorts."

"Malorts. I feel like I've heard that before."

"It's the name of a really awful-tasting liquor."

"Oh, okay, that's why."

"It's so silly, right?" She laughed. "The name. My people. They take it very seriously. Or, some of them do, at least. But as a name it's really lacking. Not like 'human.' I mean, 'human' just rolls off your tongue. It's so pleasant to say. *Human*. When I first got here, I used to lie in bed at night and just say it, over and over again to myself. Human human human human human human human human."

"Human."

"Human."

"Human human human."

"Human human human. Ahhhh. Right?"

"Yeah."

"When I first got here . . ."

Anne had checked into a Marriott hotel in downtown Louisville, Kentucky. For two weeks, she watched television and ordered room service. She sampled the complimentary soap, but it wasn't delicious. She stockpiled shower caps. Shower caps! How wonderful! Plastic half-sacks contained in teensy cardboard boxes. She couldn't decipher what purpose they served, beyond existing as a repository for plastic, which, on her home world, was a highly coveted commodity, susceptible to re-formation but limited in its availability. They couldn't make more. Plastic, they said, back at home, didn't grow on trees. Except on Earth, it did! On trees, in trees, and in the ground around them! The wife pilfered a whole big cardboard box full of tiny cardboard boxes full of shower caps, and it felt like she'd struck gold, until an identical box appeared on the housekeeper's cart the next day, and she watched enough commercials to understand what Earth's currency meant. She spread all her shower caps out on the bed, beside the ice bucket plastics and the garbage bags and the single-use plastic silverware sets she had saved from her half-dozen daily room-service meals, and she rolled around in them, naked wife in her human body on a bed of luxury plastic. It felt, she explained to her husband, like gold flakes in the bathwater, or a bonfire of hundred-dollar bills.

"But what about microplastics in our water? What about the island of plastic floating out there in the ocean?" Blaine had said this to her before, and she had told him, *Gosh, Blaine, I'll try to be better! I'm sure they'll figure out how to recycle it all soon.* But they didn't, and she couldn't help herself. She continued buying salads in misleadingly non-recyclable plastic clamshells and bottled water and bulk bags of plastic novelty toys; miniature rubber duck-animal hybrids, spinner rings, kazoos, single-use glow-stick jewelry.

"I thought you—the humans—would figure it out. How to repurpose all that amazing plastic!"

"Do you know? Could you teach us?"

"Me?" She laughed. "I'm not a scientist. I have no idea how to recycle plastic."

"But your . . . your people . . ."

"My people . . . You know, you're taking this really well, Blaine."

"Did you think I would be upset?"

"I don't know. Yeah. That I'd lied. I thought about telling you. So many times I thought about it, and I wanted to, and then . . . every time I played it out in my head you were upset and shocked and I . . . I didn't want you to not love me anymore."

"Anne . . ."

"Yeah?"

He stared into her eyes. At the gleam. At her. "I could never not love you," he said, and she felt relieved, and grateful. She scooted closer, so she could touch him.

"Same. Me too. I love you more than anything. But still . . . I'm sorry for lying."

"You know, I guess . . . I guess part of me always kind of knew that you were . . . different. But that's one of the things I love about you."

She rested her head on his shoulder. "Thank you," she said.

"But . . . back to the plastics," Blaine said after a minute. "If they can all be recycled, could your people show us? They could save our planet."

"Yes. They could. If . . . if they even come back."

They had left Anne on Earth for a two-Earth-year immersive mission: live among the humans, gather data, observe. They dropped her off and flew away in their stealth ship. They had other parts of the galaxy to explore, and she had no way to reach them. They couldn't risk equipping her with a communication device. Such a device might lead to her detection, or get snatched by the wrong human hands. They left her with a spare set of clothes, a fake ID, several million dollars—

"What?"

"Several million."

"You have several million dollars."

"Well, I made some investments, so it's more than that now."

"Okay . . . okay . . . this is crazy." Blaine seemed more shocked by the revelation of millionaire wife than he had by space alien wife.

"It's just paper," she said. "Or not even paper. It's mostly digital." The money was hardly plastic.

"Okay, but . . . why have you been working?"

"What do you mean, why have I been working?"

"You work as a lawyer. You work, like, sixty hours a week when you could just retire. Why?"

"I like it."

"You like it working that much?"

"Well, why else would I do it? Isn't that why you work?"

"What? *No!* I mean, I don't dislike my job. But I don't spend eight hours taking samples and driving the city van around with Dave just because I like it. People work because they have to work."

"That's silly! No one has to do anything."

"Everyone has to pay the bills."

"I *know* that," Anne said. "But everyone could get a monthly stipend, or there could just not be bills."

"So we could just get rid of our economic system altogether."

"Of course!"

"Okay, that's just . . . I mean, no one would ever go for it. Not in America."

"Because they like it the way it is."

"Yes. No. It's . . . It is what it is. Some people like it. The ones it works for. The really rich people. They don't want it to change. A lot of them would do anything they could to make sure it doesn't and to protect what they've already got. And everyone else, all the people it doesn't work for, well, it's complicated. Some of them think they'll be billionaires someday. They think the system works for them even though it really just sucks them dry. Or they want things to change, but they're tired or busy or afraid or disillusioned, or they can't even imagine where to begin, or what a different world might look like."

"I see."

"Maybe your, um, people, maybe they've just got more imagination."

"Ha! No," Anne said. "It's more like . . . discontent. We get furious about things. Especially having to do things we don't like."

"Oh. Like cleaning."

"Yep."

"But you like work."

"Do I ever! Everything about the legal field is so weird and fascinating."

"That's great," Blaine said. "But . . . you know, I swear I remember you complaining about it."

"Sure! But I didn't mean it."

"Then why complain?"

"I thought that was just what humans liked to do."

"That we complained about work because we like complaining?"

"Exactly! I mean, why else do it?"

So, the Malorts dropped Anne off at the Marriott with her single change of clothes, her fake ID, and her millions of dollars, and Anne watched a few weeks of TV and discovered bacon, and eventually she ventured out of her hotel room. Why, she wondered, would anyone ever leave a hotel room, when they could laze in bed and watch TV and eat bacon all day, every day? She rode the elevator down to the lobby to see if she could find the answer, but instead she found the breakfast buffet. The buffet bacon lacked the delicious crispness of the room service bacon. It had a rubbery texture. She tried dipping it in maple syrup, in yogurt, coffee, orange juice. She tried bits of bacon torn and stirred with chocolate cereal spheres and milk. She observed which combinations of breakfast foods garnered strange glances from the humans at adjacent tables. She avoided combinations that invited puzzled head shakes. She refrained from sucking ketchup straight from the packet and taking shots of half-and-half and collecting the packaging afterward, her little white plastic cup prizes. She tried shots of bourbon at the hotel bar, and she overheard humans talking about horse racing. She wondered: *What is a horse? Might she be one?* The human who delivered food to her hotel room had remarked that she *ate like a horse.* The bourbon dissolved her Malortian inhibitions. She introduced herself to the chattering humans: *Hi, my name is Anne Smith from Marriott. I would like to join the horse race. Can you tell me where I can find it?* Her English back then sounded like a strange amalgam of proper British, Japanese tourist, and hillbilly twang. But she learned quickly. She learned how to identify a horse, to place a bet, to catch a cab from the hotel to the racetrack and back again. She learned how to drive a car, how to eat at a restaurant, how and where to procure the accoutrements of the American Human Female. By the time she checked out of the hotel, two months and thirteen days after she had checked in, she had learned to pack her belongings up in a suitcase, to tip the valet who brought her car up from the garage, to thank him, and to wish him a lovely day in the voice of a practiced American, with just a touch of refined Kentucky drawl.

No commitments, the Malorts had instructed. No sustained human interactions. No physical entanglements. No electronic trails. No television appearances. The Malort Earth-scouts groaned when their leadership issued the don't-be-a-TV-star edict. They all loved TV. At least half had volunteered for the Earth mission because of TV. But the humans loved TV too, and the scouts understood. No eliciting attention. No enrollment in anything. Stay alert and mobile. *Stay alert and mobile*, Anne had reminded herself as she drove from Lexington to Mobile to Tallahassee to New Orleans to El Paso to LA. She took photographs and notes, in the form of a human woman's travel journal on her new laptop. The laptop's glow reminded her of TV, so she loved it. She loved the radio. She creatively interpreted Malortian rules to conclude that yes! she could subscribe to satellite radio. Lots of human women had satellite radio. Not a lot of them listened to an endless stream of disco. Anne had disco fever. In LA she found a disco nightclub and she danced and danced, night after radiant night, until the bartender called her a "regular" and she looked up what it meant and freaked. A Malortian Earth-scout did not get to be a regular.

Her patience for Malortian rules waned. She wanted to do

what she wanted to do, which was dance at disco night clubs, and perhaps try to win a game show. She bought wigs and glasses so she could dance incognito. She bought a tiny disco ball to hang from her rearview mirror. She drove north, through San Francisco, Eugene, east to Boise, Billings, Cheyanne, Denver, Des Moines, Chicago. In a bar in Chicago she heard someone order a shot of Malorts, and she thought: *Oh no, they're early! I can't go! I'm not ready! I need more TV!* But then she saw the bottle behind the bar. She ordered a shot for herself, and its strange taste made her laugh so hard that the Malorts came out her nose.

She drank enough shots to feel wobbly in her human form, which had ceased to feel like a stiff suit that she had crammed herself in and begun to feel instead like her. Herself. Herself. She wandered the downtown streets of Chicago beneath a cold sliver moon, her jacket pulled tight around her, her pockets stuffed full with the plastic straws that she had, impulsively, pilfered from the bar. She thought: *I am Malorts. I am Malorts. I am Malorts.* She laughed and fondled the straws in her pocket and imagined the journey home, the exalted parade arrival of the plastic-bearing Earth-scouts, the pure plastic award trophy she would earn, and display on a shelf in her room on the worldship. Except that in her mind, her room looked like a Marriott hotel room, and back in her hotel room she already had a plastic trophy. *Number One Mom*, it said. She had found it at a novelty store in Cedar Rapids and bought it for herself, as a reward, for existing as the number one version of herself, whoever that was. *I am Malorts. I am Malorts.* She wandered back to her hotel room. *I am Malorts.* She turned on the TV. She sat on her hotel bed, with her Number One Mom trophy and a collection of snack foods and she calculated how many months-weeks-days she had left, in Earth time, before the Malorts came back to retrieve her.

Not enough.

From Chicago she traveled east, all around the eastern coast of America, watching TV, racking up hotel points. No commitments, the Malorts had told her. But she couldn't *not* commit to the hotel loyalty program; it rewarded her with complimentary gift totes and free water in plastic bottles and tiny chocolates on her pillow at check-in. She endeavored not to hoard the plastic bottles, but she couldn't help it. She had a trunk full of them. *I am Malorts*, she reminded herself, when she opened the trunk and gazed at her stash. She was also Malorts in the paradise aisles of the Value Valley, where everything came encased in plastic packaging. Fruits and vegetables in plastic clamshells. Cardboard boxes filled with plastic bags. Plastic toy pets sealed in plastic eggs arranged in plastic cartons with protective plastic shrink-wrap outer-layers. She bought a carton, and the clerk swiped her plastic card and tossed her unhatched pets into a plastic bag and told her to have a great day, and she squealed. *I will! It's fantastic!* Back in her hotel room, she cradled each egg in her hand, warming it until it cracked apart. She saved the broken eggshells. She arranged the infant toys in formation on her plastic-coated wood-grain hotel table. *I am not a horse*, she told them. *I am Malorts*. But she was also an aspirant Earthling, a future renegade. Her allegiance had, throughout that inaugural year of bacon breakfasts and television game shows, already begun to shift.

After two Earth years, eight-hundred-some seasons of TV, countless hours wandering Value Valleys in every state, fondling plastic products in their innumerable forms, collecting travel-sized shampoo bottles, rubber finger monsters, lip balm tubes, to-go coffee cup lids, hotel points, and Polaroid pictures of herself snapped in front of massive plastic painted groundhogs, pumas, cowboys, and dinosaurs, a Malort with a fake Kentucky driver's license identifying her as Anne Smith checked back into the Marriott in downtown Louisville. She stayed three nights. She gambled at the racetrack. She drank several bottles of bourbon and gobbled obscene quantities of bacon and watched TV until her bleary eyes burned. Then she packed her suitcase full with Earth souvenirs and drove out to the rendezvous point in the dark forests of the Red River Gorge and waited.

She waited and wept. *I am Malorts. I am Malorts.* She ate chocolate bars and played disco music on her car stereo and wept until the dark sky was tinged with pink and the stars twinkled out. She waited through the hot day. She checked and re-checked her Earth calendar. She thought about the world's largest prairie dog petting zoo, the dinosaur museum with its animatronic T. rex, the Buck-a-Bacon plastic farmyard family playscape, the endless highway miles through the flatlands, desert lands, mountain lands folding down toward the funnel-cake seashore, where bits of plastic flotsam washed up along the sandy beaches, where she felt, for the first time, like a pirate, when she realized what the word meant. A Malortian pirate with her plastic booty.

I am Malorts. I am Malorts, she reminded herself, but her heart yearned for Marriott.

She was Malorts, and dedicated to the mission of surveilling and exploring.

"To what end?" her husband asked.

Her husband had bought her a diamond engagement ring; a cheap trinket for Malorts. She had laughed and kissed him and laughed, *yes yes yes I will I will!* But later, she plunked two quarters into a toy vending machine in the Value Valley entrance, and out popped a plastic egg with a plastic ring inside.

"Because," she tried to explain. "To see. To see how it works."

"You're scientists?"

"Hmmm . . . I don't know. I mean, there are scientists among us, sure. But to say that's what we are . . ."

Malortian worldships zipped past planets a-plenty, no thanks, nothing fun there. They didn't take rock samples or send probes to the watery moons of Jupiter.

"You're explorers?" The husband tried to frame it in terms understandable to his human brain. She loved his human brain. Sometimes she wished she could cut open his head and give that brain a love-squeeze.

"Maybe? Kind of? We're attracted by shiny objects."

TV-shiny. She had entered the Earth-mission lottery and won. Her mission training required hundreds of Earth hours of television viewing, but the sitcoms she watched had aired half an Earth century ago.

She had no inkling that she wouldn't want to leave.

For an Earth month she parked at the rendezvous point every night, and through the days she hiked and snacked and brooded. She watched TV from a Red River Gorge motel room. *I am Malorts*, she told her bathroom-mirror image, but her image looked like pretty human female Anne Smith. Anne Smith found a local diner, breakfast bacon till two p.m. It didn't compare to room service. But she ate every strip of bacon as if it would be her last. She wept and waited and fantasized about Anne Smith the game show contestant, Anne Smith the reality television star. The motel had lousy cable, and she watched a lot of Court TV. She envisioned Anne Smith the judge, Anne Smith the lawyer, Anne Smith the accused.

The defendant is charged with illegal immigration, of fraud, of Being Malorts. How does the defendant plead?

Not guilty not guilty not guilty! Please, Your Honor, just give me a chance! To prove myself! To prove my loyalty! To bacon! To Marriott! To Earth and humans and this life here! Let me have a chance at this life here!

She drove to the rendezvous point and sat out all night, night after night after night. Malorts never came. Then one night, she didn't either.

She checked out of the motel and drove back to Louisville. She went home to Marriott. She cuddled in her king-sized bed with the remote control and her plastic travel-sized bottles and slept like a Malorts baby, which is to say she slept for a few hours, uninterrupted, and awoke famished.

Anne Smith ordered room-service bacon and eggs. After breakfast, she took herself out for a second breakfast of bacon and biscuits. She watched TV. She waited for a signal. Malorts had missed the rendezvous, but they knew how to find her. She had a tracking device embedded in her human arm. But then, after thirty-six double-breakfast days, she saw something curious on TV.

His name was Jack P. and he had gotten himself a slot on *Jeopardy!* She knew the moment she saw him.

Answer: "Malorts, downloaded in a human shell."

Question: "What is Jack P., really?"

She didn't know how she knew, exactly. He looked human enough. He had mastered the accent, the proper cadence, the mannerisms of a human American male from Long Beach, California. She didn't recognize him. Protocol required that Malortian observers remain ignorant of one another's whereabouts and human identities. She might have met Jack P. on the worldship, in his small, squirrely Malortian form, before he got that chiseled jaw and sun-bleached man-bun, but nothing about that Malorts looked anything like the Jack P. on the set of *Jeopardy!* Yet somehow, she knew. He was peculiarly giddy. He evanesced. He had a certain manic glint in his eye, when he said, "What is *Three's Company?*" She had seen that same glint in her own eyes, in the mirror, after binging on 1970s sitcoms. He was Malorts.

He was on TV.

He won *Jeopardy!* and got invited back. Anne Smith packed her car full of plastics and snack foods. She drove, nearly straight through, stopping only for gas and beef sticks and drive-through burgers, to Burbank, California. She waited outside the TV studio until Jack P., *Jeopardy!* victor, won again.

He came trotting out, looking tanned and spectacularly human, and then he saw her and knew. "Hey!"

The same way she knew.

"You're . . . you made it to TV!" she gushed. She felt unexpectedly starstruck.

"Malorts?"

"Malorts."

"I'm staying at the Marriott in Long Beach. Come check in. We'll go out to dinner. You can meet the others."

Three other Malorts had seen Jack P. win *Jeopardy!* on TV, drove to Burbank, and waited for him outside the studio. One Malorts watched Jack P. win from a close-up studio audience seat. They all shared the same fantasy of a human life in game shows or reality television. They had all traveled to their rendezvous points at the designated date and time. They had all waited for Malortian ships that never came.

"Any idea why?"

"Nope."

"No idea."

"Nothing."

"Did you try the meat loaf? Holy Batman, I love meat loaf."

They shared ten entrées and seventeen sides at a private room in the human steakhouse, passing dishes between them, fork-feeding bites to each other, Malortian-style.

"I don't think they're coming back."

"Obviously. You just went on TV."

"I know."

"I know!"

"Half the Malorts on Earth are probably heading to Hollywood right now."

"Or they're already here."

"Ooh, try this Hasselback potato! It's got snippets of bacon!"

They shared a love for decadent human foods, for dance clubs, for novelties, toys, illuminated devices. They debated the prudence of full immersion in the human world, in which they now found themselves abandoned.

"But Malorts will return, won't they?"

"They can't just leave us here."

"Why not?"

"They did leave us."

"We're humans now. We might as well accept that."

"Says the *Jeopardy!* champion."

"So, what, we forget the rules?"

"What rules?"

"If they come back, if they see us all on TV—"

"You realize Malorts don't have to come back to see us on TV."

"They probably saw Jack on TV already."

"But why make it worse?"

"Worse!"

"I'm going to sign up for one of those roommate shows!"

"That's a whole season! That's a terrible idea!"

"You really think you can manage to live with human roommates?"

"Without them noticing?"

"As you finish your third cut of prime rib."

"So I'll be the human female that can eat like a horse," one of the other Malorts said. Anne's human heart raced. Her mind galloped back to her first weeks in the Louisville Marriott. A horse could devour fifteen to twenty pounds of food each day. She had done her research. She had converted racetrack french fries and burgers into pounds.

"Maybe a foal," she said. "Or a pony."

"Not unregardless, the humans will notice."

"So I'll be another freak in the kingdom of freaks."

"I say go for it."

"I think it's too dangerous."

"Malorts will know."

"They could be on their way right now."

"They could all be dead."

"That's bleak."

"It's pragmatic."

"But still—"

The debate digressed to fisticuffs. Malorts slapped and pinched each other. Anne poked the other human female horse in the shoulder with her fork, not because she disapproved of her reality-TV agenda but because it felt like the right thing to do at the time. It felt like the chaos of her worldship home.

But she didn't break the human skin. Humans got testy about bloodshed. The dispute didn't require bloodshed. A few yowls and whimpers made them all feel better. They ordered all twelve desserts on the menu, plus a bottle of port, a bottle of limoncello, a round of Irish coffee.

"I'm glad Malorts didn't come back," one of them said.

"They could be dead."

"Have you tried the tiramisu? Here. Try it."

"If they're dead, there's nothing we can do."

"So what do we do?"

"What we want."

"What else?"

"I'm going to become TV."

"I'm going to ride an elephant."

"I'm going to get a cat."

"Yes!"

"A cat!"

"I'd like a whole family of cats!"

"I love cats."

"They won't let you have a cat at the Marriott."

"They won't?"

"That's shameful."

"Silly humans."

"I'm going to order more desserts."

And they did.

The Husband

BLAINE'S HEAD FELT swimmy. He looked at Anne, at her soft human skin, the curvature of her imitation human frame, the glowing orbs of her cosmic eyes. He envisioned Anne in a rocket ship, blasting away, sailing at light-speed through milky deep space, the glitter blur of asteroid belts witnessed out the spaceship windows, the plump miracle of life-sustaining planets, scattered Easter eggs of sentient life hidden throughout the vast fields of empty space. His thoughts whirled around. His wife could eat a dozen candy bars in a single sitting. This hadn't alarmed him. He had watched her tear open the value pack, had watched her shove bite after inhumanly large bite into her pretty mouth, and thought, *Oh, wow, look at her go. The wife sure can eat like a horse.*

"A foal," he said, seizing a disjointed thread from her narrative. "Or a pony."

"I had wanted to get one."

"I remember."

"You said the yard was too small."

"But have you ever eaten that much? Fifteen pounds in a day?"

"A few times," she said. "But I had watermelon . . . Blaine?"

"I'm okay."

"You don't look exactly okay. Here, have this." She fed him a bite of chocolate nougat.

"What . . . Anne, what do you look like? Really?" He loved his beautiful starry-eyed human-bodied wife, but that other body, the one sewed up inside her human form, made him anxious. That other body might have sloppy tentacles, suckers growing from its slime skin, tar-pit eyes, a lipless orifice capable of slurping down fifteen to twenty pounds of pureed horse per day.

"Right now? What you see is what you get."

"So . . . you mean, Malorts look human, or—"

"Oh no! I look human because I mostly am human. I'm . . . well, it's kind of like I got downloaded."

"Like a computer program."

"Exactly. My consciousness got downloaded into this human body. That, and some proteins and microbes, and a little bit of Malortian DNA. So, I'm mostly human. Ninety-five percent. Or maybe eighty percent. Seventy. But it's not like there's some weird squid creature living inside your wife's body, if that was what you were wondering."

"Your body . . ." He touched his wife's arm. He examined her lips, her neck, her collarbone. "Was it . . . did it belong to someone else?"

"Yes," the wife said. "She died."

"Oh."

"We didn't kill her."

"Oh. Good. I was—"

"Of course. That would be terrible! No, she died, and we found the body, and . . . well, that's how."

"You got downloaded into her dead body."

"Malorts had to sew her back up first. And fix all her broken bones, and some of her organs were, like, yuck. Crushed. She was kind of a wreck."

"But you . . . Malorts couldn't bring her back?"

"Dead is dead," Anne said. "You can fix the body, but once the mind goes . . . It's like, like if your computer gets wiped. And then dropped from the roof of a ten-story building. You might be able to bring parts of the mind back, but they'd be disjointed. There might be fragments of thoughts or memories that you could extract, but they wouldn't piece together. They wouldn't be you. Once you die you're, well, who knows! I don't know. But I know this human, Anne Smith—thank you, Anne Smith, for the gift of your body—she was dead."

"So," Blaine asked, "Malorts, in their own bodies, are they . . . What do they look like?"

"Um . . ." The wife pondered. "So you know meerkats?"

"Yes."

"Like that."

"Meerkats." Wide-eyed, sweet-snouted, adorable creatures. The children fawned and squealed about meerkats at every visit to the zoo.

"Yes. Except much bigger. And our fur is more velvety. And our snouts are longer, with bigger, sharper teeth. And our hands are a little more like human hands, except we have three of them. One on each arm, and then a third retractable one that folds up into a pouch on our bellies. That one's called the chlor."

Blaine tried to envision his wife as a woman-sized meerkat, velvet furred, razor-toothed, carnivorous, with two small meerkat pups scurrying behind her. He looked at her.

"Anne . . ."

"I'm still me, Blaine. I'm Malorts but I'm . . . I'm also human. I'm Anne. I'm the woman you married."

"I know. But . . . the kids—"

On cue, the motel room door opened. Avril and Jas ran out.

"Mom!"

"Dad!"

"Mom and Dad!"

"Where are you guys?"

"Over here!" Anne called.

"Anne—"

"The kids are fine. They're great!"

"But are they—"

"They're our kids Blaine. Ours."

"But do they know? Are they . . ."

* * *

They had plenty of beer but they needed light bulbs, cat food, fuel for two not-human human children who required horse-sized servings of salted snack foods and powdered donuts, wine and food for the wife. His wife. The horse. The three-armed giant meerkat stuffed inside the body of a dead girl. He had kissed every inch of that body. His wife. She needed cheeses, olives, highly processed meats, preferably individually packaged in plastic wrapping that she could fondle. He needed to unzip his own skin and step out of himself.

"I'll go out," he volunteered.

"You don't have to," she said, but what she meant was *please come back*.

He got into the minivan, packed with all their belongings, by a wife who told the kids *Disney World* when what she meant was *Moving Day*. He drove from the motel into the nearest town, a two-horse blip in Missouri-nowhere. He found the one shop, the only shop, about to close. He strolled the short aisles, gathering chips and sugared cereals. For the wife: boxed wine, jerky, string cheese, American cheese, all the filmy plastic a wife could dream of. He thought: *I am losing my mind I have lost my mind I am crazy.* As crazy as his father, spouting alien conspiracies, purchasing excess candy bars. *My wife! My wife! She's an alien! You know they've been here on Earth this whole time! Procreating!*

Blaine believed every word the wife had said. He believed in the wife. It all made sense, and yet, when he gazed down at the complete picture, alien-style, as if witnessing Earth from space, he couldn't believe it. He had lived with the wife all these years. He had known her better than he had ever known anyone. But he hadn't known.

* * *

He must have checked out, because then he was outside, loading groceries into the passenger seat, hands shaking, wondering how exactly he had gotten here, to this weird moment of his life, which had all gotten packed up into this minivan. He closed the door and walked around to the driver's side. Then he saw the bar across the street. The bar was called the Polynesian, wholly incongruous with the rural Midwest. The wood front door was carved with tiki faces. Neon palm trees danced in the window. It made him think of vacation. He was on vacation, but he really wasn't on vacation, and maybe he needed a moment to just step away, to clear from his mind the uncertainty, the fear that he had gotten it all wrong, not just the wife but everything. Everything might change, just like that. Peel off the skin. Find a different reality underneath.

The inside of the Polynesian was thatch and palmetto, balmy, coconut-scented, not the grounding dive-bar place he had expected. Tiny UFOs dangled over the thatched-roof booths. A miniature spaceship scene had been constructed on the far end of the bar. A model ship with blinking red-blue-green lights hovered over a tropical seaside. The tiny plastic humans on the beach raised their hands and gazed up in awe. A plastic dolphin floated in the air, halfway between the blue-glass sea and the beaming ship.

Blaine sat at the bar. He ordered a shot from a country bartender in a Hawaiian shirt. The bartender poured a shot and a mai tai in a coconut cup.

"Looks like you could use more'n just a shot," the bartender said.

Blaine tossed the shot back. His throat burned. The country music on the jukebox transitioned to Beach Boys. Blaine wanted to bury his head in sand. Or he *had* buried his head in sand. Or his neural paths had gotten all sandy and clogged and his brain didn't work right anymore. Like how it had manifested this tiki bar, this alien wife, this crazed, homeless-looking fellow who slid up to him at the bar and ordered them both another round of shots.

"This bar," the guy said. He pounded the physical bar with his dirty fist. "This bar! You know, the thing about it is, it's not really here!"

"Right, sure." Blaine nodded. He chugged back mai tai.

"I see, you don't believe me. But it's not! This bar, it's in Denver! That's where. It just *seems* like it's here in Missouri. But that's a glitch!"

"Uh-huh."

The guy babbled on about the bar that wasn't real or maybe it was real but only in some other place that maybe also, according to the guy, wasn't real. Blaine didn't get what his point was. Blaine only half listened. His mind kept dredging up old wife moments and examining them for signs of extraterrestrialism or insanity. Like the sliders from the last party they threw in their old pre-spaceship normal (seeming) life. How many had she eaten? Twelve? Fifteen? She called them *just a snack*.

"But names are irrelevant," the guy told Blaine. "They decided to name me Walter. Walter! Their intent was to turn me into a Walter-type. Obviously. But I renamed myself Mewtwo. You know? The Pokémon? But I go by Mewt for short. Anyways, I bet you're wondering, how'd Mewt confirm that it all wasn't real?"

"Uh-huh."

Blaine drank. Mewt ordered another round of shots. Mewt had a distinctly Davian vibe. Dave but dirtier, with the eccentric-meter ramped up to full insane.

"I got a job working cruise ships in the Bermuda Triangle. I wanted to get lost there. Yes! So it would, uh, uh, reveal itself!"

"Uh-huh."

"But it never did. It was nothing but a lotta shrimp cocktails. Hot damn! So then I changed strategies, and I went back out into the desert and wandered around out there until I saw the shimmer. Found myself a black hole. Pulled it open. Hopped inside. And it shot me out here! Yep! So that's how I know! What's your story, buddy? How'd you end up here?"

"My wife," Blaine said. He wanted to say it out loud. To hear it back in his own ears. To gauge whether it sounded true, and right. And Mewt could never alert the authorities, because no one would believe a word that came out of Mewt's deranged mouth. "My wife's an alien."

It sounded true. It sounded right.

"So?"

"So my wife. She's an alien."

"Hm. She look like an alien?"

"No. She's . . . She's beautiful."

"She got like, weird alien bugs inside her, that are gonna bust out and try to swallow your face?"

"No."

"So?"

"I just . . . I didn't know."

"Welp. You love her?"

"Of course. Of course I love her."

"Then there you go."

The Brother

THE CAT WANTED a motorcycle. The sturdy Spyder-style, with two wheels up front, it told him. Or a vintage Harley, teal and white with brown leather seats and a nifty sidecar.

"But cats don't talk," Oliver told it. "Cats don't ride motorcycles."

Pshaw. Where are you getting your facts, buddy? Who says we don't ride motorcycles? Is that a verifiable assertion? Sounds like fake news to me.

The cat suggested that they bid farewell to the roach motel, catch a taxi to an even grittier part of Baltimore, find a used-car lot, and purchase said motorcycle for themselves.

The sort of outfit where they won't ask to see your driver's license, the cat said. *Since, you know, you haven't got one.*

Which begged the question: Should post-catatonic, questionably sane Oliver Smith and his talking cat go cruising the highways on a vintage motorcycle without a driver's license?

I have a name, you know.

"You didn't tell me."

You didn't ask.

"Okay. Okay, what's your name?"

Bouchard.

"Bouchard? What kind of cat name is that?"

What kind of stupid human name is Oliver? Bouchard is at least more dignified. In my opinion.

Oliver had no plan, no purpose, no aspiration or destination beyond his itchy inclination that he needed to get out of here, wherever here was; that he ought to go someplace mountainous, where the pines grew tall and the blue ridges rippled as far as he could see, all the way to the edge of the earth. So he packed up his suitcase. He picked up Bouchard and set him down in the astronaut cat-pack. Bouchard hopped right out.

"I thought you said you wanted to go."

I do. But I don't like to be stuffed into the carrier like some sort of, I don't know, dog. I can climb in myself.

Bouchard circled three times around the pack, then hopped back in. Oliver zipped the pack up and strapped it onto his back. He checked out. He walked down the sidewalk until he saw a taxicab. He waved his arms and called for it to stop. He had the distinct sense that he had not ever in his life called for a taxi, but his arms waved naturally. His mouth knew what to say when he climbed into the back seat.

"Nice cat," the driver said. "Where to?"

Bouchard gave Oliver an address. The address came out of Oliver's mouth. The streets of Baltimore blurred past. The cab stopped in the city's sprawling outskirts in front of a used-car lot. Oliver paid and climbed out. He stood and blinked in the blinding midday sun. He wondered why he had come here, and whether he ought to go check himself back in to Brookwood, where they could slice open his skull and peer inside. They might find worms. Squiggly crazy worms gouging crazy holes in his brain.

Nope, Bouchard said. *I know, it'd be easier that way. If you could just throw your hands up and yell, "Wheeeee! I'm Crazy Oliver!" It'd be easier for me if I could just go home and nap all day. But I can't. That's not how this works. And you're not crazy.*

"I'm not crazy."

Not more than any other human. See?

He saw, there in the used-car lot, the teal-and-white motorcycle with the brown leather seats and sidecar.

"How . . . How did you know?"

It's magic, Oliver.

"Magic?"

No, I'm just messing with you. I walked past this place before I found you.

"So." The used-car salesman ambled over. "You looking for a motorcycle? This one's a beauty."

* * *

Half an hour later, Oliver loaded his suitcase and his cat into the sidecar of his new motorcycle and drove off.

Do you know where you're going? Bouchard asked.

They stopped at an intersection. They could turn left, right, full throttle onward. They could coast past the Buck-a-Bacon drive-through, or stop for milkshakes, or equip the hog with a sick car stereo, a subwoofer so bassy it made the asphalt quake.

"I don't know."

Turn left.

"Why?"

Let's take the freeway.

"To where? Why?"

Because that's how we get the fuck out of Baltimore, Oliver.

"Oh. Okay."

He would listen to the cat, because what the hell else did he have to do with or for himself? He veered left. He saw a sign for 695.

Take the ramp.

"Sure. Right. I'll listen to the cat."

He turned onto the ramp. He merged onto 695. He flew. The wind rushed at his skin. The sun sparkled down, catching chrome, warming his back. The verdant world unfurled around him, the trees lush with fledgling leaves, the neon grass, the smell of fresh-laid mulch, of lunchtime strip-mall carne asada, deep-fried chicken, sweet grease. The cues, here and there, that something had shifted, something seismic. That the superficial sameness of the world betrayed its transformation, the heart stir, the flutter of eyelids, the palpitation beset by quickening breath, the latent animal stretching its limbs from placid years of long slumber, awakening. There were, Oliver saw, opposing billboards and bumper stickers. The disk-shaped UFO sticker. The classic gray, inverse tear-drop head, big black eyes. Some embraced: MY OTHER CAR IS A SPACESHIP and OUR FAMILY OF ORE AND FLESH WELCOMES OUR ALIEN FRIENDS and BEAM ME UP! Others promoted isolationism: EARTH IS FOR EARTHLINGS and EARTH IS FULL: GO HOME! and NOT YOUR PLANET. But the messages felt like a different iteration of the same dispute. The NRA billboard with its gray-alien-head bullseye, GET YOURS FREE FOR TARGET PRACTICE, felt like a red herring. The real shift burbled beneath the stars-and-stripes surface. Every morning the sun rose in an empty sky, and every night it set, and the sky was still empty. But everyone knew, and the vast expanse of empty blue-black space served, always, as a reminder. We had got it all wrong. First the flat Earth. Then Earth as the center of its solar system. The primacy of man. Now this. We were not alone. And we weren't the best. We drove around our potholed freeways with these silly stickers on our cars, professing our wisdom, our certainty in something. But we didn't travel between the stars. We didn't know. Not really. And maybe we never would.

Take the exit. Interstate 70, half a mile, the sign said.

"I-70?" Oliver yelled into the wind.

You don't have to yell. I can hear inside your head.

"Where are we going?"

In the right direction. Can't you feel it?

"No. I can't. I'm …" Just a lost man. A man who lost a large chunk of his life. Which made him not so different from many.

But you are. Different. Oliver.

He took the exit, around the loop, onto I-70. He had never driven a motorcycle before, and yet its motor purr felt familiar beneath him. The freeway felt familiar, though he did not recognize it.

Because you've been here.

"I don't remember."

Except then Oliver saw a snowdrift on the road ahead. He heard the faint pulse of a disco beat. Fat flakes swirled down from the cloudless spring sky. He heard a woman's voice. *Faster, Ollie, faster faster … You ever seen flakes this big? Holy moly—*

You're drifting! Bouchard yowled. Oliver blinked. He straddled the white line. A passing car swerved and honked. Oliver swung back, into his own lane.

You were drifting. You almost got us killed.

"I'm sorry."

I'm sorry you lost her, Bouchard said. *But at least you have me now, Oliver. I'll love you.*

"What do you mean?"

I'm sorry. We'll talk later.

"Bouchard! *What do you mean?*"

The snowdrift turned silver, then black. Then it was gone. It had never been there. It was Oliver's faulty wiring. His frostbitten brain hadn't thawed out right. Everything was unfamiliar and familiar at the same time, the monotonous unreeling of a highway dreamscape. It went on for three thousand miles, which seemed like a great distance but was really just a blink. He could see all three thousand miles of it in his mind's eye, the forests and factories of Pennsylvania, the rolling farms and fields and flatlands, the point where the mountains rose up in the distance, those magnificent snowcapped peaks, the parched mesas beyond them, the green valleys, the salt flats, the desert sands. He saw himself, much younger, in a Polaroid posed in front of the world's largest prairie dog statue, more than twice his height on its hind legs, its diminutive painted arms bent, its impressionable eyes gazing up at the sky. *What's up there, buddy?* he heard himself say. *What up there? Is it aliens?* Then the frame widened, and he could see more than just his youth, and the prairie dog.

He could hear too, her voice, singing along to a song on the radio. He saw his young Polaroid self with his arm slung over her shoulder, platonic, brotherly. He saw her face, clearly now for the first time since before the blizzard, her bright eyes, a cascade of chestnut hair down her back. Her.

Jo. Jo Anne.

The Wife

ANNE STAYED OUT late while the children watched the motel TV. She could see them through the window, their faces close enough to kiss the screen.

Yeah. It's pretty. But damn. I can't see shit
Maybe you should pull over.
Pull over where?
We could just stop.

She dragged two vinyl-backed chairs from the room to the shadowed center of the parking lot, away from the mistrustful light bulbs. It was paranoid, she knew. She didn't really think the humans or Malorts would bother bugging a two-star motel in rural Missouri. But she didn't want to take any chances.

She had told her husband, and then he left. He hadn't come back. He had been gone too long, and she started to wonder. When would he come back? Would he come back?

She loved him so much.

Her human heart would burst.

Screw you. What were we really talking about?
I'm serious. Bear corpse sleeping bags.

It's not yours, she had told herself, when she stepped out of the chamber, when she stared down at the strange limbs, the dewy skin, the peculiar bulbs on her chest, the tufts of coarse fur between her legs. *It's not yours. It's borrowed.*

Hey, turn the radio up. This song—
What, you like this?

She liked the bacon-cheddar-flavored potato chips. She liked the salty residue they left on her human fingers. She liked the crinkle-sigh sound the bag made when she pulled it open. She bought every bag from the vending machine. She bought four bottles of Fizz Wizard Orange-Pizazz. She chugged one down in a single gulp.

She liked the small soft voice she heard inside her own mind. The human voice. The voice that belonged to the dead girl. She heard the girl in fragments. She saw disjointed scraps of memory, of dream. She didn't entirely understand it. She wasn't a scientist. She was a lawyer. A Malortian explorer lured to this blue-green planet by its television waves.

I love this song!
Uh-huh.
It makes me feel like . . .
Like what? Like you want to dance?

She was a wife and a mother, and she couldn't let the humans take that from her.

They had come for Jack P. during breakfast, she had heard from John, who heard it from another Malort who lived in LA. They tossed him in the back of an unmarked van and no Malorts had heard from him since. Jack P. had a kid, too. He was the first. Anne had held little Alex in her arms when he was still toothless and bald. *This*, she thought. This tiny being stared up at her with his big eyes and her heart swelled. *This is it.* That was before she knew Blaine, but she felt the same thing that first night, after she hustled him at pool and he bought her a drink and their eyes locked. *This is it.*

Inside the motel room, the children retreated from TV. They leapt in tandem from bed to bed, high-fiving each other midair. They were like everything and nothing she had imagined.

Sometimes, late at night, when Blaine slumbered, she would lie on the couch in the dark and her mind would replay the daily reel of family life and her heart felt at once impervious and fragile. A heart of titanium and steel. A heart of wind and dreams. She would slink upstairs, into her children's bedroom. She would rest her head on the pillow beside them, where she could hear the patter-patter of their hearts and bask in the soft breeze of their breath. She would marvel: what miracles, to bring them all together here.

I love this song!
Uh-huh.
It makes me feel like . . .

She had a vague recurring vision of herself in a constant phase of blooming, of herself busting out of herself, shedding the skins of her past. But always, when she passed close to her husband in the kitchen and felt that slight electric bolt between his skin and hers, when she saw the kids, huddled heads together on the floor coloring the same sheet of paper, when she caught her reflection in the mirror, she thought: *I've bloomed!*

She unscrewed the cap on her second soda bottle. She saw

the ghost of a memory of her fingers opening a bottle, holding it to her lips. The wheels slipped on the ice. The snow fell. There was a brother, and she remember how she had loved him and how broken she had felt inside about what had happened.

You ever seen flakes this big?
Nope.
Me neither. I—

Right before the car slipped, had the girl seen eyes in the dark? Maybe. Maybe two feline eyes had watched the crash from the side of the road. Maybe her own eyes had glazed the past with the tint of her present.

She saw headlights. The lights of her minivan, pulling into the motel parking lot. Blaine got out. She ran to him. She threw her human arms around him. He smelled like rum. He smelled like love.

"Blaine! You're back! I was . . . I was worried. I thought . . ."

"I would never leave you," he said. "Never. No matter what."

* * *

They placated the children with more snack foods. They fed the cat. They sat down in the vinyl chairs in the parking lot, out of the light. Anne peeled the plastic wrappers from three American cheeses and four string cheeses. She built herself a double-decker cheese sandwich.

"I didn't want to leave," she said to Blaine. "I don't want to leave. That was why . . ." She glanced down at the scar on her forearm. "I had a chip. So Malorts could find me. But when the ships showed up, I panicked. I didn't want them to make me leave. So I carved it out."

"Your arm—where I had to sew you up—"

"Yeah."

"Are they coming back?"

"Malorts? I don't know."

"You don't know."

"They didn't tell me. They were supposed to come and get me eighteen years ago. They never came. And after a while I just figured they never would."

"But you don't know why they didn't come then, or why they came back this year and then left so abruptly or if or when they're coming back—"

"I don't know anything!"

She started to cry. The sensation still felt peculiar, even after all these years; the shaking empty-chestedness, the leaking eyes, her inability to control it.

"I'm sorry," Blaine said. He wrapped his arms around her.

"It's okay. It's just, I've been so stressed-out about this whole thing. And no one knows. I mean, none of the others. I was too afraid to even contact them, but John reached out to—"

"Wait, John? Our neighbor John?"

"John. Yes—"

"Is he—"

"Malorts."

"John is Malorts."

"Yes, that's why I was, why we were spending so much time together. We were trying to figure out what was going on. Or freaking out. Okay, both."

"Does Elena know?"

"I don't know. She didn't before."

"Anne . . ."

"Yeah?"

"You could have told me."

"I know."

"I would have loved you. I love you."

"I know."

"Why didn't you?"

You could love someone, and you could also believe them, but love and belief didn't always coincide. Anne had an old friend from Jack P.'s *Jeopardy!* days, Carolyn, a Malortian geologist. Carolyn fell in love with a human. She told the human her truths. *That's crazy,* the human said, but he meant *You're crazy.* He made a psychiatric appointment and everyone suggested this pill or that pill and eventually she decided to pretend. She had suffered an acute episode of psychosis. But the delusions were all gone, thank you. She convinced the humans, but the story seeped through, rerouting her circuits, establishing itself as the dominant narrative. She began to believe it. It was one thing to keep a secret, but maintaining an outright lie required advanced mental gymnastics, and sometimes things got tangled up. Carolyn moved to Texas and stopped returning Anne's calls. Carolyn had three kids, and surely those kids believed, as Carolyn now believed, that their mother grew up Catholic in a Scotch-Irish household in Cleveland and that their mother had once experienced a brief mental breakdown having something to do with aliens and rock samples but she was all better now. She was a stable, somewhat boring middle-aged soccer mom, and the only remarkable thing about her was her metabolism, and her seemingly boundless enthusiasm for school bake sales.

"I don't know. I wanted to. Sometimes. But then I'd think about your father."

"Yeah."

"And I wasn't sure whether it would be worse if you didn't believe me and you thought I was crazy, or if you did. Because if somehow it got out, if humans really knew, what do you think they'd do, Blaine? You think they'd let us live peacefully in our little house? You think we could keep on throwing cocktail parties and sending Jas and Avril to the public school?"

"No. Obviously. But . . ."

"They've got my friend. Jack P. The feds picked him up."

"The one you said won on *Jeopardy!*?"

"Yeah. That's why we left home. John and I both thought, you know, at least it's spring break. We can make it seem like we're just going on vacation. And . . . Blaine, I'm so scared. And I feel so bad for Jack P. Who knows what they might do to him? Or what they might do to make him talk?"

The Stepchild

HEATHER INTERNET-SHOPPED FOR swimsuit cover-ups with matching beach bags. *Do something useful with yourself.* She browsed vacation rentals in Cabo. *You could at least tidy up, for when the housekeepers come.* She hoped, secretly, that her mother would blame the housekeepers. Jack P. paid the housekeepers in cash because the housekeepers did not have Social Security cards and had entered the country illegally, and if the universe had any sense of irony, it would have been them who informed Homeland Security that Jack P. was an illegal space alien.

Heather forgot to tidy up. The housekeepers came and went. Heather's mother texted: *Not thrilled about the last lawyer. I'm going to meet with another one. Did you call your brother?*

Her mother tried to peddle family togetherness like it was a miracle tonic. A dose of matching family sweaters could cure every ailment. Bodily sickness derived directly from the loneliness and isolation inherent in the absence of family game night. Jack P. likewise believed in the therapeutic primacy of weeknight croquet and boccie ball. But Alex excelled at lawn sports. Alex always won, until he matured to the point where he knew, as his father did, that he should deliberately lose. And yet despite the tacit handicap, Heather felt as if the games were rigged against her.

Heather had already suffered through one post-government-abduction emergency family call. She didn't want to call Alex again. Alex wasn't even really her brother. Alex was Jack P.'s kid. Alex adored the nautical-themed team-family hoodies that his father had specially made, which made Heather loathe them. The hoodies. The family. She pretended to have lost her hoodie at school, but *lost* implied an inadvertence that the sweater's disappearance lacked. She left it on the bleachers and never checked the lost and found. *Oops!*

Her mother texted the same message again—*Did you call your brother?*—followed by: *He's probably very upset. I know you are both upset. We need to stick together as a family and support each other.*

If her mother had been physically present, she would have added an *I don't need to remind you that, of course,* which contradicted the fact she had just reminded Heather of exactly that, and which they both knew in their hearts to be demonstrably false. Heather repeatedly slunk out of family movie night or suffered headaches that lasted the duration of the family lawn games or intentionally forgot to turn her cell phone ringer on so that she missed calls. *Oops.* The consequence of Heather's half decade of practiced avoidance was that Alex attained, in Heather's mother, the mother he never had, his own biological mother having passed away after a car crash during Alex's infancy, whereas for Heather, Jack P. remained Jack P., her mother's husband or whatever, and she didn't love him.

She texted back, eventually: *I will soon.*

Soon was amorphous enough to not occur until her mom returned home from the lawyer circuit, at which time her mom could call, and Heather could sit in the room and listen to how chummy the conversation sounded and feel bitter and relieved.

And guilty.

Did she feel guilty?

She felt something uncomfortable that she didn't want to think about. She felt an overwhelming irritation directed toward *that whole alien thing* that had disrupted the blissful idleness she had hoped to cultivate with her gap year. If only Jack P. had not permitted her to eavesdrop on his alarmingly suspicious telephone conversation with some other alien somewhere probably. The feds had traced the call, no doubt. Jack P. should have gotten himself a burner phone like a proper fugitive, instead of calling from the landline. The landline! As if it was 1990-whatever. Jack P. should not have made them all wear those silly propeller hats to his annual Fourth of July barbecue, and he should not have been so trusting.

"He trusts me," Heather's mom had said, the day that the feds carted her husband away. "If he thought he was in any trouble, he would have told me."

Jack P. had told Heather that he grew up in Connecticut playing lawn games at the country club. In the winter they played Trivial Pursuit. They played along with television *Jeopardy!* He had dreamed of that day in the spectacular future where his game show dreams came true, and then they did. Jack P. told Heather that his family had died and left him a hefty inheritance but now he had a new family to share with. Jack P. said nothing about aliens or spaceships.

"And don't you think he would have said something, if he was an alien?" Heather had said, during the emergency family call that her mother insisted on, even though she could have talked to Alex without involving Heather. "I mean, we probably would have all gotten matching family space alien T-shirts, right?"

"Maybe he was just trying to protect you," her mom replied.

Alex, who had flown back to his fancy Massachusetts school for exceptional geniuses, claimed to not have been informed of any alien heritage.

"Protect me from what? Because, I mean, he's not an alien, right? Alex? He never said anything to you?"

"No," Alex said. "I mean, Dad can be kind of silly sometimes, but an alien? No. But, Mom, do you want me to come home? I can come right now. I'll hop on the next flight if—"

"No, it's fine, Alex. It's important that you try and focus on school."

"Are you sure, because—"

"I'm sure it'll all be fine. I'm sure it's all just a big misunderstanding."

"Yeah, you're probably right. But, Mom, if you need anything, I'm here."

Heather knew she should have said something similarly supportive, but instead she said, "Well, at least they probably won't need to torture him to get information, since he likes to talk so much," which prompted accusations from her mother that she had freaked out the golden child and demands that she call said golden child to check in when she really didn't want to call him.

He was so good.

He had flowers delivered to her mother, with a card that read *Mom, we'll get through this together. Love, Alex.*

Heather contemplated the temporal distance between now and *soon*, when she had said she would call. Soon was relative. She could stretch soon out. She could throw in an *Oops, I forgot* or an *I fell asleep* or maybe both. Maybe her mother would buy it. Maybe her mother knew already: Alex was good, and she was not.

She wandered into the bedroom that her mother shared with Jack P. She searched through Jack P.'s drawers for evidence of his alienism. She found perfectly ordinary boring human things: cell phone charging blocks, socks and underwear in perfectly aligned rows, a whole dresser drawer devoted to hokey souvenir T-shirts from the places he had traveled. *Orange I Glad I Sailed Lake Orange!* What a dweeb. She moved on to his walk-in closet. His suits and shirts and sweaters hung on their own separate bars. He had bow ties in assorted colors and patterns. He collected cheap snow globes, also from vacation spots, and plastic lunch boxes with television show adhesives. Heather opened a *Fraggle Rock* lunch box, hoping that maybe good ol' Jack P. kept his stash inside it, but all she found was a stupid matching thermos.

As she returned the lunchbox to its honorary spot on Jack P.'s shelf, she saw another box behind it, an ordinary shoe box with a name scrawled in Jack P.'s handwriting across the side: *Heather.* She pulled the box off of the shelf. On the lid, Jack P. had written: *Heather— Sentimental.* She opened the box and emptied its contents onto the floor. There were her school photos from every year since the fourth grade, her colored-pencil drawings of cats and dragons, her collection of fifth- and sixth-place swim team ribbons that she had thrown out after she quit swimming, her report cards and honor roll certificates, the birthday cards she had made for him when she was just a kid, before she'd diagnosed him as terminally lame. He had kept all this junk. She opened one of the birthday cards. A cartoon family stared back at her: kid-Heather, kid-Alex, Mom, Jack P. She recognized her own juvenile handwriting. *Happy Birthday Dad! Love, Heather.*

She stuffed the keepsakes back into their box. She returned the box to the shelf. She choked back a sob. She felt indignant, but also moved, that he had cared enough to save them. She felt wretched. She had turned him in. She had thrown him to the government wolves. He wasn't an alien. Maybe he was an alien. Fuck. He didn't deserve it, whatever befell him. Whatever *befell* him.

Kudos, Heather. Way to absolve yourself of responsibility.

Well, she thought, *he shouldn't have been acting so—*

He had been wearing an old family T-shirt the other morning, when the feds came for him. The image flashed, sudden-like, in her brain: Jack P. at the stove, frying eggs in butter, dressed in his shorts and socks with sandals and his first-ever family croquet tournament T-shirt, a shirt that Heather had designed, eight years back, when she

still got excited about game night. When she still called Jack P. *Dad.*
She wondered what happened. But the inquiry was a ruse. She
knew. Alex was a good kid. So, so, so good. Kid Midas. Every school
project or family holiday gift exchange or Pictionary game he touched
turned gold. And if someone was gold, someone else got to be bronze
or rusty iron or cracked concrete. *That's great! That's a great picture,
Heather,* Alex had exclaimed, in earnest, when Heather drew the picture
that got printed onto the first-ever family croquet tournament T-shirt.
But Alex's picture was better. They both knew it. She felt it every time
she saw that stupid T-shirt. That small seed of self-loathing began
to grow, and it grew and grew until she loathed every one of them.

Especially Alex.

Except:

Alex was so so so good.

There was his portrait, taken last summer, framed, hung in the
hallway outside their bedroom, right beside her own. There was Alex,
looking friendly and relatable, and deep-deep down inside herself,
Heather hoped that maybe they would travel together over the summer,
that maybe they would find themselves tipsy teetering toward drunk
on a Thailand beach, laughing about this stupid astounding alien thing,
*Can you believe they ever thought DAD of all people was an alien? How
ridiculous!* Staring up at those same glittery stars.

She called him.

He didn't answer. She hung up without leaving a message. She
wandered into the kitchen. She poked around in the fridge. She made
herself a salad but when she sat down to eat it she didn't feel hungry.
She felt annoyed, at Jack P., who sprinkled his salads with hunks of
bacon and blue cheese and drenched them in dressing, at Alex for not
picking up his phone when she called, at her own drunken initiative
in furthering the anti-alien agenda.

She loafed through the afternoon, brain-snacking on twenty-second video clips, deepfakes, internet quizzes, pictures of white-sand Fiji resorts, anything to distract her from the omnipresent itching in the back of her mind; the mosquito-buzz of her brother's voice (*You want me to come home? I'll come right now. Mom. We're in this together as a family*); the absence of Jack P. flapping around the house, talking too loudly into his Bluetooth headset, fixing himself a banana split, frying up another pound of bacon. Anything to dilute her incongruous feelings of guilt and vindication. Anything to blunt the sensation that she had fucked it up, seriously, for real.

She called Alex again. Again he didn't answer, and then her mom came home.

"Did you call Alex?"

"He didn't answer."

"Well, how long ago did you call? Because—"

"*You* can call him. I mean, I just did, but whatever. Maybe he'd answer a call from you."

Her mother overcooked spaghetti for dinner and they sat together on the pool deck but neither of them ate. Her mother jabbered about this lawyer and that lawyer and what the lawyers said and Heather wondered how it could actually be true, the whole Jack P.-as-alien thing. She had felt convinced when she ratted him out, but now that her one drunken phone call to the authorities had provoked a real attack-of-the-feds on her annoying stepdad and his peaceful Malibu pool house, his alienism seemed entirely implausible. How could Jack P. be an alien when her mother had seen his, you know . . . It grossed her out just to think about. And he had won at *Jeopardy!* A real space-traveling alien spy would never be so bold as to appear on a game show, not to mention all the reality television shows he had produced since then.

"I mean, you would think a clandestine alien agent would want to keep a low profile, right?" she said to her mom.

"Mm-hmm."

"And, and if they were going to be so exposed, at least they'd do it for some important purpose, like to get access to classified information or something."

"Uh-huh."

"Like, I can imagine why one of them would want to run for Senate or join the CIA or become a general or something. But *Jeopardy!*? It's just, it's—"

"Yes, yes." And then her mom blathered on about due process and human rights, which Jack P. wouldn't have if Jack P. was an alien, which he couldn't be if he was a television producer and *Jeopardy!* champion, and then her mom, who hadn't listened to her, said, "Are you even listening to me, Heather?"

"Um, yeah. I'm, like, sitting right here."

"I just don't get the sense that you're really listening," Heather's mom said, but what she also meant was *Alex would listen, if he was here with us. Alex would support his mother through this tumultuous time.* "Well, I have some calls to make anyway. Can you at least please clear the table?"

"Mm-hmm."

Her mother got up. Heather sat at the table. She watched the sun set over the Pacific Ocean. She watched for that elusive green flash, but she didn't see it. The world was calm, still, dim. Dull. Yet also stunning. This sphere of gleaming water and snowcapped peaks and life, so abundant, on Earth as in the universe. She thought of something Justin had said, between A-Day rounds of *Super Smash Bros.*, while he smoked a poolside joint and sipped Jack P.'s quality bourbon, Justin her loser ex who, despite his general stoned daftness, grasped the profound. *It's like, we thought we were, like, this totally unique magnificent rose or something,* he said, *but it turns out we're only like a single rose on this whole crazy-ass bush, and maybe that bush is only one bush in a huge garden of roses. Or like a valley of roses. Roses as far as you can see, all red and pink and fuckin' glorious.* And she was like, *Whatever, Justin. Roses are overrated anyway* because he had never given her any. No one had ever given her roses. And Jack P. gave roses to her mother all the time. Still, maybe it was all red-pink-glorious. The sunset was that exactly, red-pink smoldering along the horizon, draining into the charcoal sky. LA, City of Angels, existed under that sky, and Cabo and Fiji and Thailand, and Alex's elite super-mega-genius boy school, and Jack P. and the possibly windowless cold Faraday cell-box in which the government kept him locked up and denied him of any right to a lawyer because he was, so clearly and obviously, a threat to national security.

She cleared the table, eventually, because clearing required less effort than fielding mom-complaints that she had not. She even loaded the dishes and wiped the table clean and then, as she turned to go inside, she saw the cat.

The cat looked like the same cat she had brought home from the animal shelter. It crept through the succulent garden alongside the pool deck.

"Kitty," she whispered. The cat stopped. It stared at her.

No. I'm not so sure about you.

"C'mere, kitty."

She stepped toward it.

The cat seemed to shake its head. *I don't know.*

She almost thought she could hear it speaking. But it was probably just her stupid imagination.

I really don't know about you. And don't touch me.

"Kitty."

No.

It didn't want her. Its rejection rang inside her head. It didn't want her. But that was ridiculous. It was just a dumb cat.

She took another step. The cat darted away.

Whatever.

Dumb cat.

She went inside. She dicked around on the internet. She got bored. She called Justin, but his phone went to voicemail after one ring. He saw her name on his phone screen and rejected the call. She called Alex because she was supposed to call Alex, but maybe, maybe she wanted to hear his voice.

He didn't answer.

What the heck did he have to do that made him so important and busy that he couldn't answer when she called?

She called again, immediately, but felt immediately self-conscious of her apparent desperation to chat with Mr. Spectacular. If she ever got roses from anyone, it would probably be him, and that would make roses even more terrible.

Again, he didn't answer, so she decided to internet-stalk him.

She found him.

Someone filmed what happened and they posted it and there he was. Her brother. He was walking across the campus at night toward his fancy ivy-covered dormitory building. The feds ran up. *Sir, can you please come with us?* Alex stopped and stared. His brow furrowed. He glanced behind, left, then right, for whoever it was that the feds had come looking for. *Homeland Security. Yes. You. Now. Please come with us.* He looked confused. What did they want? Did they want him? They didn't say. The agents flanked him. They led him away. Into the back of a windowless van. His head shook. His mouth hung open, aghast. He didn't understand. He was such a good boy.

The Husband

THE CHILDREN MADE forts with motel towels and bedspreads. They sack-raced down hotel hallways in four-hundred-thread-count pillowcases. They established ice machine assembly lines and carted enough ice back to the room to fill the bathtub. They fought. They fondled the television. Oh, glorious television! How the half-lings loved its cartoon animals and its ability to condense complex issues into succinct plot points. On television, stories had purpose and people existed free from any biological imperatives.

"But do they poop?" Jas asked.

"Who?"

"TV people."

"No, silly," said Avril. "Why would they need to? They're just pretend."

"But they eat. So where does the food go?"

Maybe the food was pretend, too. Holographic pizzas, apples crafted out of wax. The children drafted lists. *Things That TV People Eat that Don't make Poop. Reasons How Some TV people don't Half to Sleep.*

"But that's not how it works," Blaine tried to explain. "They're real off the TV. They're actors."

The children prepared a list on hotel stationery called *TV People Who are Really Probly Aliens But You need to Peel Their Skin Off to No For Sure.* The children were, in some capacities, brilliant. They were math wizards, speed readers, crafty, artistic, brutal little creatures. Yet some basic concepts eluded them. Like actors.

"So, you peel their skin off and that's how you know it's an actor inside?"

"No. No!" Blaine snapped. "No one is getting their skin peeled off!" Especially not the children. He would not let anything bad happen to the children. Anne wouldn't either. Anne had, years in advance of their hasty spring-break departure, in preparation for the possibility that someday some fanatic or government agent would endeavor to capture and skin-peel or Guantanamo her precious family, procured fake IDs and credit cards and opened Cayman Island accounts owned by byzantine networks of LLCs that Anne assured him could not be traced to her.

The children had more reckless ideas. They ran up the down side of the escalator. They lifted the hotel television onto the luggage cart and pushed it out through the lobby, where they were predictably caught. They pinched each other, kicked each other, poked each other with forks. They played dress-up with Mr. Meow-mitts and the cat scratched them both. They introduced themselves to hotel desk clerks using their real names.

"But if we use fake names, then we're actors."

"Yeah, Dad!"

"And actors get their skin peeled off when they're not on TV!"

"I don't want my skin peeled off!"

"And they can't poop, Dad! If I couldn't poop, I might *explode!*"

The children were, and had always been, marvelous and strange, but it was impossible to discern whether and what portion of their strangeness derived from Malortian DNA, as opposed to the usual human variety. Fully human children likewise exhibited violence and illogic. Fully human children certainly sometimes bit their siblings and refused to release teeth-grips, or sucked the peanut butter from their sandwiches and shoved the soggy mass of bread into the seat-back pocket of the brand-new minivan, or spoke in special intonations and baby-words to their travel cat companion.

"Ohhhh, himbs loves chimpkin and fishlasticks."

"What a wittle chonkster."

"Wook at himbs with his hecka screm."

"Peets and beans and peets and beans and—"

"It's Blep City over here. Dad, we're taking a trip to Blep City!"

Blep City, wherever that was, was just a diversion en route to their primary Disney destination, where the children still believed themselves to be headed, after three days driving in the wrong direction.

They drove circuitously, through Branson, Oklahoma City, Albuquerque, Santa Fe, Colorado Springs, north to Denver. They stopped at scenic overlooks and souvenir shops. The wife yielded to her Malortian hankering for plastics, apparently shared by the children, who wanted to own every cheap plastic snake, every dart gun, every plastic egg full of slime. The wife indulged, because what if her Golden Era of Plastics was drawing to a close?

The wife's direction seemed motivated predominantly by food. She saw a restaurant billboard for fried chicken and a macaroni buffet, and the minivan changed course. She drove through fast-food takeout lines for bacon burgers or stopped for milkshakes or called ahead to place a Cracker Barrel biscuit order, a dozen for the family's midmorning snack.

"But where are we really going?" Blaine asked, in the evening, after they had checked into a winterized cabin at the Blue Antler Lodge. The children were busy inside, planning events for their Winter Cat-lympics, arguing about whether Mr. Meow-mitts could pull them both in a sled, periodically taking a break to stroke the television. Blaine and Anne stepped out onto the deck, into the hot tub. Snow drifted down from the mountain sky.

"It reminds me of something," Anne said.

"What reminds you?"

"The snow. The cabin. It feels . . . I don't know. You were asking—"

"Where are we going? *Really*?" He had asked in the car, and the wife had answered *the Buck-a-Bacon drive-through*. When he asked again, the kids answered for her. *Duh, Dad. We're going to Disney World!* Never mind that Disney World was in Florida and it didn't snow in Florida and the kids had read the road signs. WELCOME TO COLORADO! The kids had studied basic geography in school. They had a Cracker Barrel map displaying restaurant locations nationwide. Somehow, things still didn't click.

"I don't know," the wife said.

"You don't know."

"I don't."

"You must have some idea. I mean, we've been driving west, basically. Is there some destination you had in mind, or—"

"No. I just . . . When we left, and I started driving I didn't really have a plan or anything. It was just like, I felt like I needed to go west. Like . . . I could hear this voice in my head saying, 'Go west, young lad,' and it just felt right."

"So should we stay?"

"What, here?"

"It's remote. No one would think to look for us up here."

"Probably not. But no. It's too . . . I don't know . . . I don't know what it is."

"So where do you want to go?"

"Honestly? If I could go anywhere . . ." Anne trailed off. She slid up to the hot tub ledge. Steam rose from her wet skin. Her eyes sparkled. She looked up at a sky brimming with stars. "If I could go anywhere, I'd go home."

"To your own planet. Your people. I—"

"No." The wife turned. She looked at him. "You're my people. You. Avril. Jas. Earth is my planet. If I could go anywhere, if it was safe, I'd go back to our home."

* * *

In the morning, Blaine awoke early to find the wife still asleep in bed beside him. He looked at her human lips, her human eyelids softly fluttering, her human hair spilled across the pillow. He thought, *No. She's human. My wife is human. She can't be an alien.* Occam's razor says she's just a human woman suffering an understandable post–A-Day psychotic episode. He would be crazy and reckless to indulge her alien story.

But then she woke up and told him she planned to take a long run up a steep mountain road.

"But what about mountain lions?" Blaine asked.

"I've traveled across the galaxy, honey," the wife assured him. "I think I can handle a little ten-mile jog on a frosty morning."

The children thought their mother should bring Mr. Meow-mitts along to protect her, but Mr. Meow-mitts had other ideas. He claimed a couch spot in a strip of sun and refused to move.

"Awww, himbs is a sweepy-sweepster."

"The fur baby just wants to stay inside and warm his chumbis."

Blaine fretted about mountain lions, slippery ice, broken ankles, no cell phone service (not to mention no cell phone), so the wife couldn't call for help. He thought that the time had come to purchase burner phones, like a modern half-space-alien fugitive family. The wife had dropped the *fugitive* word the day before but had since tried to claw it back. Their status as fugitives was unknown.

Maybe Jack P. wouldn't talk. Maybe he would forget to mention her. Maybe the government agents who had hauled Jack P. away really just wanted a Malortian game-show-winning television-producer celebrity BFF.

"I'll be fine," the wife insisted. "I can outrun a mountain lion."

Sometimes the wife—the remarkable, brilliant, foxy wife—had, despite her obvious intelligence, adaptability, and decades logged on Earth, strange ideas about things. She knew how to bake perfect croissants, and could give a lecture on corporate law in her sleep, and could describe the myriad varieties of arthropods in an adorable way that made you want to own them as pets, but she lacked a basic understanding of how fast a mountain lion might run, for example, in relation to her own velocity.

Blaine could not convince her otherwise.

While the wife ran, he took the children to the lodge for a pancake breakfast.

"Can Mr. Meow-mitts come with us for breakfast?"

"I'm pretty sure they won't allow cats in the restaurant."

"But, Dad!"

"I don't think we're even supposed to have a cat in the cabin."

"But, Dad! How would Mr. Meow-mitts ever come with us to Disney World if he couldn't sleep in the cabin on the way? I mean, he can't be expected to sleep in the car!"

The children believed, fervently, in the Disney World future, both theirs and Mr. Meow-mitts's, which was grounded in the Disney World past, as described by the wife. She had seen advertisements for it on TV, as a Malortian child. Her own children drew pictures of Mr. Meow-mitts with mouse ears, Mr. Meow-mitts on Space Mountain, Mr. Meow-mitts seat-belted between them on the Matterhorn. They asked their father, between syrupy bites of pancake, whether he would buy a child's admission ticket for the cat, or if the cat would need to pay full price.

"Because he's small," said Jas.

"Compared to a child," Avril added. "For a cat, he's a chonskter."

"Sir Chonksalot."

"The Chonkasaurus Rex."

"But he's, like, an old man in cat years."

"So could he get, like, a senior citizen discount?"

"Or both! A double discount!"

"But, Dad, is it going to be snowy like this at Disney World?"

"Yeah, Dad, because then we might get cold."

"And Mr. Meow-mitts will get cold, even with his rainbow sweater. He doesn't like the cold."

"And then if we ride any of the water rides and our clothes got wet they might freeze!"

"Kids—"

They had not told the kids anything. To protect them, the wife said, from the government, and from each other's experimental inclinations. They couldn't have one kid attempt to peel off the other kid's skin to reveal the alien inside. Blaine agreed, and yet it seemed unfair to withhold from the children the fundamental knowledge of their own selves and their destination.

"What?"

"What, Dad?"

"Well . . ."

"Hey, look!" Jas pointed out the window. "There's a cat! That lady's got a cat!"

"Look, Dad!"

"Two cats!"

"Dad!"

The window looked out upon a frozen lake, accessible from the lodge by trail. A woman traversed the trail carrying a cat in her arms. A second cat trotted alongside her.

"Can we go pet them?"

"Can we, Dad?"

The children did not wait for his reply. They both leapt up and ran for the door.

"Avril! Jas! Coats!" Blaine ran after them with coats and hats. He watched them from the window while he waited for the check. They sprinted toward the cats, coats in hand. They dropped their hats in the snow. They swooped. The cats, surprisingly, did not flee. The woman set the carried cat down beside the other, and both cats wove circles between and around the children's legs and let themselves get pet by small, syrupy fingers.

By the time Blaine paid the bill and zipped up his own coat and headed outside, the cats had gone, and the children had both punched each other, and Avril refused to give Jas his hat back because he had packed her hat full of snow.

"Dad!"

"Dad! Jas hit me!"

"Well, Avril's a big borthole!"

"And he tried to shove snow down the back of my coat!"

"But she did it first!"

They both did it again, while they yelled, *Dad! Dad!* But their protests turned quickly to whoops of excitement as they recalled the cats.

"Dad! You should have seen them!"

"They were such fine bois!"

"The short furred one had little booties so her peets wouldn't get cold!"

"She was a slonk. They were both slonks."

"One was named Piñata!"

"And the other one was called Carmen Kitty."

"And one was from Orange Country—"

"Orange County, stupid!"

"You're stupid!"

"Well, you're a poop face!"

Kick. Slap. Pinch. Ow! Ow! Dad!

"And the other one was from this place called Santa Barbie—"

"That's where we want to go after Disney World."

"And they didn't know each other before but now they're all best friends!"

"They're adventure cats."

"And they can talk!"

"They go everywhere together now."

"They're going skiing!"

"And after that they're going to take a trip to outer space!"

The Brother

OLIVER AND BOUCHARD rode their motorcycle southwest through Virginia. They crossed a bridge, and Oliver heard her voice in his mind, singing. *Oh, Shenandoah, I long to see you. Aaaawayyyy, you rolling river.* Shenandoah rolled over in his mind and he found himself taking a southbound exit, driving toward it. He heard Bouchard purring approval. Then something in his mind snapped.

A cold snap. A bitter torrent of memories blew through. He saw a road sign: SHENANDOAH NATIONAL PARK. He meant to take the exit, but then he drove past it. He drove miles past it.

Oliver, where are you going?

"I don't know."

You should turn around. Turn around and go back.

Oliver pulled over into a scenic overlook. Blue mountains rippled across the land, as far as he could see. Cotton-fluff clouds dappled the crisp spring sky. The trees were tipped with redbuds, white blossoms, fledgling greens.

Turn around, Bouchard urged.

"It's too close."

But it's special. I can feel it. Turn around.

"It's too close. It's too easy to get pulled back," Oliver said. He didn't understand why, but he felt it. He felt pulled, inexplicably, in a different direction. Bouchard hissed, vocalizing his displeasure with his irrational human. But the cat acquiesced.

Fine, Oliver. If you need to keep going. But let's be swift about things, hmm?

Oliver merged back onto the road. He drove through Staunton, Lexington, Lewisburg. He stopped overnight in Beckley. He smuggled Bouchard into his hotel room. They ate fried chicken and biscuits. They watched TV. Bouchard did not speak. The cat lapsed into lengths of feline silence, some long enough to make Oliver wonder if Bouchard was just an ordinary, albeit exceptionally amenable, cat, and his lonely post-psych-ward brain had invented the talking cat companion. Then Bouchard would say something like, *I cannot fathom why my old humans liked to mix their tuna fish flesh with that awful sour green stuff. Bleck. By the way, do you think we could get some of that fish juice soon? I love that stuff.* Or he would say, *I had a neighbor who got injured and was forced to wear a cone, like a common dog. Please, Oliver, don't ever make me wear a cone.* Or, once, *I'm so glad we found each other, Oliver. I feel as if, after all those idle years, my life at last has a purpose.*

From Beckley, they traveled west through Charleston, Huntington, into Kentucky. Oliver dropped a Shenandoah Valley postcard into the mailbox, addressed to the Transition House. *I am doing well,* he told them. *I've got a pet cat. I am starting to remember.* Oliver thought about his sister, Jo Anne Smith. Jo. They had different mothers, but Oliver didn't remember their mothers. He didn't remember where he had lived or who he had been. He remembered little Jo in jelly-shoes, darting sprinkler spray, skipping across the cracked concrete. He remembered Jo in snippets, untethered to any timeline. Jo chasing the ball across a soccer field in her Keds. Jo playing ponies while background TV blared cartoons. Jo cloaked in an oversized sweatshirt at a high-school party. Jo sipping a warm can of Natty Lite. Jo behind the closet door, refusing to come out. Black-eyed Jo. Jo with her head cracked. A white bandage wrapped around her scalp. Jo in the passenger seat of his car, while around them the world receded, supplanted by endless snow. *No one else gives a shit,* he remembered her saying, but the setting shifted. *No one but you, Ollie. You're the only person in the entire world who cares about me at all,* and he remembered thinking the same thing. Samesies. No one gave a fat flying fuck about Oliver Smith except Jo. He remembered her face when she turned up the disco music. Once he had a love and it was Jo, crunching graham crackers as she walked, leaving a trail of crumbs. He wished she had left a trail of crumbs for him to find her.

There was nothing so solid as crumbs. He had only the vaguest inclination, pulling him westward.

Bouchard rode in the sidecar, enclosed inside his cat-bubble backpack. He had tried riding with his head exposed, but the wind and speed hurt his ears. He slept from Charleston through the hills of Kentucky, but as they neared Lexington he woke suddenly.

Oliver! he exclaimed. *Oliver, I've got it!*

"Got what?" Oliver yelled into the wind.

Our destination. Take the exit.

"What, that exit?"

Oliver saw a sign ahead, EXIT 123 FOR US-60 TOWARD SALT LICK/OWINGSVILLE.

Yes, Oliver! Yes!

"I don't know. I kind of feel like I want to keep on going."

Oliver! Take it! Trust me! The cat was insistent. Its psychic howls rattled Oliver's brain. *Take it! Take it! Take it!*

"Okay. Fine. But stop yelling."

Oliver took the exit. Bouchard purred. *Take the next right.* Sure. Why not follow the path proposed by the talking cat? Oliver turned right. He followed Bouchard's instructions, through the forest, toward the gorge.

At the cat's direction, Oliver turned off the winding two-lane road into a parking lot in the Red River Gorge.

"Okay."

Okay.

He unzipped the cat's bubble pack. They both stood up and stretched.

"What now?"

What do you mean?

"You said we should come here. We're here. What now?"

This is it.

"What, this parking lot?" The parking lot had picnic benches and trail access, and not much else. "Do you want to hike?"

Not particularly.

"So why are we here?"

This is the spot. It's special.

"Why is it special?"

I don't know. Why would I know? I'm a cat, not a physicist.

"You're a freak," Oliver grumbled.

You're the one talking to a cat, buddy.

"Well, I think we should hike. If we're here we might as well."

Only if I can ride in the backpack. I don't want to get my paws muddy.

Oliver strapped on the cat-pack. He carried Bouchard up the steep trail, up and up until they reached the natural bridge rock formation at the top. From the top, he could see a landscape of green hills, pine valleys, rock cliffs. *It's pretty.* He remembered Jo's voice. *It's not Shenandoah. But it's pretty.*

"We're free, Bouchard," he said. The statement felt true, but borrowed. Bouchard didn't answer. Bouchard was asleep.

Oliver headed back down the trail. He passed other hikers on his way down. One of them, he noticed, wore a backpack just like his own, with a cat inside. A modern thing, Oliver thought, when he saw the identical cat-pack. He had missed twenty years of life.

The world had changed in those twenty years. Technology advanced. Fads dissipated and started and spread. Modern cats rode around in backpacks. Oliver did not presume them capable of speech, like his own Bouchard. He had not pressed Bouchard as to how or why their psychic link existed. Cats were skittish. He didn't press because he didn't want to scare the cat away. Jo was gone. He had no one else. No one but Bouchard. Bouchard was the only creature in the entire world, as far as Oliver knew, who cared about him at all.

"Where to now?" he asked the cat, when they got back to their motorcycle.

I'm hungry, Bouchard answered.

"Me too. Where should we go?"

Just a cat, Oliver. Just a cat. Why don't you ask those humans over there?

Oliver asked a group of hikers for recommendations. He drove a few miles down the road to a pizza place, Miguel's, in a vibrant yellow wooden building flanked by picnic tables and campsites. He ordered a beer and a pizza for himself, topped with extra chicken for Bouchard. He sat down at a bench outside to wait. He sipped his beer. He thought, *How strange, I haven't drank a beer in twenty years.* He didn't know what had compelled him to order it. It tasted bitter and wonderful and awful, and he wished he understood. He wished his sister was there to explain. He remembered her being smarter than him, and then all of a sudden she wasn't anymore. He remembered her being in the car beside him and then *it was a miracle he survived.* But what about Jo? *Sure doesn't look like a miracle to me.* Bouchard climbed out of the cat-pack. He sat on the bench beside Oliver. He cleaned his forelegs. He licked his paws to smooth the fur on his face. He turned and watched another cat, a black cat with white spots, hop out of a car, trot over to the entrance to

Miguel's, and wait outside while his human went inside to order.

"Bouchard, there's ..." Oliver watched the cat. He had a shivery sense that something strange was happening, something more than just a modern era of freewheeling cats.

What is it, Oliver?

"There's a cat."

Hmmm. Indeed. He looks nice. Not so stylish as me, though.

The cat's human exited the building. She walked to a nearby picnic table. The cat followed. She sat down. The cat hopped up onto the bench and sat beside her.

Stop staring, Oliver. It's not polite.

"Oh. Yeah." Oliver shifted his gaze. He watched the other cat from the corner of his eye.

You want me to watch it? What should I watch it for? I don't think it's going to do anything. It doesn't look very threatening.

"No, it's just ... it's strange ..."

Then someone called his name.

"Oliver?"

Oliver!

His pizza was ready. He retrieved it. He picked off the shreds of chicken and set them on a plate for Bouchard.

Ugh, yuck! Bouchard hissed at the chicken.

"What?"

You hoomans. I don't understand why you have to ruin perfectly good chimkin with this spicy red stuff. Bleck.

"Barbecue sauce? Are you talking about barbecue chicken?"

Chimkin.

"Chicken."

Chimkin. But if you want to say it wrong, that's your prerogative.

"You want me to see if they have any plain, um—"

No. I can tolerate it, I suppose. But next time ...

Bouchard choked down spicy chicken bits. Oliver devoured his pizza. He washed it down with beer. He got up to leave.

"You coming?"

Carry me. Bouchard flopped onto his back.

"Okay."

That chimkin was exhausting. I require naps.

Oliver scooped the cat up into his arms.

"Hey." He heard a man's voice behind him. "Nice ham sandwich."

"What?" Oliver turned around. He saw a long-haired man dressed in cargo pants, a striped poncho and hiking sandals.

"Nice ham sandwich," the man said, smiling.

"Huh?"

"The cat." He pointed at Bouchard.

He means me, Oliver. I'm the ham sandwich.

"Oh. Um, thanks."

"Right on, dude. Sure is crazy, right?"

"Um, yeah ..." Oliver agreed, though he had no idea what the man meant.

"I got one, too." The man's poncho squirmed. A cat head popped out, right beneath his chin. "Moritz. He followed me home. Moved himself right in. And then he starts saying shit, and dude, I thought I was having, like, a bad flashback or somethin'. But my lady, she was like, 'Maybe you should listen to Moritz. If he says to go, maybe we should go.' She's, like, she's into crystals and stuff, so it didn't seem weird to her. So here we are!"

"That's ..."

"Crazy. Dude. Aww, look at that chonk." The man scratched Bouchard's head. "What's his name?"

"Bouchard."

"What a hammy. Bouchard. And you?"

"Oliver."

"I'm Gonzago. Nice to meet you, dude. Well, I gotta go get some grub. My lady's waiting back at the cabin. We'll see you guys!"

The man went inside to order. Oliver looked over at the other cat, the black one with white spots. It nibbled meat bits from its human's pizza.

"Bouchard?" Oliver asked. "Bouchard, what's going on?"

But Bouchard didn't answer. He was one hefty ham sandwich stuffed full of chimkin. He was fast asleep.

The Stepchild

HEATHER WAS ASLEEP when her bedroom door banged open and her mother stomped in.

"Heather! Heather, wake up!"

She knows, Heather thought as the covers were torn from her bed. *She knows what I did.*

"Noooo," she groaned. "Let me sleeeeep." The blinds flew open. Sunlight blazed through. Heather pulled the pillow over her head. "It's too early."

"It's almost eleven. Jack is about to call."

"What?"

"My lawyer said he talked to someone and they said Jack could talk to us, but only for a minute, and they were going to listen of course but at least it's something so you need to wake up! So you're up when he calls!"

"Me?"

"He would want you there."

"But, Mom . . ."

"You know he would. We're a family. We're in this together. Now come on!"

Her mother snatched the pillow. She opened Heather's drawers and pulled out clothes.

"Ugh. I can dress myself, Mom."

"Then do it. Come on! Chop-chop!"

* * *

The landline rang at exactly eleven a.m. Heather's mother took the call outside on the patio, on speakerphone, subjecting Heather to effusive exclamations about how fervently Jack P. yearned for her mother, and how her mother could not wait to be in his arms again, and all their gushing made Heather feel nauseous. It was too early for parent-level verbal canoodling.

"But is Heather there? Heather are you there?" Jack P. asked.

"Yeah."

"Good. Good. Heather, I'm so glad you're there. This must all be terribly difficult and confusing."

"Uh-huh."

"I just want you to know . . . whatever happens," Jack P. said, "we're family. You're my family. And I'll love you no matter what."

Heather closed her eyes. *No matter what.* Jack P., that dweeb. The sentimental dweeb who kept a box of her childhood artwork and school photos in the back of his closet. The dweeby dad, the only dad she knew, whom she had outed.

An unexpected tear slipped from the corner of her eye.

"Heather?"

She opened her eyes. She saw a streak of fur in the bushes.

"The cat," she whispered.

"Heather, are you there?"

"I'm here. I—"

"Jack," her mom interrupted. "What's going on? Can you tell us anything? They're going to let you out of there, right? I mean, they can't have any legal basis for keeping you. You didn't do anything wrong, so—"

"Honey—"

"Jack—"

"That doesn't matter."

"Jack, no—"

"I just have a second, okay? And then they're going to make me hang up. But I have to tell Heather."

"Do you really think that's—"

"What? Tell me what?"

"Felicia," Jack P. said. "She needs to know. She needs to hear it from me."

"Hear what?" Heather asked. "Mom? What's going on?"

Heather's mom sighed. "Okay," she said. "Okay. You're right. We're all in this together."

"Heather. Honey, I know this is going to sound shocking, but that thing you heard about me, well, it's true. I'm not human."

"That's . . . no. *No!* Mom? That can't be . . . I mean, he was on *Jeopardy!* You were on *Jeopardy!*"

"Heather—"

"They must have tried to brainwash him. What have they done? Mom? Jack?"

Heather's mom shook her head. She did not look shocked. Why was she not shocked?

"Mom? Is this . . . Did you . . ."

"Heather, I'm sorry," Jack P. said. "I know this is difficult to understand. I never intended . . . I didn't think the ships would ever come back."

"The ships? Mom?" Heather felt light-headed, dizzy, like she had gotten sucked up into space except she could still see herself, a million miles down; lost, trembling, insignificant Heather.

"They were supposed to pick me up eighteen years ago and they never did," Jack P. went on. "I thought I was here for good. I just wanted . . .

I wanted your mother. I fell in love. I wanted a family. You, Alex . . . I love you all so much. You have to know that. I love you."

Heather sank down onto the floor.

"Heather?"

"Heather—"

She stared, unresponsive, at the sunlight ripples of Jack P.'s pool. His novelty taco pool float drifted on the surface, a cartoon float in a make-believe world straight out of a Jack P. reality TV special, where reality wasn't reality. Where stage lighting and dramatic plotlines made it impossible to parse the fiction from the fact. The fact. Her stepfather was an alien.

"Heather?" Jack P.'s voice sounded smaller, less certain. "Felicia?"

"She's okay," Heather's mom answered for her. "She'll be okay. We just need to work on getting you out of there. I've got a lawyer lined up, and—"

"Felicia, I'm—"

"—and she's looking into this. You have rights. You have rights as an American and . . . and Alex. Is he even—"

"I don't know."

"They haven't told you? They took him too, Jack. And I'm so worried—"

"I know. I know. Me too. And I don't know what's going to happen, but—"

"Oh, Jack . . ." Heather's mother gazed up, into the endless blue. Tears slid down her cheeks.

"I have to go."

"No, Jack, please—just, please. Come home. We'll be waiting for you, as soon as they let you come home," Heather's mom sobbed.

But she knew. They all knew. Jack P. couldn't just come home.

"I . . . Whatever happens . . . You mean more than the world to me. Both of you. More than all the worlds."

The line went dead.

A motor rumbled to a stop in front of the house. Car doors slammed shut.

"What was that?"

More vehicle sounds came from the street side of the house. But Heather didn't notice. She was suspended in a reality-fiction Jell-O salad of E.T. stepdads, faceless feds, taco pool floats, all those taco Tuesdays where Jack P. ate like ten or twenty, loaded with cheese, globs of guacamole, a half-dozen margaritas to wash them down as he exclaimed how awesome, how spectacular this tortilla-meat-topping combo was, like some genius should win the Nobel Prize for thinking it up, and all the while she knew in her heart that this dude Jack P. was weird, and yet she didn't know. Her mom knew.

"You knew."

"Heather—"

"You knew. And you didn't tell me."

"Heather . . . Yes. Yes, I knew."

"For how long?"

"For almost as long as I've known him. But . . . look, I know this is a lot, but I think there might be something happening out there that . . ."

Another vehicle pulled up in front of their house. They couldn't see it from the pool deck, but they could hear the angry voices of people who emerged.

"Look, why don't you go inside, okay? I've got to find out—"

"Fine. Whatever," Heather said. Her mom turned and walked into the house. Heather followed after her. She went into her bedroom. She flung herself facedown on her bed. She screamed into her pillow, but no sound came out, only the sorry steam of her wasted breath.

"Heather!" Her mom ran in. "Heather! We need to get out of here!"

"No. Why? I don't want to go anywhere," Heather groaned.

"It's not safe here. I'm serious."

"Ugh."

"We need to go. Heather. Listen to me. Pack a bag. Everything you can't do without. Okay? Heather? I need you to trust me."

When she hadn't trusted Heather.

For the next few minutes, as Heather's mom flitted frantically around, selecting clothes, shoving them into suitcases, Heather idled in her bedroom. Her finger scrolled absently across her phone screen. Her heart beat too fast, but her mind was a product of the television era, where things weren't safe, where government agents in tinted-window cars ferried you away, where aliens revealed themselves, and in the end none of it was real. A nefarious spaceship appeared above the city, but in the end it was defeated and everyone ate plenty of popcorn and Milk Duds and went home happy.

"Are you packing, Heather?" her mother yelled across the house, but why would Heather pack when none of this could possibly be happening? It was unfathomable, more so than the spaceship, which might have been a projection or a mass delusion or a dream. It felt dreamlike, observed from the even stranger vantage of the present. It felt like a dream that had spun out, over the cliff edge, down down down. Any minute now, she would wake.

She pinched herself, hard enough to leave a mark.

"Heather! Come on!"

She walked out of her bedroom, toward the room her mother shared with the alien Jack P. The alien impostor. She resented him, loathed him, loved him, pitied him. It was all her fault and she felt terrible. He was a fake and he deserved it. It would all blow over. Maybe it was over, forever; farewell, Malibu. She didn't know what to feel or what to think. She would tell her mother *Forget it, I'm not going anywhere* because why go if she could just change this channel to something else, a lighthearted sitcom, a stand-up special. *Aliens, folks. The thing about those aliens is, you ever try to take an alien out for dinner?* Jack P. would order two entrées, a salad, a side, a bottle of wine. He'd still have room for dessert, and Heather hated how he savored the cheesecake, how he sipped port wine between bites of chocolate cake, how he licked his fork clean of ganache. *Oh, Heather, you must try this. It's divine.* As in, heavenly. As in, it came from the heavens, like Jack P., while wretched Heather, child of Earth, would transform into a human blimp if she ate a minute fraction of the cake that her stepfather sucked down on a weekly basis. And her mother was even worse, feeding him like that, knowing what he was the whole time. No, she would not take travel recommendations from Mrs. Ganache.

But then the shock faded and she started to hear things. First, her mother sobbing. Then the motor-hum of another car outside the house. Then she pulled back the blinds and looked at the truck parked right in the middle of their front lawn. I-♥-USA bumper stickers plastered its back. Two flags fluttered above the cab: the American flag and a flag for planet Earth. Two men stood in the truck bed. One held a sign: GO HOME ALIEN. They both carried rifles.

"Mom . . ."

Heather stepped back from the window. She slumped down.

"Mom . . . Mom!"

"What is it, Heather? Because I'm trying to pack and—" Her mother stomped into the room. She looked down at Heather on the floor. "What are you doing? We need to get ready! Do not tell me you're not coming. Because that would just be, I mean, I've tried to be patient with you, but you can't always be completely selfish about everything. And this is—"

"No . . ." The tears burst. "No, it's not . . . I . . . The window . . . Out the window . . ." She pointed. She couldn't get the words out. Sobs engulf her.

Her mother walked to the window and peeked out through the blinds. "I tried to tell you," she said. "It's not safe here."

"Mom, I'm . . . so . . . suh . . . suh . . . sorry, I . . ."

Her mom crouched down beside her. She brushed the tear-damp strands of hair behind Heather's ears. She kissed Heather's forehead, softly, contemplatively, the way she had when Heather was just a girl.

"I'm sorry, too."

"No, Mom, you don't . . . I . . . I told them . . . You don't understand. It's my fault! All of this is my fault! I'm horrible! I'm a horrible person and I . . . I . . . Just leave me! Leave me here!"

"Heather, honey . . . whatever happened, we're a family. You. Me. Alex. Jack. We're in this together. I don't know what you did that makes you think you're a horrible person, but you're not a horrible person. You're just a person, trying her best to make do in a horrible world. But the world is also beautiful. I didn't used to see it that way. But I can see it now, and I have Jack to thank for that. He gets so excited about the smallest silliest things, you know? Inflatable pool floats. Commercials. String cheese. And it makes you think, gosh, maybe the world is better than I thought, if it's got things like string cheese. And I know, he's . . . Well, I understand how you could have felt . . . overshadowed. And I'm sorry for that. But whatever happened in the past, we need to put it aside. That's the only way we'll get through this. We put the past behind us, and we stick together. Can you do that for me?"

Heather choked back a sob. She nodded.

"Good," her mother said. She took Heather's hand in her own. "Come on. We can't waste any time. Those people out there . . . We need to get packed."

* * *

Outside, more trucks and cars arrived. People with signs and flags and guns gathered in the street. They yelled and chanted. *Go home! Go home! Earth is for earthlings! Go back to space, you alien freaks!*

Inside, Heather and her mother frantically packed. Heather filled one large suitcase and a duffel with clothes. She started to pile even more clothes into her last suitcase, but then she saw in her mind a sudden flash of the future, an alternate future in which she and Alex spent the summer traveling through Thailand. She didn't need to pack so much. She stopped. She dumped her clothes out onto the bed. She rolled the empty suitcase into Alex's bedroom. He had taken many of his favorite possessions to boarding school with him, but he had left behind the treasures of his childhood; the dragon books he had read a hundred times; the tiny robot he constructed in the seventh grade; his beloved stuffed rabbit, now armless and missing an ear. She packed them all in the suitcase. She filled it three-quarters full with his belongings, and then she wheeled it into Jack P.'s bedroom. She went into the closet and found the box of her notes and ribbons and pictures that Jack P. had saved, and another box beside it with Alex's name scrawled across the top. She shoved them both into the suitcase. She wheeled it out to the foyer.

"You ready, Heather?" her mom asked.

This couldn't really be happening. Her stepdad could not really be an alien. There were no armed protesters in the street. She would never be ready.

Heather nodded. Her mother sighed and wiped a stray tear from her cheek.

"Me neither. But it's time."

She opened the front door. Protesters had gathered in the street.

They trampled the yard. They chanted and waved their signs. *Go home, freaks! Get the hell off our planet! Earth is for humans! Earth is for humans! Earth is for humans!* One of the two armed men Heather had seen from the window aimed his gun toward her.

"Go home!" he yelled. "Go back to space, you alien bitch!" His eyes gleamed with vitriol.

This couldn't be happening. It didn't happen like this. Not in Malibu. Not in America.

But it did. It was.

For a moment Heather thought that nothing would ever happen again, after this. That angry man would shoot her. She would bleed out, blood and spattered brains all over the pristine grass. Then nothing. No trips to Thailand, no college, no family boccie ball tournaments, no sunset pool-deck dinners beside the glistening Pacific, no green flash, no end to this awful gap year. No redemption.

Then she felt a hand, her mother's hand, tugging her forward, toward the car.

"Yeah, you better run!" the hateful man's voice rang out, above the sea of chanting. "You better get the hell out of here, you freaks!"

Heather's mom threw their suitcases into the car. Heather stumbled toward the passenger door. She climbed in. She saw a sudden swift movement. Something hurtled toward her, into the car. *The end,* she thought. The tragic end to a story she had believed belonged to someone else. But this story was hers.

She felt a sharp sting. She cried out. She looked down, expecting blood. Instead she saw the cat, the same cat she had brought home from the shelter, that had, until now, evaded her. Its claws dug into her legs. Tears streamed down her cheeks. Her mother slammed her door shut, tucking her safe inside the car. Her mother climbed in, started the engine, backed up slowly, at first, then faster, forcing the protesters to scatter or get hit. The car turned onto the street. The cat's claws retracted. It curled itself into a cat ball on Heather's lap. It looked up at Heather and purred.

* * *

They didn't make it far. A mile down the winding hillside road, traffic stopped. They couldn't see the source of blockage around the curve. Heather's mom drummed the wheel nervously. The cat perked up. Its claws came out.

"What's going on?"

"I don't know."

"If there was some way we could—"

They couldn't. Another car rolled up behind them. The cars ahead inched forward. They turned the bend. Two black SUVs blocked the road. Half a dozen Homeland Security agents stood beside them, directing traffic. They waved a car past, then another. Heather and her mom pulled to the front of the line. An agent approached them. He signaled for Heather's mom to open the window.

"Mom—"

"Don't say anything, Heather. I'll talk."

"Mom, what is—"

"It's going to be okay," she said.

Then the Homeland Security agents swarmed.

"Mom!"

One of them opened the driver's-side door.

"You're coming with us," the agent said. He had a gruff voice and a bulletproof vest.

"I'm not," Heather's mom said. "Where's your warrant? You

want me to go anywhere, you've got to establish reasonable cause and—"

"Nope," the agent growled. "This is a matter of national security. Out of the car!"

"You can't just—"

He grabbed Heather's mom by the wrist and yanked her from the car. Heather screamed. The cat dug its front claws into her chest. Her door opened. An agent yelled.

"Out! Out of the car!"

"No, please—"

The agent loomed at her door. He had the same eyes as the armed man in her yard, cold and spiteful. Heather clung to her cat. The cat clung back, digging its claws deeper. She could feel the fast patter of its heart against her chest.

"Hey," the agent at Heather's door called. "She's got a cat. What do we do with it?"

"A cat? Just, I dunno, toss it."

The cat shivered. Heather held it tighter. It burrowed its head into her neck. She would not let it go. It had chosen her. It wanted her, and she wanted it. At that moment, she wanted the cat more than she had ever wanted anything in her life. "Please," Heather begged. "Please don't take him!"

"Come on! Get out of the car!"

"Not if you take him. I won't! I won't!" The agent reached for the cat. It hissed. "Don't take him!"

"Fuckin' cat. Fine," the man grumbled. "Fine, whatever."

He reached again, this time for Heather. He pulled her out of the car. He led her to an SUV with tinted windows and government plates, shoved her in the empty back seat, slammed the door shut. She could see her mother in the back seat of the adjacent SUV, pinned between two government agents. Heather closed her eyes. She held the cat tight.

At least I found you, she thought. *At least we have each other.*

But the thought was an echo; a voice, not her own, that resounded in Heather's mind.

The Wife

THEY TRAVELED THROUGH the Rocky Mountains, down the arid Western Slope, to where the land looked like her homeland, her planet: dry, rocky, resplendent with reds and browns, low brush, scraggly trees, broad mesas, endless sky.

Except her homeland wasn't her homeland anymore. She scarcely remembered it.

She had boarded the worldship as a youth, the Malortian equivalent of a human teenager. She had run through the holographic savannahs and scaled the holographic hills of the speckled brown-blue sphere that had gifted her life, but the holograms never looked quite real, not like they did in *Star Trek*. Her feet could feel the difference between real dirt and the worldship running wheel. The worldship breeze blew stale. She remembered her first run on Earth, in Louisville, after she had finally gleaned enough television knowledge to feel confident running outside the confines of the hotel. She remembered the stifling humidity, the terror of crossing the street, the elation when she had made it, unharmed, to the other side, the abundance of plastics—plastics embedded in vehicles, molded into stoplights, illuminated signs, plastic shaped as bottles and straws and coffee cup lids left out on the street, free for the taking. She remembered green life sprouting from the sidewalk cracks. Trees grew taller than she had ever imagined. Vines, ferns, flowers, lush grass, green everywhere she looked. Life proliferated.

How would she answer, if asked: *Where are you from, Anne Smith?*

Her body came from Pittsburgh, and after seventeen years in Pittsburgh it went west, to California, where it slipped on an icy road and sailed off the edge of a cliff. Her mind came from a distant planet in a distant galaxy, where it had formed inside the small fuzzy body of a creature resembling Earth's meerkat. But if she thought about the question, if she endeavored to pinpoint her origin, she would focus on the moment she stopped, breathless, drenched in sweat after five miles running in the sweltering Louisville heat, and crouched down to observe a dandelion flower growing out of the broken sidewalk. And another moment, not long after, when she watched a child pick a white-tufted dandelion, hold it up to her lips, and blow. She copied the child; plucked, marveled, blew, scattering the seeds. Life proliferated.

If asked, she said: *I am Anne, officially Jo Anne Smith, born in Louisville, Kentucky.*

The plateau lands of Western Colorado reminded her of her Malortian home, but there was something else, some memory she couldn't quite dredge up. Another past-life memory, elusive, like the tail of a mouse that scurried away every time she turned to chase it. She had this sense that maybe, if she moved at the right speed in the right direction, she might catch it.

Malorts were omnivorous and enjoyed hunting, with claws and teeth, for food and sport. They hunted tiny hairless rat-tailed creatures with salty flesh and delightfully crunchy bones. During Anne's first month on Earth, she had seen a baby rat and instinctually chased after it, caught it, crammed it into her human mouth. It squirmed fitfully. Its skin tasted awful, like spilled beer and rotten banana peels. She had caught it in the dumpster alley behind the Marriott. She spat it out. She stood in the alley, shaking, appalled, terrified by her own acute unfamiliarity with this foreign planet, its creatures, its customs. She was marooned. She had no one to tell her not to eat the rats or explain why. Jo Anne Smith of Louisville, Kentucky, was an orphan.

She would never let her own children eat rats, or hunt back-alley creatures on lonely urban nights after the hotel restaurant had closed, or leave them stranded. She would do everything she could to protect them, and not just because the human parenting books she had read suggested that good mothers shielded their offspring from dangers and rodents. She loved Jas and Avril in their tinfoil Faraday suits; Jas and Avril salivating over television; Jas and Avril on the carpet, foreheads touching as they colored a picture together; Jas and Avril pinching, swatting, squabbling the way Malorts did, incessantly, but without any malice; Jas and Avril fawning over their cat, because somehow, on some unconscious level, they knew that cats existed on a different frequency from the rest of Earth life.

When the first Malortian worldship approached Earth, twenty-some Earth years back, some Malorts believed that cats were the planet's dominant species. TV said humans ruled the planet, but scientific probes and scans suggested Earth belonged to cats. The furry little chonks looked finer and more intelligent to the Malortian eye than those mostly furless, gangly, puffy bipeds that strode around in funny costumes. The Malorts fought amongst themselves. There was some biting and scratching. Several Malorts assigned to planet-scouting missions refused to survey Earth, if it meant getting confined in one of those weird human skinsuits. When they backed out, Anne won the Earth lottery. She spent three Earth weeks in a cloaked scout ship, floating around the mountains in the lower atmosphere, waiting for a body. The first time she saw the body, it was horribly mangled, bloody, broken, and she felt unspeakably sad for the human who had owned it. The first time she saw herself inside the body, her own Malortian form now sealed up in cryo-stasis, she laughed.

Human bodies made her laugh, with their silly elbows and belly buttons and their exposed skins. Then she met Blaine, and she felt something else about his body entirely.

Then she met Avril and Jas, and their little bodies were tiny and perfect. She fed them from her own strange, hairless teats. They grew bigger, and she fed them cheese and eggs and bacon, to make them strong. She wanted to tell them how special they were, how amazing, how unique, how improbable; how, in all the universe, there were almost no others like them. She held them in her arms while they all watched TV together, and she thought about that first dandelion she had seen blooming out of a sidewalk crack. She thought about life, scattered across the galaxies; life, blown through space on a world-ship, from a speckled blue-brown planet to this luscious green one. And yet from here, in the Colorado plateau, the two worlds looked remarkably similar.

In the back seat of the car, the real cat slept and the children drew crayon comic strips about the lives of fictional cats. The car stopped, for gas and jerky and potato chips. They stopped to visit a dinosaur museum and archaeological excavation site. They stopped to buy souvenirs and matching family hats and milkshakes. They stopped overnight at a hotel near Salt Lake City. Anne unscrewed all the hotel room light bulbs and replaced them with bulbs from a fresh pack, just to be safe. The children caressed the hotel TV. They took its picture; TV portrait, TV family photo, TV with Mr. Meow-mitts perched on top. Anne had bought Polaroid cameras for the children so they could photograph their family trip to Disney World. Half their photos depicted Mr. Meow-mitts in his two primary states: annoyed and asleep. The other half were of TVs.

The children went swimming in the hotel pool. They ordered room service. They watched cartoons. They drew crayon pictures for their comic strip, *Trek of the Chonks*. The comic described the adventures of a cat who, not unlike Mr. Meow-mitts, took a family vacation to Disney World, except that the fictional cat and his clan traveled in a light-speed-capable flying car constructed out of television parts, and each cat got its own travel-TV so they never got bored, so they never had to torture their parents with are-we-there-yet refrains or back-seat cat fights or ceaseless off-key bottle-on-the-wall songs in assorted beverage iterations.

"They're very advanced," Avril explained, about the trekking chonks. "They built the flying car themselves because, like, they're waaaaay smarter than humans. But also they knew how to build the car because their future selves traveled back in time in the car to give them blueprints for how to build it." Avril spread all the completed comic strips across one of the two queen-sized hotel room beds.

"So it's a paradox," Blaine said. He reclined on the other hotel bed, his arm slung over Anne's shoulder. She examined the strange fur on his forearm. Even now, after years living with this forearm, its hair growth still perplexed her. But she loved it. She loved the sparse tufts of hair on his arms and chest. She loved his hands, his fingers, his stray moles and scattered sunspots. She kissed the back of his hand.

"No, Dad," Jas said.

"No! Dad, it's a flying car, not a paradox."

"It's also an ice cream machine."

"So the cats can have ice cream whenever they want. Each seat has, like, its own nozzle where the ice cream comes out and there are, like, a thousand different flavors."

"These chonks are supersmart," Jas said, waving his paw above the comic-strip cats.

"They're highly advanced," Avril added. "They're so advanced that they don't need to talk because they're always psychically linked. They just all know what the other ones are thinking."

"Like the Borg."

"Except they won't try to assymbolate you."

"Unless you're a cat, and you're a chonk. But if you were a chonk you would want to join them anyway."

"Because of the ice cream."

"Yeah," Jas agreed. "But how come Mr. Meow-mitts can't talk?"

"Yeah, Dad?" Avril asked. "How come?"

The children always posed how-come questions to their father. Anne had coached them early on to ask Dad. *Hmmm, that's curious. Why don't you ask your father?* Anne didn't know the answers to Earth questions and felt equally perplexed. She spent countless late-night hours asking Google, both the children's questions and her own. Why do we have toenails and not toe-claws? How many jelly donuts is too many? Why do humans not bring home bacon when they say they're going to bring home bacon? Are chipmunks good for eating? Is the Great Pacific Garbage Patch for sale? How do I buy it? What are hiccups? Why do humans suppress their burps? Why do they pretend that burping isn't funny? Can I kick my coworker when he is being annoying? Why do I want to watch my children when they are boring and asleep? Why am I in love?

She had felt love, in her Malortian form, but not the way she felt it for Blaine, or for their children.

Sometimes she felt like her human heart would explode inside her chest.

"Because Mr. Meow-mitts is a cat," Blaine said. The children persisted with their accusatory questions.

"Yeah, but why can't he talk?"

"Yeah, Dad?"

"Because he's a cat. Cats don't talk."

"But why?"

"Yeah, Dad, why?"

"Because that's just how it is. Their brains aren't like our brains. They don't have the right vocal cords for speaking."

"Yeah," Jas said, "but how come Mr. Meow-mitts can't talk to us tele . . . tele, um—"

"Telepathically," Avril clarified.

"Yeah. Telepathically. How come Mr. Meow-mitts can't talk like that?"

"Because," Blaine explained, "cats just can't do that."

"They can too."

"See!" Jas pointed to the comic strip as evidence. "They can."

"No, unfortunately, no one can do that," Blaine said. "Not cats. Not us. Telepathy is just, well, it's science fiction."

"But, Dad," Avril said, "those slonks we met at the last place we stayed—"

"Piñata and Carmen Kitty."

"Yeah, Piñata and Carmen Kitty, they could talk inside our heads."

"And they could hear us!"

"Yeah, Dad!"

"So how come Mr. Meow-mitts can't talk inside our heads like that?"

Anne's heart did a jolt-sputter-skip. *How come Mr. Meow-mitts can't talk inside our heads?* Her fingernails-not-claws dug, inadvertently, into her husband's arm-flesh.

"Ow!" he exclaimed.

"Sorry. I'm sorry." She rolled out from under his arm, off the bed. She stood up. She felt dizzy. The children swooped in on their father.

"Yeah, Dad. How come Mr. Meow-mitts can't talk like that?"

"Or do you think we can make him do it?"

"Yeah! How do we make him do it?"

Anne walked across the hotel room, to the balcony. Her heart thudded: *cats cats cats cats cats.* Malorts loved cats. Anne opened the door and stepped outside. She stared out across the glittered expanse of Salt Lake City. The air felt brisk. The clouded sky had a sorbet glow, softly orange from city light. Beyond the clouds, beyond the atmosphere, way out there in the deep-deep dark of space, things happened. Things were happening. She felt concurrently gleeful and terrified.

The balcony door opened. Her husband stepped out behind her. He wrapped his weirdly semi-hairy arms around her. "You okay?"

"Yes. No. I don't know. I don't know."

She didn't understand it. Not really. She knew only that she wanted to stay, here, in this human's arms.

"You want to tell me what's going on?"

"The cats . . ."

"Yeah, the kids are—"

"No, they're right, I think. About being able to hear the cats. It's just a guess, I don't know for sure but . . . I think the Malorts, the ships, I think they're coming back."

EPISODE 4

The Brother

I REALLY THINK we ought to stay here, Oliver.

Bouchard paced across the motel bed. He refused to climb into his cat-pack.

"No." Oliver shook his head. "No. There's something I need to do. I need to find her."

You won't find her.

"I might."

It's a moonshot. You told me yourself. About the crash. It's a miracle you survived. It's highly improbable that your sister survived as well.

"She might have."

Even if she did, you don't have the faintest clue where to find her.

"But . . . but . . ." He needed to do something. He fixed himself a single-serving coffee, three sugars, two packets of powdered cream. Bouchard gave himself a bath.

And even if she was alive, Bouchard said, between licks, *and you could find her, then what? She's certainly moved on with her life by now.*

"But . . . Jo would . . . You know what? I'm not going to listen to you," Oliver said. "Why would I listen to you? You're just a cat! And you won't even tell me what's going on! Why are we here, Bouchard? Why'd we come here? You obviously wanted us to come here! Why?"

Bouchard stared at Oliver. He blinked.

It's complicated, Oliver.

"So, explain it."

It's . . . I can't . . . I'm sorry. I can't.

"What do you mean, you can't?"

I just can't.

"Well, fine. I'll find someone else. You know how many cats I've seen since we came down here yesterday? Too many. There are at least three others staying at this motel right now, and they're all acting strange. If you won't tell me, then . . . then I'll find another cat or, or, or someone else who will!"

Oliver headed toward the door. He felt annoyed and confused. He had no intention of striking up a psychic conversation with some other cat. He just wanted to get outside, away from the maddening pessimism of his own cat.

Oliver, wait. Bouchard leapt down from the bed. He galloped over toward Oliver's feet. *Wait. Don't go.*

"Or what, you'll bite me?"

I can't tell you why we're here because I don't really know.

"You don't know? You knew exactly how to get here. And now you don't want us to leave, but you expect me to believe that you don't know why?"

Will you scratch my head? Bouchard nuzzled his head against Oliver's foot. *I'll tell you what I do know, but I would really like you to scratch my head.*

"Fine," Oliver sighed. He bent over and scratched Bouchard between the ears.

More, please. Sit down. I will sit in your lap.

"You're ridiculous," Oliver said, but he sat. The cat spiraled in his lap three times before he found a decent seat. He rammed his head into Oliver's hand.

What I know . . . Bouchard purred. *What I know is* . . . *it started before I found you. Something happened. It happened inside my head. It was like* . . . *how do I explain it? It was like, how one moment you're sitting peacefully in your spot by the window and then all of a sudden that confounded vacuuming device comes to life. Like that, except not terrible, like the vacuum. That was what happened, inside my head.*

Oliver nodded. He understood. Something just like that had happened inside his own head.

And then, Bouchard continued, *I felt as if I had to get out and go. I had to find a friend. I didn't know why. All I knew was that I had to go and find one. I ran and I ran, and I found many other cats, but that wasn't* . . . *it wasn't my purpose.*

Bouchard found groves of cats, woodland gatherings teeming with cats, mass cat confusion. Every cat had fled their home at the exact same moment, even the pampered indoor chonks like Bouchard. They swarmed. But as the days passed, the cats began to scatter. They wandered, or returned home. Whatever switch had flipped on inside them flipped back off.

Not for Bouchard. Bouchard felt increasingly intensely aware of himself, of the world, in a way he had never before understood it, of his purpose. He understood that he needed to find a friend. *Find a friend. Take them there. Find a friend. Take them there.* His brain replayed this directive, as if programed to repeat it. *Find a friend. Take them there.* Bouchard befriended a human woman, a child, a couple. All of them seemed nice enough. They all scratched behind his ears and under his chin. But bells rang inside his ears when they reached down to pick him up. His body recoiled; a cat spring, bouncing back.

Then Bouchard met Oliver, and it felt like late-afternoon sun through the window. Oliver warmed his belly. Oliver made him purr.

"But why me?" Oliver asked.

I don't know, Bouchard said. *I don't know. You just felt right.*

The repeating message in his brain changed, once he found his friend. *Take him there,* it said. *Take him there.* So he led Oliver here.

"But why here? How did you know to go here?"

Beats me. Why do the geese fly north in the summer? Why do the salmon swim upstream?

"And how do you know about geese and salmon?"

All this extraneous knowledge was just suddenly there, drifting around in his head. He knew that the blaring torture device of his sleepy early years had a name: vacuum cleaner. He knew about motorcycles. He had a map inside his head, with directions from there to here.

"What's here?"

I don't know. The directions end here.

"In Kentucky. In the Red River Gorge."

Yes.

"Whatever map you've got inside your head says, go there, to the Red River Gorge, and then stop."

Well, yes. It's an endpoint.

"And then what?"

I don't know.

"What would happen if we leave?"

I don't know. Maybe the map would tell me to go somewhere else. And it might be loud again. It's hard to sleep well when it's loud inside my head.

* * *

Oliver pulled open the motel room blind. He had spread pillows on the floor for Bouchard, in the spot where the sun shone through. He went outside. He paced the motel parking lot. Cats watched him from the windows. He pondered his sister. Jo. Jo Anne. The blizzard in his brain had stopped, but Jo still lay half-buried beneath the drifts. He had to dig her out.

He went back into his room.

Good, you're back. You can pet me now..

Bouchard rubbed against his leg. Oliver found the prepaid phone in his bag, and his social worker's business card.

What are you doing, Oliver?

He dialed the number.

Whatever you're doing surely does not require both your hands. Pet me.

"Brookwood Institution, this is Rachel speaking."

"Hi . . . this is Oliver Smith—"

"Oliver! Are you all right? Where are you?"

"I'm fine. I . . . I'm in Kentucky."

"Kentucky . . ." He could hear the click of her keyboard. She was taking notes. "Gosh, I am so glad to hear from you. I've been so worried! Everyone's been worried. All your friends at the Transition House, no one had any idea where you'd gone!"

"I . . . I'm sorry. I didn't mean to make anyone worry. I just wanted to travel."

"Is everything okay?"

"Yeah."

"Because you sound upset. What are you doing in Kentucky?"

Don't tell her about me, Oliver.

"I'm just . . . I've been hiking."

"That sounds pleasant. Where in Kentucky are you?"

If you tell her about me, she'll think you're crazy. But could you really please resume the petting? I'm getting itchy and impatient.

"Clearly."

"Where?"

The Red River Gorge.

"Oh, um, the Red River Gorge?"

"It's a small world. You know one of your doctors here at Brookwood, Dr. Moody, he's vacationing there right now."

Oliver remembered Dr. Moody, perplexed. *I'm just trying to understand why, Oliver. One day you were, well, catatonic . . . But now, all of a sudden . . .* Dr. Moody adorned his office walls with mountains. He dreamed of trading his urban life for a mountain cabin. *You should get out of here. If that's what you want.*

Maybe the doctor had. Maybe he had brought a cat friend with him.

"Is he vacationing, or did he quit?" Oliver asked.

"What?"

"Never mind. Look, I . . . well, the reason I called is I'm just trying to figure out what happened. Not, like, why I'm not catatonic anymore. But the accident I was in . . . it's just, I had a sister. And I'd like to find her."

"Of course. Of course. But I'm not sure how much I can help you, Oliver. We looked for next of kin before we released you to the Transition House. We always check, so that patients can be with their families, if that's what they want."

"And you didn't find anyone?" Oliver asked.

"Not that I recall. But I can pull up your records and take a look."

The social worker retrieved Oliver's records. Oliver scratched Bouchard's head. He stroked Bouchard's back. Outside the motel room window, a car pulled into the parking lot, its hatch packed full of suitcases. The car parked. A family climbed out, two moms, a girl, a boy, and a cat.

"Here it is," the social worker said, reading. "It looks like . . . well, we didn't find any living next of kin. I'm sorry, Oliver."

"What does it say, exactly?"

"Your mother passed about twelve years ago. We couldn't locate your father. And it looks like your sister is presumed deceased."

"What do you mean, 'presumed deceased'?"

"The crash you were in, Oliver, twenty years ago, they never recovered the wreckage. Your car went off a cliff. And how you managed to climb up the cliff in the snow, with your injuries . . . Honestly, it was a miracle that you survived."

All of life is a miracle, Oliver.

"But my sister—"

"There was a police report," the social worker went on, reading from Oliver's records. "That's where it says your sister is presumed deceased. Looks like the police spoke with your landlord or your employer or something? Some guy who said he'd rented a cabin to you and your sister. Anyway, I guess the police deduced somehow that she was with you during the crash."

"Oh."

"I'm sorry, Oliver. I know this wasn't what you were hoping to hear."

"No. It's just . . ." Oliver felt a sudden strange tingle up the length of his spine. Bouchard bristled. "Where was the cliff?"

"Plumas County."

"Plumas?"

"California."

"How did I end up at Brookwood?"

"It looks like . . . let's see, you were at some state institution and then there was a request to transfer you here. Because, it says, we had a specialist in catatonic conditions? This must be referring to Dr. Singh. She's retired now though."

"Who made the request?"

"The records don't say."

"But the crash was in California?"

"Yeah."

California. He remembered driving west, Jo in the passenger seat, Jo belting along to the music, shaking her shoulders to the disco beat.

"Did I have an address?"

"You did. You want it?"

Oliver wrote the address on the complimentary pad of paper on the motel room desk. He folded the paper and put it in his wallet. He started to pack.

What are you doing? Bouchard panicked. *Are you going? We can't go!*

"I have to."

You don't have to do anything. Except stay here. You have to stay here. This is where we're supposed to be!

"Didn't you say something just like that when we were in Virginia?"

No.

Maybe.

"You did. But it doesn't matter. I need to go. I need to go to California. If I can just go back to the same place, the cabin. We lived there together. . . ." He remembered waffles with maple syrup. He remembered Jo in her bathrobe, Jo gazing out the window at the glistening white world. The world was a miracle. Snow was a miracle, but it was also what you made of it. It was death and it was beauty. It beckoned beginnings, and ends. "We went there together . . . My sister . . . I loved her, Bouchard. No one else did."

No one loved either of them but them.

And me. I love you, Oliver.

"I need to go there. To California. If I'm there . . . maybe it'll come back. Maybe . . ." *I'll find her.* He did not dare to hope. "Maybe I'll be able to move on."

Okay.

"Okay?"

Of course we'll go.

"You're not going to insist that we stay here?"

Bouchard hopped down from Oliver's lap. He trotted over to his bubble cat-pack.

I feel that we should stay here. But that's not what's important, Oliver. What's important is that I'm your friend, and that we stay together. So if you really need to go, then we'll go. Of course we'll go.

The Stepchild

THEY TOOK HER to an army base. At least, Heather figured it was an army base. She and the cat had been asleep when they arrived. She still had claw-print scabs from where the cat had gripped her tight. But she didn't blame it.

Those jerks.

Her head felt swimmy and cavernous, full of echoes. Those jerks had taken her phone. They gave her a windowless room with a hard bed, itchy blankets, stiff bleach-scented sheets. There was an empty desk with a metal folding chair, a threadbare rug, a television that only had basic cable, no HBO, no Disney+, nothing to watch but boring sports and talk-show news and reality television shows; Jack P. had produced half of them. Jack P. haunted her every attempt to watch in peace, to forget, to pretend herself back to Malibu.

"Aw, princess is pouty today."

The army jerks and homeland security goons made fun of her. They delivered trays of greasy meaty food, food that only Jack P. could love. Heather picked apart her sandwiches. She fed ham and sausage to the cat. She tried to sop up the grease with her napkins, but they never gave her enough.

"Why are you keeping me here?" she asked.

"'Why are you keeping me here?'" a goon replied, in venomous singsong. "Why'd you hang out with that alien freak, huh?"

As if Heather had a choice.

The goons weren't universally cruel. Some of them tried to be nice.

One of them, a slim guy with an indivisible strip of eyebrow, delivered salad when she asked. He brought a brush for her cat.

"Why are you keeping me here?" she asked him.

"Just doing my job. Following orders."

"Yeah, but why are *they* keeping me here? I didn't do anything wrong. I was the one who called and reported my stepdad."

"Who?"

"You know, Jack P. That's why I'm here, right? Because he's an alien? I just don't understand why they're keeping me locked up. Like, what am I even going to do?"

"Are you talking about Jack P. the TV producer?"

"Yeah."

"Wasn't he, like, a *Jeopardy!* champion?"

Jack P. had deceived them all.

"That's him."

"Yeah, I know who he is. And you turned him in for being an alien?"

"Well, I mean, yeah."

"Lady," Uni-brow said, "that's a dick move. Ratting out your own family. And that guy, you know, I don't make the calls around here, but that guy, Jack P., he seems pretty cool. Even if he is an alien."

After that, Uni-brow and the other nice goons turned cold. They wouldn't chat. They delivered food and left. Heather rinsed oily dressing from mealy tomatoes and wilted lettuce. The room, at least, had a half-bathroom with toilet and sink. Heather ripped the buttered crust from her white-bread bun. She hand-fed bits of bacon to her cat. She cuddled with her cat and felt nostalgic for her *Super Smash Bros.* past, back when the biggest obstacle to a happy life was her video-gaming boyfriend, back before the whole alien show. Or at least before she had seen it.

They let her out of the room once a day, to bathe and exercise. The showers had no stalls or curtains. The towels were thin and scratchy. The cat meowed through the duration of every shower, as if the pelt of water on Heather's skin *tortured it* personally, even though it waited in the farthest corner of the locker room and didn't get wet. The cat clearly hated the locker room, but it insisted on following Heather. It followed Heather wherever she went, trailing behind her, its fat sack swinging jauntily. The goons tried to contain it, the first time they let Heather out. The cat responded with claws and teeth. They didn't bother after that.

For exercise, they let Heather wander around outside the base. The cat wandered with her. There was no view, nothing to see. Just drab barracks, scattered vehicles, brown grass, barbed-wire fencing. Once, she saw her mother, on the far distant end of the base, being led from one building into another.

"Mom!" Heather yelled. She waved. "Mom! It's me! I'm okay!"

But her mom didn't hear her, or she pretended not to.

The hours and days merged together in an endless sulky binge of reality TV reruns and nature documentaries and pseudo-news-show debates on the moral and practical repercussions of detaining suspected aliens. The US government had rounded up exactly three, according to the news, which made no mention of the suspected aliens' relatives and associates. Heather, as far as anyone knew, had ceased to exist.

"Do I?" she asked the cat. "Do I exist?"

The goons were probably recording her. They were probably watching the *Malibu Princess Breakdown Special* right now through some tiny camera hidden in the light bulb, laughing their government asses off.

The cat stared and said nothing *because it was just a dumb cat*. It perched in front of the television, blocking her view, staring at her with its judgmental eyes. At night, it stole her pillow. It played early-morning pounce and swipe games while Heather tried to sleep. If her foot moved, the cat attacked. It seemed to like to wake her up.

Just like Jack P.

Morning, sunshine! He was eternally chipper. *It's another gorgeous day here on Earth! It's the perfect day for our annual family croquet tournament!*

It wasn't. She couldn't see the sun from inside her windowless room. Still, he woke her up.

Thud thud thud. Despite the knock, the army goon didn't wait for Heather to answer and marched right in.

"You got a call, princess." He tossed the telephone onto Heather's bed.

"Who—"

He turned around and marched back out. Heather picked up the phone.

"Hello?"

"Heather!" It was Jack P. "Heather! This is Jack P.!" As if that gusto in the face of indefinite internment could belong to anyone else. "I'm so glad to hear your voice. I didn't know until this morning that Homeland Security had picked you up. I don't think one hand knows what the other hand is doing, if you know what I mean. Golly, that's a great expression! But are you doing all right, Heather?"

"All right? No! What kind of question is that? No, I'm not all right! They locked me up! These government agents took us and locked me up and they won't tell me anything and, and they won't let me see Mom and I don't understand! I didn't even know. I didn't know anything until—"

"Heather, I understand you're upset—"

"This is all just ridiculous!"

"Yes, but, you know, I think the government is doing its best, considering the situation."

"This is the government doing its *best*? *Are you serious?*"

"It's understandably all confusing, even for me, and unless we can make contact with the ships—"

"We? So, are you, like, working with the government? And you somehow didn't know I was locked up here?"

"I called as soon as I found out. And I'm not . . . Well, I'm just trying to navigate this situation as best I can, so that if the ships come back we can be prepared."

"Are they?"

"Coming back?"

"Yeah."

"I don't know."

"Well, can't you, like, reach out to them? Make some kind of deal? Get them to come back and pick you up, so . . ."

Jack P. sighed. "If I could—"

"I mean, couldn't you, like, entice them with something? Because otherwise—"

She had traded Malibu views for a windowless room. She could only see, at that moment, the walls right in front of her.

"Well, they do love television." Jack P. chuckled. After a pause, he added, "And plastics."

The Husband

WHY DID SHE think they were coming back?

Her inklings had not quite congealed into talking points. She needed a moment to think, away from the clamor of cat-obsessed children, and she also needed a bottle of wine and some crackers. Crackers, cheese, salami, olives, several packages of salty snack foods, chocolate. She gave Blaine a list. He went downstairs to the hotel bistro and wine bar. He left the wife on the balcony. He fretted about the wife on the balcony. If the children suspected that their mother was an alien, they might try to lock her out there. They might bolt the hotel room door, sequestering Blaine and his snacks in the hallway. *You can't come in, Dad. Your judgment is clearly impaired.* They would make unreasonable demands. *Maybe if you cut off your finger so we can make sure you have the right parts on the inside, maybe then we'll open the door.* The children could not be trusted.

The children were vicious inquisitors.

The moment he returned, they pounced. "But why can't Mr. Meow-mitts talk?"

"Yeah, Dad?"

"What's in the bag?"

"Is it snacks?"

"Can we have snacks?"

"Ooo, did you get salami? Thanks, Dad!"

"Hey, you have to share it! You can't take the whole salami!"

"*Maybe* I'll let you have a little piece."

"But we have to share with Mr. Meow-mitts."

"Do you like salami, Mr. Meow-mitts? Do you?"

"He's not going to answer."

"Maybe we could send him to school, and they would teach him how to talk."

"Dad, is there a school for cats?"

"Yeah, Dad, is there? And could we send Mr. Meow-mitts when we get home from Disney World?"

"And why is Mom outside on the balcony?"

All Blaine could think to say was "She's waiting. For the salami."

"Is something wrong with Mom?"

"What's wrong with Mom?"

"She's acting weird."

"Is she having a midlife crisis?"

"Did something happen?"

"What happened?"

"Nothing!" he shouted. The children excelled at needling. They effortlessly pestered their father into an explosive rage. "Nothing! Mom is fine!" he shouted again.

Jas held Mr. Meow-mitts up. His forelegs dangled. He stared up at Blaine with a disgruntled expression, as if to convey that his present state of suspension and chimkin-less-ness was entirely Blaine's fault.

"If any cat would talk, you'd think it would be Mr. Meow-mitts. He's very smart."

"Just look at himbs!"

"Maybe Mom would feel better if she could rub the chumbis."

"Yeah, Dad. She should rub the chumbis." Avril rubbed the cat's floppy belly.

"Do you think Mom is upset because Mr. Meow-mitts can't talk?"

"It's not very fair."

"Other cats get to talk."

"Maybe we could find a talking cat to teach Mr. Meow-mitts to— Ow!"

"That was my idea!"

"He just hit me!"

"She stole my idea!"

"Ow! Dad! Make him stop hitting!"

"No, *you* stop hitting!"

"Look what you did! You made Mr. Meow-mitts run under the bed where we can't get him!"

"Hey! Ow! That was your nail! No fair!"

"Kids!" Blaine bellowed. "Stop! Kids! Just stop!" He stepped between them. He held them apart so they couldn't reach each other. Their slapping arms and kicking legs continued to flail. "Stop it!"

"But, Dad!"

"Mr. Meow-mitts can't talk because he's a cat. Your mother is fine. But she won't be fine if you don't cut the crap right now. Got it?"

"But, Dad—"

"I'm going to go outside onto the balcony and join her. And you two are going to stay in here and watch TV and *not fight*! No fighting!"

He released the children. They scrambled for the remote control. Blaine abandoned the salami and half the snack foods. He headed to the balcony. He turned the TV volume up louder on his way. He glanced back at his children as he slid the door shut. They sat together on the floor, enrapt, their arms entwined, their hands holding the log of salted meat, the cat cuddled between them.

The wife stood on the balcony where he had left her. He draped a coat around her shoulders. He opened the bottle of wine and poured her a glass. She gazed up, at the stars over Salt Lake. She looked so human, and yet there was something otherworldly about her eyes.

He had always known, just as he had known of his own father's tenuous hold on reality; of the inhuman peculiarities of his two children; of the mocking fallaciousness of his partner Dave's flat-earth declarations. Dave didn't really believe, in his heart, that the earth was flat. He just thrilled at Blaine's reaction when he said it.

"You know I would love you," he said, to Anne, "even if you were, like, a giant cockroach inside your human shell instead of, like, a meerkat-type creature."

Anne laughed. She nestled her head against his shoulder.

"It's the cats," she said.

She gulped back half a glass of wine. He had always known, from the way she drank her wine like water, impervious to its ill effects. He had convinced himself that the wife's metabolism ran remarkably but not aberrantly fast. He was a master of self-delusion. No human could eat pork and cheese like Anne.

"The cats?"

"It's what makes me think that the Malorts are coming back." She devoured a hunk of Gouda. "You know I never had cheese before Earth."

"You didn't?"

"We don't have it. We have milk . . . well, things like milk. But we never figured out cheese. Isn't that wild? Cheese is one of the most spectacular things in the whole universe." She took another bite. "Anyway, the cats. When we first came to Earth—I think I mentioned this already—a faction of Malortians thought that cats were Earth's dominant species. There was a big spat about this. That's just how it works with us; we have lots of factions, lots of spats—"

"Kind of like them." Blaine nodded at the balcony door. On the other side, the salami truce had ended. Jas, on all fours, had stuck the whole salami in his mouth. Avril, standing for leverage, tried to yank it out. This was how children lost teeth.

"Exactly." The wife finished her first cheese. She poured herself a second glass of wine. "It wasn't just because cats are ubiquitous, or because they're such skilled hunters, or because they look more Malortian than humans. Cats also have unusual brains. They perceive things we can't. The way they process the world, the frequency of their brain waves, it's almost as if they're existing in some different version of the world. And those frequencies—the cat-waves—they're malleable.

"We did some experiments," the wife continued. "When we were first trying to decide how we would survey Earth. The only way to get the true human perspective is to get inside the human head, literally. But with cats, you can ping them. You can transmit a message. And they can transmit back. We didn't get very far along with the technology before our ships left. Just some simple stuff, geographically limited. Like we could make a stray cat follow a human home or an inside cat go out. Nothing that would have been useful. But if Malorts kept working on the technology . . ."

"You think when the ships were here—"

"They pinged the cats."

"That's wild."

"I know. But it fits. Think about it. As soon as the vessels appeared, the cat ran away. And Mr. Meow-mitts wasn't the only one. Our neighbors' cats. The partners at my law firm, they had cats who ran away—"

"There were Lost Cat signs up all over."

"Something affected them. And even though our cat came back, there may have been others who didn't. If Malorts sent out some sort of signal, cats who were in just the right range might be . . . It might have changed them."

"Okay," Blaine said. "That's crazy. But . . ." The whole unfurling narrative was crazy. He heard a thud as the salami smacked against the balcony door, marking the glass with a greasy smear. "I mean, the kids keep insisting that these cats they met could talk. They couldn't actually make cats talk, could they?"

"Well, not physically. At least not without surgery. But telepathically, sure."

"Really?"

The wife shrugged. "It's all just a matter of brain waves and frequencies."

Blaine looked at the wife. The wife unwrapped another wedge of cheese. She ate it like a slice of pizza. Could she read his mind? He felt exposed, but also awestruck. Was she reading his mind right now?

"Why are you looking at me like that? Oh, shoot, I'm sorry! I'm hogging all the cheese. Here, do you—"

"I'm good."

"Are you sure, because—"

"I'm still full from dinner. But, Anne . . . can you—*are* you telepathic?"

"Me? No!"

Blaine sighed.

Then the wife added, "Not in this body anyway."

She set her cheese wedge down. Her human body climbed onto Blaine's lap. He could feel the beat of her human heart, the warmth of her breath. She looked at him with her cosmic eyes. He thought about Anne when he met her—how she hustled him at pool, drank him under the table, dragged him along to disco night at the dance club. She had a remarkable wellspring of trivial knowledge, about astronomy and geography and twentieth-century sitcoms. She knew practically nothing of sex. She understood the mechanics. She had read a manual, she told him, right before her first time, and he had assumed it was a joke. But she didn't feel entirely at ease in her human skin. He loved her skin and every part of her inside it.

He didn't want Malorts to take her back.

"Assuming that Malorts sent the cats a signal," Blaine asked, "why would that mean that they're coming back?"

"If they didn't," Anne said, "what would be the point? Why signal cats but not come back to see what they do?"

"Could they have signaled the cats by accident?"

"Maybe? But I don't think so. Malorts are very deliberate. And they were working on this tech with the cats. And I don't see how the ships could just randomly send the signal out, so . . ."

"So . . ."

"It's the only thing that makes sense."

"So, if you're right, if they're coming back . . . Anne, what then?"

Anne shook her head. "I don't know."

"I don't want you to leave."

"I don't want to leave. But . . . if people knew what I was, if they knew about the kids . . . God, Blaine, I can't even bear to imagine what might happen. The kids would never be safe. None of us would. But . . . I guess if I had to go, maybe you could come with me?"

"You think they would let us?" Blaine asked. Malorts would fight about whether the wife could bring them along, Blaine assumed, from how she had described them. He envisioned the future where Malorts permitted their presence: lunching with hyperintelligent alien meerkats in the ship's cafeteria, sampling the assorted flesh from the cafeteria's all-meat buffet, the children extracted from their human child bodies and downloaded into all new furry forms more befitting their essential nature, the wife resuming her Malortian shell, himself the lone hulking human, ducking through doorways, all the space-pod beds too tiny, all the chairs too short. What it must feel like to be relentlessly obvious, exotic, uncertain. To be alien.

To feel the way the wife had felt, all this time.

"I don't know," the wife said, as he knew she would. "There wasn't a policy for what to do with a human spouse and kids. We weren't supposed to have them. We were only supposed to be on Earth for two years. But ... Malorts might be quarrelsome, but they're not cruel. If they had reason to believe that you'd be in danger if you stayed ... but maybe, if Jack P. didn't say anything about me and the government didn't pick up any other Malorts and ... You know, I'm not even going to think about that. We don't have any way of knowing who the feds got to or who talks or doesn't talk. So we have to be prepared. In case, if Malorts come back ... if we have to go with them. Blaine. Would you? If we had to, if they let you, would you come with me?"

Anne looked at him. He could see, behind her luminous eyes, a latent fear.

"When we board the ship," he said, "we'll tell the kids it's Disney World."

"Disney World!" Anne laughed. "Wonderful ... I'm so glad, Blaine, that you'd want to come with me."

"Of course I would go with you!"

"Now we just have to figure out where Malorts will land."

"What do you mean?" Blaine asked.

"It's not like *Star Trek*," the wife said. "Nobody just beams us up to the ship."

"So would we go to DC, or LA or someplace where the vessels were last time? I mean, they'd go back to the same places, right?"

"Same problem. Those vessels don't land. Obviously. They'd crush half a city if they tried to land. You need a shuttle to get up to the ship. And if Malorts send shuttles down, they probably won't send them into the cities, where there will be mobs of people trying to board the shuttles and other mobs trying to steal parts or destroy them. Malorts have seen enough TV to know better than to do that. No, if they send shuttles, they'll probably send shuttles to the vortex points."

There were places on Earth—on most planets, really, the wife explained—where electromagnetic energy amassed, or where geological attributes caused frequencies of sound and light and dreams to harmonize in peculiar ways. Vortex points, where a small alien spacecraft could land and take off undetected, where the craft would appear as a malfunctioning radar blip, for the briefest of moments, and then be forgotten—forgetful spots where time seemed to slip differently.

"In Kentucky," the wife said. "Where Malorts left me—"

"At the Marriott?"

"No, I mean, where the ship landed, in the Red River Gorge."

Malorts flew the wife's new body from California to Kentucky, where she would start her new Earth life. They gave her a drug cocktail so she would not freak out or remember the trip, on the back of a motorcycle driven by another Malort who was only sampling human form to ferry Malortian scouts from ship to hotel, who had learned to drive by watching it happen on TV, who had no idea where to go or what the road signs meant, or chose to disregard them, the speed limit sign in particular.

"It'll take us days to drive back there," Blaine said. "What if the ships come before then? Are there any closer vortex points?"

"Probably. I don't really know where they all are though."

"You don't?"

"Well, there's one near Sedona, in Arizona. But everyone knows about that one. I even saw it on TV. There were a bunch of humans camped out there, waiting for the ships to come back."

"Shoot."

"There is one more I know," the wife said. "And it's closer than Kentucky. It's in California, in the mountains. The place where Malorts found my body."

The Brother

OLIVER DROVE WEST. His memories unfurled across the miles and years. *Go west, young lad. Like, you know, the mouse. Fievel.* Except he wasn't young anymore. He wasn't high on hope and skunk weed. He wouldn't save her. Maybe destiny had manifested as a patch of ice on the road. Maybe it blustered in, all blizzard-like, demanding sacrifices. *That one*, Destiny had said, pointing its icy finger at Jo.

Oliver drove through Nashville, Memphis, Amarillo, Albuquerque. He took the southern route to avoid the mountain snow. He drove past cities where humans carried on with their lives and tried to ignore the hasty arrival and departure of alien life, the rippling changes wrought by uncertainty. The uncertainty. Life had always been uncertain; its nature was just more evident now. He drove past faded flyers for missing cats, past roadside stands selling home-planet pride-wear, Earth flags, novelty spaceship piñatas, spaceships stuffed with fireworks that would explode in a jingoistic fountain of crackling fire. He drove past militia marches, E.T. parties, newly opened offices of business entities with names like StarTrust LLC and Space Tours Inc. formed to establish intergalactic contacts, information exchanges, IP trades, immersive tourist experiences. He drove past billboard offers of redemption:

THE HEALING SAVING MIRACLE POWER OF OUR LORD AND SAVIOR, OUR INNER, IMMORTAL, SPIRITUAL SELF.

OUR FAMILY OF ORE AND FLESH, YOUR CHOICE FOR BELONGING AND PURPOSE!

SALVATION FOR THE FAITHFUL, WHEN *THEY* RETURN TO SMITE THE REST . . .

LOW MONTHLY PAYMENTS OF $49.95 TO SECURE YOUR ONE-WAY TICKET ON THE SPACE-TRAIN TO HEAVEN . . .

A reasonable fee, for the Truth.

The Truth was that most everyone had no idea—not the vaguest inkling—as to why alien life had come and gone, or whether or when it would return, or what it all meant. This mass confusion was, from Oliver's perspective, equalizing. His role—as the catatonic, amnesiac, invalid—had shifted; he knew as much as anyone, save those few privy to the secrets of government. He knew that the billboards made false promises. One could not ride out the coming invasion in a twelve-by-twelve underground bunker for the bargain price of $2,999, no money down, zero percent financing. One could not purchase answers. Answers came when they damn well wanted to come, which was sometimes not at all. Answers were, in that respect, like cats.

The cat, Bouchard, slept in his cat-pack in his motorcycle sidecar, tucked down low, where the world felt as safe and windless and dark as a traveling cat could hope. Sometimes Bouchard startled awake, like a cat-switch flipped suddenly on. *Take the exit, Oliver! Take it!* he would yowl, insistently, in his most grating telepathic voice. His cat map had its own programmed agenda. Oliver ignored it. He kept on driving west, even when Bouchard hissed and scratched at his pack and called Oliver a dim-witted human.

But I didn't mean it, Oliver, Bouchard told him later. *It was just that I felt a very strong need—a pull, Oliver, like something was pulling me—to go in one direction and you drove us in the other direction, and it made me very irritable and itchy. It was quite intolerable. It would be so much better if I could just sleep straight through this drive!*

In Albuquerque, Oliver brought Bouchard to a drop-in veterinary clinic.

"He's taking a road trip," Oliver told the veterinarian. "But he's not enjoying himself. Can you give him a tranquilizer?"

The vet prescribed a feline sleeping pill. Oliver had to shove the pill down Bouchard's throat. Bouchard's claws came out, reflexively. They got stuck in the sleeve of Oliver's jacket.

I'm sorry Oliver, I'm not trying to be difficult. I just can't swallow pills. It's a reflex.

Oliver pried the cat loose and tucked him into his pack.

"It's okay. I hope you can sleep now. Good night, Bouchard."

Good night, Oliver.

Bouchard slept peacefully for about three hundred miles, but as the motorcycle neared Flagstaff he began to whimper and thrash. He spoke in his sleep. Oliver heard the cat's disjointed whispers inside his head. The cat spoke of vortexes and portals and the spot in the desert where they *had to go, they had to, Oliver, or we'll get left behind and we can't be left behind. Oliver. The spot. The vortex. Our destiny, Oliver. Our destiny.*

"What did you mean—our destiny?" Oliver asked Bouchard afterward, in a hotel room on the flashing outskirts of Las Vegas.

Destiny? I don't know.

"You said it when we were driving. You were dreaming. You said we had to go. That it was our destiny."

I honestly don't recall that. All I know is that I had the absolute worst dream ever. It was horrendous. You might want to give me two of those pills next time, Oliver.

"What was the dream about?"

It was just awful, Oliver. I was strapped down on some kind of table, and I couldn't move at all. My paws didn't work. And I was all alone, Oliver. I . . . I felt as if the only one I had ever loved was gone.

Bouchard blinked. He looked sad, almost on the verge of tears. Oliver picked up the cat and cradled him in his arms.

"That sounds terrible."

It was. Oliver?

"Yes, Bouchard?"

Promise me you won't leave me.

"I'll try," Oliver said. "I'll do my best."

You're the only one I love, Oliver.

"Really?"

Truly. Scratch my head.

Oliver stroked the cat's silky head.

"Thank you. Thank you, Bouchard, for finding me."

Do you love me, Oliver?

"Of course," Oliver said. He could feel the rapid pat-a-pat of the cat's beating heart, and the steady beat of his own heart, improbably alive and unbroken. "Of course I love you. You're my best friend."

The Stepchild

SOME BEEFCAKE ARMY jerk dragged her out of her cot in the middle of the night. The room went from dark to blinding fluorescent. Agents stole her covers and ruffled through her belongings, shoving them into her suitcase. They threw shoes at her feet. They ordered, "Out! Now! Time to go, princess!"

"But my cat!"

The cat was a streak of fur and sharp teeth. For a moment, as the agents carried away her suitcase and pushed Heather toward the door, she feared she had lost him. Then she felt a claw in her calf, more claws in her thigh, her butt, her back, as the cat scrambled up its Heather-tree.

It climbed onto her shoulder and rode there, through the ammonia-scented halls, out the metal doors, past the barracks, into the night. The agents led Heather to an SUV, the same black window–tinted variety that had brought her here. They threw her suitcase in the back and told her to climb in.

"Where's my mom?"

"She left already."

"Left? Where? Where are you taking me?"

"Tahoe, princess," the agent said, snickering. "You're going to Tahoe."

* * *

The cat rode on her lap all the way to Tahoe. They both fell asleep near Bakersfield and woke up outside of Stockton, in the early morning, when the car stopped for gas. Heather went to use the restroom. One of the Homeland Security goons insisted on escorting her. He seemed less frightening in the daylight, less gruff, more human. The cat trailed after them, across the parking lot, into the gas station, through the salty-road-snack aisle. It paced outside the ladies' room door until Heather emerged.

Beef jerky.

Heather was ten and oblivious to the threat of front-butt the last time she had dabbled in beef jerkies, so she couldn't fathom why her mind had struck her with this jerky craving.

Beef jerky.

The craving was audible; perhaps generated by technological advances in impulse-buy marketing, speakers hidden in the shelves, subliminal pro-snack whispers embedded in the gas station Muzak.

"Hey, I'm hungry."

"Good for you."

"Yeah, but they took my purse. Can you—"

"It's in the back," the agent said. "With your suitcase. But here." He handed her a twenty. "Get me a candy bar. But next time, leave the cat in the car. He's conspicuous."

There wasn't a next time because the SUV drove straight from Stockton to Tahoe. The cat reclaimed its spot on Heather's lap. Heather fed it nibs of beef jerky. They finished all the jerky by the time they reached Tahoe, except it wasn't really Tahoe. Tahoe had an immaculate lake, deep azure at its center, lustrous emerald around the edges, flanked by tall straight pines, existing beneath a perpetually clear blue sky. Tahoe had ski-in cabins with resort privileges and private hot tubs. When, on their way out of the army base, the agents said they were bound for *Tahoe*, Heather envisioned herself in a white cashmere turtleneck sweater, sipping pinot by the fire after a long day on the slopes. She understood now why they had snickered. The place where they took her wasn't Tahoe, and it was definitely not a resort.

The Twin Pines Motel boasted low rates and cable TV, as if cable was even still a thing. They had no hot tubs and no Wi-Fi. In the motel office, the Homeland Security goons exchanged papers with two other nearly-as-goonish government types dressed in jeans, alpine sweaters, and matching Sherpa coats and boots, à la Sierra Tourist and Winter Weather Enthusiast. One of them had a trapper hat and the other wore earmuffs, but otherwise they matched, which Heather thought was creepy.

"She's your problem now," the Homeland Security goons told the others. The man in the trapper hat checked Heather in. He handed Heather a key, her suitcase, her purse. He did not tell her why she had been brought to this lonely two-star motel, or where her mother was.

Heather let herself into her motel room. She locked and chained the door. She paced. The cat paced. She dug her phone out of her purse. Its battery had died. She found her charger and plugged it in, but it had no service. Heather dialed zero on the motel room landline to reach the front desk.

"What do you mean, no Wi-Fi? I mean, how can you not . . . It's . . . There's Wi-Fi everywhere."

"Not here."

"But . . ."

"There's a café down in Blairsden. One of them internet cafés. You can drive yourself down there, if you need the Wi-Fi."

Heather couldn't drive herself anywhere. Instead of a car, she got two government handlers occupying one of the adjacent motel rooms. Periodically, one would emerge to stalk the motel grounds, trying to look casual.

"What are you doing?" Heather asked the earmuffs goon when he circled past her door, because she had nothing else to do.

"Surveillance."

"What are you surveilling?"

"Look, can you just try to stay in your room and out of my hair?"

He evidently did not like her.

Trapper hat was more forthcoming.

"We're keeping a watch out for dangerous individuals. You know, fanatics. Thieves. Potential terrorists."

"Terrorists? Is that why I'm here? Do you think my mom, I mean—and why would there be terrorists?"

"You don't need to worry, ma'am. There won't be. We're here to make sure everything proceeds in an orderly fashion."

What struck her, when she thought about the exchange later, as she lay on her motel bed, gazing up at the popcorn ceiling, listening to the drone of cable news, was that he had called her *ma'am*. She had only recently celebrated (if you could call two blunts and a bottle of rum while Justin and his buddies played dumb video games and she sat alone by the pool a celebration) her nineteenth birthday, and already she had begun the transition from *miss* to *ma'am*.

What struck her, far later, when the course of her life's drastic immeasurable changes became fully apparent, was how she had focused on something so meaningless; how she had, for too many of her nineteen years, allowed trivialities to absorb her. She had missed the magic that unfurled before her eyes.

Where were you when it happened? someone would ask her, later, and their inquiry would inundate her mind with agonizing moments. She would recall her petty fights with Justin; her Alex envy; her resentment of Jack P., his rocket metabolism, his generally recognized awesomeness, and his gall to be not merely excellent but genuinely nice; the annoyance stoked by her mother's love for Jack P. and Alex both, when she could scarcely stand to look at them. She could not see them, not really. She could only see, reflected by them, the inadequacies of her own self. Her self, who gave her father and her brother to the feds, who got her mother and herself evicted and taken here, to this third-rate no-spa motel in the middle of Boringville, where there was nothing to do but wait.

"Heather?"

A knock came through the door. Not the outside door, but the one that led to the adjoining room.

"Mom?" Heather rolled off the bed. "Mom, is that really you?"

"It's me, Heather. Can I come in?"

Heather felt a surge of relief. But guilt and betrayal muddied her initial reaction. She remembered: Her mother had chosen Jack P. Her mother chose him, and she never told Heather the truth. Despite all their proclamations of togetherness, despite the matching shirts and annual Ping-Pong tournaments and pro-family accolades, they kept Heather in the dark.

And then she proved them right—she snitched on her stepdad.

She didn't want to see her mother. Her mother would blame her. Her mother *should* blame her. They had lived together in a very lovely Malibu house with ocean views, and Heather's mother had expected to continue living there, with her television-producer husband and his unusual collection of inflatable pool floats. She had anticipated annual trips to Carmel, Baja, intermittent Europe, and instead she got a trip to the army base before checking into this stone-age motel void, with its scratchy polyester bedspreads and stained carpets and grade-F soap bars that left a residue whenever you washed your hands.

And instead of Jack P., her dashing, otherworldly husband, she got Heather.

"Please, Heather . . ."

Heather opened the door. Her mother stepped through. Her mother hugged her.

"Oh, Mom . . ."

She let herself be hugged. She buried her head. She wept, as the cat wove circles around her legs.

"It's okay, Heather. It's going to be okay."

"Will it? I want to go home. What are we even doing here?" Heather complained.

"I don't know."

"And how long are we supposed to stay? Are we just, like, stuck here forever?"

"I don't know. All I know is that I spoke to our lawyer, and they're working something out."

"What? Like what are they working out?"

"I don't know. But what matters now is we're okay. We're together. We just have to have faith that everything will work out."

Her mother had boundless faith in Jack P. and the inherent goodness of the universe.

"How? How can I? After what just happened—"

What happened because of Heather.

"I'm sorry, Heather. I'm so sorry, for all of this."

"Me too. I'm sorry, too."

* * *

Heather's mother used to drink all the best wine, and now she had to ask the government agents: When they drove down to Blairsden to pick up their pizza dinner, could they stop by the grocery and select a bottle of wine? And then the agents returned with a *box* of wine, and the pizza was not wood-fired. It was soggy with grease. No one outwardly laid blame for the subpar refreshments on Heather, but they both blamed her, in their hearts.

Heather's mother's heart had more time to mature, and after dinner she poured herself a plastic cup full of boxed wine and sat down next to Heather and tried to explain. None of what had happened was really Heather's fault. She hadn't made the aliens appear and then abruptly leave. She hadn't married one of them.

"But I'd do it again," her mother said.

"Even if you knew this would happen?"

Her mother flinched. Her eyes gazed at the dark beyond the window, her murky reflection on the glass.

"Jack is Jack. Regardless of where he came from. Jack is Jack," she said, but it wasn't until much later that her words sunk through. Jack's heritage didn't matter. It withered beneath the hot glare of the larger truth: *Jack was Jack.*

"I just don't get why you didn't tell me. You could have told me. If I had known . . ."

She would never know what she would have done, in that other universe where Mom and Jack P. disclosed the truth. But maybe the truth would have looped her, in body and spirit, into the family unit. Maybe she would have felt included, instead of always lousy, always last place, always stuck with rice cakes and dry lettuce while Jack P. dined on pies and cakes.

"We just wanted to protect you," Heather's mom said.

"By leaving me out? And what about Alex? He got to be a part of it. He was included."

"No."

"No?"

"He didn't know."

"He *didn't?*" He had claimed not to, but Heather assumed. Perfect Alex. Of course he would know.

"Jack didn't want to tell him. I mean, he was going to, eventually. We were going to tell you both. But Jack didn't want him to feel like he didn't belong, or wonder . . . Jack wanted him to feel human."

* * *

Her mother—*thank the Space Angels*—had the adjoining room. The government agents had tried to make them share but Heather's mother demanded separate rooms. It was the least they could do, she said.

Thanks, Mom, Heather thought. *Whatever. I don't want to sleep near you either.* But she misunderstood. Her mother didn't insist on a separate room because she wanted one herself. She did it for Heather.

Heather's mom persuaded an agent to pick up a stack of thrillers from the Value Valley even though she didn't read thrillers and had packed enough books to entertain herself. She arranged delivery of Heather's favorite snacks, nail polish, coloring books, crossword puzzles, magazines. She complained about the greasy egg-and-sausage breakfast. Heather couldn't stomach all that grease, literally and insofar as its outward effects on her stomach. Mom came to the rescue. And Mom came to the rescue again after Heather's misguided visit to the motel vending machine in the middle of the night, in her robe and slippers. She neglected to bring her key. She assumed the door wouldn't lock unless she deliberately locked it. She assumed the vending machine would accept Jack P.'s credit card. The machine only took cash. The machine only offered the sorts of snacks she would eat if/when high. Her imprudent brain conjured a fantasy in which the vending machine journey yielded not only snacks but the necessary weed to fully enjoy them.

Beef jerky, she heard a voice say inside her head. *Tuna fish. Fried chicken.*

The voice sounded oddly like Snoop Dog, which made her think of getting high, which reinforced her vending machine whimsy. The vending machine had none of these things, and she had no cash. She scurried back to her room. The door, of course, had locked. She had been stuck inside the room all day, stuck in the car the day before, and now she was stuck outside in the cold.

Winter had ended, but mountain spring got cold enough to snow. Languid flakes drifted down from the dark sky. The windshields and rooftops had frosted. Heather went to ask the motel front desk for a spare key, but the office was dark. The signs said CLOSED; NO VACANCY; PETS WELCOME.

She walked slowly back toward her room. In the periphery of her vision, she caught a swift motion, like the flick of a tail. She turned and looked. She saw, in the window of the nearest room, a cat. It stood on the windowsill, staring out. Its tail flapped against the glass. Heather walked past, to the next window. She saw another cat, in sausage pose, its belly pressed against the window glass.

She muttered to herself, "This is fucking weird."

She walked on, past the next cat, and the next. There were cats perched in each window. Some windows looked blank from further back, but when she approached, cats popped up onto the windowsills. They watched her, their eyes impassive, whiskers twitching, tails dancing to an enigmatic pipe-flute tune that only cats could hear. *But at least my cat is just a normal cat,* she told herself as she neared her room. The thought gave her comfort, but also resentment. She wanted it to be true, but she didn't. It wasn't. There was her cat in the window, standing regal, staring at her with eyes that said *Where's the chicken?*

She rapped on the window. *Tap tap tap.* She shivered. Her toes had begun to freeze. Her cheeks had an icy flush.

Magellan.

The cat blinked.

"Magellan," Heather said, out loud, not understanding why the name had popped into her head. As soon as she said it, she heard it again.

Magellan.

She frowned. The cat blinked.

That's my name.

Heather shook her head. This was all too weird. Maybe she had found a stale joint in the bottom of her bag and gotten high enough to forget that she had gotten high? It was too weird and too cold to stay outside, and she didn't know what else to do besides knock on her mother's door until her mother woke up and let her in.

"Jesus, Heather."

Mom to the rescue.

"My key . . ."

"You need to be more careful."

She fell asleep in her mother's bed. Cats stalked her dreams. Her own cat woke her in the morning. Her mother had procured a spare key from the office and unlocked the adjoining door between their two rooms. Heather felt a claw on her lip. The cat wanted to cuddle, but it wanted to wake her first, so she would know. It purred. Its breath smelled like chicken.

"I fed your cat," Heather's mom called, from the other room.

So now it was *her* cat.

Heather and her cat watched cable cartoon reruns and game shows all day. Heather kept waiting for the *why-don't-you-do-something-useful* mother call, but it never came. Her mother passed the day reading. She watched a few episodes of a reality TV show her husband had produced. She did calisthenics. After dinner and a glass of boxed wine, she went to bed.

Heather could hear her sobbing through the flimsy wall.

Heather lay on her own bed with the cat. *Magellan.* She drifted, but she couldn't sleep. She felt itchy and antsy. She wanted to know the status of window cats. She had walked past the windows during the daytime and tried to glance inside, but she only spotted two cats, and both were sleeping.

She got out of bed. She poured herself a glass of water.

Magellan meowed.

"What is it?"

He meowed again. Then she heard a knock.

Heather crept toward the door, the cat at her feet. She peered through the peephole. Her heart stopped.

She opened the door.

"Alex?"

Her brother threw his arms around her.

"Alex!"

She hugged him back. She had never felt so glad to see anyone in her life.

The Wife

WHEN THE SPACESHIPS appeared over metropolitan skies, Anne had been in her office, reviewing corporate-merger documents, snacking on bacon-flavored chips, multitasking a weekend fantasy of home-baked éclairs and happy hour with the neighbors and an all-day TV binge. Then her email froze. The internet sputtered. Larry from Estates and Trusts ran through the hall, shouting. Larry's wife was on a business trip to DC and had texted him a scenic photo: *Alien Vessel over the White House.* And now the damned clocks had stopped.

Oh my god, oh my god, that can't be real, right? That can't be real!

Anne feigned skepticism, but her shock was genuine. She couldn't believe it. After two decades of empty skies. Two decades gazing up at the stars, wondering, worrying that something had happened, something far worse than the characteristic Malortian bickering and political infighting that could, and often did, cause the ships to alter course. She had not expected them, after so long, to turn back.

Her work-neighbors—Phil from Corporate and Diane from Antitrust—emerged from their respective offices. They all gathered around Larry's phone.

"No way."

"That's got to be a fake."

"My wife is right there, she saw it."

"Turn on the news."

Anne's heart pounded. She texted Blaine: *Are you watching the news?*

Larry and Diane surfed browser windows until one of them found news. There it was: massive, unmistakable, Malortian.

She texted Blaine. *I am freaking out.*

If you are not watching the news, you should turn it on right now.

But he wouldn't have time. The internet blacked out. She sent two last texts, into the ether.

I love you.

Whatever happens Blaine, I love you.

* * *

Anne went back into her office. She stared at the photos of Jas and Avril on her desk, in Popsicle-stick frames the children had glued and painted themselves. There was a wedding photo beside them: her in a white dress, dapper Blaine with his beard trimmed short. She had other Jas and Avril pictures encased in glitter-frame cubes, sea-glass paperweights, plastic flowers blooming in a kid-made pot. She had paper clips and highlighters and a letter opener—decorative, because her secretary opened all the mail—and she picked it up and stabbed herself in the arm. Blood spurted out. She hadn't bothered to close her office door, and Lisa from Tax appeared in the doorway. She lingered there. Words spilled out of her mouth, but they sounded foreign, and Anne just stood there and nodded and bled until her partner went away. Then she closed the door, rammed the letter opener into her wound, and dug the tracking device out.

She thought: *Whatever happens Blaine, I love you.*

She thought about the first night she had gone disco dancing at an LA club. She thought about how she would never work a job that required roller skates. She would never own platform shoes with real live goldfish inside of them, and it broke her heart.

Oh, Earth!

She thought about her human heart when Blaine held her close, how she could feel it beat against his chest, as his heart drummed back. She thought about her running legs, her arms that twirled and pointed skyward with the disco beat, her human womb that grew two miracle children, the second and third of their kind, as far as she knew. Little Alex had been the first.

Oh, Earth, with its shimmering oceans and chirping valleys and mountain spires, its Top 40 *Billboard* hits and feathered bangs, its roller derbies and horse races, its single-serving plastics, its bacon, its cats.

She didn't want to leave it.

* * *

She rented them a house on a hill above a mountain road. The house was just a vacation rental, but someone had lived there once. A Maine coon cat had lived there, until the night of that horrible crash, when the snow blew like mad. The cat went out that night, and it never came back.

"So how will we know when they're coming back? When do you think it might happen?" the husband asked when they brought their luggage into the house.

"I don't know." She didn't know when they would come. Blaine had accused her, on occasion, of clairvoyance. But she was just clever. She couldn't see the future. She couldn't detect the scent of Malortian vessels on the solar wind.

"But soon?" he asked. He looked nervous, understandably. He had never contemplated leaving the planet, or watching his wife be flown away. "What if they don't let me come?"

"I don't want to go anywhere without you. We're going to stay together."

"At Disney World?" the children asked.

"Yes. At Disney World."

The vacation rental house had four televisions, which made it almost as spectacular as Disney World. The children migrated from TV to TV, sampling the view from different locations. Blaine drove to the nearest library, in Portola. He wanted to check his email and messages, he said, but what he really wanted was a last glimpse at the connections of his human life.

He returned a few hours later. His eyes looked red and wistful. He had groceries—all her favorite meats, cheeses, ice creams.

"Anything interesting?" she asked.

"Greg and Rebecca are all settled in Costa Rica. They invited us to come and visit this summer."

"That's nice."

"Jeff and Marshall said they're feeling lonely with everyone out of town. They were wondering when we'd be back from Disney World."

"What'd you tell them?"

"I said we'd be back in about a week. Oh, and Dave is getting married."

"Dave your coworker? That Dave?"

"That's the one."

"Huh. Well, good for him! That's great!"

"He invited us to the wedding."

The wedding would also serve as a Whitesnake Raider recruitment event. Their numbers had gone down. Snakes had begun to slither back to their urban lives after one of them got speared in the back during a night hunt, and it turned out the home-brewed beer tasted like vinegar, and then there was that botulism incident. But Dave had climbed the snake ranks from Anaconda to Cobra. He had met a devoted Squirrel who baked a great sourdough, and they had decided to get married and make a dozen or so babies who could grow up to fight as Earth warriors in the coming alien siege. They had wedding registries with the Bass Pro Shop and Guns-R-Us.

"We should send them a gift," Anne said. "If we go back to the library—"

"I took care of it already," Blaine said. "His and hers matching fishing rods."

"Oh good."

"Because, you know . . ."

"Yeah . . ."

Anne didn't know when Malorts would come, but she knew it had to happen soon because before they found the rental house, they had tried to get a motel room. The motel sign said VACANCY, but the front desk clerk had just rented the last room to a nice fellow with a cat. *I swear*, the clerk had told them, *I've never seen so many folks traveling with cats in my whole life. Nearly every one of our rooms here has got a cat. And you folks, too. Now what's the deal with that?*

Anne cooked bacon-and-cheese sandwiches for lunch and then she went outside for a run.

"I don't know how you can run after eating two of those sandwiches," Blaine said. "I mean, how does that work, exactly?"

"Genetics," Anne said. "Or, biome—maybe my Malortian gut bacteria, or something like that."

"Well . . . at least if we're leaving, you'll never have to worry about getting kidnapped and dissected by the dieting industry."

She wrapped a third sandwich in foil and stuck it in her fanny pack, in case she got hungry during the run. She jogged down the gravel driveway, out onto the road. Blaine had felt nervous about her running along a curvy mountain road, but the speed limit was twenty-five and the road had a decent-sized shoulder.

She jogged a quarter of a mile and she stopped.

How fast you think we can go around these curves? Sixty? Seventy?

Faster, Ollie! Faster faster faster!

I bet we could take that next curve at seventy-five. You think?

It had happened right here.

You ever seen flakes this big?

She saw the curve ahead. The spot where the car had hit ice and sailed off the edge of the earth. She jogged toward it. She peered down, over the guardrail, at the spot where she had died. Where Jo Anne Smith had died, and poor Oliver. Poor Oliver.

* * *

Malorts thought Oliver was dead, too, when they plucked him from the wreckage and carried him into the shuttle. They started the transfer preparation process: genetic alignment, bacterial modifications, radiation treatments. Then, all of a sudden, he wasn't dead anymore. He wasn't Malortian, but he wasn't entirely human either. He was an unexpected assemblage of murky DNA, human soup with Malortian crackers. He moaned, *Jo, Jo, Jo . . .*

They couldn't use his body now. They didn't know what to do. They bickered and scratched, until a consensus was reached. They hauled him off the ship. They left him on the side of the road. They hid in the trees and watched. A car stopped. *My god, is he alive? He's alive!*

It was a miracle, but it wasn't really. He was alive, but he wasn't really living.

Anne wasn't conscious for any of this. She was suspended in a tube of jelly, undergoing transfer and transformation. Malorts filled her in when they dropped her off in Kentucky. She found Oliver later, at a state facility in Sacramento. She set up a trust and had him transferred to some fancy institution in DC that had a specialist in catatonic disorders. But there wasn't anything the humans could do. Poor Oliver.

She wiped a stray tear from her cheek, her own tear, but also Jo's. They were inseparable now.

She took off running. She sprinted around the curve, up and down the hills, as fast as she could go for several miles. Then she saw a gravel driveway just off the road. She slowed down. The driveway had an old rusty gate propped open with cinder blocks. It had an inviting familiarity.

She knew this place.

She turned into the driveway. It sloped up a hill, flanked with pines and patches of old snow, and dead-ended at an A-frame cabin with an old picnic bench out front. The front window was boarded up. The roof was a patchwork of popped nails and missing shingles. The green trim around the windows had begun to peel off.

She knew this house. She had lived in this house.

She sat down at the picnic bench. She took out her sandwich and ate it slowly, savoring every salty bite. The mountain sky was blue and cloudless, but she could see its gray version. She could see the green-needled pine-tree branches heavy with snow. She could see herself inside the house, with a plate of waffles. She could almost smell the maple syrup.

She finished her sandwich. The afternoon sun was waning. She didn't want Blaine to worry, so she stood up to go.

Then she heard the sound of a motor. The crunch of wheels over gravel.

A motorcycle rolled down the driveway. It stopped. The driver got off. He took off his helmet. He looked at her. He looked puzzled at first, and then recognition blossomed. His eyes lit up.

"Jo?"

"Oliver?"

The Brother

HE STARED, AGHAST and elated. He had tracked down the address of his last house, the alpine A-frame where he and his sister had lived. He hoped that if he came here, he would find closure. He hadn't expected to actually find her.

"Jo?"

"Oliver?"

She looked the same as he remembered, except older, brighter somehow. Young, frail Jo had a spark in her eyes that Bill couldn't beat out, and that spark had finally caught. The fire inside had blossomed. This woman's eyes blazed.

"Are you ... Is it really you? *Jo?*"

"It's me ..." She touched her hand to her chest. She sounded uncertain. "But ..."

"I thought you had died."

She looked at him. Her gaze turned quizzically skyward.

Sudden meowling resounded from the motorcycle sidecar. Oliver went over and unzipped the cat-pack. Bouchard leapt out. The cat galloped toward his sister.

"Bouchard—"

They're here! I'm so excited! They're here, Oliver! They're here and— Bouchard circled her legs. His whiskers twitched. *Wait a second ... is this the right spot? Oliver? This isn't the right spot. I must have gotten confused. I must be groggy from napping for so long.*

"It's okay, Bouchard."

But we have to get there. Oliver! Tonight! Come on! The cat bounded back toward Oliver. He jumped up onto the motorcycle seat. He batted Oliver in the ribs. *Come on!*

"Ow! Don't scratch me." Oliver picked up the cat and dropped him onto the sidecar seat. "I'm sorry," he said to Anne. "He's been really agitated all day."

"Your cat? Bouchard?"

"Yeah."

"He's lovely." She looked at the cat. Her face was a tapestry of emotion, delight and sadness, panic, bewilderment, conviction, awe. A tear leaked from the corner of her eye. "This world . . . I love cats. And he's a good one, isn't he? Does he talk to you? Can you hear him speak inside your head? Or is it more like a feeling?"

"He talks . . ." Oliver trailed off. "But how did you . . ."

He wondered whether he had just dreamed this all, from his chair by the window at Brookwood, where the blizzard never stopped. His mind returned, the alien vessels, his talking pet cat, his sister back from the dead; it was all too astonishing to be real.

"Oliver?"

Oliver.

"How did you know that?" Oliver asked. "How are you here? The crash . . . they said it was a miracle that I survived. And they couldn't even reach the wreckage for you—how are you not dead?"

"I did die," she said after a long pause. "Your sister, Jo . . . she died. I'm so sorry . . ."

"You're not Jo?"

"I am, and I'm not. I'm . . . I'm sure you heard on the news about how there are . . . aliens, here on Earth, who've been living here on Earth for years?"

She's one of them! Bouchard proclaimed.

"Are you—"

She nodded. He looked at her; Jo but luminescent; Jo who had bloomed into someone else.

"But Jo . . . she's gone?"

"Yes . . . Well, a part of her still exists, I think that's what brought me here. There are, like, fragments of her, still floating around in my head. I don't entirely understand it."

"Are there . . . is there anything you can tell me about her?"

"I . . . remember a blizzard," Anne said. "The car crash. I remember this place—this house. It was . . . It was happy. Your sister was happy here. She felt free. And . . . she loved you. I know that. You were her favorite person in the whole world, and she felt this immense gratitude for you, that you were in her life."

Oliver wept. His eyes flooded. Memories of Jo surged back, a deluge of every memory he had missed, all at once. Jo in pigtails on the swing set, legs pumping. Jo eating Popsicles, her sticky orange fingers, her fingers holding a crayon, drawing a stick-figure pair, Oliver and Jo. *See, it's us!* Them watching *Gremlins* on TV, them playing video games, them lighting sparklers in the street. Them packing their bags, driving away, away, away. *Aaaawayyyy, you rolling river.* The taste of warm cherry pop, bubbling over his tongue, down his throat. *We're free, Ollie. Ain't no one'll come looking for us all the way out here.*

Bouchard climbed onto Oliver's lap. *I'm so sorry, my friend.*

Anne wrapped her arm around Oliver's shoulder. She hugged him. She wasn't his sister. His sister had gone, and yet he could still feel her, a faint happy shadow of the girl he had known, loving him still.

"Also," Anne said, "disco. She loved disco."

Oliver laughed. He wiped the tears from his cheeks.

"I did, too," he said. "But I would never admit it."

"I think she knew."

"Yeah. Yeah, I think she did. Will you tell me?" he asked. "What happened? I mean, how are you—"

"Yes, of course," Anne said.

They sat together on the picnic bench outside the house they had shared, long ago, when she was still just Jo. Anne told Oliver the story of her twenty years on Earth, condensed.

"But you, Oliver," she said when the story finished. "What about you?"

"Yeah, there's not much to tell. I was just . . . catatonic. Nothing much happened to me, until I found Bouchard."

I found you, Oliver.

"I felt really bad about what happened to you. I tried to find a specialist who could help. I set up some accounts, and—"

"The money, that was you?"

"Yes. But it wasn't enough."

"Still, thank you. For trying."

Can we hurry this up? Bouchard paced across the table. *I'm antsy.*

"Just give me a few minutes, okay?" Oliver said to the cat. He turned to Anne. "Sorry. He's in a hurry."

"He's in a hurry. Why is he in a hurry?"

Well, it's obvious. What else would it be? We're going up there. Bouchard stared up at the sky. *We're going up to the stars.*

"He says we're going up to the stars."

"We are . . ."

Oh, is she coming with us, Oliver?

"When?" Anne asked.

Soon. Tonight, if you can hurry this up. Otherwise we might miss it!

"He says tonight," said Oliver.

"Tonight. They're coming tonight?"

"Wait, Bouchard," Oliver asked. "Where are you getting this? You didn't tell me this before. How come you know now?"

I can't explain the mysteries of the universe, Oliver. All I know is that me and my friend—that's you, buddy—we need to be at the right spot at the right time so we can board the ship.

Oliver told Anne what Bouchard was impressing upon him.

"Of course." She laughed. "Of course they'd want the cats. But I guess you're invited, too."

"That's . . . That's crazy. I just . . . We're supposed to board the ship? Bouchard? Is that what's going to happen?"

Yes, yes, if you can wrap this reunion up!

"And you're sure—"

Yes. Sure. And if we're not going yet, can you at least scratch under my chin while we wait?

"I bet that whatever they did to program him," Anne said, "there was some sort of switch programmed to flip right before the ships came back. So he'd know to be ready."

"Do you think maybe that explains what happened to me? That they programmed me somehow? Because when the ship flew over DC it was like, like a switch flipped inside my brain and I came back on."

"They might have. They might have done something when they botched the upload and didn't know how to fix it, in case they figured out how to fix it later. But I don't really know."

"Well . . . maybe I'll get to ask them."

"Yeah, so, assuming your cat is right, which, knowing Malorts, it makes sense . . . do you want to do this?" Anne asked. "Board the ship? Leave Earth?"

Oliver closed his eyes. Earth's sun felt warm on his face. The air smelled like pine. He tried to imagine a different air, a different sun. There were so many out there—a whole vast universe of suns. He remembered back to when he and Jo packed up and drove west, dreaming of Malibu. Except this time the darkness wasn't at his back. The only thing behind him was pure, cold, blank, and from that blizzard void he could forge something new.

"I . . . I think I do. I think I'd really like that. And maybe that's why Bouchard picked me. Maybe he sensed somehow that I'd want to go."

I can smell it on you, Oliver.

* * *

Oliver thought about the different course his life might have taken if his car hadn't plowed off that snowy cliff. How Jo might have gone to cosmology school. *Cosmetology* school. He could never get those words straight. How he might have traded his duct-taped car for a truck with four-wheel drive. How they might have driven west, down the mountains, to the sea, where gleaming water lapped at white sand, where blue stretched on, to the edge of the earth. How they might have gone out dancing, him and Jo with glitter on her eyelids. His sister would never go out disco dancing again. She would never find love, like Anne had. Her heart would never break. She would never weep in frustration from the limitations of a broken brain. She had ended, and Anne had started anew. So had he.

"I'm just glad I found you," Oliver said.

"Me too."

"You know the life you have, your family, it's . . . it's what I always wanted for Jo. To be loved. To have family like that."

"She did," Anne said. "She had you. And . . . and she still does. I might not be her, exactly. But I'm here. If there's anything I can do, I'll be here for you."

And me, Oliver, Bouchard purred. *I'll be here for you, too.*

"So you're coming on the ship?" Oliver asked. "That's why you're here, right?"

"Oh . . . I, I don't know. I don't know. I need to get back to my family. I need to get my husband, our kids. And we need time to pack. Does Bouchard know where the ships are coming, exactly?"

I can feel it. Left, then right, then right again. Bouchard circled, left, right, right, the way a cat did when seeking out the perfect spot to nap. He glanced up. His whiskers twitched. *Up the hill. There.*

"Um, it seems like he knows, but not to the point that we can give you good directions. We're staying at a motel about fifteen miles from here. Why don't I give you a ride back to where you're staying and then you can pack up and meet us at the motel? Then you can follow us from there."

You need to hurry, Oliver.

"That works."

"Bouchard says we need to hurry."

Anne carried the cat to the sidecar, climbed in, and settled him on her lap. Oliver mounted the bike and revved the engine before taking one last look at the house.

"Goodbye, house."

"Farewell."

Au revoir!

They drove back to the cabin that Anne and her family had rented. They found the children waiting on the front porch.

"Mom!"

"Mom!"

"Where were you, Mom?"

"Dad's been worried!"

"Who is that guy?"

"Is that a cat?"

"Are we getting a new cat?"

"Does it talk?"

Anne pulled herself out of the sidecar. She tucked Bouchard into his cat-pack. She hugged Oliver.

"Mom!"

"Mom!"

Anne turned to the children.

"This is your uncle, Oliver," she said. "And his cat, Bouchard. And yes, it talks. But that's not for right now. You need to go inside and get ready as fast as you can."

She looked at the husband. "It's time. We're going to Disney World."

The Stepchild

THEY COULD GO on a great adventure.

For thousands of years, humans had gazed up at a brilliant plethora of unreachable universes; they had pondered the expanse between the flat Earth and the starry heavens, the meaning of Earth and sun and sky, the existence of life elsewhere, life in all its wondrous forms. Throughout the short span of their existence, individual and collective, they wondered: What did it all mean? What was out there? Was it brutal and merciless? Ravenous? Curious? Soft and kind? Would they find in the heavens, as on Earth, life across the spectrum, from kitten to shark, from clever child to brainless worm? No one knew. No one had ever gone out there, past the cold hunk of orbiting moon. Not until now.

They could go on an adventure because Jack P. had made a deal.

"What do you mean, he made a deal?"

"I don't know. I don't know the specifics," Alex said. "All I know is that I was stuck at this army base and they wouldn't tell me why or what was going on. But they made me take all these tests. Like, cognitive tests, but also physical tests. They drew blood and made me run on a treadmill and stuck me in the MRI, all that kind of stuff. I was so scared, Heather. But then I got a call from my dad and he explained, you know, the whole thing. . . . And he said he had made some kind of deal. And then they put me on a plane and brought me out here."

"And then what?"

It would be a great adventure, one they could go on together. Better than Thailand, Alex said. They could forget about college. Maybe they didn't want college anyway. Maybe they didn't want degrees and titles and weekend workdays. They could live lives unburdened by transcripts, certificates, licenses, applications, dissertations, diversifications, stocks and bonds and dividends, insurance and annuities and 401(k)s, fashion trends, pantyhose, stuffy suit coats, bow ties, boring parties where the humans squandered irreplaceable minutes on suffocating small talk and no one partook in Dionysian pursuits and everyone went home early feeling empty inside despite the excesses of the cheese tray.

The cheese on those trays never satisfied.

It got dried out around the edges and rubbery in the middle. Imitation spaceship cheese was bound to taste better.

They didn't have real cheese on the ship. Apparently, cheese was one of humanity's superior creations. Cheese and television and products that came in plastic twist-tubes—lip balms, deodorants, push-pop ice cream. These were the things, Jack P. had told his son, that he would miss about Earth. He would miss floating on brand-new inflatables in his backyard pool. The chemical smell of fresh plastic. The sun setting over the shores of Malibu. Miniature golf. Black-light bowling. Paddleboats. Disneyland.

But they were going on a great adventure!

But Jack P. and his son didn't have a choice about their bacon-less, cheese-less, Earth-less future. They were known aliens. They had gotten outed. *Because I'm terrible I'm terrible I'm a terrible person,* Heather thought, until Alex told her how the feds had kept a file on his dad for years.

"They knew? How did they know?"

"My dad isn't the only one. There are others. One of them went to work for the CIA."

"Seriously?"

"He got himself through the background check and then reported himself. He told them about my dad. Which, like, was totally Dad's fault. The CIA guy—or alien or whatever—he only knew about my dad because of *Jeopardy!* Not to mention all the TV Dad's worked on since then. The CIA guy saw my dad on some late-night TV interview talking about plastics, and he was like, 'That guy. That guy is not a guy.' And I guess he told the government, but they left my dad alone because they thought he was harmless. Which, I mean, he totally is."

"So then why'd they pick him up? And you?"

"Part of it was about public perception. People see spaceships and then feel like the government isn't doing anything about the 'alien threat' or whatever, and it undermines public confidence. They need to make a show. Like, 'Watch us. We big strong government. We solve alien problem. Hooray!' But also they were hoping he'd have some idea why the ships came and went."

"Their CIA guy didn't know?"

"Nope."

"Does your dad?"

"He does now."

"So why?"

"It's like . . . So I'll explain it the way Dad told it to me. He was like, 'Alex, you remember that nice young Japanese fellow who came to live with us for a few months, who brought us all those fantastic Hello Kitty artifacts—'"

Heather laughed. "Oh my god, of course. Hello Kitty artifacts. I remember that. What was that guy's name?"

"Akihito."

"I don't know how you remember that."

Alex shrugged. "So Dad was like, 'You remember how he came to live with us as a foreign exchange student? That's why the ships came.'"

"To pick up foreign exchange students."

"Well, I mean, not students per se. Just humans who could come and live with them and learn about their culture, the same way they came to Earth and learned about us, as like an immersive intergalactic exchange program. And they haven't picked anyone up yet."

"They haven't?"

"When they came last time, it was just so they could find the humans who would go with them. They're coming back to pick us up."

"Find them how?" Heather asked.

The cat, Magellan, hopped up onto her lap. It gazed up at her with its big, stormy eyes.

How do you think?

Heather looked at the cat. Its gaze shifted, from her to Alex, then up, skyward.

They're coming back to pick us up.

It sank in slow.

We're going on a great adventure.

She could not quite believe it. Even when she heard the cat inside her head. Even when it asked her, a moment later, to *Please turn the heat up as high as it will go.* Even as Alex described the political fighting and genial squabbling endemic to his lineage, which had stranded his father on Earth for twenty years. Someone had decided to extend his father's two-year Earth trip in pursuit of more robust sociological data, obtainable only by lengthy immersion. Someone else had decided, later, that cultural understanding ought to cut both ways.

They're coming back to pick us up.

But Heather couldn't quite believe that *us* might include her. That space was an option. She tried to envision a reality where she was something more than a rich girl taking a gap year; where Alex chose neither Stanford nor Harvard nor Thailand; where Jack P. wasn't making this year's hit reality TV show and getting all worked up about his latest plastic Pokémon figurines and whisking Heather's mom off to Carmel. But the vision played like a movie with a dashing rescue ending. A few explosions, a dramatic *take my hand* moment, a hunky scientist soldier type who through sheer bravado would thwart the aliens' nefarious foreign-exchange-human plans. Something would happen, and they would all go back to Malibu, better off for having learned some valuable lesson about compassion or bravery or family. Something like: Nothing is more important than family.

Heather—

And that cat voice in her head—that was just a narrative device constructed in furtherance of the movie plotline, or a stress-induced auditory hallucination easily eradicated by a twice-a-day pill.

Heather. We're going on an adventure. You're my friend. Can you scratch my head?

"This isn't really happening, is it?" she asked.

Scratch my head. Right there behind the ears.

"It is," Alex said.

"This is crazy."

He nodded. "Dad told me he spent the past two days helping the government pick out action figure toys and plastic novelties to go inside the piñatas, as a part of the welcome gift from Earth. They're gifting the aliens, like, a hundred piñatas. And a shipload of TV show merchandise. Oh, and get this—apparently as part of the deal, the aliens are going to help humans set up some sort of advanced plastics recycling program, but in exchange we have to give them the Pacific Garbage Patch."

"The *what?*"

"It's, like, a floating island of garbage in the Pacific Ocean," Alex explained.

Heather stopped scratching. Her head snapped back toward her brother. "We're giving them garbage. Seriously."

"Specifically, plastics. You should hear Dad when he talks about it. He gets all excited and does this little flappy dance with his hands, like it's the best gift in the universe."

"That's crazy. This is all crazy. Right?"

"Yep."

* * *

Heather and Alex did the only sensible thing they could think to do as two teenagers about to potentially embark on a galactic journey aboard an alien vessel with no end date, no return ticket, no travel guidebook, no idea what to expect beyond Jack P.'s vague assurances that everything would work out fine and that the spacecraft had television and could produce foods with a bacon-esque flavor: They got last-night-on-Earth *wasted* on boxed wine.

"But what if the bacon-whatever, the bacon-flavory food, what if it's made with, like, ground-up space bugs?" Heather asked.

"I don't think Dad would (hiccup) tell us," Alex said. He refilled their plastic motel cups with wine. "He would be like, 'Kids, (hiccup), kids, you're going to like this bacon flavory flavor. It's stellar. It's really great. Why I (hiccup) ate two pounds of it just this morning and I'm doing great!'"

"Ha! He totally would."

"I've never had (hiccup) the hiccups before."

"No. Really? No way!"

"Maybe I'm finally (hiccup) becoming a real boy."

"You were always a real boy," Heather said. "You were, like, everyone's favorite real boy ever in the entire universe."

"But I was . . . I'm (hiccup) not. I'm like a, like a (hiccup) replicant, or one of those, you know, I'm not (hiccup), I'm not real."

"No, you're real," Heather said. "Just because you're not like, *totally human*, you know, you're still real. Everything that makes you who you are, I mean, it all really happened. See?"

She pinched him.

"Ow! What was that for?"

"See, you felt it. That means you're real."

"It made my hiccups go away."

"If one of us is not real," Heather said, "it's me. I'm superficial and fake and I'm always worrying about the most stupid-ass shit. And I'm . . . I'm such a selfish bitch. . . ."

Alex's eyes went wide. "You're *not!*"

"I am! Like, even now I'm thinking about me, about what a bitch I am, and here you just found out you're not human, and that Jack P.'s not human—and that's so fucked."

"Yeah but . . . it's not. I mean . . . I think maybe I knew?"

"That you were, like, half alien? You're half, right? Because your mom—"

"Yeah. My dad met her on the set of *Jeopardy!*"

"So she was human."

"Yeah, but . . . so it's not like I knew what I was—what I am. Dad never said anything. I just kind of always knew that I was different somehow."

"Alex the genius. Remarkable Alex. Wonder-boy. Boccie ball champion. Master violinist. Published poet. What else? Like, you're so excellent it's impossible for us regular humans to even keep track of all your accomplishments. Oh—always remembers everyone's birthday *and* picks out the best birthday presents. That's a fucking feat. Sheesh."

"I'm not that . . . I'm just . . ."

"I'm sorry. See, my tone was super bitchy."

"I can see why it was hard for you," Alex said. "That's not what I wanted."

"I know. I know because of how you'd lose at games on purpose, so that I could win, and I just . . . it's not that I even ever felt anything bad toward you. It's just that, I guess being around you always reminded me about all the things I didn't like about myself."

"I'm sorry."

"You don't need to be."

"I like you."

"You're so good."

"I'm serious. I'm glad you're my sister."

Alex looked at her. He was radiant with goodness, and sincerity. He hiccuped.

"Really?"

"Really. (hiccup) Darn it, they're back!"

"Me too. I'm glad you're my brother. Even if your awesomeness is sickening."

"And we're (hiccup) going on a great adventure together."

"Together!"

Together.

The Husband

THE CHILDREN HAD unpacked Every. Single. Bag. They had dispersed their toys throughout the house, crayons scattered under beds, stuffed animals stashed in pillowcases, beloved pony figurines grazing on the windowsill, staring wistfully up at the starry sky. The same sky that looked down upon Disney World. The children had played a fun game called try-on-all-the-clothes, converting the stack left folded on the dresser into a dirty mountain on the floor.

They had almost no time to pack.

"You sure? It's tonight?"

"It's tonight," the wife said with a nod. "This evening. Or sooner. We need to be all packed up and on the road in an hour."

"How are we going to—"

"I have no idea. But go! Go, go, go!"

They did not have time to deliberate. Wife and husband whirl-winded through the rental house. They filled suitcases. They packed sandwiches, crackers, cookies, cheese. They showered, brushed, dressed, searched for missing boots, plush runaway cats, the real cat who did not want to go anywhere, especially not back into the minivan, and then into space. Mr. Meow-mitts wanted to stay Earthbound.

"But how can we go to Disney World without Mr. Meow-mitts?"

"Yeah, Dad?"

"How can we?"

"Who will ride Space Mountain with us?"

Not Mr. Meow-mitts.

They Tetris'ed the last suitcase into the minivan. They scoured the house for Mr. Meow-mitts. The children moaned.

"We can't go without himbs!"

"Kids, we've looked everywhere—"

"We'll look again, okay?"

"But if we don't find him—"

"Himbs."

"If we don't find *himbs*, then—"

"Why don't you kids go watch some TV while your dad and I look, okay?"

* * *

One hour came and went and Mr. Meow-mitts would not emerge from wherever *himbs* had gone to hide.

"We need to just go," the wife said to Blaine.

"Anne . . ."

"I don't want to leave the cat either, but—"

"Yeah. You're right. But what do we tell them?"

"I don't know."

"Maybe they won't ask."

"Yeah, right," Anne said. "Well . . . at least there will probably be a lot of cats on the ship."

But the children didn't ask because their full focus had shifted to TV. They stood inches from the screen, slack-jawed, unblinking. They appeared to be holding hands, but their hands were both just mutually holding the remote.

"Kids—"

"It's time to go."

"But TV!"

"The TV!"

"There will be plenty of TV at, at Disney World, but for now—"

"But TV!" Jas yelled.

"Look!"

"Look!"

"We know that guy on TV!"

"He comes on the Christmas card!"

Anne's heart skipped.

"He's famous!"

"Look!"

"We can't look with you both standing right in front of the TV like that," Blaine said. "You're blocking the view."

The mesmerizing pull of TV held the children statuesque. Anne grabbed ahold of their arms and gently pulled them back. She stared at the TV screen. Jack P. stared back.

The camera showed him close up, smiling, waving, like the winning contestant on a television game show. Except the game show was happening in real life, on the Capitol steps, with the chyron practically shouting: LIVE FROM THE CAPITOL.

. . . and we just heard from the Chief of Staff. The government believes that the extraterrestrials do not pose a serious threat; that they have come to Earth on a peaceful mission of exploration.

The camera panned out, revealing the other contestants: twelve men and women in navy blue jumpsuits flanked by generals, senators, military guards.

For those just joining us, we are awaiting arrival of the extraterrestrial craft. The vessel is expected to touch down in the Capitol in one hour to pick up all extraterrestrial operatives located in the United States. Twelve

ambassadors from North America, including six from the US, will also
board the vessel for what will be a historic mission . . .

"All operatives . . ." Blaine said. "Did she just say *all?*"
"Dad!"
"Shhhhh!"
"We're trying to listen, Dad!"

. . . president will be speaking soon, but first . . .

The camera zoomed back in, on Jack P., as he stepped up behind
the podium. He spoke into the microphone.
"Earthlings . . ."
He paused, then shook his head. He placed his hand on his heart,
right beneath the American flag pinned on his lapel. "Americans . . . My
fellow Americans . . . I came to this planet, to this country, twenty years
ago. I wanted to come here—I volunteered for this mission because I
love TV. I watched your TV growing up, on our worldship. All of us
Malorts did. We only had black-and-white TV back then, sitcoms and
news programs from the 1940s and '50s that traveled across the vast
reaches of space, for us to find. It wasn't as good as the TV we have
here now, but it spoke to me. It made me laugh and cry and it filled me
with hope, that someday I might come here and meet the species that
made it. Earthlings, Americans, you have made my dreams come true.
"My name is Jack P., for those of you who don't know me. About
two decades ago, I went on a little television game show called
Jeopardy! From there, I built a career here on Earth, producing *new*
television shows. It was the most amazing thing I can ever imagine
doing. My fellow Americans, thank you. My name is Jack P., and
I'm an extraterrestrial.

"I love Earth, and I love the United States of America. If I could stay here and keep on making television shows, I would. But the time has come for me to go back where I came from.

"There are a total of five of us extraterrestrials who had the great privilege and honor of calling America home for the past twenty years and living here among you all; myself, and the four folks you see here standing right behind me. Tonight, the five of us Malorts will begin the long journey back to our home planet. We will also be joined by these twelve human ambassadors you see standing here on the Capitol steps, as well as ambassadors from many of Earth's other nations." Jack P. looked straight at the camera, through the television, right at Anne. "Not one of these ambassadors is being forced to go—they could choose to stay on Earth if they wanted. They are all going, as I did, voluntarily.

"Folks," Jack P. continued, turning toward the ambassadors, "I can only hope that your experiences learning about our culture are half as good as mine have been, though I daresay I got the better end of the deal. We don't have TV back on my planet. So, with that, I say, farewell, and thank you. Thank you all, and God Bless America."

The gravity of the television had kept drawing the children toward it. By the time Jack P. finished speaking, their little noses grazed the screen.

"Did he just say . . ." Blaine started.

"Five," Anne said.

"A total of five, in America."

"But that's not true," said Anne. "There are more of us. He knows there are more of us."

"So do you think, maybe . . ."

"Not one of them has to go. That's what he said. He said, they could choose to stay if . . . if . . . He wouldn't just say that."

"So do you think he meant . . . Was he trying to tell the others they could stay?" The simplest explanation, per Occam's razor, was . . . What *was* the simplest explanation? Blaine wasn't sure. "What do we do?"

"I don't know."

"Do we go, or—"

"The car is all packed. And Oliver, I told him we'd meet him, and Jack P. might be wrong, or maybe he meant something else. I wish I had more time to think. I don't know."

"You know him. Do you think he meant what he said?"

"I . . . Probably . . . but I don't know."

"So, what do you want to do?"

The Stepchild

SHE FELT TERRIBLE. Abysmally hungover. Her head throbbed. Her stomach felt acidy and gross. She had stayed up all night guzzling boxed wine and then gorged on salty snack foods.

BEEF JERKY.

"Ugh, no ..."

Had she eaten beef jerky? She couldn't remember. She remembered Alex having his first ever hiccups and something about Hello Kitty artifacts and—

Oh. Shit.

Space.

BEEF JERKY.

Magellan jumped up onto the bed. He climbed on top of Heather's chest, claws out. He stared down at her.

BEEF. JERKY.

Like she was some sort of jerky-dispensing machine. She swatted the cat away. She pulled the covers up over her head.

We are going to be late. Feed me.

She pulled the covers down. She peeked out at the cat. Magellan extended a paw toward her face.

"I am too hungover for talking cats."

I am too hungry for humans to be stupid. Do you see these claws? Look at these claws. I want breakfast.

"Oh my god, fine! Beef jerky!" She pushed the cat away. She flung off the covers and rolled out of bed. Her head spun. She fed the cat a can of wet food and a strip of beef jerky. She chugged a glass of water. She looked around the motel room, for Alex.

"Alex?"

His suitcase was gone. Had he brought a suitcase? She thought so, but her thoughts were hazy. She knocked on the door to her mother's adjacent room.

"Mom?" No one answered. "Mom, are you in there?" She tried the handle. The door was locked. She walked over to the window and looked out. Things were happening in the parking lot. People were loading luggage into trunks, getting into cars, milling around talking while cats circled their legs. People were checking out and driving away.

Heather closed the blinds.

"Shit. Shit, shit, shit! What do I do?"

Alex's bag was gone. Alex was gone. Her mom was gone. They had left her. Everything Alex had said, about great adventures . . . They hadn't even left a note.

She started to cry. But she felt all cried out, stripped down, too worn to hold on to her doubts. She looked over at Magellan.

The cat smiled. *Come on, human. Adventure time.*

Well, maybe it was.

And maybe they didn't want her. But if so, she hoped they would change their minds.

She wanted them.

She wanted them, and she felt more certain than she had ever felt about anything in her life. She wanted her mom. Her brainiac brother. Her dorky stepdad with his stupid plastic lunch boxes and his action figure collection. She wanted her family. She wanted adventure, and no adventure would be the same without them.

She looked at the clock. It was 4:32.

She hadn't packed. She hadn't showered. She felt gross and

horribly hungover. But there were still cars in the parking lot. She could find herself a ride. She could make it, if she hurried. She would make it.

"Okay." She took a deep breath. "Okay. Yes."

She chugged another glass of water. She took the quickest shower of her life. She put on the first pair of jeans and T-shirt she found and shoved everything else into her suitcase. She grabbed Magellan and ran outside.

There, in the parking lot, was Alex.

"Alex?"

She ran to him. She dropped her suitcase and flung her free arm around him. They hugged, the cat sandwiched between them. "Oh, Alex—"

"You're crying," he said when she stepped back. "Why are you crying?"

"I . . . I thought you had left without me," Heather said.

"We would never leave without you!"

"I didn't see you, and your suitcases were gone and, oh, god, I drank way too much last night, and I just thought . . ."

"We just went to get some food and load up the car. And Mom's just checking out, she'll be back in a sec. Oh, and we got breakfast for you. It's in the back seat. We got pancakes and eggs, hash browns, bacon, French toast, everything. Because who knows what kind of food they'll have on the ship."

She wiped away a tear. "I . . . Thank you."

Heather's mom returned from the motel office with an armful of vending machine candy bars.

"For Jack," she said.

She got into the passenger seat of the car. Trapper Hat drove. Heather rode in the back seat, next to her brother.

It smelled like butter and bacon and maple syrup. Like home. But Heather was too excited to eat just yet. She stared out the window at the trees, the mountains, the winding road. It was her last car trip on Earth for a long, long time at least. She felt her doubts drain away. In their wake, an unfamiliar feeling surfaced. Hope. Hope that she would find her best self, out there in the universe. Hope for her family, that they would stay together. Hope for all the great adventures they would share.

The Wife

THEY PRIED THE children away from TV. They ran out to the car, sans cat. They drove fast down the mountain road, where twenty years ago a girl named Jo had died but her miracle brother did not. But life, all of it, always was a miracle.

Two little miracles sang Disney theme songs in the back seat.

"When you wish upon a cat—"

"Then you wonder where himbs at—"

"Any chonk your heart desires—"

"Will coooome to you."

"When you wish upon a chonk—"

"Himb so purr-fect, chonk or slonk—"

"Teef and peets and bleps and beans—"

"Will coooome to you."

"If a floof is in your dream—"

"Or himbs does a hecka screm—"

"When you wish upon a chonk . . ."

"Are we there yet?"

"Yeah!"

"Yeah! When are we getting to Disney World?"

"It's already dark out. Will they still let us in in the dark?"

They pulled up in front of Oliver's motel, an L-shaped one-story roadside motel with a pool, surrounded by a chain-link fence, closed for the season.

"Hey, this doesn't look like Disney World."

"The pool is closed! And where's the waterslide?"

The parking lot had nearly emptied out. Oliver was already outside, on his motorcycle, waiting. Anne rolled down her window.

"Sorry we're late," she said.

"It's fine," Oliver said. "I mean, Bouchard is annoyed. But he'll get over it."

"Should we just follow you?"

"That works. Bouchard says the spot's not far."

"Okay, we'll be right behind you!"

* * *

They followed Oliver's motorcycle along a paved forest road to the point where the pavement ended. The road narrowed into a one-lane gravel path, barely wide enough for the minivan.

"This definitely doesn't look like Disney World. . . ."

The path turned, and up ahead they saw lights. Oliver pulled off to the side of the road. He waved them ahead. Anne drove on, several more yards, around a bend, to where the road merged into a meadow teeming with people.

They parked along the edge of the meadow. The children leapt from the car.

"Hey . . ."

"Hey!"

"Mom?"

"Dad?"

"Where is it?"

"Where's Disney World?"

Anne stepped out of the car. The children stared up at her, dismayed.

"Kids," Blaine said, walking around the car to join her. "Kids, we're sorry. We're not going to Disney World."

"We're not?"

"Not at all?"

"But why?"

"Well," Anne said, "we came here because—"

"Hey! Look!" Jas yelled. He pointed toward the throng of people. "Look! There's a cat!"

"There's two—three!" Avril squealed "No, more! There's a bunch of cats!"

"Mom!"

"Dad!"

"Look! Look!"

The children took off running. Anne reached for her husband's hand. They followed the children through the meadow, toward where the travelers had converged. There were dozens of humans, mostly younger adults, but also a couple of families and spry older folks who would likely live out their last years in space. They gathered around small campfires, roasting marshmallows, sharing stories of their lives before, and where they had been when the ships arrived, and about the cats who had found them. And in the meadow all around them, the cats frolicked.

"Anne?" said a voice behind her.

She turned around.

"Alex! Oh my gosh! And Heather! You're all grown up! You're— are you in college now? I can't believe it."

"Not quite," Alex said. "Next year. At least, I would have been."

"He was going to go to Harvard or Stanford," Heather said. She had a fluffy gray cat in her arms. "But now we're going to outer space."

"It's so good to see you," Anne said. "I think the last time I saw you, you were maybe twelve?"

"I was eleven. Heather was twelve."

"The time here has just gone so fast . . ."

"It's good to see you too, both of you," Alex said to Anne and Blaine. "You're the last people, um . . . ones I thought I'd see."

"Your dad told you everything?"

"Yeah. A few days ago. And it was like, 'Oh, *now* it all makes sense.' The staying up all night. Eating twice, three times more than any regular human."

"The action figure collection," Heather added.

"But my dad said he didn't think you'd leave Earth. That you loved it here too much. And no one should have to leave the life they've built for themselves. Not if they don't want to."

"He said that?"

"Yeah." Alex nodded. "He made sure of it."

* * *

She loved Blaine. She loved their kids. She loved Earth. She was sure of that.

"So, what do we do?" Blaine asked. They stood together in the meadow, watching their children play chase games with cats. "If you want to go—I just want to be with you. Here or there. It doesn't matter to me."

"I'm just thinking about the kids," she said. "And what this means for them. If we go, if they grow up on the ship, it'll be—"

"They'll love it."

"Yes. They will. But, I just wonder if that's the best for them, to grow up as humans—or, well, half humans—on a Malortian ship. And in space, I mean, you never know what's out there. It could be dangerous."

"Earth isn't doing too great, though, when it comes to danger."

"Well, yes. But if they're here, if we stay . . . you know, it's hard, to be different. To be in a strange place, where you always feel like you're struggling to fit in or even just understand. And as much as I love Earth, I felt like that when I came here. Less so now, but still . . . here at least, to the extent our kids are, well, different, it's not so obvious, to them or anyone else. They just get to grow up like regular human kids. They get to feel like they belong."

"We should tell them, eventually."

"But not until they're . . . I don't know—"

"Past the skin-peeling stage?"

A full-throated laugh erupted out of her. "Exactly."

"So?"

Anne gestured toward a campfire not too far off. "So . . . let's go roast marshmallows. I'm starving. I could eat about a pound of chocolate."

Anne and Blaine joined Oliver and a campfire circle of travelers. They warmed their hands and stared up at the blaze of stars, watching for the swirl of spaceship light. But it wouldn't arrive for a while yet.

They shared their own stories, while wild children prowled the meadow, chasing the flocks of cats, or being chased, or running silly circles while the cats practiced beatboxing like the children had taught them. The children's voices echoed across the meadow, but Anne could hear the cats' voices too. She heard them as a whisper inside her head, a soft purr, a prayer, almost.

Peets and beans and peets and beans and peets and beans and cat-fat-sacks.

The beatbox resounded as a prayer, and Anne understood exactly what it meant. It meant: Life is a miracle. Life is miraculous and absurd and . . . so what? We celebrate. We run dizzy circles. We ride Space Mountain, and we beatbox, and we find the love of our lives, and we hustle him at pool, and then we marry him and marvel at the miracles of our lives and the lives we make together.

Peets and beans and peets and beans and—

Anne huddled close to her husband, their arms wrapped around each other for warmth. They told Oliver how they had met. They told him about their lives together.

"If things had been different—" Anne said.

"But they weren't," said Oliver.

"I'm sorry you lost so much."

"I don't know what would have happened to me if I hadn't," he said. "If things had been different. I . . . It's impossible to know. But I know now that I'm going on a great adventure."

The night grew late. Cats stopped frisking and settled around the campfires to warm their bellies. The breeze shifted, and all the humans and cats in the meadow knew. Their ride would be here soon.

The children flopped down in the middle of a fluffy cat pile.

"If I fits, I sits," Avril said.

Jas yawned. He mumbled something about silly hoomans and hambois. He rubbed his sleepy eyes.

Anne gazed up at the glittered expanse of stars. She loved this view. She loved Earth's myriad skyscapes: flanked by mountains, gleaming over ocean waves, hazy with skyscraper light. She looked over at her children, nestled in a heaven of cats. Avril purred softly. Jas had fallen asleep. She looked at her husband.

"Blaine," she said. "I think it's time to go home."

The Brother

THE CATS FELT it coming. The slumbering cats awoke. Warm-bellied fireside cats leapt to their feet. All at once, every cat in the meadow began to meow and pace and weave between their human's feet. Their eyes turned to the sky.

It's happening, Bouchard said. *It's happening.*

"I know."

I'm scared.

"Me too," Oliver told the cat. "But it'll be okay. It'll be good. We're going together."

Together.

Oliver wished that Anne was coming too, but he understood. Anne wasn't Jo. Jo was mostly gone. He felt glad, at least, that he had gotten to glimpse her one last time. That he had gotten to say goodbye.

Bouchard swirled and meowed, swirled, meowed, carried on about his nerves, swirled, meowed. Then, all of a sudden, he stopped. A low purr filled his chest and bellowed up through his throat. The purring grew louder and louder, until its thrum resounded throughout the meadow. It poured from the mouth of every cat, a hundred cats, purring in tandem.

Then the lights appeared.

Blue-green-red. They flashed down from the sky, directly above. A patch of starry sky turned shimmery, then opaque. It became the hull of a small spacecraft.

The craft looked like a miniature version of the larger vessels that had appeared over Earth's cities. It was silvery, smooth, wheel-shaped, illuminated in blinks of blue-green-red. It hovered over the meadow, as the humans and cats dispersed to the edges. A short blast of air burst from its hull. The campfires went out. Slowly, the craft descended.

Oliver watched from the forest edge. Bouchard sat by his feet, his cat motor still purring. The spacecraft flashed. It hovered about twenty feet above the smoldering campfires. On its side, an unseen door opened. A plank rolled out, forming a walkway from ground to ship.

A voice, amplified by speaker, sounded from the ship.

"WELCOME, HUMANS."

A pause.

"WELCOME, HUMANS. WELCOME, *CATS*."

Oliver recognized the voice, but he didn't know where from.

TV, Oliver, Bouchard said. *Don't you watch TV?*

"WELCOME, HUMANS. WELCOME, CATS. WE ARE MALORTS. WE ARE VERY GLAD YOU WILL JOIN WITH US IN MANY HAPPY JOURNEY. WELCOME. THANK YOU."

The purring intensified. Bouchard pawed at Oliver's leg.

Oliver?

"Yes, Bouchard?"

Will you hold me, Oliver?

Oliver scooped the cat up into his arms. He held the cat close. Bouchard's purr vibrated through Oliver's arms and chest, filling him with a strange warmth.

"HUMANS, PLEASE BRING SUITCASE AND ARTIFACTS TO DIRECTLY UNDER SHIP. ROBOT WILL LOAD ONTO SHIP. ROBOT WILL MAKE SURE SUITCASE FIND YOU. THANK YOU. WELCOME."

All around the meadow, human travelers gathered their belongings and hauled them into a spot of light beneath the ship. Robot drones drifted down from the ship. The drones were silver and cat-shaped, with retractable limbs and tails that latched on to the bags and boxes. The robots secured bags and zipped them up through a portal in the ship's underbelly. They hummed softly, a hum that harmonized with the collective purr of the earthling cats.

Bouchard clung to Oliver's shoulder as Oliver carried his own one suitcase over to the loading area. He set his suitcase down and watched as a robot snatched it up and delivered it to the ship. Then he detached the claws from his jacket and cradled the cat in his arms.

I'm sorry for the claws, Oliver.

"I'll be okay," Oliver said.

A line of humans had formed to board the ship. All of the humans held cats in their arms. All of the cats purred in tandem.

"WELCOME, HUMANS. WELCOME, CATS."

Oliver and Bouchard joined the end of the line.

"It's totally awesome, right, yo?" said the man in line in front of Oliver. *"Space."*

The man had a companion, another man about his age, and they both had cats. They introduced themselves. "Tommy Fisher. And this is Bradford, but we call him Fatty Bratty."

"And we're best friends, and our cats are best friends, too."

"Yo, you should come hang with us, once we're up on the ship!"

Oliver looked up at the ship. One stray snowflake drifted down from the sky, but then it was gone.

The robot drones collected the last suitcase. They disappeared inside the ship. The lights flipped off. The ship went dark.

Then it twinkled, a sparkle of red, a dazzle of green, blue glitter across the hull. The hull was covered in tiny light pixels. The lights twinkled faster. They formed constellations, fireworks, swirling rainbows. They flashed, faster and faster, until a picture appeared:

a cat, emblazoned in rainbow light. One cat became two, four, ten. A parade of pixelated cats marched across the spaceship hull. Stars and hearts of light burst around them.

"WELCOME, CATS."

The voice from the ship was ethereal, melodic, embedded with alpha waves.

"WELCOME, CATS."

Down in the meadow, the cats resumed their collective purr. Oliver held Bouchard close. He felt Bouchard's purr resonate through his chest, into his heart. His heart and Bouchard's beat in time.

"NOBLE CATS, YOUR ILLUSTRIOUS FUR AND TAILS BRING JOY AND HONOR TO MALORTS. WE WELCOME YOU ON MANY WARM SOFT SPACE JOURNEY."

Thin beams of radiant light poured down from under the ship. The first, most adventurous cat, a dark gray longhair with sharp green eyes, leapt from its human friend's arms. It galloped across the meadow, ears perked. It stopped beneath the ship, surrounded by a beam of light. It gazed up. It lifted off the ground. It floated up, slowly spinning. Its tail swished. Its paws batted at the beam. It reached up and touched the bottom of the spaceship. A cat-sized door opened. The cat wiggled its butt and jumped up, into the ship.

"WE MALORTS WELCOME ABOARD FIRST CAT PASSENGER SMOKEY BOI. WELCOME!"

Down on Earth, another cat ran toward the ship, fat-sack swinging. It, too, stopped to bask in a beam of light. It rose up. More cats followed. They gathered beneath the ship. They basked. They floated. They twirled and played in the light. They boarded the ship, and the ship's voice called out their names and welcomed them aboard.

I'm nervous, Oliver, Bouchard said. *I've never floated before.*

"You'll do fine, Bouchard."

I've never done anything like this.

"Neither has anyone."

It will be good, though, right?

"Yes. Yes I think it will be."

Okay. It's time. I'm ready. Bouchard jumped down from Oliver's arms. He trotted toward the ship. *I'll see you up there, Oliver!*

COMING SOON!

A FORGOTTEN STRING-AND-CAN alien trap still hung across the back stoop. The apocalypse beer in the garage was cold enough to drink, thanks to a recent spring chill. Dave's official wedding invitation waited in the pile of mail. The children had missed several weeks of school, but the official school district truancy notice professed to be understanding. These were uncertain times here on Earth. The children were eager to return to school, so they could brag about their amazing long vacation.

"Foster will be so jealous!"

"It was the best vacation ever!"

"Now children, look," Blaine told them, "instead of telling all your friends where you went, why don't you just tell them you went to Disney World."

"But, Dad!"

"Dad!"

"The Cat Camp was soooo much better than Disney World."

"The Cat Camp was the bestest most awesomest thing ever!"

"In the whole entire universe!"

"Yeah!"

"Plus, Dad, we're not supposed to lie."

"You said so yourself."

"You said, 'Jas, Avril, no lying! No biting! No skin peeling! And don't stand so close to the TV!'"

"That is exactly what you said, Dad."

"Sometimes," Blaine replied, "every once in a while, it might be better to break the rules. Like here. If you tell all your friends you went to the Cat Camp, well, they might feel jealous that they didn't get to go."

"But, Dad, that's the whole point!"

"But if they feel jealous, then that might lead to them feeling sad. You don't want anyone to feel sad."

The children pondered this.

"Well ..."

"I guess not."

"But does that mean there's also times when biting is okay?"

"And skin peeling?"

"No! Not those! No!"

* * *

In the living room, the children built their own Cat Camp around the warm glow of the television, with all the stuffed cats and Mr. Meow-mitts, who had finally emerged from hiding just before they packed up to drive home. Mr. Meow-mitts wouldn't talk, but he was floofy and chonky, and that was good enough.

In the kitchen, the wife baked welcome-home cupcakes.

"But we're out of cream," the wife said, "and I need cream to make frosting."

"What happened to all the cream? I thought you got some when we stopped at the store on the way home."

"What do you think happened?"

"Oh, right. The kids."

"They filled a bowl for every cat in the camp. So can you run to the grocery?"

"Sure."

"And also maybe pick up some bacon? Ten pounds? Wait, no. Just, make it one pound. Two. I'm going to be good." The wife opened the fridge. She took out the last slice of American cheese. She unpeeled its precious plastic wrapper. She tucked the wrapper into her pocket.

There was a crayon picture of Earth taped to the fridge; egg-shaped blue-green Earth, colonized by massive cats. A stick-figure family floated in the yellow-scribble airspace around it—the wife, the husband, two kids with claw-studded puff-ball hands, the family television. The wife studied the picture, as she nibbled on a slice of Earth's finest in cheese-engineering.

Blaine kissed her.

"Thank you," she said.

"For what?"

"I don't know. Bacon? Cheese. Cats. You. Everything. Look at that TV." She tapped on the refrigerator picture. "On the screen. That gray splotch with the sharp teeth. Is that supposed to be an alien?"

* * *

Blaine drove to the store. On the way home, he saw the RV parked outside John and Elena's house. The RV door opened and Elena stepped out, hauling a suitcase. Blaine pulled over. He rolled down his window.

"Hey there!" he said. "Welcome home."

"You too! How was your trip?"

"Oh, it was . . . good. Shorter than I thought."

"Yeah . . . Where'd y'all go?" Elena asked.

"Disney World."

"That's funny. That's where we went, too."

* * *

The suitcases got unpacked. The children returned to school. Blaine drove around in a Dave-less city van. He felt, admittedly, strangely nostalgic for Dave, speeding through red lights, loading unmarked crates in the back of the van, his menthol smoke, his spy-drone flat-earth pro-militia rants. The wife ate more soy-based fake bacon and less real bacon, which was still a lot of bacon. She tried not to select fruits and vegetables *just* for their plastic packaging. She took the family on a weekend trip to the downtown Louisville Marriott, her birthplace.

"Hey!"

"Dad!"

"This doesn't look like Disney World!"

"Yeah, *Dad*. This is just a common hotel."

"But there is *TV*."

The children took its picture. They awarded it second place, runner-up in the ranking of hotel TVs, for which it received a hand-drawn award, affixed by crafty children to its base with a hot glue gun. The children were lured from TV land with the promise of salty meat sticks, loaded into the minivan, and driven to the racetrack, where their mother ate like a horse. They returned to the hotel, to their precious silver-medal TV.

"Dad!"

"Dad! TV!"

Blaine tried to take a nap. It didn't last.

"Wake up!"

"Dad!"

"Aliens!"

"TV!"

He rubbed his eyes. He sat up. The wife sat too close, close enough to touch the screen. She was smiling, enrapt.

"Blaine, look," she said. "On the TV."

On TV, a Malortian worldship flew through starry space.

Was it the real ship?

It might have been CGI, a model ship, a studio screen. Nevertheless, in front of the ship, a word appeared:

EARTHLINGS!

The camera zoomed in, toward the ship. It passed through a window, into a futuristic corridor of silver panels and trailing lights. Malorts traveled the corridor in pairs and packs. They swatted and bickered merrily. They looked like meerkats, except for their longer snouts and sharper teeth, and the plastic Mardi Gras beads they wore; a gift to Malorts from Earth.

On the wall of the corridor, a panel opened. A paw darted out, swiping the foot of a passing Malort. Another Malort laughed, and got punched. The paw retracted, then emerged again, followed by the whole cat, a plump calico with mismatched eyes, one green and one blue. The cat strutted through the hall, looking dignified. Malorts smiled. They gave the cat a cheesy human thumbs-up with a sharp-clawed digit.

The camera followed the cat through a panel door into a larger room where Malorts sat at cafeteria tables eating food that looked like cheese but wasn't. At some of the tables, Malorts and humans sat together.

"*Earthlings!*"

A deep voice announced the series title.

"*Brought to you by the acclaimed reality show producer and patriotic American, Jack P.*"

Jack P.'s smiling human face flashed across the screen.

"When Jack P. and his fellow Malortian travelers returned to their worldship, both ambassadors and ordinary people from all over the world—along with their cats—decided to join them for the adventure of a lifetime. Earthlings! *is the real story of six of those human explorers and their cats, as they travel together on a Malortian vessel into the farthest reaches of space."*

The cafeteria scene faded into a montage of spaceship moments. Humans studied Malortian text and drawings in a star-view lecture hall. Pairs of humans and Malorts played doubles tennis in the holodeck courts. Humans showed Malorts how to juggle, shuffle cards, thread elastic bands through neon lettered beads, dance the Hokey Pokey, catch thrown pretzels in their mouths. How to lure a cat with a catnip mouse on a string. They played Candyland and Red Rover and Uno with eager Malortian pups. Cats piled together around the ship's warm core. A woman gazed wistfully out the window, at the luster of deep space.

"Season one of Earthlings! *arrives next spring. This epic journey is not to be missed."*

THE END

ACKNOWLEDGMENTS

For my husband, Steve, who encouraged and supported me through every step of this journey, from wrangling our children while I worked, to reading drafts, to inspiring me with all those blurry photos of unidentified spacecraft. You always believed in alien life, and I thought, *Aaww, aliens, isn't that cute?* You always believed in me, too, even when I had no faith in myself. I am so grateful. This book would not exist without you, Steve.

I am also endlessly grateful for my agent, Holly Root, whose steadfast commitment and relentless effort toward wresting the publishing chimera into a real ink-and-paper book exceeded all my expectations.

Thank you to my brilliant editor, Adam Wilson, whose understanding and insight helped transform a silly manuscript teeming with cats and half-feral children into the polished hunk of awesome that you all just read.

Thank you all for reading. I am so happy that I got to share this story with you.

Many, many thanks to all the folks who have helped this book along the way. To *The Antiheroes*, and Ryan Aoto in particular, for convincing me that I ought to try writing a novel. Without you, I never would have gotten started. To my brother Anthony, who read and laughed and made me laugh. You'll get your Jet Ski someday, I hope, if this book sells enough copies. To Taylor Hughes, for the author photos, for helping me design a nifty website, and for being a generally awesome human. To my children, Ella Jane and Sammie, for your patience while I work long hours, and for inspiring me always. And to the team at Hyperion Avenue—Tonya Agurto, Jennifer Levesque, Monique Diman, Ann Day, Julie Leung, Alexandra Serrano, Kaitie Leary, Amy King, Sara Liebling, Guy Cunningham, Mark Amundsen, and Dan Kaufman—thank you for all your contributions.

Thank you, Earth, with all your remarkable creatures and artifacts and your movies and books and television shows about extraterrestrial life. If the aliens ever come to visit, I hope we can sit down with a pot of fondue and laugh about how absurd it is, all of it.

TURN THE PAGE
TO CHECK OUT
EMILY JANE'S
NEXT NOVEL

HERE BESIDE
THE RISING TIDE

Love, fun, sun, and . . . sea monsters?

JOURNEY

Present Day – The First Day of Summer

NOTHING HAPPENED THE way it was supposed to happen according to novels and TV shows and the self-help manuals Jenn had gorged on, naively, in the optimistic early years of mother-slash-wifehood.

And the magazines. A woman could *Do It All*, the magazines said.

The husband, for example, was not supposed to file for divorce because, as he explained over a series of text messages in which he did not even bother to fix the typos caused by autocorrect, he did not feel *actualized*.

He had not *cultivated his innermost potential* or *activated his Power Nucleus*.

It was not, he insisted, because he had read that self-help manual— *Bond with the Man You Were Always Meant to Be* by Danz Landry, motivational profiteer and CEO of the Male Actualization Society (MAS).

It was not *because* of *her*. The book said he had to seize ownership of his actions.

But it was because of her.

He was a salesman. He had a name that belonged to a salesman, or a mortgage broker, or a mid-level mob boss: Charles (Chuck) Lanaro. When she met him, he worked at a car dealership. He had a special talent for upselling. Warranties. Fake-leather leather seats.

Sunroofs. Her name was still Jenni Farrow when they met, but then she got married and became Jenn Lanaro. Then she wrote a book and became, in pen name only, Jennifer Lamour, *New York Times* bestselling author of the Philipia Bay series, now on paperback book number twenty-nine.

Philipia Bay was not acclaimed, poignant, powerful, meaningful, or particularly well written. Philipia Bay was action smut. But the people wanted what the people wanted.

Chuck Lanaro wanted to know:

Chuck: *What were you trying to say when you picked that yodel for the book cover?*
Chuck: *It was insulting.*
Chuck: *Just another thing to add to the List of Underminstances.*

Jenn could only assume that "yodel" meant "model." There was nothing yodelish about the man on the cover of *Philipia Bay and the Castle of Castaways*, with his resplendent hair and rippling abs. The mystery was why her husband's autocorrect had converted *model* to *yodel*. What did this say about him as a person? She made a note for her lawyer.

"Underminstances" was not a word, except in MAS-speak. Jenn had looked it up on the internet. *Catalog your underminstances*, Danz Landry directed in his instructional video series. *Catapult your awareness of events in which the shemale voice attempts to undermine you. Understanding is the first step on the road to control.*

It was a fallacy, Jenn wanted to tell her husband, to assume that any of us could have control.

After they got married, and the first Philipia Bay book appeared on the impulse-buy endcap at the checkout line at the Value Valley, and the first double line appeared on the pregnancy pee test, Chuck

Lanaro was glad—elated, over the moon—to give his two-weeks' notice to the dealership and trade his sales pitch for rubber dish gloves and embrace the stay-at-home-dad lifestyle. He mastered sleep cycles and potty training. He met other baby-strapped dads for playdates at the park. As the children grew, he filled the school-day hours with hobbies and projects—woodworking, drywalling, aerobic kickboxing, disassembling and reassembling the washing machine, cryptocurrency trading, stalking the backyard racoons with his BB gun. The racoons had been digging through the trash again, *underminstancing* his efforts to contain it neatly in its proper bin.

Jenn should have known, when she spotted him hiding in the bushes, in camo, with night-vision goggles.

Chuck had never gone hunting. He had never fired a real gun. He had grown up in New Jersey, a subway ride away from Manhattan. He had, as a dealer of cars, professed to enjoy art museums and symphonies and duck-pin bowling. Yet his hobbies bespoke a stereotypical masculinity, a reactionary pattern, as if selected in outlash. Against what? The rubber dish gloves? *He* was the one who said they protected his hand skin. He didn't *have* to wear them.

He didn't have to hire a process server to serve her with his petition for divorce either. He didn't have to start the ending chapter of their marriage by lawyering up. He could have just conveniently disappeared, like her own biannual-greeting-card father. He could have waited at least until she'd finished edits on *Philipia Bay and the Pirates of Pandago Cove*. Or until the children had finished school for the year. Or until she had figured out what to do with her mother's Pearl Island house, which was, after several years, no doubt overrun by dust mites, spiders, ants, palmetto bugs, and all the detritus left in the wake of sudden departure.

But no.

Chuck Lanaro rented himself a furnished town house, three bedrooms, two baths, in a gated community with a pool and tennis courts. In April, when Jenn Lamour flew to Las Vegas to attend a romance writers convention, Chuck Lanaro packed his bags and moved out.

Jenn: *Can't we at least talk about this in person?*
Jenn: *What about the kids?*
Jenn: *You think you're the only one who's been unhappy?*
Jenn: *Fine, I'm hiring a lawyer*
Jenn: *I can't believe you.*
Jenn: *You are so petty. Seriously. And after my mom just died.*
Chuck: *That was three bears ago*
Chuck: *I am noting that you have perpetrated yet another underminstance*
Jenn: *Because I called you petty?*
Chuck: *Don't pretend you don't know damn well what you did*
Jenn: *What about the kids?*
Chuck: *What do you mean, what about the kids?*
Chuck: *I always take care of them. It makes more sense for them to live with me*

The kids were supposed to react to the news of their parents' divorce with anguish, angst, blame—self- and parent-directed—perhaps misconduct and shenanigans. A fistfight, for example. Biting, hair-pulling. Intentionally neglected school assignments. They were not supposed to passively accept their broken-home fate.

"So?" Jenn asked them after she'd explained that sometimes mommies and daddies didn't get along, but that didn't mean that it was anyone's fault.

"So?" Evie replied.

Mason put on his cat-ear headphones and pressed play on the video-gaming talk show-esque program that he had, resistantly, agreed to pause for the divorce spiel.

"So . . . we are getting divorced."

"So?"

"And I just wanted to talk to you both about, well— Mason, could you please take your headphones off?"

Mason tapped on his headphones to indicate that he couldn't hear her with them on.

"Is this because of the underminstances?" Evie asked.

"What? No. No. Is that what Dad said?"

"He has the list taped to the fridge in his kitchen."

"He— That is just— *No!* I have been nothing but kind and respectful to your father, and this is just, it's—"

"He asked me to report any trash-talking," Evie said. "For the list. But can I go now?"

"Go? Where are you going?"

"Just, you know, to the couch." Evie pointed to the couch, where the tablet and the console sat together without her.

"This is— Don't you want to talk about it? As a family? Evie? Mason?"

Jenn pulled the earphones away from Mason's ears. Mason snarled. He yanked them back on and clamped his hands down over them.

"You just told us," Evie said. "But we already knew, because Dad told us when he moved out, like, six weeks ago. What else is there to say?"

These were children born into a world that was, according to every scientific measure everywhere, careening toward its own destruction.

These were children who had heard their parents discuss, in hushed but drunkenly audible voices, the tragedies that permeated Modern Life. Hurricanes. Droughts. Shootings. Et cetera. When adult talk started up, these children put on their headphones, turned on their screens, and then complained at bedtime because six straight hours hadn't been nearly screentime enough.

She was supposed to say something heartfelt, something meaningful enough to permeate the child-screen bond. Something her own mother might have said, in the slim band of time between work and bed, or work and work. She should have held them in her arms and assuaged the doubts that . . . well, honestly the doubts belonged to her. She had been, in her distraction, unwittingly lenient with the children. She ignored them, and this led to excess YouTube. Too many snacks. Too often she let them subsist on plain noodles with butter. Now they were detached. She had sacrificed Quality Family Time for Mom's Gotta Work. She had a flimsy excuse.

Someone had to work, she had told herself.

Chuck: *It could have been me. But you insisted.*

Had she insisted?

Chuck: *Admit it. You wanted to work.*
Chuck: *You love work more than you love me.*

Well, maybe now she did. Now that he was keeping a list on his fridge where the kids could see it.

She should have at least sat on the couch between the children so they could all stare at their devices together as a family. But Mason had already requisitioned the center cushion for his stuffed animals. Evie made a shoo-shooing motion with her hand. *Get away, Mom.* So Mom went into the kitchen and poured herself a beer-glass full of wine, because Chuck had given himself full custody of all the wineglasses.

She sat down at the table with her laptop and a tube of Potato-Wizard Cheddar Crisps. She was supposed to work on edits. She was supposed to feel grateful for the continued success of Philipia Bay. She had loved Philipia Bay when she wrote the first book. Maybe more than she loved Chuck, though present-day-Chuck inevitably colored her memory of past-Chuck with a douchey tint. She had wanted nothing more than to write more books with Philipia Bay, books brimming with treasure and romance, where villains got sent to prison or mauled by bears or devoured by snakes. Where everything turned out the way it should. Her readers wanted the same. More Philipia Bay. But by book five, she was bored. In book eight—*Philipia Bay and the Congress of Sabotage*—she tried something new. She made Philipia Bay fall in love. Then she killed the lover. Then Philipia discovered she was pregnant with the lover's child and was faced with an untenable choice: give up the child or let the sabotage of democracy go unpunished. Her editor said no. No tough choices. Her readers hated tough choices. She was supposed to stick to the formula.

Almost thirty formulaic books in, she was inexorably stuck. Jenn Lanaro was Jennifer Lamour. Jennifer Lamour was Philipia Bay. Philipia Bay paid the bills. Jenn had no time or inspiration for anything else.

Her phone buzzed. A text, from her editor.

The editor's name was Betsy Rankleman, a name that the editor lamented as lacking in romantic flair. She was fifty-six. She had no children, which meant that she had time for karate lessons, kickboxing, fencing. The editor herself was svelte, with toned arms and pampered skin and a regimen of Botox. She had a husband who, when they married, in their beautiful bangable twenties, had looked like the cover model from *Philipia Bay and the Arrow of Algiers*, but now he had a shiny bald patch and a beer gut and a proliferation of moles with hairs growing out of them *but he won't let me pluck the hairs* the editor said *and he won't pull them out himself. What am I supposed to do?* They did what they could, with the dashing Adonises of Philipia Bay.

Betsy: *So…???*
Betsy: *You promised me edits by last week* ☺
Betsy: *Everything alright?*

Jenn replied with an amorphous thumbs-up. She put her phone down. She stared at the words on her laptop screen. Holy Shakespeare, these were terrible words. Absolute crap. She took a gulp of wine. Her phone buzzed:

Chuck: *My lawyer will be sending proposals for alimony and child support*
Chuck: *Since the kids will be staying mostly with me*

No. *NO!* She fumed. She started to type:

Jenn: *Screw you, you selfish asswipe. You are not taking my children. I'm not paying you a cent. You can go fuck yourself*

But she didn't hit Send. Chuck would screenshot the message and add it to his list of underminstances. That message would make a great exhibit for divorce court. Evidence of her motherly ineptitude and incivility. She took a gulp of wine.

She needed to get away.

She needed to go someplace where she could forget all about Chuck.

She needed to put the life she had known behind her.

Her glass was empty.

She refilled it. She typed another cathartic screw-you-Chuck reply. She deleted it. In two days, at nine a.m., Chuck would knock on the door. He would take the children. Mason still in pajamas. Evie with a rat's nest of unbrushed hair.

What, you can't even handle getting them dressed in real clothes, Chuck would chide. *You can't even make them brush their hair? They should have been ready.*

She wasn't ready. She wouldn't see them for five whole days. Chuck would return them with swimming pool tan lines and Whippy Dip stories and new Pokémon cards, but only for the weekend, and then nine a.m. on Monday would arrive and they would disappear again.

Unless Chuck couldn't find them.

A devious idea hatched in her mind.

If Chuck couldn't find them.

If Chuck couldn't find them . . .

If he knocked on the door at nine a.m. but no one answered. Because no one was home. Because they had left. She took a gulp of wine. The school year had ended. She could work on edits anywhere. She didn't need to stay here, where Chuck would bogart the children and mansplain her blunders and lambast her with MAS-speak.

They could just leave. The thought made her giddy. She envisioned herself in Cabo drinking a pina colada from a coconut shell while the children splashed in the crystalline waters. She envisioned Santorini. The Florida Keys. The Gold Coast. The rage on Chuck's face when he found out. His cheeks red. His nostrils flaring, like a horse.

Except how would she explain a Cabo summer in family court? She couldn't let the horse win. She needed a plausible excuse for their departure. A sensible destination. A task to accomplish. Such as . . .

Pearl Island.

Her childhood home. Her mother's house. She *had* to clean it out. Her mother had died three years ago and the house had sat vacant ever since, collecting mold and ants, springing leaks, stockpiling complaints about the overgrown grass. She had a *responsibility* to deal with the house, one which now seemed more appealing than procrastination, her long-standing approach. Her mother's house made for convincing testimony.

Though they couldn't stay there. The house was—

She saw the house in her mind, as it had been, long ago. Sunlight streamed through the kitchen windows. Her mother stood at the laminate counter, scooping ice cream into the blender, singing along to Joni Mitchell on the record player.

Jenn felt a churning, clenching pain in her gut. A pain she dismissed as *just gas*. Too much wine. Not enough fruit.

If they went to Pearl Island, they would need a rental house. Something not ghosty, with ocean views. She opened a browser window. She searched for Pearl Island summer rentals. *Booked. Booked. Mostly booked except for one week in July.* Naturally. Summer had already started.

Except then she saw a house with *New Listing* written in yellow letters above the picture. She clicked the link. It was beachfront. Four bedrooms. Two and a half baths. Outdoor shower. She swiped through photos. It didn't look new inside. The kitchen boasted chestnut cabinets, gold-plated hardware, a dial-microwave, ancient appliances in shades of pale yellow and pea green. It opened onto a weather-beaten deck that overlooked the ocean. A spiral staircase led up to a second deck with a French door to the primary bedroom. Jenn took a gulp of wine. She clicked on the rental calendar. No bookings. Available all summer. It had either just gotten listed that day, or it was haunted. Or a scam. All of the above.

Her phone buzzed.

Chuck: *You didn't respond to my text.*

Chuck: *Are you trying to be rude?*

She finished the wine. She felt drunk. Impulsive. Reckless. Furious. She felt like a hurricane force, like Philipia Bay with a pair of nunchucks, a katana holstered to her back, a bladed throwing star that never missed. Except that Chuck was safe inside his town-house fortress, protected by lawyers and threats. Her only weapon was a credit card. She wasn't a force. She was more like a shingle torn from its roof by hurricane winds, hands whipping uncontrollably, tearing the credit card from her wallet, pounding the numbers onto the screen.

Done.

Her face was drenched in tears.

Her phone buzzed.

45299: *This message confirms your booking of SEA-LA VISTA*
Check in 29-May after 4:00 p.m.
Check out 19-Aug by 10:00 a.m.
No cancellations.
Thank you and enjoy your stay on Pearl Island!

Philipia Bay and the Return of the Red Sea Raider

(highlighted excerpt)

She needed to forget that awful day. To forget him. Her life had moved on. And yet his absence continued to shape the contours of her days. The echo of his laughter lingered in the hallway of her Manhattan apartment. She flipped off the light, rolled her suitcase out the door, locked it behind her. She took a cab to the airport. She said goodbye to the life she had known.

Twenty-four hours and six martinis later, Philipia Bay stepped outside into the steamy Thailand night. The automatic airport doors closed behind her. The air smelled like sea salt, fried fish, the exhaust from a million cars. All around her, Bangkok clamored.

She felt fresh, exuberant, wide-awake despite the mere hour of sleep she'd managed on the plane. No one would ever find her here. His ghost would never find her.

She stepped up to the curb and waved for a cab.

"Philipia?"

Somewhere behind, someone called out her name.

But that hadn't really happened, had it? She had bought her ticket and packed her bag just hours before her flight. No one knew she had come here.

"Philipia!"

Philipia Bay turned around. Her jaw dropped. There he was, staring straight at her. Like a ghost, or a dream. The last person she ever expected to see.